All the Land to Hold Us

All the Land to Hold Us

RICK BASS

Houghton Mifflin Harcourt

BOSTON • NEW YORK

2013

www.hmhbooks.com

Library of Congress Cataloging-in-Publication Data is available.
ISBN 978-0-547-68712-4

Printed in the United States of America
DOC 10 9 8 7 6 5 4 3 2 1

For Nicole Angeloro

Prologue

He was not the first seeker of treasure upon the landscape, was instead but one more in the continuum of a story begun long ago by greater desires than even his own. Richard was a geologist, a prober and a searcher, dedicated to uncovering certain things, though he tended to ignore or obscure others. Even in his youth, he understood he was tiny against the world, his desire burning no more and no less than that of any other traveler who pressed against the world like one great animal swimming by itself in a vast sea, each traveler's life passing through that sea like the equally brief phosphorescent specter of time or memory that trailed in the traveler's wake: though always, after that phosphorescence faded, there would be one more traveler.

There was once, and still is, a place in the West Texas landscape, Castle Gap, that drew travelers toward it as the eye of the needle of heaven is said to draw human souls.

Castle Gap rises from the greasewood plains as a wall of rimrock formed from limestone deposits in the warm, shallow Permian sea of 270 million years ago. It was through this eroded notch between broad valleys and the desert that all travelers were drawn — Stone Age man, then Comanches and Apaches, Spaniards seeking gold and souls to convert like bullion for the King, and later, white colonists and the cattle drivers and wagon trains that would supply the colonists with their many whims and needs. It was the gate through which they all had to pass, to cross the river, and then the great desert.

The Gap was a bottleneck on either side of the Pecos River. To scale the vertical cliffs of the mountains would have been next to impossible, fraught with peril for even a lone climber; and certainly neither livestock nor wagons could have made such a sheer ascent. And not only did the Gap attract every traveler, it seemed also to summon every myth, every tale of deprivation or longing, every fear and every desire, from the first moment a traveler's eyes fell upon it.

It is said that even today an odd whistling occurs from the cleft in the early evenings as the winds of the day are bent by the landscape's wishes to moan one and only one song, so that even a traveler blind to the world, or on a blackened night, with his or her back turned to the cleft, might know by that sound the shape of that cleft; and from that shape the knowledge of the stories buried there, stories which had no choice but to pass through.

The inland salt lake below Castle Gap — Juan Cordona Lake, fifteen miles farther into that westering desert — had for centuries drawn the wandering Paleolithic clans, who sought its salt for both sustenance and trade, and who passed it on their journeys up onto the Edwards Plateau to hunt buffalo. The first known recorded reference to the Gap comes from 1535, when Cabeza de Vaca, lost, wandered inland from the Texas coast.

De Vaca had had a hard time of it, having been held hostage on the Texas coast by both the Karankawas and, slightly farther inland, the Coahuiltecans, who, not knowing enough yet to kill all white men on sight, instead kept their captives bound with leather in thorn cages, feeding them fish swarming with maggots, and a meal de Vaca would later call indescribable: the "second harvest," a collection of partially digested nuts and grains gleaned from the remnants of human feces.

De Vaca — not the last dreamer of glory upon that landscape — had taken to using his mother's name, which implied higher social standing. He survived his first exploration of the area, and eventually returned to Spain, where once back in the court of the King, he did not dwell on the hardships, but instead told the Spanish Viceroy, Viceroy Mendoza, that although he had not exactly seen gold, antimony, or iron, he had glimpsed signs and clues of such, and had been told of great cities and civilizations farther west.

Maps and dreams: as if in evidence that all that he dared to dream or believe was true, de Vaca gave Viceroy Mendoza a map he had stopped long enough to sketch of the unmistakable landmark of Castle Gap, beyond the sharp bend of the Pecos River, and the deep-water crossing into Castle Gap, known later as Horsehead Crossing, named for the skulls that would wash ashore there.

The Viceroy dispatched one of his old hands who had marched with Pizarro in Peru — Fray Marcos, who would know gold if he saw it — to further investigate the rumors. And like de Vaca, Fray Marcos came back claiming that he too had at long last sighted one of the fabled cities of Cíbola, repository of an entire continent's gold and silver, though he had not quite had time to enter the city, and instead viewed it only from a great distance.

Before turning around and heading back to Spain, however, Fray Marcos had built a cairn of stones and cried out to the western wilderness, claiming it for the possession of Spain as far as the eye could see, as well as any kingdoms beyond, in the name of God, King Charles V, and Viceroy Mendoza.

Another expedition was planned. Francisco Coronado, only thirty years old, was chosen to lead this exploration, provided that he match Mendoza's funds with his own, which Coronado did, after looting his wealthy wife's estate.

Hence five years after de Vaca's crude map, Coronado too wandered beneath the stone gateway of Castle Gap, searching for Cíbola (which proved to be nothing more than a rock pueblo of the Zuñi tribe, sun-glinting in the distance; in disgust and frustration, Coronado and his men killed some of the Zuñis).

They staggered farther then, lost — to Kansas, to the Grand Canyon, to Mexico, to Louisiana — a great fevered wandering that was fueled by the fabrications of their guide, El Turco, as he whispered intimations of gold just over the next rise, gold just around the next river-bend — though finally Coronado's army gave up their dreams and began pining solely for water.

They killed more Indians. They captured some two hundred Puebloans, planning to burn them at the stake. As the captives approached these stakes, however, they broke and ran, and were cut down by rifle fire and swords. In the end the Spaniards were able to burn only about thirty of their captives successfully, with the captives' women and children witnessing the torture, and after the burning was done, Coronado embraced his lieutenant heartily.

Coronado finally understood that there was no gold and had El Turco garroted, somewhere in North Texas or Oklahoma — the journals are barely legible — but the garroting occurred somewhere over the vast underground lake of the Ogallala Reservoir, that sweet and seemingly eternal fountain which supplied all of the plains with their astounding bounty; and El Turco's scheming blood filtered down through those loose sands, draining away in micrograms to be spread throughout the underground veins of the earth, resurfacing here and there, in no pattern that we the living might discern, but always, eventually, resurfacing.

⤙ Book One ⤚

1

1966

FOR MONTHS AFTER Richard first visited Horsehead Crossing
— he had been sent by his employer in Houston to explore the
largely worked-over oil and gas deposits in the Permian Basin
near Odessa — he would dream nightly of what he had seen: the salt-
preserved skulls of thousands of horses and cows tipped up in the saline banks of the Pecos, and in the surrounding, shifting sand dunes
— horse and cattle skulls trapped in the sand and silt like the pale fossils of the limestone cliffs above.

Richard would awaken nightly to the dream of being amidst those
churning horses, fighting the river's fierce current, trying to make the
crossing at the only possible spot for a hundred miles in either direction. He would dream also of trying to push the maddened cattle
across, their legs and horns entangled. In the dream, the herd tipped
sideways in the current, thrashing and goring one another and chok-
ing on the terrific waves of their own making, the sunlight disappearing beneath the frothing waters, with thousands of pounds of wild
horses or cattle riding atop the backs of others, pushing the others
down deeper.

Then the chain of animals would begin to break into tatters, like
an ice floe swirling in loosening fragments downstream, with most of
the cattle or horses drowned now, drifting into eddies along the banks,
where later that night, after a good day's heat, they would begin to
swell, and would line the night-dark shores like the whitened bellies of
so many dead fish.

Too often, in the dream, Richard would find himself beneath the darkened mass of animals in the river crossing, surging with the other animals, trying to find air and sunlight but unable to. Though other times an opening would appear, and he would move quickly up to that clearing of light, would get his head above the water, and would survive; and he would know with exquisite, shining relief the feeling of his hand clutching the far and stony shore. He would pull himself out, drenched and battered, back out onto the land, safely across, along with the rest of the herd, or what remained of it.

There were human bones all up and down the Pecos too, and back among the sand hills. The sand dunes flowed and shifted with the unpredictable movement of a creature pacing across the land, towering dunes of white sand appearing one morning outside an unfortunate homesteader's window, where none had existed for fifty years before.

Richard had never found an entire human skull out in the dunes, but had found pieces of skull, and arrowheads too, and broken arms and bones of his fellow kind. He carried some of the loose bones back to the drilling rig where he had been working at the time. He did not protest when some of the older roughnecks entertained themselves by building a small log-cabin structure out of the bones, which was disassembled later that night by the workers' dogs, who scattered the bones and clacked on them steadily for the next several days; and for days beyond that, the desert was littered with the scat and offal of the dogs, in which the white cracked pieces of human bone were discernible, like nuts or seeds undigested.

Once atop the desert, on the stone reef overlooking the flatlands below, Richard would find in his wanderings the prehistoric grinding basins, as deep and circular as if cut with posthole diggers, where people had sat across the centuries, grinding roots and nuts at bluff's edge while staring out at the depths and the void beyond.

It seemed to Richard then, even in the midst of his careless youth, that he could feel their presence, thick and dense along the cliff's walls, still seated around those empty grinding basins — as if the grinders had stepped away for only a moment, or as if they might be returning, having merely not yet shown up for that day's waiting work — and he moved carefully around the holes, careful not to bump into any of the ghosts, which seemed to him to be everywhere.

Something about being up there on top of the fossiled reef, so much closer to the sky, and with all of West Texas spread beyond — something about the dryness of the heat, and whiteness of the limestone caprock on which he walked, and the pale blue of the sky above — made him crave sex even more than the general background steadiness of his youth demanded; and sometimes he would bring girlfriends out to Castle Gap, to stare out at that horizon, and to spend the night, to bear witness to the sunset, and the stars that night, beside the windy campfire, and to the sunrise the next morning, and to the glories of each other's bodies in the warmth of the next day.

Other times, however, alone, he would wander the shifting, swirling dunes below, with the fortress wall of the reef above like some outpost sentinel or surveyor.

Strangely enough, there was water out in the dunes — remnant fresh water from millions of years ago, both trapped and transported in mysterious unmappable lenses of sand that changed nightly, daily, beneath the hot scouring breath of the wind.

Richard had occasionally come across such sparkling water. There would almost always be colorful songbirds gathered around these brief blue puddles, and surprised by Richard's approach, the birds would leap away on a whirring of wings, water splashing from their wetted beaks and feet and wingtips, differentiating for him the mirage ponds from the real ones — and always, in such moments, Richard would be reminded, with longing, of kisses.

He would crouch at the water and drink from the little pond like an animal, drinking as much of the ancient water as he could hold, and then he would travel on; and by the next day, the pond would have vanished.

Sometimes, while walking through the dunes, he would see flocks of small colorful birds go flying past — scarlet tanagers, golden warblers, vermilion flycatchers, all flying together — and he would hurry over the dunes, following the direction they had flown. But he had never been able to find water in this manner, and had instead encountered the brief ponds only and always by stumbling chance, like a sleepwalker in a dream awakening to find him- or herself standing ankle-deep in a river.

His company's drilling rigs pushed deeper into the desert, seemingly scattered here and there, but located according to some master plan of the drillers and geologists, who pursued the deepest reservoirs of oil and gas, probing around the edges; seeking the center always, but with their misses defining the rough perimeters.

Every well drilled brought both mystery and knowledge. A dry hole could be as valuable as a producing well, in that it would help define the limits of the field, and would point the geologists in their next direction.

Between wells, and during bit trips and circulations for washouts, Richard continued to hike the reef country above, and the dunes below. Down in the dunes, on three separate occasions he found old wagon wheels. Two appeared to be the remnants of failed crossings — the bent wooden staves that housed the iron rim were still intact, sand-pitted and varnished by both time and the flow of the dunes (as if, just beneath the crests of the dunes, the wagon had still been traveling); but the third wheel was charred: not burned completely, as it might have been had it been damaged and used for firewood, but burned only in a three-quarter arc, which suggested to Richard that the wagon train had been set aflame while still standing upright in the sand: the echo of one of the ritual massacres that took place regularly beneath the notched visage of the Gap.

The landscape gathered all men, across the ages, as the anguished, hungry, confused blood of man surged this way and that, sloshing around in the soft human vessels as if such blood no more belonged in them than a flock of wild birds, bright birds, would belong in a rusting wire cage.

During his crumbling reign, Maximilian, the Austrian ex-archduke who served as emperor of Mexico from 1864 to 1867, reportedly sent wagon trains northward with all his family's treasure. Maximilian was eventually placed before a firing squad in the spring of 1867, where, before being blindfolded, he handed each of his executioners a single gold coin; but the rest of his immense wealth had vanished, and the stories surrounding its disappearance, and its eventual burial at Castle

Gap, carry at least as much authenticity of detail, and faintly corroborative evidence, as any of the other stories of treasure.

There is always an escapee. The gold is placed in a cave and sealed with a charge of dynamite; Indians thereafter massacre all but one survivor, a Negro slave who eludes capture by submerging in the river and breathing through a straw or reed. He returns to the scene in the night, unearths one of the locked strongboxes, smashes it down on a boulder, and a shower of gold and silver coins cascades onto the ground.

He scoops up a few, caches the strongbox, and heads north, where he is captured, charged with murder, and taken to prison. After seven years of saying he knows where the treasure is, he returns with his jailers, traveling all the way down from Ohio, to show them the cache in exchange for his freedom. When they arrive, however, the cache is gone; and rooting in the dust and gravel, all he is able to produce are a few individual coins, entirely unsatisfactory to his captors, and he is returned to jail.

Or the survivor is a one-hundred-year-old woman who had been but a child on the runaway priests' expedition, the Catholic Cross Cache. In the 1870s, near the end of the old woman's life, she returns by burro to Castle Gap with her two great-grandchildren, one of whom is ten-year-old Susie, who in the 1900s will go on to become Cat-House Susie, an ex-madam servicing oilfield patrons in the region.

According to Cat-House Susie, her great-grandmother left her and her sister playing in camp and rode the burro up to the summit, and then returned, assuring her great-granddaughters that the treasure was still there, that it had not been disturbed.

Or an old barfly, for the price of a drink, will produce a gold nugget and a tattered map, and the story of having been privy to the deathbed conversation of an outlaw or a priest; and the next day, when the treasure seeker goes out to the mountain (sweat already streaming down his back, not so much from the warmth of sunrise as from the heated palpitations within), he will find a veritable minefield of previously dug holes and cairns and freshly blazed trees, and false graves in which, upon being excavated, no bones are to be found — though no treasure either.

The seeker will wander the mountain for a day or two or three, digging in the sun and resting in the heat of noonday in the shamble of the adobe hut at the base of the mountain, the hut that once served as a rest station for the stage.

(It seemed to Richard, when he came to the landscape, that this hut was the only place on the mountain that had not been disturbed by the shovels and pickaxes of man; and if he were going to look for any of the treasure, or treasures, that is where he would have looked. But he didn't. He had come looking for other treasures, other things.)

There was one woman in particular with whom he spent time, during the period that he was developing the oilfields in the region. Her name was Clarissa, and she had grown up in Odessa, and hated the oil business — hated the familiarity and sameness of it, as well as the landscape — and though she and Richard were only together for about four months, they were good months, and seemed timeless to the lovers.

Clarissa's hair was as black as a Comanche's, and her eyes were a pale green. She had thick arching eyebrows that could give one who did not know her the impression of perpetual surprise, and flawless, pale skin. Unlike the other girls she had grown up with (whose skin, by the time they were eighteen, already looked like that of forty-year-olds), Clarissa did not endeavor to spend her every sunlit moment in pursuit of bronzing her skin, but labored to keep it the color it was.

She hated the desert, and loved to soak in water for long stretches — in the bathtub, in the salty rivers, even in warm stock tanks — and she and Richard spent many nights just sitting in the shallows, after having loved; and it seemed to him that her pale body, almost luminous when wet, was a phenomenon in such a harsh country — exceedingly rare, and daily imperiled.

Clarissa had no goal other than getting out: away from West Texas and away from the oil business, which meant away from any and all of Texas. When Richard met her she was working in Odessa as a receptionist for one of the drilling companies. She could smell the odor of crude oil on the men who came and went through the office as a farmer or rancher can smell the scent of horses or cattle in another's clothes, or on another's skin; and lying next to Richard, there in the eddies of the salty, muddy river, she could smell it on him, and could taste it on him, though she forgave him, because she in no way loved him, was interested only in the luminescence she sometimes sensed emanating from him. Her own light was hidden, but his seemed at times to leap from him.

There was a place inside him she was drawn to. He would not let her into that place, for she did not love him: but she could sometimes see the glow of it from far within; and for those four months, while he was drilling the various fields, she stayed with him.

The consensus of her high school (she was twenty when Richard met her) and of the community had been that she would go to Hollywood and become an actress or a model. They overestimated her in this regard. She had no desire to work, nor, necessarily, to improve or "better" herself; she wanted only to keep her skin looking the way it did, pale and creamy-soft, night-dreamish, for as long as possible, and to escape the wind and heat.

She sensed intuitively that her power, her physical beauty, lay in this emotional detachment, and ambition of any kind would have jeopardized and perhaps even marred that trance in which the dreamy mental languor was so tied to the physical.

As if everything in her sphere was hypnotized: her viewers, her suitors, the innocence of her skin and beauty, and the ravages of time itself; as if she had momentarily betranced even time's pendulum. So frightened was she of losing her beauty that she lived almost as if in a state of narcolepsy — seeking, as often as possible, not to let the drying winds of the world rest upon her for more than a moment, and moving from one body of water to the next, and bathing, always bathing.

They spent the nights out near Castle Gap, among the reefs and caverns of the bluff, searching for fossils. It was easier to search for them in the daylight, but Clarissa preferred to be out at night, and so they would walk along the rim with flashlights or lanterns, looking for the most perfect and interesting specimens; chipping them out with rock hammers and collecting them in canvas pouches.

Richard kept most of these for his own interest, a personal collec-

tion to be placed along his windowsills, while Clarissa saved hers to
sell to the museums, to help raise enough money to leave Odessa and
make another life as soon as she could.

"This one is over a million years old," he would tell her, handing her
some intricately spiraled snail, "while this one is only about six hundred thousand." The smell of ancient lime-chalk both fascinated and
repelled her — it was the stuff of geology, the stuff of her hometown
— and yet neither could she pull away entirely from him, or the fossils.

They worked in the evenings along the old strand lines, and along
the fringed edges of ancient reefs, and then deeper — cracking open
vertical seams with rock hammer and crowbar, collecting not just
the fossils on the surface, but reaching down into the strata of their
predecessors.

Even then, and about a thing so meaningless as a mild hobby, he
always kept maps, and they found fossils no one had ever seen or described before, and after a while he was able to predict where they
might be able to find a certain kind of fossil; and after a while longer
— beginning to follow the journey of his dream as if riding on a small
raft, feeling the water take it and lift it, feeling the current's center — he
was able to predict where they would find certain types of fossils that
they had not even seen yet, did not even know existed for sure — hypotheses, musings, based on how a certain sea current, and a certain
temperature and water chemistry, might sculpt them: the world shaping them like a potter spinning clay, or a woodworker tending a lathe.

Like a magician, he would sketch the imagined creatures in a note-
pad — gone-away beings that were fantastically ornamented, bold, and
multiantennaed — and then, a few nights later, and several feet farther
down into the crevice, they would find those very forms.

The impression such discoveries gave both of them was that the
world was infinitely varied, and that the ground upon which they
walked was studded with a colossus of change below, vertical columns
of magnificent fluted architectures and symphonies that no man or
woman had ever seen or heard, dreamed or imagined.

Clarissa's father, in addition to working in oilfield wireline services,
was a Baptist preacher who felt that Clarissa's beauty was more a curse
than a blessing, and who would have been appalled at her wanton en-

gagement with evolution: prowling the reefs and cliffs with the tusks of cephalopods and bivalves and the ribbed shells of trilobites kept safely in a pouch between her breasts, and Clarissa believing more and more deeply, with each swing of the hammer, in some story larger and grander than the same but simpler version on which he had raised her.

Their work was dirty, climbing among the slot canyons and brushy draws and smashing apart the old lime reefs that were sometimes so riddled with fossils as to seem like the honeycomb of bees. Their bodies would be covered with grit and dust and chalk — newly cracked, freshly broken Cretaceous odors that had not been in the world for several hundred million years — and their arms would be latticed with scratches from where they had reached down into the stony crevices to extract their treasures, as if dissecting the tiniest and most integral gear-works of some huge and calcified machine that had once been the grandest thing on earth.

They camped down along the river, and would swim back across it — Clarissa was not as strong a swimmer, and used a life jacket — and they would bathe in the eddies. They would ride inner tubes through the rapids, making the long run in the horse-drowning current and then walking back up along the shoreline, picking their way around the salt-encrusted skulls of the last century's horses.

Sometimes under the cover of so much darkness it would feel to both of them as if all the sky above had already been transformed into the strata of time — that they were already sealed beneath such a sky, as if below so many trillions of tons of stone — and that at any moment their movements would cease forever and they would be stranded there with the horses' heads, caught ankle- or knee-deep in the mire. Like the children they had been not long ago, they would ride the inner tubes down the moon-bright current, the river bright as magma, again and again, until they were both clean and exhausted, or as clean as they could get, bathing in a salt river.

They would sleep beside the crossing on air mattresses, lulled by the sound of the river. On clear nights, they could hear (and sometimes feel trembling within the earth) the ceaseless throb and clatter of the faraway rigs, as the drillers sought to reach ever deeper, focused on only one thing, and chasing that one thing, the shape of it like the outline of a fleeing animal, hounding it, as if believing like blind converts that that one thing had more significance than any other, and that there was nothing else of comparable worth in the world; or, most blindly of all, that there might truly one day be an end to their searching, and a stanching of their hunger.

Clarissa rarely slept, there on the air mattress. She would lie awake watching the stars while Richard slept, and she would wait. When she swam she kept her hair up in a bun, to keep the salt in the river from damaging it, and only the hair at the nape of her neck would get damp.

On the riverbank, she would lie very still, conscious of the need to conserve herself — her energy, and her passions — sensing that if she was to escape Odessa successfully and forever, she would have to do so, despite her great beauty, by somehow staying beneath the world's, or time's, notice. To wait, and wait, until a gate or door opened.

She did not even know what the door looked like, nor certainly to where it led: only that it had not yet opened, and she felt the need to wait, as if sleeping.

Richard would awaken shortly after dawn, on those mornings when they were able to spend the night out along the river — when his work did not call him back to the oilfields that next day, for one rare reason or another — and Clarissa would already be sitting up, just watching him, a sheet drawn around her shoulders, as if even the first pink light of day might somehow be able to burn her fair skin.

He would feel himself being studied, and would rise and embrace her. They would make love on the sand, the sheet over his back above her for protection against the sun, like a billowing tent — the day's dry breezes already beginning — and then he would make a driftwood cookfire, and would catch and fry a catfish for his breakfast, and make eggs and bacon for hers.

She would eat nothing that came from so wild and rank a place as the river, though she enjoyed with a perfect mix of distaste and longing watching him hunker naked by the fire, cock hanging down to the sand, spiny gutted catfish dipped in batter and leaning out over the skillet head and tail, Richard using a sock as a hot pad for the iron skillet, so that in that first pale light, pink turning already to copper, the scene could have been from a hundred or two hundred years ago, a nomadic Comanche or Apache.

After breakfast, Clarissa would paint her body completely with zinc oxide, as would Richard, and they would go walking in the desert, naked save for their sandals, hats, and sunglasses.

This was the most dangerous thing she did; the most dangerous thing she would ever do. She could feel the heat trying to burn through the crust of her white shell. She carried the tube of zinc with her and stopped to reapply it whenever a trickle of sweat revealed even the thinnest trace of flesh, and Richard carried a canteen on a strap slung over his shoulder.

On they marched, like ghosts reanimated, following the sensual hills of the dunes, searching for nothing, only wandering; and knowing that if they got lost, or ran out of water, they would die, and die horribly.

In the dazzling heat and blowtorch winds, their zinc coatings baked and continuously cracked and fell off in patches, so that they kept having to stop and mend each other's gaps, as if repairing chinks in armor. Sand and grit and even husks of insect shells and stray feathers and the fur of jackrabbits and the occasional wind-tossed glittering scales of skeletal fish and reptiles would become affixed to the sweating sludge of their whitened, protective coating, so that it might have seemed that they themselves were evolving, and at a pace approaching light-speed, into some melded, awkward admixture of landscape: a crude experiment, and reeling, lost, frantic.

None of these emotions were in them, however, when they were in the dunes. They took their time, gave themselves over to following the curious, shifting slopes as they might follow behind a herd of circus elephants, or camels, or some other odd and extravagant grouping; and they did not panic.

Occasionally they would happen upon the little temporary oases, the just-appeared ponds of wind-rippled, sparkling water, once again attended to by birds, and sometimes by coyotes and kit foxes; and again, they would crouch on their hands and knees at water's edge, or hunker, and drink from the lens of water like wild animals (the colorful birds swirling overhead), or they would drink with cupped hands, would let the cold water run down their arms, and would sprinkle the water on the backs of each other's necks and faces: and then, reapplying even more zinc oxide, they would turn back, heading for the wide salty vein of the Pecos.

And once back in their camp, they would bathe in that salty river. They would dress in cool long-sleeved shirts and light cotton pants and drive back to Odessa, feeling free and glorious to be shed of the old fur-and-grit paste-skin that had become like a part of themselves; and on the drive back, bleary-eyed, they would drink a gallon of fresh water, drinking straight from a plastic jug.

Once back in town, Clarissa would sleep for the rest of the day and that night, and almost all of the next day as well, so drained would she be from the sojourn and its strange challenges; and it would not be until the next day that she would use her parents' car to take the fossils she had collected all the way to Austin, a five-hour drive each way, to sell to a museum there, lying about the provenance of the discovery, saying only that she had found them in cardboard boxes upon cleaning out the estate of her grandfather.

She would put the money in an Austin bank. She wasn't sure how much she would need to go to wherever she was going, nor when or where that would be. In her first two months with Richard she had made almost $10,000, collecting and selling fossils, but she did not think that would be nearly enough. It would have helped to know where she wanted to go or what she wanted to do, but the door simply had not opened.

She was certain that it would. It never occurred to her that it might not. And there was never a gathering of people — an office party in Odessa, a routine shopping trip, a Sunday morning in church — when, if a real door opened, her eyes did not turn to that door, to see who or what might be entering.

There was another collector in the region, a Mr. Herbert Mix, an elderly man who had lost a leg to diabetes and who had once been enraptured with the search for the various caches of gold.

Before his leg had been taken, Mix had evidenced a hunger not only for the gold itself, nor its legends and lores, but for everything else that might have been peripherally associated with it. Any trace of iron or steel he happened across in his diggings, or any other human artifact, he was compelled to save. He had begun searching for the treasure when he was seven; he was now seventy-four, and had lost his leg only ten years before. Over the years he had established a substantial hoard, one that filled numerous adobe huts in town.

Old horseshoes, knife blades, wagon wheels, clay pots, human skeletons: anything was fair game, his hunger was nondirectional and unquenchable, and he hauled it all home, affixed an index card to each item stating the date and location of when and where it had been found, along with a brief narration of what Mix perceived to have been the circumstances of its deposition.

Always lurid, his descriptions confirmed without fail his suspicions that there had never been an arrowhead that had not pierced human flesh, nor any skeleton that had perished under any circumstance save for a massacre or a sun-maddened wandering. The most intricate trinkets — a single rusted link of chain — were physical proof of the Emperor Maximilian's exiled wanderings. *Here,* he had camped for the night, with only half a day's lead on his pursuers, who intended to bring him back to Mexico to execute him for, among other things, having failed their expectations; *here,* this shard of pottery, was where Coronado sat with the chief of the Zuñis and informed him that the Zuñis were now subjects of the nation of Spain. *Here,* this fragment, was where the chief rose to his feet, broke the clay dish over his knee, and stalked off, vowing to make war upon the white man "until the ocean turned to stone again." *This* tattered songbook, this hymnal, could only have belonged to the wife of the first pastor in the county, the pastor who had received the deathbed confessions of so many, and who, in turn, prior to breathing his last, murmured more treasure clues, scrambled, to his wife . . .

It was all there, in little dusty earthen-floored storage sheds out back off the main streets of Odessa, the blood-and-guts matrix of his dreams, as well as the dreams of so many others; and, enthusiastically quantified and cataloged, it was for him as irrefutable as any history book.

Mix opened a museum that showcased the trappings and residues of the treasures, if not the treasures themselves. He catered to the lonely and the unfulfilled; and in addition, to the long tables of mementos he kept on display in an abandoned garage — charging fifty cents per head to walk in and take refuge from the heat of the day (the eternal wind slinging sand against the curved metal roof of the garage, which had the shape and cavernous sounds of an airplane hangar), and charging a dollar for those who wanted to touch.

Horseshoes, square nails, old coffee cans, and other refuse from the hundreds of searchers earlier in the century: nothing was sacred, and though Mix was unwilling to part with any of the hundreds of human skulls he'd accumulated over the decades, he was not above selling various lesser body parts — a vertebra, a phalange, or even a pelvic bone — to a motivated buyer.

In the yard behind his house, amongst the weeds, were enough rusting and rotting wagon-train wheels to supply three cavalries across five centuries. It had long been said that a person could not safely ride a horse through the dunes, because one of the horse's hoofs would sooner or later snag on one of the thousands of abandoned wagon wheels; and until about the 1930s and '40s, until Herbert Mix's insatiable appetite had been unleashed fully upon the landscape, that had been true.

In addition to selling wagon wheels to decorate the front-gate entrances of ranches and ranchettes, he sold pickaxes and canteens, tents and army cots, to would-be searchers; and he had his own maps for sale too, diagrams of the position and orientation of what he perceived to be some of the more significant of his discoveries: and from those orientations he had offered interpretations.

He rented these maps out to novice prospectors for hard cash as well as a contractual agreement that stipulated a fifty-fifty split of any bounty that was found. And though Mix could rarely any longer get into the mountains, he offered himself as a consultant, and for a fee could be persuaded to haul himself up onto a midget burro and, beneath a pink or purple parasol gotten for $1.99 at the department store, head laboriously up into the mountains or out into the desert with one of a new generation of seekers, sipping whiskey and pointing out places to dig, while ruminating upon and interpreting each spadeful of dirt.

Across the span of over half a century of his disease, he made a lot of money; not as much, perhaps, as he might have been able to produce from the liquidation of a single strongbox of bullion, but enough — more than enough, had he lived prudently, conservatively, moderately. And in a cautious, considered manner, he might have been able to summon, across time, some approximate and perhaps satisfactory semblance of the wealth not from any discovery of the treasure itself, but simply from the sustained dream of it.

He failed in prudence, however. He was unable to restrain his appetite, nor the terrifying euphoria he would sometimes feel, midmeal, when he first realized that, despite prodigious consumption, enough would never be enough.

And so he had not only sold, he had bought. His goal was to sell the unworthy, the duplicated, and the common; but because it all had value in his eyes, he was rarely able to refrain from purchasing the dregs of memorabilia that came sweeping through his museum, brought there by fellow treasure seekers like the cracked and salt-corroded leavings of some reverse tide, running always counter to his own.

No sooner had he closed a sale on a pickax, or a time-pitted cannonball, than some wayfaring derelict would come in with yet another skull, or a sun-mottled medicine vial, or a bird-point arrowhead with the cedar arrow-shaft still attached, wanting to trade it for whiskey money. He had once bought a saber for four hundred dollars; a conquistador's helmet for seven hundred. A rust-gutted six-shooter for a hundred dollars; an odd-shaped stone with an etching on it — perhaps authentic, perhaps not — for two hundred. Even tattered articles of clothing — a faded straw hat, a pair of sand-blown chaps stiff as the sun-dried hide of some bone-bleached steer; a salt-crusted boot — were not beyond his desire.

He spent what he had, for the tide was always coming in.

Always, the skulls were what intrigued him the most. In the early days of his obsession, he had been enamored with the entire skeletal carriage; but as he aged, and then even more so as he shed one of his own legs, it became only the skulls that held interest for him: and of those skulls, his favorite part was the upper; the smooth, boulder-rounded curve of sutured cranium, repository of an infinity of gone-by senses, of sparkling cells of memory now dried to dust and blown forgotten back into the world, leaving behind only the curious whorls of geometry, the empty skull as smooth and lifeless as the inner sweep of a wave-polished, long-vacant conch shell or some other calcified vessel, like the specimens held up to one's ear in childhood in order to hear the echo of the sea's roar.

The other, lesser skeletal parts he kept piled about in his weedy backyard. At first he had attempted to arrange and catalog them, with painted reference numbers corresponding to their detached head-pieces, but over the years he abandoned that practice and now merely stacked them into one general boneyard.

Before the physical limitations of his age and his condition had caught up with him, he had rented a great balloon-tired tractor, and with a deep-toothed harrow had combed the troughs between the dunes with the patience of a deep-sea fisherman, keenly attuned beyond the throttled tremblings of the tractor to the dull snag and clink of iron tooth finding rounded bone; and when he felt or sensed such interruption, he would throw the tractor into neutral and hop down and trot out through the warm sand to go gather up his dis-covery: examining it eagerly, searching for clues to the wounds of battle.

Despite the intensity of his hoarding, his remained always an ama-teur's interest, and he was never able to ascertain any ethnicity of the skulls, nor sex, nor age. He simply gathered them, like pumpkins, and dropped each one into a burlap bag that he kept hanging from the rear fender of the tractor.

Other times he would not feel the harrow's tug, but would ride for unknown stretches of time as if hypnotized by some lulling com-bination of the tractor's idle and purr, and by the sight of the dunes all around him like waves, and by the heat, and by the brightness. Crossing-over seagulls, traveling from the Gulf Coast to some inland lake — Yellowstone, farther north, or the Great Salt Lake, or even the smaller Juan Cordona Lake — would see the tractor trawling below, and from habit would veer and follow it for a while, as they did with the shrimpers' boats at sea, or the threshers tilling the wheat fields farther north, churning up worms and insects.

But there was nothing for them below but dry sand and the occasional skull or arm bone (the radius or ulna sometimes crooking up from the sand in the precise position of a swimmer executing a perfect crawl-stroke, as if having labored all this time to come back up from the depths).

In his reverie, Herbert Mix would travel on for some great distance, until some stray thought or image finally awakened him; and he would look back and see, in the long furrowed row behind him, a wealth of risen skulls, shining like melons in the sunlight, and the gulls circling; and again he would shut his tractor off, and throw the burlap bag over his shoulder, and wander back into the desert to gather time's harvest, retracing the furrows of his path.

The bag would grow heavy as he wandered that long furrow, and he would sometimes be made uneasy by the thought and then the belief, as the heft of the bag grew greater and the skulls clanked and rattled, that he was not so much walking on sand as he was on skulls; that were the teeth on his harrow longer, they would find even more skulls; that the world was nothing *but* skulls, and a tangle of skeletons, all the way down — that even the mountains themselves were but a thin patina of earth drawn taut across that tangled assemblage — and when he turned to look back at his tractor, as if for reassurance that he was still in this world, he would be further discomforted by the distance he had traveled, without having realized it.

The tractor would be only a shining glint in the faraway blending of haze and dune, barely even identifiable as an artifact of man, and Mix would be overcome with loneliness; but still, he would turn around and press on, harvesting his skulls, for it was less frightening for him to pretend that the feeling was not real, than to acknowledge it, and to turn in fear and loneliness back to the tractor.

Like a coward as well as a stoic, he pushed on. Ravenous. A slight pain in his leg, twenty years before the fact, as he wandered the bone fields collecting the legs of those he had never known.

• • •

A miracle had happened to Herbert Mix only once, and in many ways his life was poorer for it rather than richer, for it had been so many years since the phenomenon had revealed itself, and so many years had he spent in the dunes awaiting expectation of others like it, that his waiting had turned finally into disappointment, and the disappointment to frustration.

He had seen the phenomenon when he was forty years old. He was out prowling the dunes, as he often did, walking with a backpack and compass, ribbons and long willow poles. A shovel and a sack lunch; a straw hat. Anything of interest that he came across that would fit into the pack, he would load into it before continuing on his way; and anything that was too bulky or heavy, he would do his best to mark on the map, and would drive a willow pole into the sand, affixing bright pink and blue ribbons to the top of the pole like prayer flags, and would hope that the dunes would not change so much by the time he returned.

The miracle had occurred on the summer solstice. Such an event was of no special import to Herbert Mix, other than the fact that the day would be long, and, still being in relatively good health, he intended to travel a long way, to utilize the fullness of the day.

He had been traveling already for half the day — trudging bronze-skinned beneath the sun — when he crested a tall dune and looked down and saw, in the opposing and balanced wind-scalloped trough on the back side of the dune, the most astounding sight: what he took at first to be a modern-day wagon train, complete with gaunt horses and gaunt travelers, laboring to get the mired wagon back on track.

Mix's eyes blurred in the wind, and his heart froze with terror, as in that first moment his eyes tried to inform his brain of the impossible: that these lost travelers were still wandering from the last century; that time had stranded them — had braided around them, leaving them untouched.

He stood petrified on the ridge, the ribbons on his flags flapping in the wind like the pendants of some child playing conquistador; and it was some time before the chill in his heart subsided and his true vision returned to him, so that he was able to see that the wagon train was not captured by ghosts but was simply the remains of the past, little touched and well preserved.

He hurried down into the basin with all the greed and astonishment of any seeker. Already the swirls and back currents of wind were bringing a fine flashing sift of sand into the basin, as when rising waters seek to fill a low spot. He hurried over to the wagon train and marveled at the story before him, examined all the parts of it with his hands, still not daring to believe what he was seeing.

There were but two huge horses in the traces: all bones, now, and crumpled to their keels in various states of collapse. Mix got the impression they were down on their knees, pawing for water, and in the back of the wagon (canvas top long gone, but hooped ribs still intact) lay a skeleton in perfect grinning repose; not as if he had been fever-wracked at the point in time when the wagon had finally gotten bogged down in the sand, and not as if he had already been dead at that point, so that it was merely his lifeless and soulless body that the wagon had been transporting (why else had he not gotten out to try to help, nor even stirred?), but instead as if he had been enjoying everything so immensely — the sickness, the bouncing ride, and then the agony of getting stuck yet again; and enjoying, above all, the waterless, blazing heat — that he had been unwilling to bestir himself from this position of ecstasy.

The rider's hands lay clasped across his chest. His gnarled and rodent-chewed boots were still on the remains of his feet, as if he had intended to lie down for only a little while; as if he had intended, once the euphoria had passed, to get back up and go out and help.

It was the figure kneeling at the right rear axle that intrigued Mix the most. She, too, still had her boots on, and her hat, still sand-filled, had not traveled far from her bright shining head. Her blouse or shirt was long gone — scraps of that fabric shredded by time and used in the lining of the nests of generations of mice and birds — though her skirt, evidently of a hide material, was still partially intact, tattered but drawn taut around her, as if it had been her skin, not another animal's, all along.

The woman had had straight long reddish-brown hair — hanks of it still lay attached to the hat, and on the quilt on which she seemed only to be resting — and to Herbert Mix's great horror and discomfort, he found himself aroused. As if the woman were somehow still living. As if time had vanished, or never occurred. As if the elegant shapes and suppleness of flesh were but a layer of clothing, obscuring or covering something even more beautiful, stark, and vital.

He shook these thoughts from his head and moved a step closer. The woman was leaning against the stuck wheel, collapsed against it as if praying — still praying — and Herbert Mix took out his shovel and dug cautiously but easily around the wheel.

At its base he found more quilt.

The sand was still sifting into the newly uncovered basin, like that which runs through an hourglass. Herbert Mix went over to the left rear wheel and began digging, and found another quilt; and under each front wheel, more quilts.

It was obvious to him what had happened. The iron wheels had been just a little too narrow, and the wagon a little too heavy (perhaps if the man had been able to get out and walk — had he been a big man — or even been able to help push, things might have been different; perhaps, perhaps), and the horses were too tired to continue to pull the heavy load.

The woman had been pushing them on, three feet at a time, making the journey easier for them, if even only slightly, by positioning the quilts under each wheel, so that it was for the horses as if they were pulling across that quilted surface, rather than plowing so deeply — muscles quivering; sweat pouring from their huge bodies, and not a sip of water for miles ahead — and finally, the heat had killed one of them, horse or woman first, Mix couldn't tell.

Perhaps when the horses went down, it was at that point that the woman had leaned her head for the last time against the stuck wagon wheel.

There were twin oaken water barrels mounted upright on the back of the wagon, and out of morbid curiosity, Herbert Mix pried open the lids and looked inside — *Still empty,* he thought, fingering the heft of his own canteen.

He gave the wagon a cursory search for any possible bullion — what but treasure, he wondered, could have inspired such ferocious and dogged wandering? — and finding nothing of real worth — an ancient cracked Bible, pages fluttering back and forth in the wind as if some unseen reader was furiously scanning for some certain passage only dimly remembered — Herbert Mix pondered and debated on what to fill his pack with, knowing (the rising sand was up over his calves now; had risen to the kneeling woman's wind-sharpened haunches) that when he returned, all would be vanished — knowing that trough would become ridge, and ridge, trough.

In the end, he settled for the mundane, the seemingly trivial: a pair of reading glasses, a pocket watch, a diary that he would later examine for clues to treasure, though there were none. An old Dutch oven; plates, knives, forks. The wind-whipped Bible, if only to cease its furious movements.

Nothing from the man or woman — not even their skulls — but from the back of the wagon, a riding saddle, still in tolerable condition, one that might possibly be restored. His mind was already racing, thinking ahead to the text he would put on the index cards. Surely they had been headed to the gold fields in California, if not already on their way back. What else was there?

He turned and stared back in the direction from which they had come.

From all the trouble they'd been having — laying down those quilts, lunging through the sand three feet at a time, stopping to pull the quilts out, dig under the wheels, clawing with bloodied hands, laying them down again — it seemed certain that they must have jettisoned any tonnage of gold elsewhere; and it was one of the few moments of truth in Herbert Mix's life, one of the few times he was ever given pause to realize how vast the desert really was, and what tiny space such treasure might truly occupy.

The wind continued to carve funnels of sand out from beneath the cornice: cutting it lower and lower, and as the lip of the undercut cornice fell, re-formed, and fell again — moving ever closer to the scene below, like some stalking giant — Herbert Mix set about the planting of his flags; scrambled with drowning gold-lust up the sand slope, sinking to his knees under the weight of his useless bounty. He quickly began setting the poles along the windward rim of the basin, even as that rim continued to be scalloped downward.

Drenched in sweat, he succeeded in ringing the caldera with eight of his poles before the skeletons had disappeared beneath the sand, not like victims but like divers choosing to descend. Mix watched as the sand dimpled in waves that showed only vaguely their sleeping shapes below, and then nothing: the wagon sinking too in that manner, as if it was the weight of the wagon, the thing to which they clung, that was pulling them down, and that if only they could have released themselves from it, they might have been borne back up to the surface.

His poles were leaning and then toppling as the ridge advanced across the basin, again like something walking; and as the level of the ridge lowered itself to meet the rising trough of filling sand, the sight gave him the most disorienting feeling — as if he were surfing; and without his moving, it seemed nonetheless that he *was* moving, riding some immense and powerful wave: and he knelt there, grit stuck to his sweating body, skin broiling, lungs heaving.

It was not until the ridge had leveled itself completely with the trough, with the pioneers suddenly beneath that astounding burden, that Herbert Mix realized he was sinking, descending into a new sandy basin much as a doodlebug falls prey to the ant-lion's simple but cunning trap of gravity.

Fighting the shifting substrate, he labored halfheartedly up the new ridge, the one that seemed to be walking away from him, and began gathering his fallen flags. He would place them elsewhere in the desert on his walk out — planting them in what he hoped would be more trustworthy locations, near the scarce patches of semipermanent willow, saltbush, and tumbleweed; and he would attempt, with his drunkman's trudging stagger, to measure approximate distances, in leagues and varas, while sketching a crude map of his backtrack: but he knew even as he paused to construct these tiny markers that there was no hope, that the miracle was as good as gone, and in some strange way more ungraspable now for having been seen and lost than had it been only imagined and not yet found.

The physical toll would rock him as nothing ever had before. A hundred and then a thousand times that day—*he had gone too far*—he knew that he should lay down the burden of his foolish pack and focus instead simply on getting out alive. He could feel the tender organs inside his pale skin, sheathed only in thin muscle, beginning to bake inside his body, could feel the blood soup that bathed the fragile meninges of his brain beginning to simmer, and as he trudged on, he dreamed of wading through reeds into the warm shallow water of a stock tank, the mud soft between his toes, and lying back then and floating on the surface of that water.

After that, he imagined nothing, only pushed on, seized with some implacable and uncalmable ferocity—not even greed, but some primal essence of hunger, which surprised him, aware as he was of the hugeness of his need.

The glistening sweat kept leaping from him, evaporating quickly, until he had no more to give, but still he struggled on, tumbling and falling, his pack full of treasures, or things that might have once been associated with treasures.

He barely made it back out. He hauled the sledge of his pack up one dune after another. There was no clear path out, no trail, and each mistake or inefficient choice seemed to cost him tenfold.

Twice he had gone into fibrillation, his body so dehydrated as to venture over into the territory of cardiac arrest and sunstroke, and he had lain down the last time, barely able to breathe—his lungs and breath quivering staccato now, within sight of the river, though he had not been able to make himself rise.

He lay there, chest pounding and breath racing, and stared at the not-too-distant and extraordinarily familiar notch of Castle Gap, and Horsehead Crossing below.

He was close enough to smell it. A pair of ravens drifted in the distance, black against the blue sky of summer. Had it been earlier in the day, he would have lain there and baked to death. As it was, dusk rescued him after only a couple of hours, and when he awoke again it was evening and the desert stars were out, and he was still lying on his side and looking at them upside down, so that they seemed to be the lights of some endless civilization far below.

He did not have the strength to carry his pack any farther — each time he tried to stand, his heart leapt with the fright of a trapped wild animal — but he was able to drag it down the hill to the river, and to the river's road where his jeep was waiting.

And such was his weakness when he got there that he was unable to lift the pack into the jeep, but had to unload it, item by item — again lifting out the most mundane objects with the greatest reverence.

He managed to haul his cracked and fried body up into the familiar seat of the jeep, but was too addled to take the key from the ashtray where he kept it stored. He sat there staring at the ashtray for the longest time.

He was comforted just to know that the key was close, that he had made it all the way to within sight of it, or to within sight of the place where it was kept, even if he could not close that final distance, and he fell asleep — or into some chasm deeper than sleep but not all the way into unconsciousness, some floating, pre-embryonic place, his mind unmade and unformed and instead simply a tangled mass of electrical synapses emitting low and random signals — and it was not until dawn the next day that his life returned to him with any semblance of function.

He drove on into town, slowly; had one glass of water, and then a second, drinking it carefully.

He lay down on his bed — his chest was bruised purple from the severity with which his runaway heart had pounded — and he slept for thirty-six hours, rising only once to use the bathroom and drink another quart of water.

For a week, every part of his body felt as if it had been beaten with a wooden club, and for the rest of his life, his kidneys ached whenever he encountered any kind of physical stress; and he was certain it was because of that one ordeal that he eventually lost his leg.

But his treasures! They occupied a special place in his museum — the Ghost Wagon Train wing of the garage — and though he went out again and again looking for the man and the woman, he never saw them again; and in this regard, across the years — or so he told himself — the value of his treasures from that day grew and grew: the old

Dutch oven, the broken saucer, the rusting knife blade, the Bible, the arrowhead with spear shaft still attached. That was all there was. That was all there would ever be.

He might as well have traveled to the moon. And to his credit, he did not put those items up for sale.

2

CLARISSA FOLLOWED RICHARD that summer as if in a trance, and he let her, made no effort to speak the truth of their differences (partly because it was so unnecessary; it was only too evident). He led her around town, and around the desert, as if escorting some haltered or bridled animal that was being led to slaughter.

As if taunting love, Richard would often come by Clarissa's house just after daylight. She kept irregular hours, like those of some rarely seen animal, waking and then sleeping in small naps through the night, and wandering the world and performing her tasks and errands in the cool and lightless hours (as did a surprising number of the town's residents — not out of fear of the light, but simply in order to avoid the heat).

By nine o'clock, Clarissa would be showered and dressed and in the air-conditioned office, ready for the short run of the workday. Sometimes she napped in a back room on her lunch break, lying down on the carpet with neither sheet nor pillow, an alarm clock by her side, sleeping the unconscious fish-mouthed drooling slumber of the pole-axed; awakening on the alarm's beeping, forty-five minutes later, with the carpet's impressions deep upon one extended arm and the side of her face, and the day really only beginning for her, at that point.

But in those few hours between the rise of the soft prairie dawn and the time when she had to leave for work, Richard would occasionally come by her house and make breakfast for her as she slept: fried eggs, from a neighbor's henhouse, and corn tortillas wrapped in a damp clean cotton dish towel and steamed in the oven, and black coffee, filter-dripped, and thick bacon, cooked sizzling in a black iron skillet, and salsa made from cilantro and tomatoes he'd clipped from her garden there at the edge of first light.

It was the sound of the blender that would awaken her, on those mornings when he came over to her house, and the chagrin she felt at being awakened so early was tempered by the pleasure of the knowledge of the meal he would be bringing to her.

She would lie there between those two places, annoyance and anticipation, and would rise and fall between sleep and wakefulness, until finally he brought the meal to her in bed, as if he were in love with her: as if she dominated his almost every thought, and shaped the direction of his days.

Other mornings, they ate out on the front porch. She lived at the edge of town, so that she was able to look west to the buff-colored desert, soft and luminous at that hour, with no waves of heat and mirage rising yet from its hardpan surface, nor any dust devils or curtain of blowing sand. The lift and plunge of the eternally throbbing pumpjacks would be the only movement.

To the east, they could see and hear already the wakeful sounds of town — the mongrel coyote-dogs trotting down the brown streets in brown light, going from garbage can to garbage can; the whishing sound of sprinklers in the yards of the few people who still kept a few spindly fruit trees, and dying lawns; the groan of the delivery trucks, potato chip venders and beer and soda distributors and bakery vans, and the paperboy on his bike (the solitary *thwap* of each thin city-paper skidding onto the sidewalk or porch, and the almost musically arranged chorus line of barking dogs noting his passage through the neighborhood).

The pumpjacks throbbing, not just to the west, but in all directions, pumpjacks set up even on empty lots within the city limits.

Farther east, over the tops of the houses, they could see the modest rise of the sparkling new office buildings, constructed in only the last few years — and on such mornings, their hands clasped together, it would seem to Clarissa that she and Richard were emotionally in some similar place and time, and that for the time being that might even be how they preferred it — neither east nor west, nor past nor future.

Richard would brush her hair some evenings for over an hour, and would stroke and rub and caress and otherwise administer to her sometimes for just as long, before beginning the interior acts of love. And there was always some trace or lingering resentment, and sometimes even fear, on Clarissa's part, believing or suspecting that with such kindness — the prepared breakfasts, the extraordinary food, and his generous lovemaking — he was attempting to ensnare her and pull her out into the light; and when faced with such thoughts, every inch of her body would recoil, retreating again to some safer, darker distance; and each time, always, he would follow her calmly into that place, and lead her back gently to where she had been before she had become frightened: though never would she venture any farther, out into the heat and light.

She was honest about it: he was an antidote to loneliness. He could be a balm against the heat, even if she was frightened of his force, and the temperature, the excitement, that seemed often to be attendant to both his ideas and his actions.

She was content to only pick at the breakfast — the gleaming melon, the bright strawberries, blackberries, and blueberries — and to take the odors of these things with her black coffee. They would sit, one hand loose in the other's — he admiring of her beauty, and she respectful of his radiant force, even as she was frightened of it — and Richard would end up having to finish her meal for her as the day came slowly to life; and still she would sit there next to him, desiring his body and desiring to share hers with him, even as that defensive part of her was stirring with a thing almost like hate.

Whenever Richard, admiring her, stopped to consider how much time of perfection she might have left, the number he usually guessed was ten years, but from his vantage point that was nearly half his life, and it still seemed like such an extraordinary span of time that it might as well have been twenty or thirty years of knock-dead beauty she had remaining, or even forty, or even the rest of her life.

If Clarissa had dared to think about it, she probably would have given herself only two years of remaining perfection. But she didn't. She didn't even assume that it would last until the end of each day. She huddled beneath the weight of that remaining time as a quail chick remains frozen beneath the shadow of a hovering hawk.

The strong wind blowing the grass in waves, laying it down flat in shifting meanders, the bird remaining crouched. The wind gusting, swirling, rearing, and all the rest of the world hurrying past. *Hide.*

All the rest of the town coming to life. She and Richard would hear the streetcar-like clack and clatter of the football team trotting through the streets on their morning training run. The holiness of that sport exceeded even the rites of the fundamentalist sects and churches to which most of the town belonged. In the height of summer, as football season approached, and then in the autumn, in the full pitch of battle, the tenor of the village differed very little from how it had been in Aztec villages centuries before, farther south, or the bloodlust rituals of the Roman gladiators, in which the ultimate pleasure came not in seeing one opponent triumph, but rather, the vanquishing of the weaker.

The only saving grace might have been that the townspeople loved the players, or believed that they did. It was a poisonous trap in which the town's greatest love could, however, be reached only by their boys' victories; and no matter, really, whether in close and dramatic fashion or by overwhelming crush — the boys had only to win, to be most fully loved; the entire town baying like hounds, when this happened, a Friday-night chorus in the autumn that would set the coyotes out in the desert to howling, answering across that thin space between village and wilderness.

And of this seemingly unconditional love that was in fact not at all unconditional, the players, even though still yet children, understood the nature or boundaries of it in ways that were never spoken to them, and of which they never spoke, even amongst themselves.

The connection, though perverted and tenuous, was at least a connection; for the townspeople did endeavor, in their crude way, to raise the boys as they would a crop, bestowing gifts and favors as a farmer in a dry land would haul water to his or her crops, so that the crops might flourish, even if unnaturally, in that hostile environment.

The songs were what the townspeople would hear first in the early mornings, in any season. The coaches pushed the boys as if driving them to their salvation, and as the boys ran, or pulled a wagon, fitting six in the harness at a time (the other players jogging alongside them in full combat gear, cleats tatting the pavement like some brute parade of tap dancers, with the players' feet looking cloven and dainty beneath the monstrous bulk of their pads and helmets), the boys would all sing the school hymn and fight song, usually a cappella (though sometimes if the boys' play had been laggard in the previous game, or if the worst and rarest tragedy, a loss, had befallen them, the coaches would punish them by having the boys in harness pull the marching band on a string of wagons, with the brass ensemble playing the full blaring, rousing piece, over and over); and it was like a parade, each and every morning one by which the townspeople could set their clocks.

The song, and the demon-frightening tinny banging and tooting of the band, was the first sound a sleeping or resting citizen would hear, followed by the shouts and curses of the coaches, who also rode the wagons; and then, closer, the grinding and rasping of the steel wheels of the wagons.

Closer still, the listener would hear the strangely rhythmic pattering of fourteen hundred and forty cleats rising and falling — sixty boys, twelve cleats to a shoe — and finally, the individual breathing of the boys as they passed: the sibilant intakes of air by the flyweight receivers and running backs, and the torturous wounded-bull gaspings of the out-of-shape linemen.

The players' faces would be limned with saintly agony as they pushed themselves further than ever before, entering each morning into a new country, and almost always not so much out of a love for the game as out of a perversion of that love, desiring foremost only to please the fans, and the coaches, and the other players — beginning to disappear in that manner, as if swallowed by some cleft in the world, even before they had fully emerged as individuals of any merit, worth, or interest: and from that point, the coaches pushed them still further and harder.

The boys staggered and stumbled and hacked phlegm and spat clumsily. They ran drenched in sweat — the townspeople they passed could smell the fresh salt-odor of them, and could feel the radiant heat from the train of them — and when one of the boys in the harness stumbled before his time was up, the other boys in the harness would snatch him up quickly, before the rest of them tangled legs and they all went down together; and once again, it was as if no hitch had occurred, so that a viewer watching it could not be sure that the stumble had even happened.

Generally they were clumsy, and the training process looked like what it was, work. Sometimes, however, there would be moments in which a purity of glide appeared not just in the pace and movements of one or even two or three of them, but in the whole conjoined body of them, and in which all the previous tension was released from their faces, and there seemed to be no torment or even effort required at all.

On all their faces, in those brief and strange moments, would be expressions of calm rapture; and in some strange shift of realignment, their cleats would all be lifting and falling at the same time, rising and striking not with fourteen hundred and forty patterings, but one sound, and one voice.

In these inexplicable moments, as unpredictable as desert rain, the boys ran like men, or with the grace and power of animals; and in those blissful moments there would be only silence, save for the steady, hungry grind of the steel wheels, and the one steady striking rhythmic slap of all cleats on track and on line, all in the same moment; and if the band were riding with them, its members would fall silent in slightly envious awe — a silence somehow more eloquent than even the most rousing compositions they had yet been able to muster — and both the band and the coaches would simply ride, in that breezy, gliding silence, behind the sweating backs of the harnessed pullers.

So silent was their passage in these moments of grace that to an on-looker glancing out his or her kitchen window, the procession would have seemed utterly soundless, and that the carriage, the stage coach, was traveling with a smoothness of movement that is usually seen only in dreams.

As well, the simple confidence they received from experiencing these moments of fluency gave them a strength in the world, an authority of bearing, that was an added advantage, enabling them to defeat even superior opponents, on the few occasions when such foes were encountered; and to their advantage also was the plain and grueling nature of their training regimen.

And aiding them still further, though sending them also further down the road to ruin, was the twisted love the townspeople lavished upon them.

Many of the locals parceled out not only the thing they called love, but also the physical treasures of the world: bushel baskets of withered fruit and sun-stunted vegetables from their hot, sandy little gardens, and cases of soda pop, and the latest albums, and new clothes, and even money, as well as surprises from whatever foreign or exotic lands any of the boosters might have visited recently. King salmon, gleaming and wolf-toothed, resting on a bed of ice; Japanese silk kimonos and gilded martial arts swords; autographed footballs and baseballs from famous athletes; ivory trinkets from Alaska, loose gemstones from Thailand; and all other manner of the many layers of dross in the world.

The more able-bodied of the town's and team's boosters would be listening for the boys' far-off but thunderous approach, and it was a joy for those fans to be able to run down out to the street with their offerings and, for a few strides, to keep pace with the rushing-past herd of boys.

The boosters would run a short distance farther with the boys, grinning wildly, as if in amongst a herd of wild cattle or mustangs. But then the wagon, the football players as well as the loose herd, the coaches and the band, would be pulling away, and after that short distance each booster, man and woman, would have to slow to a stop, gasping, bent over and huffing, hands on his or her knees; and as they watched the wagon growing smaller and smaller, not like some tide receding or being pulled by the boys but as if drawn away by some larger, hungrier force, with the boosters' donations piled high on the sides of the wagon, those left behind could sense further that their lives were draining away: and as if some wild little spark burned stubborn within them even still, they would begin already, in that moment of loneliness and failure, to consider what gifts and offerings they might be able to bestow for the next morning's run, and the next; and for most of them, no matter what deals they closed later that day, or what transactions occurred, that brief morning's chase would be the highlight of their day.

For those of them who were too old or infirm to run briefly along-side the wagon — for those who might totter out in front of it and be crushed — they would place their contributions on the sidewalks, and the street corners, on the night before; or, worried that coyotes and stray dogs would wander into town and carry away the perishable items, they would wait until that first gray light of dawn to hurry out with their streetside emplacements for the boys to take as they gal-loped past; and it was a thrill for the old people to sit by their windows and watch as their offerings were received — the velocity and hunger with which the gifts were scooped up seeming somehow crudely rep-resentative of gratitude.

And it was a thrill, or at least a pleasure, for the boys, too, in the monotony of their run, to know that they could always keep looking forward to the next block, and the next; and as with their memories of those rare moments in which a nearly silent glide was achieved, so too in later years would they remember how it had been for each of them when they had first caught sight of the morning's distant, shining gift, glinting in the new-rising light, and of how they had surged slightly, unconsciously, thundering toward both their reward and their goal.

It made them stronger. They left nothing behind.

The games were murderous. The fans wore shining hardhats (the team was called the Roughnecks), and banged on their own helmeted heads with pipe wrenches after every score, or any particularly dra-matic play. It was a deafening, maddening sound, not only to the fans inflicting this upon themselves, but to the players and referees, more disturbing than even the primal wailing of bagpipes, and deeply unset-tling to the opposing team.

Cannons boomed blue smoke into the thin dry air every time there was an Odessa score, and trumpets blared so that the night's sounds were nothing less than those of war; and adrenaline, musky as dog piss, flowed uselessly through the veins of everyone in the stadium, and exited their pores and rose from the circular confines of the new stadium like mist or fog rising from a swamp as the morning light first strikes it on a summer day. The mist intermingled with particles of cannon smoke, and the raft of it was illuminated to a shifting, pulsing glow beneath the halogen intensity of the overhead stadium lights.

Out in the desert, on their nighttime geological digs, or their riverside camping trips, Richard and Clarissa could hear the distant cannons, and the crazed and arrhythmic pipe-and-helmet clattering; and hunkered there on the high reef, they would be able to see clearly the round bowl of incandescence from which those distant sounds were emanating—howls that again elicited in return, from all across the prairie, the savage yelps and wailing of the packs of coyotes, squalls and barks rising all around them from out of the darkness. It would seem to Clarissa and Richard in those moments that the two of them out there on the old frozen reef were the only ones not speaking the language of that excitement, and it was a lonely feeling for them to feel so voiceless, so disempowered.

In that loneliness, Clarissa might have let her heart move in closer to Richard's, there in the safety and distance of the darkness. She had not traveled this far into life, however, hoarding across the span of her days that one rare and delicate treasure, only to release it over the course of a single lonely or frightened evening, or even a hundred or a thousand such evenings.

It could seem to her sometimes though, in Richard's company— whether lonely or not, and whether in the distant-desert darkness or the full white light of day—that that tightly held cone-shaped muscle, the frozen stone-treasure of her ungiving heart, no longer rested on as secure a ledge as it once had, safe from the reach of the world, but was emplaced now on some slight slope; and that the substrate on which that stone heart rested was no longer as firm, but disintegrating, with siftings of sand grains fine as sugar being whisked from beneath it by the steady force of wind and water—forces she had once long ago, as a child, perhaps, viewed as dispassionate, but which she now perceived were hungry solely for her: hungry for the fairness of her skin, the tone of her muscles, the luster of her dark hair, the corona of her beauty.

There were the world's sounds, then, swirling and howling and shouting at one another, with Clarissa and Richard caught voiceless amidst that wild conversation; and there was the steady rushing of the night breezes above them, winding above them like the braids of rivers they could hear but never see; and visible before them was the mushroom-globe dome of blue-white light.

Scattered beyond the stadium and its dying, fading lights, after the game had ended, were the little lights of the town; and beyond that, the lonely vertical towers of incandescent white light that illuminated the outline of each solitary drilling rig, the men and their machines hunting always the elusive green-black swamps and seas of buried oil, hunting the last of it; and beyond the town, in all directions, the wavering yellow lights of the gas flares of the oil wells.

The effect of seeing all those orange fires out on the prairie below was that they might have been viewing a sprawling encampment of Kiowa or Comanche from a century before; or that they had come to the edge of some bluff from which vantage they could see a sight unintended for them — the plains of hell, or at least the gathering encampments of those waiting to be judged and sentenced.

But up on the reef, away from it all, Clarissa and Richard were safely beyond that queue, and knew it; and like lost or clumsy but diligent miners, they kept searching on their hands and knees, with claw hammer and pry pick, the corrugated stony earth before them, with their own lone lantern hissing and casting around them a tiny umbrella of light not unlike the larger one thrown by the distant stadium, or even the wavering gas flames from those little tents set up on the outposts of hell, awaiting their final reckoning.

Moths swarmed their one lantern as they crept through the darkness, searching with their eyes but also their hands for the finest and rarest of the fossils. Sometimes the rivers of wind above would shift direction — as if, in their ceaseless flow, they encountered some imaginary or invisible boulder and were momentarily rerouted — and in that stirring, Richard and Clarissa would be able to hear new sounds, the faint and far-off clunk and rattle of one or more of the desert's pumpjacks. And to Richard and Clarissa, working down on their hands and knees, with the old reef's river winds carrying the sounds toward them, and then away, it sounded sometimes not monotonous or arrhythmic, but like a kind of music; one that was as graceful as those rare moments of animal glide were for the running boys. Moments — fragments of moments — that they would remember forever.

They could both taste the peculiar and specific flavor and odor of the chalk dust as they broke the ancient fossils from the limestone grip of history: and Richard worked for the mystery and romance of being out on the plateau with Clarissa, and beyond the reach of the regular world.

Clarissa worked for the money, pocketing each Jurassic nugget, each Cretaceous sheet of fan coral, as if it were a typeset character from the ruins of the printing press of some grander civilization.

But despite the brute economic accounting of her search, and her desire to ride out of town, out past time's reckoning, she too was beginning to feel the faintest flickers of warmth and mystery, and the romance of it — those waves lapping at the previously firm sand beneath her bare feet, swirling loose sand now around her ankles — and like babes, or the ancient and the infirm, they crept on, groping the twisted, clastic texture of the reef, focusing on one tiny fossil at a time, while above them the world bloomed huge and alive; and with each swing of their rock hammers, more dust filled their lungs, so that it was as if they had reentered and were swimming in that reef, swimming in choppy waves, and were descending.

They began to like the chalky, acrid taste of the dust. It began to fill their throats and lungs, so that it was as if they were literally eating the mountain.

Whenever they stopped to rest for the night — shutting off the lantern and laying their rock hammers by their sides and curling up in a blanket and staring up at the stars, and listening to the rivers of wind above them — it would seem to them, those evenings, stranded out on the frozen reef, that they had finally crawled out some exciting and necessary distance ahead of the waves — had reached the unknown shore — and closing their eyes for a short and intimate nap, they would lie there on the bare pale stone, every bit as motionless as the myriad fossils around them.

• • •

The inland salt lake — Juan Cordona Lake — was perched above the plains just a few miles north of Horsehead Crossing. The lake was a scalloped basin that sat balanced like a shallow dish atop the buried cone of a subterranean salt dome, an entire underground mountain of salt.

The weight of the overlaying world was constantly squeezing down and re-forming this shifting, malleable, underground salt mountain, so that its movements were like those of an immense animal lying just beneath the surface, and almost always stirring.

The inexhaustible breath from this animal, the plumes and glittering grains of salt vapor, mingled ceaselessly, through simple capillary action, with the shallow waters of the lake or playa, saturating the lake (which was fed only by intermittent seasonal rains) with its brine and then supersaturating it, until the lake was no longer a lake but a sea of floating salt sludge, thicker than cake frosting.

The breath of salt kept rising, pulsing to the surface, salt being milked upward by every ounce of fresh water that happened to fall within the dish of the lake; and all that water then evaporated almost immediately, beneath the brain-searing heat (a heat that was magnified by the walls of pure white sand dunes that surrounded the lake, building in times of high wind to crests in excess of fifty feet tall; and the heat was magnified too by the gleaming-bone radiance of the salt flats) — so that what was left behind was a residue of pure salt, oozing slowly, steadily, from the salt mountain so far below, as if from some wound that would never heal.

The lakebed became saltier each day — the thing that would have diluted it, rainfall, ended up only contributing to the increasing salinity, luring or summoning ever more salt upward — and any lost traveler staggering across those dunes who might have happened to take the maddened trouble to climb, for some random and inexplicable reason, any of those fifty-foot hills that helped form the high wall around the lake, would have been confused at first, believing that an unknown inland passage might have just been discovered; and in the blazing, brilliant heat, the thirsting traveler might have wondered whether the ocean below belonged to the Atlantic, or the Pacific, or to some other and perhaps newer ocean, entirely uncharted, running narrow and sinuous through the country's center.

The sun-blistered traveler would be able to sit on the cornice of the giant sand dune and taste the spray of salt that the drying winds hurled, so that if the traveler stared long enough, there would soon be a thin mask of rime in the shape of his or her face, gritty but clean, and the traveler would be able to wet his or her lips and taste the brine of the grains of salt.

The traveler's eyes would sting and tear from the spray, and with the sides of a thumb, the salt would be wiped away, and the traveler might then turn, without venturing down that last perilous slope to visit the great and seemingly useless lake of salt — he or she frightened, for some unknowable reason, and like a balky animal unwilling to go that last short distance.

There would however be other travelers who, after wiping away that glistening salt-mask, would forge ahead; who would push on over the edge and run cascading in ankle-deep heated sand down the front wave of the dune, and out onto the salty floating sludge of whitened crystal, their skin baking as if they had wandered into an oven.

There, at lifeless shore's edge, they would behold the detritus of generations of despoliation and meaninglessness. It might seem to any of them that they had been led here by accursed destiny; but thinking back on their journey, some of them would remember there had been signs and clues all along that they were bound for this place.

All cultures of man had been coming to the lake, determined to find use in the abundance, the excess, of that most basic and mundane of elements, salt (had it been a lake of shit, they would have mined it and carted it away for fertilizer); and in their remembering, the travelers would recall that there had been footpaths worn deep in the desert hardpan, seemingly all ascatter but actually lying upon the desert like the widening spokes of a wagon wheel, radiating from some unknown hub.

The paths of the old salt traders were scored with the labored cuttings of wagon wheels, and lined on either side with the bleached bones of man and animal alike, the skulls looking at first like so many stones or boulders, so that even on a lightless night the traveler would have been able to continue along the trail, navigating by those pale markers alone.

Some days the density of the floating sludge, the bog of it, was such that a man or woman could walk gingerly across it, testing and re-testing with each footstep, avoiding the weaker or soupy places and stepping only on the firmer patches — the traveler's footsteps sinking nonetheless a few inches into the salt crust, so that his or her tracks would be clearly visible for the return trip; though most insidious of all, the localized densities were in constant flux, and never with any discernible physical differences, so that on the traveler's return trip, the route would have to be changed completely.

Patches of salt crust that had been dutifully firm only moments be-fore, which still bore the glistening proof in the form of the traveler's own footprint, were now no longer trustworthy — were less than trust-worthy, in fact, treacherous and beckoning — and the traveler would have to pick and choose, step by cautious step, a new route back to where he or she had come from.

Sometimes such a route could not be found, and the traveler would fall suddenly through a crevasse or abyss, a soup hole, vanishing from sight and history. Other times the traveler would simply become mired, as the sun baked to a thin salt crust certain sections of the lake while melting the sparkling, glistening glaze of others: and in those spots, the traveler would perish, baking in the brilliant heat long before he or she died from a lack of water.

Sometimes the traveler would, in the repose of death, slump forward, in those final moments, dying on all fours; and the wind-whipped sprays of salt that had so tortured him or her for a day or two would continue to lash at the unfeeling carcass, coating the kneeling form with a shining rime until finally, after a few months, nothing re-mained visible of the traveler save for that anomalous humped mound far out on the lake's surface; a shining salt mound which, if someone on the shore squinted their eyes, might be perceived as possessing the rough outline of a kneeling person, as one is able to see in the drifting rearrangements of towering cumulus clouds similarly fantastic shapes: seeing the shapes of whatever it is one desires to see.

Other times, the traveler would expire while still standing, having breathed his or her last panting breath — the traveler's burnt heart having leapt wildly, but in ever-shortening leaps, caught there in the sagging cage of its own rib bones. (He or she might last a full day, upright, and might know then the fevered respite of a short summer evening — but when the sun rose again the next morning, the dawn reflection illuminating the frying pan of salt glaze so that it looked like lava, the traveler's will would break, and by noon he or she would have succumbed, cooked to a crisp.)

Rather than crumple forward, to be baked like a roasting oven-chicken, the traveler might fall backward in those final moments, arms flung outward as if upon some shortened crucifix; and when this happened, the traveler would disappear quickly beneath the salt.

There were times too however when the salt's grip around the traveler's knees would result in him or her falling back into a leaning, forty-five-degree position; and such would be the traveler's weakness, in these instances, that no clench or contraction of leg or stomach muscles could effect a movement back into an upright position, so that for a while the backward-leaning traveler would flail and paddle his or her arms, trying to claw his or her way back up by clutching nothing but air. Such efforts were rarely successful, however, and eventually the traveler would succumb, leaning back as far as those sun-slackened muscles would allow.

The pressure on the protesting joints and ligaments, unaccustomed to such positioning, was excruciating, but the muscles required to remedy the problem simply had no fire, no powers of resiliency left, and the traveler would die quickly now, caterwauling, once he or she fell backward, or halfway backward.

And after the last cries had been uttered, and the last twitch of complaining arm had stilled — the traveler's mouth gaping open as if in song — the windblown salt would begin to shroud these carcasses, too, creating gruesome statues.

Sometimes the salt shrouded first one side of such a monument, before shifting direction and encrusting the other side. The result was that the sculptures grew in size daily, salt ghosts, as each new layer of salt accrued in roughly the same shape as that which had first been deposited upon the form; and not until some mass had been reached that exceeded the physical laws governing such accumulation would slabs of that vertical salt begin to fall from the still-upright traveler, so that again to a viewer on the shore it would now seem that the monstrous sentinel in the center of the lake was shedding one overcoat after another; and as if emerging from a cyst or cocoon, the man or woman would reappear, out in the salt flat's center.

Sometimes the gritty wind would have stripped from the traveler every article of cloth and every ounce of flesh, so that as the wind whistled through the latticework of open ribs it would make a music, punctuated by the keening that oscillated through the grinning skull, and the vacant orbitals of nostrils and eyes — a sound like the music of bagpipes, and all the more eerie for the sound's provenance, which was indisputably coming from that one lone upright skeleton, stranded just beyond reach.

Other times the salt and wind did not destroy the cloth and flesh, but cured and preserved it, so that once those salt husks were shed, it might appear that no harm had befallen the traveler.

The shirt the traveler wore would still be a brilliant blue, and the traveler's black hair might still be fluttering in the breeze. The muscle tone on the outstretched arms would still be taut and firm, and it would appear, from the distant perspective of shore, that the figure was only resting, but that his or her intent and resolve were still strong.

On the rarest of occasions, the traveler would indeed survive, and be set free, later that same day, or in the middle of the night, or in the next day's rise of the orange sun. Ever so rarely, the salt would miraculously release its grip, and after hours of the traveler's futile struggling, a swirl of water might pool up around his or her mired legs, loosening the salt's cast; and with no more effort than wading a shallow creek, the traveler would suddenly be able to lift one foot, and then another; and cautiously, he or she could resume the perilous journey toward shore — alternating the route to account for the constantly changing patches of firmness, and the constantly changing patches of treachery.

Other times, when the travelers succumbed, they acted as lures or attractants for other victims. A man might ride up to the lake and see a person stranded out there, seemingly alive and thus savable, and hurry out with a lariat, intending to get as close as he could, hoping to toss a rope to the stranded person and reel him in.

The cowboy might throw a loop over the ensnared (the traveler's back facing the cowboy, perhaps), only to find out, upon pulling, that the person had ceased moving a hundred years ago, or longer; and at the rescuer's tug the skeleton might snap in half, as brittle as the desert-bleached keel of the skeleton of some tiny shorebird.

The rescuer might end up saving only a sun-withered, mummified arm, a bushel basket of ribs, or nothing at all. Other times the rescuer would end up with less than nothing, and would become mired himself — sometimes afoot, other times on top of a spirited horse — so that there would now be a new addition to the slowly evolving diorama; and a few weeks later, a new glittering statue of salt crystals would have been erected.

Nor were rescuers, or would-be rescuers, the only ones lured out to join the other motionless travelers on the salt plain. Scalp hunters, perceiving easy pickings, sometimes could not resist; and in their greed, they were stopped well short of their quarry. Buffalo wolves, down from the north, and little red wolves and Mexican wolves, and black bears and grizzlies, also attempted to creep out onto the bog of floating salt, to nibble at the delicacies that summoned them, as did the little coyotes, after the wolves and bears had gone extinct; and sometimes they were successful, while other times they too were captured by the hungry sucking maw of the salt, so that always a menagerie or carnival was appearing out in that dangerous, glittering amphitheater, and the story remaining always the same — desire, failure, rescue, longing, foolhardiness, prudence, fortune, misfortune — with only the array of alternating characters, man and beast alike, changing across time.

Alone among the lake's visitors, only the birds were safe. The vultures and ravens were free to perch on the heads and shoulders of the stranded and sinking travelers, pecking at whatever desiccated scraps they desired, and the warblers, vireos, and flycatchers were free to ferry straw and sticks out to the carriage-bone houses and build nests upon the scoops of clavicles and in the hearts of the pelvises, raising their young in these nooks and crevices.

Violet-and-green swallows were free to dab mud nests beneath the grinning skulls, up tight against the vertebrae of the neck; so that again, when the eggs hatched and the nestlings were first attempting to fledge, the chittering, plaintive cries they sent out to the desert sounded yet again as if the skeleton had resumed singing; as if the voice of that traveler could never be stilled: and whether in lamentation or celebration, a listener would not have been able to gauge, but would only have been able to marvel at the unparalleled tenacity of life, the unstoppable longing of it.

And in this vein, it would have struck an observer how the salt plain was always on the move. It was as if the mechanical model for life were so well designed that it would continue to run by itself for some indefinite time afterward, even in the absence of life.

The vultures would shift their weight from one skeleton to another, and the skull or arm of one of the skeletons would fall off, giving the brief and sudden impression that some residue of life or energy had bestirred.

Or the final meniscus of cartilage would wither and stretch, within the skeletons' knee joints or hips, allowing them to pivot in the wind like weathervanes; and sometimes the winds would gust, spinning the sentinels as if they were all partners at some select cotillion: and for those that were still robed in tattered garments, or whose sun-dried skin had been pecked and peeled away to curl like cowhide, so that from a distance it looked as if they were wearing leather coats and vests, the jackets would flap, as the weathervanes spun, adding to an unsettling image of gaiety.

Occasionally, in gusting winds in which the weathervanes spun around and around, as if enthused with glorious indecision, the heated friction of the spins would be too much, and the skeletons would snap off at the knees and topple over with a faint clatter into the salt, where sometimes they would become detrital mounds, though other times they sank quickly, to a depth of a foot or two; and suspended thus in the saline solution, they would be perfectly preserved forever.

A man or woman poling along in a canoe or flatbottomed skiff would have been able to navigate sometimes by the upright gray-white spars of the standing skeletons, and the remnants of skeletons; and on an overcast day, one in which the sun's glare had not lit the entire lake surface into millions of dazzling, glittering salt crystals, the paddler would have been able to look down at almost any point in the journey and see suspended in the salt mire like schools of fish the motionless residue of someone's ancestors.

Richard wandered through the script of his days, unaware of any patterns of history or consequence, taking each day instead as if carrying mindlessly but enthusiastically one heavy stone that, at day's end, he placed in a pile before returning the next day with another, until finally, eventually, his vision for various things became so acute that it seemed gradually that it was as if he had been chosen all along for the knowledge of such things — and even chosen, perhaps, for Clarissa, after all: for it was not long after his fluency with the landscape began to mature that there was awakened in him, like a corresponding echo, the desire to see as deeply beneath the mask of the hidden animate things, the things that a frightened heart withholds.

And in that learning, he found that he desired to travel deeper into that territory.

He did not tell Clarissa of this newer, and secondary, yearning. But she could scent it, as it developed, as surely as the odor of salt in the air, and as surely as is felt the crispness in the autumn from the first night-wind down out of the north; and she hated feeling that change occurring within him, that developing hunger. Always before, there had been the tacit understanding that it would be just sex and companionship between them, nothing more; temporal, as shallow as the lake.

He was young and awkward. He was not to prove as gifted at gaining entrance into her hidden fears as he was at discovering treasures hidden beneath a static landscape. Hers was a moving target. There might yet have been somewhere a traveler or hunter with the ability to know her heart and gain the wildness of her trust, but such skill did not belong to the young miner Richard was then.

It did not keep him from falling. And it did not keep her from despising and being further attracted to him, in that falling.

They would picnic at Juan Cordona Lake, in the early evenings and on into nightfall, and on overcast days and, finally, in the brilliance of day, which was when Richard most enjoyed being out there, and when he most wanted Clarissa to be there. She loved the lake, too — of all their explorations, it was her favorite place — but she was terrified of its brilliance and heat, which was a step up of a quantum order from even the searing potential of the dunes. She was certain that thirty seconds' exposure to the lake would fry her creamy skin to the color of an iron skillet.

In the months before she had met him, and before she had swum Horsehead Crossing with him, and prowled the reef on her knees at night with him, and even safely wandered the sunlit dunes with him — terror high in her throat, at that last venture, but a giddiness, too, after it was over and she had emerged unburned — she would never in ten thousand years have gone out to the salt lake in the broad light of day; but because he was earning bits and pieces if not all of her trust, and because he was helping kindle some warmth if not actual spark within her — not fire, but warm, pleasing friction — she acquiesced, and followed him out into the very place that held more fear for her than any other; the place that was capable (or so in her fear she believed) more than any other of destroying the only dream she had ever had or known.

And in his company, she began to taste the freedom of what it was like to first feel that warmth, if not burning, down inside her center, beneath that carefully protected surface.

What was reckless for her — a glimpse of the salt flat's high-noon brilliance — would of course have been commonplace, mundane for another; but the borders of her fears were her own, and there were times, when with him, that she pushed against them as gamely as any high-altitude mountain climber ascended some final summit.

Even a good man is still a man, she told herself, and she feared that there was some part of him that was so bent on her seeing the salt flat at noon simply because she was resisting it; that only her fear attracted him, just as the flight of prey summons always the attention of the predator. Both of them would have agreed, honestly, that there was some of that.

But because of what he had shown her of Horsehead Crossing and the Castle Gap notch, and the dunes — because of his pagan celebration of the elemental things and places of his life, and because of his strange goodness — she gave him more faith and trust, as one would a young horse that one had been working with on a regular basis.

And she would have been honest too in admitting to herself, as well as to him, that his unselfishness was an attractant to her, so lacking was she in this characteristic; and that in this way it was also as if she was the hunter, her attention drawn by the appearance of the very thing that had thus far eluded her.

For his part, Richard wanted her to see how otherworldly the lake could be, under the cruelest of conditions; and how the world could become inverted, or so it seemed, in the blink of an eye or in the dissolution of some final impediment to the heart. Given one last breach, new rules and beliefs could come flooding in.

The thing that was her terror could become — given one more attempt, one more day of trust or effort — a source of almost overpowering beauty.

He wanted her to see how the movement of halite crystals, stirred each day by the same winds that rearranged the dunes, sometimes helped sharpen into angular prisms nearly every salt crystal on the lake, trillions of such prism-diamonds exploding the lake into a pulsing iridescence of almost maddening beauty, a phenomenon that was witnessed most powerfully either just before or just after the sun's zenith.

The curves and waves of radiance were different each time it was viewed. Sometimes little wind-driven eddies of salt would form tiny ridges, only an inch or two higher than the surrounding peneplain; but that faint topographic relief would be enough, when the sun's angle finally properly bent and ignited the bouncing, magnified, colorful rays through those crystals, to throw arcs and coronas of banded light up into the air above the salt lake, in addition to scattering the light like spilled gemstones across the lake's heated surface.

When the light entered each day's arrangement of wind-scoured halite, it was like watching energy entering a filament, like life being born. That was the good part — not simply ascending the crest of some sere and gigantic dune to look down upon the bowl of light and color, a sight all the more fantastic for the nearly absolute absence of color elsewhere in the desert (only the occasional bloom of cactus, or the lime and lemon and watermelon hues of the passing-through song-birds) — so that it seemed logical and natural to the viewer to understand that perhaps on some level it was its long absence that had finally summoned the missing thing.

Best of all was to be there already waiting for the phenomenon, and to see its birth or arrival: to hear the lake's shallow salty waves lapping against one another in the night, stirred by the wind and by the clockwise turning of a sleeping or resting earth; and to see the idea of incandescence conceived, then, in that first dim light of dawn, and to watch the light's approach, reaching its fingers in strafes through the flat-cracked tiles and the individual nuggets of salt; the light and the color being born, then, soundlessly, but with an onrushing beauty that seemed to possess a shushing sound, as the image of the salt lake be-dazzled, caught fire, and leapt into the viewer's mind.

In those moments, beholding such transformation, with the full knowledge that the dull, brown, regular world lay behind them now, it would seem to the viewers, to the travelers, that they were looking at nothing less than the biblical streets of heaven, lined with silver and gold and gemstones; and it would be both a wonderful and frightening revelation, in exchange for which privileged vision great things would be expected of them; and that they would have to reach deeper than they had ever gone, to deliver.

It was important to Richard that Clarissa witness this. He told himself he would not push her beyond that point — that she would be free to reject or accept that vision of the landscape — but he wanted her to see it, and he wanted to be there with her when she saw it.

And perhaps he was pushing her, and being gluttonous, ravenous for her heart, as he began to consider, idly at first but then with increasing imagination, what it would be like to fall in love with her, and capture, and perhaps even tame, her frightened heart.

He considered children, a life of domesticity, family.

He did not let his mounting hunger preclude gentleness or kindness. He understood her fear, or thought he did, and took every precaution to lead her tenderly into the place he wanted to show her.

When they went to the lake, they traveled with two vehicles, towing a jeep behind them as an emergency backup. Richard carried extra gas and extra tubes of zinc oxide; extra water (over a hundred gallons of it; two barrels mounted atop his flatbed truck), and a large tent in which they would spend the morning hours, drinking tea as if on safari and cooking pancakes and bacon on the hissing gas stove, peering through the mosquito netting, sweating already at first light, man and woman nude again, and once more bechalked in thick paste, should any stray ultraviolet death come slanting in through the canvas fabric.

Clarissa was constantly reapplying zinc to herself, as the sweat rivulets traced little unprotected paths across the self-cherished vessel of her body, and they would pass the morning in the tent, watching and waiting, reading paperbacks or napping or lovemaking, and sipping tea afterward.

The greasewood campfire just outside their tent would still be smoldering from where they had stayed up half the night watching the stars, and walking the lake's shore, searching by lantern light for arrowheads and other lesser memorabilia Clarissa might be able to sell to Herbert Mix, should the museum in Austin be uninterested. They would sometimes be able to pick up a few stations on the car radio — the smoke from the fire kept the bugs away, though always, the moths swarmed the flames — and they would dance to blues and waltzes, the radio's music faint and staticky, their bare feet moving eloquently across the dusty, salt hardpan, which in the moonlight was paler than their flesh, paler than bone, possessing in the night some luminosity greater and brighter than it had even in day's full light.

To a distant onlooker it might have seemed that they were dancing on the level floor of some marble ballroom; though to the dancers, so severe and well-defined and alive were the senses that there could be no misinterpretation of anything but what was: they were dancing barefoot in the cool wind-cut dust of salt, the ground soft beneath their feet, the night cool upon their unclothed bodies, their hands warm on each other's backs, the scent of the lake of salt richer smelling than even that of a churning ocean.

The Mormon crickets would be calling back in the dunes, the fire glowing and crackling as the coals popped and shifted and settled, indistinguishable from the static of the radio transmission; and perhaps sharpest of all, there would be the scent of each other's body, a scent that was for them an accumulation of the events of the day: zinc oxide and sweat and clean time-washed sand and salt, sex and barbecued shrimp from the grill, and margaritas from the ice chest.

Even the scent of the sun still echoing from the canvas of their big wall tent was so sharp as to provide for them, in their mind's eye, an outline of the tent — a kind of vision, in that regard, so deeply were the senses felt, those nights, dancing together in that salt dust.

There was no marble-floored ballroom. There was only something infinitely finer.

A hundred yards farther out, two hundred yards, the skeleton sentinels seemed to pivot, watching them. It might have seemed that they too were out on some vast floor, though without partners.

The salt kept oozing up from beneath the lake, a slow upwelling fountain of it; and under the cool stars, Clarissa and Richard were safe from the scalding sun of the next day, as well as the gone-by sear of the previous day's sun; and in the morning, after a night of such revelry, and such an intermingling of spirits — theirs, certainly, but also theirs and the landscape's, and the two of them tucked in so safely, if precariously, between the past and the future — they would crawl out of the tent in the first light of daybreak, to void in the dunes, crouching like animals, and would feel the rising, drying winds of the day already stirring around them.

It seemed odd to be able to smell so much salt, so deeply, and yet not to hear the stretch and thunder of breaking waves.

Sometimes Richard would imagine having a child, and taking her to the ocean, to hear such sounds.

They would burn their toilet paper when they were finished, setting the scraps of paper afire like the pages from some diary of adolescence, pages that had both nothing and everything to do with the adults they had become, and then after burying their spoor in the sand, they would return to the tent to nap, and read, and to wait for the coming spectacle of light.

Passing by the shoreline salt flat where they had danced the night before, they would always be astounded by the evidence of the previous night's activity. They would bend down and try to parse individual elegant arcs and sweeps of their movements — and sometimes, across short distances, they could read the sign of such passage — but for the most part the tracks they left behind were scrambled together, laid atop and beneath each other in what appeared to be an impenetrable and indecipherable scuffling.

The night's passage of two appeared as might the evidence of two hundred, or two thousand. The footprints would soon be scoured by the wind or buried beneath the next day's shining rime of wind-thrown salt; but there in day's first light, they were still visible, the proof of the previous night's evening of love, or the thing that had wandered right up to the edge of the country of love.

It was always surprising to Clarissa and Richard that the crude overlay of the tracks did not match or represent in any way their recollection of how graceful the evening's movements had been the night before.

For a few moments, they would stand and stare out at the width of lake. The sentinels would still be waiting for them, arms outstretched — as if those stark forms could hear different music; as if longing had not perished with the decay of their mortal flesh but existed still within them — as if perhaps that were the thunderous force that drove the world, exceeding even the powers of gravity; as if longing were destiny, as if longing were sacred and sacrament, as if longing were holy, as if longing were as elemental a force of the world as magma or stone, or water or fire or spirit — and as if, were this the case, great mother lodes of it might exist in vast reserves, buried deep within the earth's recesses like ore or oil, or deep within the hearts of certain men and women such as all those who still remained standing out in the lake, up to their knees and hocks in oozing salt, arms outflung, reaching for the living even from across the thin and barely discernible gulf of the other side.

Clarissa and Richard would retreat to the tent, to wait for the light. And as the day traveled on, the tent grew warmer and stuffier, acting as a greenhouse, and they would fan each other, and read, and wait, with only that thin fabric of canvas separating them from a quantity of sun, and an excess of ultraviolet radiation, that none of their kind had ever been requested to live with, in all the millennia before them.

They read poetry. They listened to the quiet ballads of folk music. They waited as if time itself were an elemental, finite resource, but one of which they had an excess, a full or overflowing reservoir.

Others, they knew, did not, but they were different, they were blessed, and time for them would behave in a different manner.

Richard could feel the light approaching before he could see it. Or perhaps it was visible to him in the distance, or even audible: certain compressions and refractions altering and repositioning themselves in the atmosphere, and driven by the rising heat of the day, like the composition of notes by some distant orchestra.

The coming arrival of the light seemed to him to be as noticeable as might be the slate-purple anvil of a towering thunderhead to the north, with the cloudbank spitting jagged lightning, and a cooler, damper breeze on one's face: though there was nothing visible at first, only an imagined or sensed difference.

Nonetheless, he would rouse Clarissa, would inform her that the change was coming; and the two of them would put on their wide-brimmed sun hats, and Clarissa would pull on her long baggy cotton pants and long-sleeve linen shirt, buttoning it at the neck (her body underneath still protected with zinc); and she would wrap a light sheet around her for extra protection. And sweating as if in a sauna, she would join him out in front of the tent, sitting on an old quilt, Clarissa in dark glasses, gripping a parasol, trembling at her audacity.

They would share a cold beer, and watch; and now Clarissa could see the change, noticeable at first in the increased stirring of the heat vapors rising from the salt lake.

As if some current had been turned off, or as if the approach of some living thing had frightened the vapors into hiding, the shimmering haze suddenly ceased, and disappeared.

A clarity appeared over the lake, swelling like a lens. It seemed to Clarissa and Richard that there was some magnification involved as well, for now they could see clearly certain distant details and features on the skeletons that they had previously been unable to: sutures in a skull, and stray tufts of grass, like the remnants of hair, protruding from the birds' nests; even the pearl buttons remaining on some of the tattered shirts, which now hung motionless on the upright spars in the total absence of breeze, the total stillness (how Herbert Mix would have loved to get to those distant buttons!); and then, like a gas lamp being lit, certain veins and ribbons within the lake's surface would begin to glow, as the spectral bands of color began to flow through them like blood.

The colors swarmed within their halite trap, surging and pulsing, as the sun inched higher. Richard felt that if he tossed a crumpled-up piece of paper out onto the salt flat, it would ignite, pierced by a shaft of fierce white light.

The lake was now a bowl of living color, aflame with sparks and flames of pigment. Richard and Clarissa kept watching, sipping their beer, Clarissa's lips lustrous with lip balm. They kept sweating, and marveled at the thing that had come right up to them.

They could have stood and waded out into it. They could have smeared the crusty sludge of halite onto their arms and faces, and tasted it; could have waded out farther into it, into that corona of wild color, in the midst of which the other sentinels stood motionless.

Instead, they watched. They watched and listened—expecting some noise, even a faint staticky crackle, to accompany such a feast of light. But nothing: only an excitement. The lake had pulled both of them farther and farther out, had beckoned; calling for them both, and whether individually or together, no real matter: calling for them both to come farther out, at a time in their lives when most people their age, and older, were already beginning to turn back and build, not just in their hearts but in all the physical ways of their lives, safe-bunkers and corrals and hen-coops and root cellars and vaults and crypts and other fences and walls and trunks and boxes for the safekeeping and hiding and huddling-down of things.

Clarissa and Richard would stare out at the beckoning; and even as they understood that they were neither special nor chosen, that it was all instead merely random, the lake taking those who would come to it and discarding or rejecting those who would not — but the lake surely as adazzle each day whether they or anyone else stood there or not — they could not help but feel tempted to try to live bigger, larger, more dramatic lives, and to step away from those little huts of safe-keeping, and out into the devastating, alluring, wondrous light.

Watching her watch the lake, Richard could not believe his good fortune, that he had gotten her to come this far. He would watch the shivery heat vapors rising from all around her ghostly turban, and he would spray her with water from a squirt bottle, trying to keep her cool.

From time to time she would go back into the tent to hide, her heart hammering; but there, too, she would become frightened, feeling incredibly alone, and would venture back out to the old faded quilt, where Richard would soak her again, as if bathing or tending to her; and as the heat and sun sucked all that moisture away almost immediately, it was a feeling like being squeezed or gripped by the evaporative action, the release and extraction of moisture from cloth; a feeling like being kissed, or a feeling like being buried alive, she wasn't sure — and she wanted to go back, and yet she wanted to go forward; wanted, even, sometimes, to have the courage to try to wander out onto the lake, picking the right steppingstone places of firmer salt, even as all the evidence that lay before her indicated to her that this could not be done.

She would come close to him, and then she would pull away from him. Through it all there remained, however, her skittish indecision, and her desire for some other, backwards, unseen land.

Richard's steady and constant hunger was always present, always pushing or pursuing, she knew, even when he pretended to be patient so that even the patience came to be like a kind of pressure and a hunger, until it began to seem to her, as the summer progressed, that she might be losing her mind.

Was she becoming the shadow of his desire, or was he the shadow of her fear? Or was there any difference?

Perhaps it was but simple and frugal mathematics. Having so little to cede in the first place, if she gambled and gave it over but came away with nothing larger in return, then she would be an even emptier vessel than before — perhaps unbearably so.

3

THE GLORY OF A YOUNG MAN is both his strength and his foolhardiness. As Richard slipped further into love — entering it as if wading out into the shallows, and a bit farther, then, to his knees, and a bit farther still — he found himself showing off for her, challenged by her heart's timidity.

To show her that no harm would come from her fears, he would sometimes, during the apogee of the day's heat and light, roll up the sleeves of his shirt from one forearm, then hold that bare arm before the sun like an offering; and the two of them would watch as the un-protected arm darkened over the course of only several minutes — browning like a piece of meat placed on a grill, and then blackening to charcoal: a streak of burnt skin as black as if smudged with cold coals from the campfire.

And not until the odor of it began to overwhelm them — the same scent as when meat burns on a grill — would he lower his sleeve back over the newly wounded area. And strangely, there was no pain; if any-thing, only a pleasant warmth.

And again, she would know two things, two responses: the horror of seeing her fear of the sun made manifest; and, later in the night, the warmth of that arm's embrace. And she would see, each time, how the black skin always peeled away and healed, every time, back to smooth-ness and strength. In the night, once the arm had healed, her mouth upon that supple arm, the arm tasting like an arm again rather than charcoal.

Each time he put his arm bare beneath the fire of the sun, and then came back away from such fire, minutes later — and not only survived such a burn, but seemed to flourish — she took another half step closer, and another, as Richard lured her closer with his own burning limbs. A slash of black across his calf; the intricate paper cutout silhouette of a mermaid burned, for a few days, onto his bicep.

His own sin? Chasing her, luring her, falling in love with her, first and foremost for the thrill of the chase, and in the loneliness of the landscape; falling in love with her because she was beautiful, falling in love with her because she was frightened, and because the summer and his job and the landscape were desolate.

It wasn't love. It was some masked thing. And what hunter could not pursue her beauty?

His strength was considerable. He could go days and nights without sleep. Out on the drilling rigs, for exercise, between short bit trips, he would perform arm curls with the thirty-foot lengths of two-and-seven-eighths-inch tubing, and clean and jerks, hack squats, and military presses with the seven-and-seven-eighths-inch steel casing, while the sun-scoured salt-wasted roughnecks and roustabouts lounged in the doghouse sucking down beer like water and stared at him through the day's heat vapors with bleary eyes. They watched his antics as if witnessing some mild hallucination, and invested no real emotion in it; only watched, and waited.

They knew he was the geologist from the city. They knew he could be walking down what they perceived to be Easy Street — working in an air-conditioned office in Houston, and hiring someone else to come out and babysit each well as it was drilled. So there was a part of him that they respected, or half-respected, even above the simmering background of socioeconomic class resentment; and there was some similar begrudging admiration for the company he kept, in Clarissa — although, as with Clarissa, they would often find themselves wrought with ambivalence — respecting him for his ceaseless and superior labor, yet hating him for his good fortune.

None of it mattered to Richard. He would never see them again. To each, the other was but like the dust of salt, swirling on each day's winds, with each staring at the other across the distance of that bright divide: the company geologist, hale and hearty, out in the sun like a madman, doing difficult exercises simply for the joy of being alive, while the laborers stared out at him in mute and sun-tempered baleful disbelief. He would be gone in another month, or two months. He was but an apparition.

Out at the lake, he continued to hunt her with both a tenderness and a lust; all passions leaving their restraining corrals now, like horses once wild but now domesticated, which notice one evening that the corral gate is swinging open, that they can return to wildness, and with thunderclouds booming all around and a wind stirring, so that it is almost as if they are sleepwalking, they slip one by one out of the gate, one after the other, until the corral is empty.

Beneath the soupy surface of the lake, the salt got thicker, dense as cheesecake. In the old days salt cutters had made a brutal living sawing it into blocks and stacking it like bales of hay onto sledges before traveling back out into the world to pawn that crudest of commodities — and Richard had discovered that with a simple shovel he could dig vertical shafts as deep as he wished, hauling the salt up in buckets and spooning foot- and handholds into the shaft's walls, the shaft no wider than the flue of a large chimney.

At first, with the buckets of residue from his excavations, he built low walls and salt igloos, as one would sculpt sand castles at the beach; but tiring of that, and digging deeper, exhuming more and more salt, he began to construct ornate and magnificent castles, glittering museums and cathedrals whose crystals at high noon caught and refracted that same phenomenon of light, so that after digging a few such holes, he had assembled enough bricks of salt to build what appeared to be a small civilization bejeweled with unimaginable wealth.

Out on the broad plains, with little vertical relief, the perception of scale was deceiving; sometimes, while Richard was down in the shaft, Clarissa could, by squinting her eyes, look at the small-scale models of grandeur and imagine that instead of viewing the structures across any near distance, she was seeing them from afar: beholding the outskirts of an immense and supreme civilization, one toward which she had been traveling and searching for all her life, and had only on that day first come within sight of it; and that although she was now closer to it than she had ever been, the journey that lay ahead would still be long and arduous — but worth it, surely worth it.

It was cooler down in the salt hole, though only slightly; and the salt and windless air trapped both Richard's body heat and the earth's, with no evaporative transfer, so that as he worked he was soon glistening with sweat, and it was hard to breathe the stale and stagnant air.

It felt at times that he was breathing salt, as might an ocean creature; and about forty feet down, he was surprised to find water that, while not exactly pure or fresh, was drinkable. Livestock would have been able to prosper on it, and even humans could have survived on it.

There was an old tin-and-wood shanty at the far end of the lake — in all of the lake's history, there was rumored to have been only one family ever to have lived there; surely this place, more than any other on earth, was representative of the farthest reaches in which an individual could survive — and crouching there in the darkness of the salt flue (the portal of sky above appearing no larger than the pearl button of a coat sleeve), Richard would imagine that the homesteaders must have dug such a well and then laid each day's drinking water out in shallow pans, waiting all day for enough of the salt to precipitate out for the rest of the water to become palatable: the residual, evaporated salt remaining in a crust around the rim of the shallow pan.

Or perhaps such evaporation made the water saltier. Perhaps they simply filtered it, like beggars, through tattered, faded cheesecloth, hoping to strain out enough of the larger, coarser crystals as to render it somewhat drinkable.

How would a person survive, he wondered, without pure water, without sweet water?

He crouched in the bottom of the hole and cupped his hands into the puddle and sipped. It was barely tolerable. Sometimes in the heat, the walls of his shaft would begin to ooze, dripping spatters of salt onto his bare back — when passing through soft spots in the salt's profile, he would attempt to shore them up with scraps of wood, gnarled branches of mesquite and bitterbrush — and for this reason of shifting instability (often it seemed to him he could feel the shaft swaying, leaning like a skyscraper in a high wind, and pulsing, too, tightening around him as if the shaft were some living organ), he never attempted any horizontal adits; and there were times when the shaft, warmed by the simple trapped coal-like heat of his presence, would begin to slump gobs of salt, a bucket's worth at a time.

When that happened, Richard's heart knew true terror, and he would grab the shovel and scramble back up toward that button of sky, before the entire gullet clenched and closed in on itself. Richard knew that if that happened, there would be no hope of Clarissa finding a shovel and digging to release him, no chance of her scrabbling and clawing bare-handed to exhume him, burrowing into the salt like a dog or coyote until her bare knuckles bled and she herself had tunneled down fifteen or twenty feet.

He imagined instead how she would rise and stand over the misshapen place where the hole had been, waiting perhaps for only a moment — as if to see whether a single hand, or a hand and an arm, might protrude, groping — before she turned and, with her long white sheet still wrapped around her, walked over to the jeep, climbed inside, started it up, and drove away.

Buckets of salt would continue to slip and fall from the walls as he hurried to the surface. He had to shut his eyes against the stinging saltiness. As he drew nearer to the top, he could taste and scent the fresher, hotter air above. Each time that he finally emerged (tossing the shovel out first, which was always a sight that startled Clarissa, watching from the tent), his head and shoulders appearing level with the surface, clambering out in the manner of a child climbing out of a swimming pool, with the world's real air upon him, he would feel in those first few moments a coolness upon him, as the sweat evaporated quickly from his bare skin.

Almost immediately thereafter, all moisture whisked away from him, he would feel himself beginning to bake again, encrusted with drying salt, like some riverine crustacean dredged from unknowable fathoms.

He would walk to the tent and open one of the chilled beers, and cover his nude salt-body with a sheet, and sit on the outside of the tent and speak to sweltering Clarissa inside, telling her of the things he had seen on his latest vertical journey, and what it had been like. And after this brief visit, he'd resume work on the cathedrals: fashioning spires and buttresses, arched bridges and porticos — working as a child might work: playing, not working — and in a way that she would not have done earlier in the summer, Clarissa put up with his foolishness.

She napped, giving herself over to the heat, and dreamed fevered dreams in which fear was no longer a factor. She dreamed of flying, of paddling dark rivers without a lantern, and of descents into cooler and darker places. She dreamed of writhing serpents, of pistols that would not fire; dreamed of burning rings of fire, and of bears, and wolves, and lions — once of buffalo, and another time, of an elephant — but never was there any fear in the dreams: only a lucid and luminous unscrolling of images so wondrous in their beauty that they could not possibly have anything to do with her own sleeping life; and she slept well, drinking in the vibrancy of the dreams, and awoke feeling rested and refreshed for having had them.

She rolled over on her cot, bathed herself with a damp washcloth, and read. She would tire of that, then, and would sit up and stare with fascination and youthful lust at the sheen of Richard's buttered arms, working the blocks and buckets of salt, manhandling the salt, giving rise to a physical dream of astounding vision, forming it as if from the materials of nothing but the vapors of heat and some magic in his heart, some dream or plan that the world had agreed to let him conjure.

She stirred on her cot, watched him, watched his salt castle rising higher: evaluating him as if anew, as her cold and frightened heart began to warm and stir like some winter-chilled seed.

For miles in all directions around the lake, pumpjacks were scattered, throbbing and clanking, rising and falling with a patience and yet also an insistence that brought to mind the notion of some single-minded living organism, rather than the machinery of man. The pumpjacks seemed like some semidomesticated stock, turned out into the fields to graze and forage upon whatever fragments they could find.

There were no pumpjacks in the immediate vicinity of the lake

— the underground mountain of salt was all but impossible to drill into, catching and bending the pipe with the unruly shifting and sliding of its gelatinous mass; and in any event, there was no known oil housed within the vast reservoir of salt — but the underground formations that had been shoved aside by the salt's rising perturbations had buckled and folded in manners conducive to trapping and holding oil and gas on the flanks of that rising dome, so that the area around the lake was an excellent place to drill; and it was in this area that many of Richard's prospects lay: so that even as Richard, on a day off, might be working shirtless with a shovel, digging a shaft down into the heart of the salt, one of his wells, only three or four miles distant, might also be sinking down into the earth.

Clarissa continued to watch him work, and tried to distinguish Richard's own force and desire from that of the land's; tried to isolate it, out there on the salt plain, so that she could be more sure of what it was she was getting into — if she even decided to go further into it.

Not realizing that even in the daydreaming or imagining of it, her hold was already loosened, and that she was already drifting his way: following the path of her gaze, as if not believing or understanding that the initial groove cut for any path is scoured first by the simple dream.

She studied him as he worked. Could she imagine becoming an oilman's wife?

Could she envision a long and rich life spent together with him, richer than even these few summer months had been?

In the blazing landscape of the salt plain, and in that country of supreme unaccountability, where a traveler was responsible only for him- or herself, it was easy to dally with the imagination.

The water was pouring out of him. She feared he was too exposed. He paused in his labors, took a swig from his canteen. Some of the water spilled from his mouth and trickled down his throat and chest, and she touched her hand to her own chest, as if savoring it, and imagined a lake in the woods; imagined the two of them living, or vacationing, at a cabin in the woods somewhere in the cool Far North.

In the dazzling heat and whiteness, she let her mind slide, and dared to imagine the two of them together in a cabin on a hill above a lake at night in the dark, early in the autumn, window squares of the cabin lit by lantern or candlelight, so that the cabin itself would be like a candle, glowing in the heart of the cool dark forest.

Finally, each time, she would shake the image from her mind. What did it matter? It was all make-believe, anyway.

Often, in his burrowings and well diggings, Richard would encounter bones. Just beneath the surface were strata upon strata of tangled arms and legs, and the long, elegant ghost-xylophones of vertebrae; the globe-like skulls, the phalanges like jewelry spilled from a snapped necklace.

Sometimes Richard would use the long bones rather than tree branches to shore up the sagging places in his shafts, but would exhume, along with his buckets of salt, the skulls, to sell to the insatiable Herbert Mix.

It seemed to Richard sometimes, such was the richness of the past, that he was lowering himself into a giant salty soup or stew in which humans had been the main ingredient.

Clarissa and Richard would assemble the skulls along the lake's edge, to dry quickly in the sun, so that the salt crust could then be brushed from their pates, making them more presentable for market. Without knowing the histories of all the centuries of people who had passed and squabbled over this place, they were learning it through their simple handling of the skulls — learning it as a child, walking along the gravel bar of a rushing stream and picking up certain polished and banded stones of sediment, might learn something of the towering mountains far to the north, from which those stones had long ago passed.

Most of the skulls, and the tangle of bones, were resting in the top ten feet of salt. And knowing this (when Clarissa was fretting overmuch about not having earned much money that week from their trades with Herbert Mix), Richard would set aside his child's-play construction of the fantastic salt castles, and would focus on harvesting basketfuls of the skulls.

Like a beachcomber digging clams, he would shovel all the way around the perimeters of the lake and, as if furrowing a garden, he would dig long, shallow trenches, working shirtless under the malevolent sun, able to tell just by the tug upon his shovel when the metal tip touched old bone; and in this manner, working a chosen shallow contour around the lake's perimeter, he would exhume a new skull every ten or fifteen yards.

As if digging up root crops, he would lift the skulls from the furrows and set them beside his trench to dry, to be gathered later, and would continue around the lake. And after he had gathered that trip's harvest and returned home, the desolate landscape would appear even more of a ruination — an abused and squandered wasteland, if such a thing was possible: the ragged, wandering furrows with the residual, cast-aside, undesired bones — femur, ulna, radius — resting beside the trenches, and the entire shoreline looking as if wild boars had been tilling with their snouts a previously untouched glade, hazed now beyond reckoning.

The desire of the world to assemble two pieces into one — to pursue and conjoin, as if for no reason other than the sake of conjoining. The two young lovers were individuals, unique and specific in the world, and yet there were moments when they felt sharply as if they were but puppets, void of purpose or free will.

It seemed to Richard already, even in his youth, that there was in the world but one breath of the single pattern that plays itself over and over again, as steady and considered as the respirations of a sleeping animal — and yet the world, not just the living world but the old world below, seemed to have some say in deciding which stories got carried forward, shaped and reshaped, and which stories got hauled back down into the abyss, as if but fodder and fuel for the maw of some heartless, forward-clanking machine.

There was no part of Richard or Clarissa that did not understand this by summer's end and autumn's beginning, even if only subconsciously. Both as individuals and as a pair, they moved with an unspoken but increasing desperation, frantic to make it up and over into the land of their dreams, or at least into the territory of those dreams that lay shimmering in the nearby haze like the oases cast from desert heat: Clarissa desiring still an opulence commensurate with the flash of her coming few years of physical beauty.

He continued to desire her further: to capture her first because she was beautiful, and second because she was moving away from him. He too envisioned a life in the woods, in a cabin by a lake, with stars above a dark forest, the cabin aglow in the darkness with yellow window-light, and a partner inside, a lover or a wife, who was made happy by the sight of him, and who was not afraid to show her love, who was not afraid of anything, really — and who could travel with him farther into new and unclaimed or unmapped or unknown country, constructing edifices and cairns and markers together as they traveled, and pausing in their travels to spend time, to lavish time, upon each other, in the brief years before their time ran out and they were covered over.

The fossils they found were not enough, the relics and artifacts they sold to the obsessive Herbert Mix were not enough, the oil and gas that Richard was finding and siphoning, suctioning, pumping out of the earth was not enough, and they both loved more intently now, squeezing each other more tightly, their arms and legs agrapple when they had sex, and daring (as if this might be the thing that had been preventing them from reaching their goals) to dive, for the first time, deeper: staring into each other's eyes questioningly, bravely, in silent interrogation; hovering over one another, and each breathing the warm breath from his or her lungs into the mouth and lungs of the other — Clarissa not running, for once, but standing her ground to examine and absorb the love that Richard had to give her; and Richard, with similar bravery, knowing that the chances were good she would be leaving.

And by October, when the heat of the desert was finally broken, it seemed to both of them one morning that they had finally somehow crossed over into that new territory; crossing over perhaps in the night as they slept, with their passage across that unmarked boundary unnoticed, at the time. And they relaxed and relished being in such a country for the first time.

And rather than pushing on with zeal and ferocity, they slowed to a walk once more; strolling, as it were, hand in hand through the richer, newer fields. They paused to revel in their bravery.

For a while, they could glide, sweeping along on the momentum of their labors, having entered, through perseverance and diligence and some daring, that small expanse and moment of grace not unlike that which the football players sometimes achieved, when pulling the loaded wagons: that same glide in which every footstep, every surge, was in synchrony, with the recipients of that glide aware of the gift, and yet also quickly, comfortably, assuming it to be their due: and assuming that once such a glide had been reached, it would never again fall away.

(And after it did fall away, they persisted in believing, for the longest time, that it would be right back: that they were only a step, two steps, away. That they had only looked away for a moment and gotten distracted or slightly off-balance, but that with a little extra surge, a little extra power, they could step right back up into that slipstream. And sometimes they did, though other times they never saw it or knew it again; though even when they did find their way back into that current, they were surprised by how much more effort it took than what they had thought would be required. And finally, one day, they stepped back for the last time, and let it go on past, and remembered, for a while, but no longer participated.)

No sooner had the new intimacy been reached between them, however, than the fear caught back up with Clarissa: as if in turning to glance at the old country, she could not help but turn back toward it.

When the fear returned for her, it came like serpents snaking their way across a tin roof in the night. The new fear returned from all its old places: the despair that she had been born into the wrong place; that she was sinking in the world, unseen — but there was also a newer bolt of fear coming at her now, the fear that new fondness, if not love, was growing in her for Richard.

She held the fear silently — pretending to be wondering to herself what she would do with it, even as the other part of her knew full well what she would do with it.

And Richard, who picked up on the echo of her fear almost the first day it arrived — discerning the return of his own greatest fear, her flight, almost from the start, as might a veteran firefighter scent the newborn wisps of smoke from a distant fire — spent a tortured week, and then a month, denying it and holding it down, and then covering it with a second layer, and a third, until both he and Clarissa were wired tight from the overburden of that pressure, and from the rivers of sand that seemed to be coming in over her.

They went to a football game one Friday evening and barely spoke to one another; lost in their fears and worries they forgot to cheer for the Odessa team. Further into the game, they tried to cover up their inattentiveness but ended up cheering accidentally for a poor play rather than a good one.

They went home and retreated again beneath good sex, but it was only another layer above what lay below, and the more she said nothing of her leave-taking, the more it became a certainty to both of them.

She still had nowhere to go to, no prospect or avenue, but so immense now was her fear and her need that she was reduced to the desperation of choosing a flight based only upon the dream of a location by its name alone. The daunting task, with her back against the wall, of being forced to convert the abstract into the real.

Nothing with a punchy, stark, one-syllable name like Minsk, or Hunt; nothing rough and guttural, like Crockett, and nothing so similar to the treacherous sinuosity of the name of her own private hell, Odessa. Nacogdoches wouldn't do, nor Laredo, nor Del Rio.

Fort Worth sounded safe and solid, but she knew of its reputation as a former cow town. Houston intrigued her, though she feared she'd be lost in the lights. San Antonio, while inviting, was too close to Odessa.

It would never have occurred to her to consider taking flight from Texas entirely. Paris, New York, or San Francisco, and the possibility of failure, terrified her almost as much as did the desert. She wanted a staging ground, an eddy, between worlds, in which she could escape the old terror and make preparations for a second flight.

Like an opium eater, that fall, she pretended to still be in love, after having first entered that country; but she kept dreaming of, and searching the map for, other places, other names.

She knew or believed that she wanted something soothing, some-

thing riverine, perhaps, after so long an absence of such. She liked the
l in Blanco, the white-blanket sound of it, and liked in her imagination
the clear waters attendant to Rocksprings or Cat Springs. She liked also
the *l*'s and the femininity in the town names of Alice, and Galveston,
and Temple; but in the end, she settled upon Dallas, as had so many
before her — the city (she had seen pictures) gleaming and gargantuan
with its skyscrapers rising above the flat grasslands and wavy hills
around it, its own ambition and self-import fortress-like amongst the
plains.

And in her mind, like a child constructing a diorama for a science
project, she began assembling the hopes of some fantastic story for
herself; and she said nothing of any of it to anyone.

Richard watched the distance between them widen, and in his mind
observed pine needles resting on a forest floor dry out and then smolder from the heat: the reckless, unstoppable smoldering.

They still went into the desert, searching and gathering; and as if the
call to her flight was rising now to full conspiracy with fate, she began
to find treasures: inexplicable discoveries for which not even the gluttonous Herbert Mix could fashion a narrative.

Chief among these was a chest full of gold-hammered goblets, with
ruby insets — two dozen of them, each heavy as lead, and spotless
— discovered beneath the sand. Digging deeper then, they found the
curve of a wagon wheel, and deeper still, the wagon itself.

More scratching revealed the tattered lace of a wedding dress — they
dug more slowly now, Clarissa being careful as ever to keep her parasol
balanced atop one shoulder — and beneath the ragged silk found the
bare foot of a skeleton, still fully clothed, as if the traveler had just returned from the wedding and had not yet had time to change.

They dug deeper. Even Clarissa worked hard on this excavation,
sometimes setting her parasol aside; and when her long-sleeved white
linen shirt slipped down off her shoulder, for once she did not panic
and slide it back over her shoulder, but kept digging, searching for the
groom, if there was any, and perhaps even the wedding party.

Richard noticed that her shirt kept sliding down but thought it was a good sign that she was willing to expose herself — to have some other passion that exceeded her own protection.

It was true that there were places on her neck and shoulders where the perspiration of her labors and the friction of the sand was rubbing off the protection she'd so conscientiously applied, but Richard believed that between the three layers of protection — the parasol, the shirt, and the zinc oxide — she would be all right. A little sun might even be good for her.

By the middle of the afternoon they had most of the sand dug out from around the wagon, and had the bride — a tall, slender woman, still fully clad — sitting up on the back of the wagon, as if watching them work. Richard kept cautioning Clarissa to drink water, but she was relentless. He guessed the goblets to be worth $10,000 as a collection, but sensed that it was not for further treasure or gold that she dug.

"Slow down," he told her, as he might caution her of some precipice ahead, but she shook off his warnings, working as if intoxicated by love; and when he took her arm to suggest to her again that she be cautious, she finally agreed, but pulled him under the faint slatted shade of the wagon and made love to him, keeping her shirt on as was his request, but nothing else.

Even for their usual energy, it was for both of them an event of surprising uncontrollability: as if they had wallowed down into some suppressed reservoir of an eros and lust so raw and overpressured that it might injure or even destroy them, upon their exodus.

They bumped and crashed against the wagon above them, in their overhead hoistings, and with their knees and elbows and the arced shape of their movements carved out deeper pits in the cool and newly exposed sand, but feeling nothing, only burning.

Their grappling and lifting threatened to shake the wagon apart, and the bride sitting above them tipped over on her side, seemed now to be holding or clinging to the wagon as she might long ago have done as it jounced over the rocky path.

There was no other sound in the desert, and eventually, the strange energy of explosive lust that they had unearthed passed on through them, and on up into the heated blue sky; and they were once more merely hot and exhausted lovers, tentative, and once again spent.

They lay there for only a short while, Richard wanting to spoon in and be tender for a while, but Clarissa was anxious, as if still with sexual energy, to resume digging. He was able to hold her for a few minutes, though, and as they lay there, sweating and gritty, latticed in sun and shadow, it began to feel to Richard as if he was holding, in both arms, an enormous fish; and though she did not struggle, he could feel the coiling of her muscles, their readiness once more for flight, and he released her.

Clarissa forced herself to lie there with him for another thirty seconds after being released, with their bare feet and ankles still twined loosely together and sticking out from beneath the wagon, so mocking of the bones that dangled likewise above them from the bride sitting on the back of the wagon as if standing watch over them.

They each drank some water afterward, and dressed, but soon Clarissa was working the shovel again with the same intensity.

By dusk they had the horses unearthed, the team of four still in cracked leather harness and dead on their knees, heads bowed not as if in defeat but only rest; though still they could find no groom, nor any other skeletons.

Clarissa grew irritable.

The sun was setting orange behind the dunes and the heat was off the land. They had brought picnic supplies with them, and they stopped now to reconnoiter. With the sun no longer direct upon them, the sand gave them less warmth now, though still it provided plenty, as if some great fire were nearby. Clarissa took off her shirt and bra, and Richard could see then that she had gotten a lot of sun. He could not tell yet how bad it might be, or if it could even be called a proper sunburn, so pale was her skin elsewhere; nor could she yet feel any pain, and if anything, she seemed to be infused with the general pleasure one sometimes feels after a long full day in the sun, purged and cleansed.

They would have liked to have sat in the back of the wagon for their picnic, but ceded that space to the skeleton, treating the bride even across the century of her death with the deference they would provide to a stranger; and there was in their deference also the acknowledgment that the wagon was still, in some manner, the possession of the bride rather than her discoverers.

They sat cross-legged in sand-scallops they carved out next to the wagon, looking like students seated at the feet of an esteemed teacher, receiving a counsel and an instruction they had long been awaiting.

Richard poured wine into two of the golden ruby-studded goblets, and he carved open a small, perfect cantaloupe. They ate the wedges of it with their hands, wiping their mouths afterward with the crooks of their sunburned arms. He had brought strawberries and chocolate bars too, and in the heat the chocolate had melted, so they stirred the strawberries (picked only the day before from the garden of one of Herbert Mix's neighbors) in the chocolate, and Richard fed those to her, and she took them from his fingers with her mouth, not with any of the old caution or hesitancy, but neither was it with any true zeal.

Instead, she regarded him, as she ate the strawberries and licked the chocolate from his fingers, with a clear-eyed, evaluating look that seemed to possess the ability, that day at least, to see into the future: and watching her watch him, as she slowly chewed the strawberries, he would have liked to have known what it was she was seeing, and how far out she was seeing it.

He leaned in against her breast, and for a moment she let him, but then would have no more of it, and rose, taking both of his hands, leaving him — they both knew now, as if that final decision had been arrived at with the help of the teacher's tutelage — and in that moment, it was a realization so strongly felt that it seemed to Richard later, in memory, that he remembered hearing something crack at the time.

She led him back to the initial treasure chest, and from that point, they each resumed digging in separate directions, still not knowing exactly what they were looking for.

As they worked, Clarissa's fervor returned, until it would have seemed to a stranger that she was maddened by this knowledge of the treasure's closeness at hand: and they worked into the night, excavating wandering ditches around the wagon, waist-deep waterless moats that were only slightly concentric, and which would have appeared from above more like the ladder-sticking of chromosomes, or the bent and groping thready arms of bacilli, than any plan or pattern.

Around midnight, exhausted, but having found nothing else (Clarissa still refused to believe a bride would travel across the desert with a four-horse team and a trunk full of golden goblets; there had to be more skeletons, and more treasures), they lifted the bride carefully down from the wagon and set her off in the dunes at some distance and then tore apart the wagon for firewood, which they burned to stay warm.

They slept in each other's arms, for warmth and for the taste of the sweetness of the summer that was going away from them forever now, the firelight flickering on their faces; and throughout the night Richard kept getting up and breaking off more firewood. And when the wagon and its wheels and axles were all burned (the steel wagon rims glowing in the night), he unfastened the skeletal horses from their yokes and harnesses as if turning them free, and burned the old leather, hardened and black as driftwood: and in that burning, the salt and minerals from a century ago, dry-caked from the horses' laboring backs, burned brightly in sputtering flames of silver and green, burning so hot that it melted the sand in their fire pit, shaping it as would the heat of a glass blower's torch into a perfect bowl, one which would years hence hold rainwater, on the brief occasions when a storm swept across the desert, and when the vagaries of the dunes had conspired to leave the glassine bowl exposed that day, rather than buried beneath fifty feet of sand and time.

And on those occasions, the desert creatures — collared lizards and desert kit foxes, coyotes and kangaroo rats — would come to the old fire pit and sip from that crystalline bowl, and then the sand would sweep back in like the tide and cover it all back up again.

The stench of the burning leather was what awakened Clarissa, just before dawn. In her dreams, she imagined that the odor was coming from her own skin, and even after she awakened, she could not shake that sensation; and like one who in the morning regrets deeply the dim memory of the night-before's revelry, upon awakening she no longer had any interest in pursuing either the treasure or the uncompleted story of their excavation, and was instead only in a panic to get back home before the heat of the sun returned: as anxious for that goal now as she had been for the discovery of more treasure the day before.

As if she had aged thirty or forty years in a single night.

The horses, free of their harnesses, had fallen over into loosened pieces of bone, as if the parts had been emptied carelessly from a large burlap sack, so disassembled now that even the idea of a horse seemed impossible.

Richard hefted the trunk of goblets onto his back, and Clarissa went over to the bride and shredded the tattered wedding dress, wrapping the gauze of it around her arms and neck, and also fashioned a crude veil.

She hoisted her parasol, and picked up the empty picnic basket, and together they hurried across the warming desert, Clarissa crying not so much from the pain of her sunburn as from the fear of its consequences; weeping at the realization of what she had done to her own precious and beloved skin.

Her skin passed quickly through all the stages of brown, and on into a blackness of char. Richard took her home and wrapped her in ice, lining her sheets with it as he might a gigantic fish that he had captured, and which he intended to keep alive a bit longer.

He stayed with her as long as possible, each night and day, during the times he did not need to be out at the rigs. When her pain was too intense, he carried her into the bathroom and laid her down in a tub of cold water and let the hose trickle water over her; and her father, who knew the pharmacist in town, was able to get morphine sulfate for her, under the condition that she use the pills only once a day.

The relief from the medication lasted but one or two hours, and the rest of a day's and night's measure was spent swimming through waves of pain: the crests torturous, and the troughs sweeter, if only by a fraction, with the dreams and memory of the last medication, and the nearing arrival of the next.

Her body, full of toxins, and with some of her flesh cooked and deadened, swelled so much that the blackened skin split in places, bursting like a hot dog left untended on a campfire grill. Richard and her parents took turns bathing these new wounds, each one as deep as the mud cracks in a gone-away pond, and these cleansings raised the scope or scale of her pain, until her twitching nerves and synapses were so frayed that her mind confused pain with pleasure; and as they tended to her she would sometimes smile and even croon a small song that at first they perceived to be cautionary, warning them to leave her alone to her delirium, but which came eerily to seem like what it was, confused or misplaced pleasure.

One day between wells and burn dressings, Richard took the goblets out to Herbert Mix's museum, where they were received with greater enthusiasm than Richard could have hoped for. Part of what made them so attractive to Mix, Richard knew, was the story of double travail that was now attached to them — not just the mysterious desert bride who had perished while transporting them, but the ruination — or so it was feared — of beauty.

Alarmed by the possible interest of other bidders, Mix borrowed from the bank the goblets' full value in gold and then tripled that number, so that he could purchase the collection as well as the story and its provenance, and ended up committing $35,000 for the purchase. (In the end it was he who was ruined; Clarissa's skin healed, and within six months the scars were unnoticeable, whereas Herbert Mix was never again able to climb out of debt; and after his death, some ten years later, a museum in Dallas was able to purchase the goblets, and the tatters of wedding dress, for one-tenth their original price.)

Clarissa almost broke. Or rather, she broke several times inside, as her skin began to crust in dark flakes and dust, and as the splits began to form scabs. She felt more reptilian than the oldest woman in town, and the irony was not lost on her: now that she had the money to leave town, there was no reason to do so. It was Richard, sunburned and with callused hands, who would be slipping away, while she remained behind, like some rock or stone sunken in a pond.

She dreamed of the lake and the cabin he had never yet dared mention to her — his own one damaged dream still held secret not like a card unplayed but like a map made on a scrap of folded paper and carried around for years, examined again and again until its lines are so known to the dreamer that it is as if the life has already been lived. But in Clarissa's own dreams, when she entered that cabin, it was not hers, nor was there ever anyone inside.

In her twisting, fevered sleep, she passed on by the cabin, and traveled farther, toward the unknown approbation of strangers, and toward a sound she perceived to be distant waves of applause — for what, she never quite knew, only that in the dream she turned in that direction; and as the splits and scabs slowly healed and the waves of pain flattened out, she no longer had the dream of the lit lakeside cabin in the woods.

Still, when she came back up out of the illness, it seemed that she had traveled far; and while she recognized the faces of those around her, she knew also that she had somehow been carried past them, and that in her absence, Richard too had traveled some distance.

For once, they had gotten out ahead of it, rather than being left behind.

Someone meek would have been tempted to pull into an eddy and wait for the current to catch up, or even to climb out onto shore and wander into the forest for a short distance, idle and blessed, waiting.

Instead, they kept traveling.

She touched the ridged scars on her arms and the back of her neck, and upon her face. An old woman in town told her that if she laid spider webs across them there would be no scars, and so each morning Richard and her parents went looking for spider webs, and brought them tangled and insubstantial to her, placing them on the worst skin-cracks. And inside herself, after having broken but not having admitted to anyone that she had broken, Clarissa determined to become a model, or an actress, regardless — whether her recovery left her with no scars or a thousand.

Because she did not have the courage to turn back, she substituted with resolve. It was all almost the same thing. She tried in her everyday conversations to keep secret from others her new knowledge and self-awareness — the almost unbearable acuity of the tiny space between courage and endurance, between determination and hope.

Richard could see it about her, however, and he wondered what she would do with that new perception. With a grace beyond his years, he made no effort to detain her, but let her flow on past: and he felt, too, that in some way he had already captured her, and that at some unknown level she would always be his, and he, hers.

He kept going out into the saltbush around town in the mornings, looking for spider webs, as did many others from town. The best way to transport the webs was to press them between sheets of cardboard; and at any point in the day, cars and trucks were driving up to her house, and passengers were getting out and carrying armloads of pressed cardboard and leaving them on the porch; and for the rest of the townspeople's lives, or those who had gathered the spider webs during the time of her illness, they would rarely be able to see a web without remembering that brief period in their lives when they had united to make pilgrimages to beauty; and of how, like a miracle, it had worked: of how Clarissa's skin had recovered completely, void of even a single scar, and of how she had gone on to continue being a flawlessly beautiful woman, by any account in the world.

All summer long, Richard's drilling success had been only average; but now that Clarissa had released him, as he had released her, his success improved. He knew this could be only an illusion, for each well location had already been decided far in advance, with Richard having plotted and selected the drill site long before he ever set foot on that landscape — but still, so dramatic was the change following Clarissa and Richard's letting-go that it was hard not to believe that there was some deeper partnership, unknown to the dreamers and participants, but existing nonetheless with foreordinance more omnipotent than the rigidity and fractured shiftings of the bedrock of the earth itself, the platey, labored movements of the groaning layers of stone. It was possible, Richard imagined, that this partnership would exist with equal dominance into the future as well.

In the last few weeks of his work in the Odessa oilfields, the ground began to cave in — gaping sump holes imploding, the skin of the earth collapsing in dozens of places each night. The belief among the towns-people was that in pumping so much oil out from beneath the ground over the last fifty years, entire caverns had been emptied; the subterranean earth had become dry and brittle, and had finally collapsed in on itself.

Such a phenomenon had never occurred or been noted anywhere else, but neither had such a volume of oil ever been extracted from such shallow depths, nor so extensively from limestone formations. The geologists and field personnel in town denied any responsibility, even though most of the sumps had occurred within a few hundred yards of an active field — but because the industry employed most of the town, there was little formal complaint; nor could anyone see much harm coming from the pits.

The land had already long ago been made nearly useless by over-grazing — one rancher had half a dozen cattle trapped for days in one of the larger sump holes, which was roughly the size of a football field; the rancher did not discover the sump, nor his herd, until the third day, by which time the cattle were weak with thirst, some lying on their sides, and he had to quickly build a ramp and scaffolding and lead them back up and out to safety.

Another rancher, an old drunkard, claimed that he had lost his best bull down one of the crevices that appeared overnight on his ranch. He claimed that he had put his ear to the ground and heard the bull bel-lowing down there. A neighbor went forty feet down, with a rope tied around his waist, before being unable to go any farther, but found no bull, nor any sign of the bull's passage.

Some of the pits and sump holes would go on to become hypersa-line lakes, their bottoms coated with an alkali hardpan, the density of which increased with each evaporation, so that although for the first few months the sump holes had been capable of holding water and attracting life, they quickly became toxic, killing the birds and mam-mals that came to their shores to drink, the evidence unmistakable in the residue of skeletons encircling the newly formed salt-shining basins, with the smaller animals dying but a few steps from the shore, and the larger ones managing to travel some farther distance; though in the end they too perished while still within sight of the lake, their arms and legs and wings and necks craned back in the direction from which they had traveled, as if to stare with disbelief at the betraying landscape: the thing that had presented itself as being able to provide succor to them turning upon them instead to be the device of their death.

When the sump holes first began appearing, some of the residents had immediate surges of water pressure in their wells, so that after years of decline, the hydrostatic levels rose all the way up the well casings and blew the lids off the well covers, water splashing onto the desert and then spreading in the night — flowing now like an artesian well blessed by some holy person.

Many of the wells were contaminated, during the collapse — oil and saltwater drilling fluids mixing with formations that had previously been kept separate. As a result, their water now had an iridescent sheen to it, and an oily taste and odor; but many residents were so pleased with the increase in volume that they quickly got used to the taste, and there were several among them who commented that the new inadvertent additive had made them more regular.

The oil companies denied any link between their overproduction and the collapses at the surface, and denied also the films and ribbons of oil that were beginning to appear in the drinking water. When the transport pipelines broke and leaked oil into the soil, they denied that too, simply patched the leak and then covered up the spill with new dirt.

Clarissa cashed the check from the sale of the goblets and left town the same day that Richard departed, leaving even as he asked her to stay and live the dream of the life at the lake; leaving after he humiliated himself and her both by pleading for her to believe in it, or to at least try it.

They drove out to the train station before daylight. He helped her board the 6:05 to Dallas, and watched, disbelieving — time for only one quick murmured endearment — as she climbed on, stone-faced, as if no pain could or ever would touch her anywhere; as if, now that it was over, none of it had ever mattered — and then the train was gone, and there was once more only a brilliant space in the desert where the train had once been, the space through which it had briefly passed. Richard got back in his truck and drove south and east, back to the Gulf, and out of the world.

He left behind a barren, sinking landscape and traveled back toward the ocean, drawn as if by his own tide, and possessing the worst scar of all — the scar of quitting, of not being able to go on any further — the death of dreams — and little by little, his once strange and powerful heart grew smaller.

He had helped despoil the landscape, even if unwittingly, puncturing it until it deflated, before leaving to return to Houston, to a life of increasing hesitancy and moderation — having failed hard at love and deciding thereafter not to pursue a subsequent attempt, some part of him understanding he could not withstand another failure. And without realizing it, he had helped ensnare her, for even as she perceived that she was escaping — had escaped — she carried in her the weeks-old seed of incautious foreplay: not quite an immaculate conception, but close to it.

A child conceived out of the ashes of her own body, forming even as her new skin formed, and with the child two months in her before she first dared to suspect that her periods, which had always been erratic, had been missed not as the result of her skin's injury, but instead because another had captured her after all.

She nearly climbed out of her own skin with revulsion — not at the child, but at herself — when the test confirmed her fears, and she cursed Richard, believing the pregnancy had been a trap to keep her from running, then cursed herself, believing that there must have been some fatal flaw within her that had desired to be trapped all along.

She lived in misery for months, unwilling to terminate the child — believing it to be a life separate from hers — and though her dreams of physical beauty were ruined, she was still the same person inside, unwilling or unable to draw close, or to allow others to come close: and rather than embracing her fear, she made the decision to give the child, whom she would name Anne, up for adoption.

Her parents had moved to Florida, for which she was glad, and she sat in her new apartment in Dallas, which was where unwed mothers from her hometown had always ended up, and with each day she was astounded by all that she had lost. She showed no talent for being able to look forward and consider that the child might be a blessing.

As in Odessa, she preferred to sleep as much as she could in the day, and move about at night. She got a job as a dispatcher for a moving and storage company, in which she was able to stay indoors, and then a better-paying job as a nurse's assistant at a hospital in Fort Worth, where her luminous beauty was sometimes the first thing to greet the injured, or the sick and the dying, as they were wheeled inside.

And yet such was her detachment, as her term grew, that other patients would sometimes glance at her and think that she too was a patient, despite her uniform, one who had just checked in to receive the best care for her unborn child.

At the hospital, it was easy to find professional if not spiritual advice. Despite having no affection for the child growing inside her, she in no way wanted it to grow up in such a backwater as Odessa, though neither did she want it in a big city, nor did she want it near her. An ultrasound had determined that it was a girl, and although one of the physicians had indicated he could help place the child with a couple who would be willing to reimburse Clarissa for her troubles, she declined the offer, thinking that if she were to profit from the baby, she might as well offer it to Herbert Mix, who could chain it in his garage and sell tickets.

In the end, she went with a church orphanage, another backwater place she had never seen, but which if she had would have given her second thoughts about Odessa — and she never wavered from her decision, not even in the last days, though after the pain and effort of the delivery (the child was not allowed to nurse), when she looked down between her legs at the spaceling that was already being wrapped and lifted slippery-glistening away, red and jerky in its movements, with an entire lifetime before it, she felt bereft. But then the nurse was gone, lingering only for a moment in the doorway to blot some of the afterbirth from the baby, and the door closed, and Clarissa was alone in the room with the doctor and another nurse, and they set about preparing her for her recovery.

For nearly a year, she felt free, believed herself to be fully on the path she had been dreaming of or desiring all her life. She switched to the day shift and became involved with a community theater group, and entertained various suitors, being boxed in at first, but choosing ultimately a lover who would not tie her down, a leading man with no fidelity to her, only desire — and it was this second world, the long evening rehearsals and the ascent into fantasy, that became most alive for her, while the hospital days became a lowermost kind of sleeping world for her.

She tensed when she saw babies in public, newborns, and told herself the silent mantras: *It's all worked out for the best,* and *I wasn't cut out to be a good mother,* and *I wasn't ready to be a mother,* and even *I'm sure she's in a loving home.*

Our Town; The Tempest; Guys and Dolls; Bus Stop. Her lover's name was Oscar. When he asked where she was from, she told him Houston.

Clarissa had seen melanoma before, in some of the patients that came through the hospital: old-woman gardeners, old-man lifelong tractor-drivers from the outlands, as well as middle-aged slack-skinned lifeguards, their arms and the backs of their necks riddled with the cancers that foretold their soon-to-be shadowy wasting away as surely as any biblical smear of blood left on their doors in the night; and when her own first appeared — showing up on her cheek not like any illness but instead merely a birthmark, a beauty mark, rising darkly through her creamy skin like a fish swimming from the depths of a clear lake and then pausing just beneath the surface — she was not frightened, nor, strangely, did she even find the mark unattractive. And the doctors, knowing nothing of the exposure she had encountered out in the dunes, were likewise lulled by the mark's beauty — if anything, it seemed to help draw into focus more quickly the admirer's glance — and when they mentioned it at all, they indicated that it was likely an aftereffect of childbearing.

She did not last the year, dying quickly, the enucleated damage within her multiplying rapidly, consuming her exactly in the manner of a fire. She was rushed through crude chemo and radiation therapies, which only fed the fire within her; and within months was unrecognizable even to herself.

She tried to get in touch with Richard, but couldn't find him. He had quit his job, someone said, when she called the company for whom he'd worked in Houston, and had gone down into Mexico, traveling; and as she was dying, she was haunted by the idea that the speed of her passing was related directly to the resistance she had put up against the world: to Richard, to the sun's rays, to her place of birth, to her own child — and on her worst days, which were frequent, she was glad that the child would never know that about her, and prayed that the child would move in an opposite direction, as she knew sometimes happened, and be open to the world.

It was the worst realization of all to understand one day that her greatest mistake had been in trying to build a life completely absent of mistakes: though in the end, there was at least some grace in that understanding, and she held on to it and pondered it long days and nights, as if she might yet somehow receive a second chance.

4

1933

SOME THREE DECADES BEFORE Richard had danced with Clarissa on the bare salt flats near the shore of Juan Cordona Lake, dancing as if to summon more life itself, or to resurrect the past, there had been another young couple in whom love had attempted to reach its roots, setting tendrils in that brilliant, searing, salty landscape.

Marie's father had been an orchardkeeper to the north, along the upper reaches of the Colorado. There was no reason to believe that Marie would be sucked down into the wasteland of salt to the south. Given her childhood in the orchard, among the peaches and pears, almost anyone might have predicted that Marie's life would be filled with blessings and affirmations.

She had been loved by both parents, loved by her brothers and sisters, attended a one-room schoolhouse. Even during times of hardship, her family and her community had had plenty to eat. She knew the love of her family and of the community, and then, as a young woman in the first year of courtship, she had known the love of a hardworking young man, Max Omo, whom she married at the end of that same first year, with the wedding held late in the breezy springtime, out in the orchards, while the blossoms blew loose from the trees, flashing through the sky like the scales of fish and catching in the hair of the wedding guests.

Marie had never heard of Odessa, nor had Max, at the time, but it was where they found themselves headed, shortly after the marriage. If Marie had been able to choose her own life, she would have envisioned the two of them staying in North Texas, working in the orchards, building a stone cottage, raising children. When she imagined their future, she pictured it as being filled always with the swirling scented petals of fruit blossoms, flashing white and pink through a blue sky.

Marie had loved Max Omo — his quiet, earnest, and even tender hardworking ways — but once those qualities began to vanish, it bothered her that she was unable to assign blame: unsure, always, of whether some harsher, inner core of his had begun to ultimately emerge, as if in some discouraging metamorphosis, or if it was the waterless land itself that hardened his tenderness, transforming it into something different.

But even there, in Odessa, love had prospered, for a short while.

They had rented a small house; Max took a job working in the grocery. They had joined the church; Marie had borne a son. She'd had friends. Max had begun to investigate the possibility of opening his own place of business in town. He was itchy, anxious for physical labor. He felt imprisoned by the absence of it.

They lived four houses down from the strange museum of Herbert Mix.

The heat was astonishing, and she had never seen a sun so fierce and bright. It began blazing early in the morning, and by midday, the streets and buildings were so illuminated that they shimmered. It seemed to Marie as if the town had already been received into a celestial afterlife. The colorless sky, in the full heat of summer, and the town, in the reflected whitewash of its buildings, was every bit as white as the ivory piles of spent orchard blossoms that blew in wind-drifts up against the sides of her house when she was a child.

For the first year, it was as if the harsh land had not yet even noticed them; as if they had arrived and tamed and mastered it through their dreams alone. As if no physical work would be required — only longing and desire.

Eighteen thousand years earlier, the glaciers that had once blanketed most of the sleeping continent were beginning to recede, leaving as their residue a detritus of moraine, time-smoothed boulders in the shape of human skulls; and though the glaciers had never quite reached the Pecos country, the cooling breath of their southerly exhalation had been enough to influence the local weather to the extent that a cool forest of fir, spruce, and pine had extended around the shore of Juan Cordona Lake.

The nomadic hunter-gatherers made lean-tos and rock cairns to shield themselves against the north winds; and at night, their warming fires flickered through the unchinked seams of the stacked rocks, so that to an observer from a later time, it could have seemed that the fire-sitters were not hunkered in front of a loose campfire, but instead housed in some warm foursquare structure. The stars glinted in perfect reflection on the dark mirror of the cold lake and burned in the tops of the dark conifer forest like decorations or ornaments.

After a few thousand years the world grew warmer, killing the spruce and pines, but cultures continued to wear footpaths to and from the lake, scraping salt from the shore and cutting blocks of it to use as a preservative for buffalo meat. Dogs pulled their sleds, and then, beginning in the sixteenth century, they used horses traded and stolen from the Spaniards, during that country's futile dreams of riches and conquest.

The residents of the new desert, the Jumano Indians, fought with the Apaches for control of the lake — as if there were not enough to share, and as if unable to conceive or understand that the salt kept replenishing itself; that the sun itself was what continued to pull the salt to the surface.

By the late seventeenth century, when Captain Juan Domínguez de Mendoza — related to the Spanish Viceroy who over a hundred years earlier had helped finance Cortés's search for gold and silver and the Seven Cities of Cíbola — encountered the lake, he found that numerous trails and roads had been developed, leading to it.

He called them *caminos,* or streets, and noted how they were curbed with white stones, so that a traveler could follow, even on a moonless night, these time-honored paths toward the same and final destination.

Finding no gold or silver — after over two hundred years of slaughter and mayhem — the Spaniards finally turned, as had every culture before them, to the ground itself, and began gnawing at the glittering salt.

As Spain helped encourage the northward colonization of Mexico through a series of garrisons and missions — the ancient march of soldiers and priests, occupying increasingly marginal agricultural lands — most of the disputes took place not between Indians and salt traders, but among the traders themselves, with the driver of one ox-pulled carreta finding himself insulted by the driver of another. It was not only the lakeshore that was littered with the bones of humanity, but the trail back to Mexico: the whitening bones of the salt traders drying flyblown in the desert next to the *caminos'* stones and boulders — as if each skeleton had belonged to an individual whose last and highest purpose in life had been, in death, to help pave and point the way to the lake, so that others of his kind could continue with similar travels.

At night, in the traders' camps, their carts would be arranged in a ring around a campfire of sage, piñon, and driftwood hauled up from the salt river of the Pecos. Rotgut tequila, crudely made and fiercely potent, would be drunk from clay jugs, and at the far edges of the wavering firelight, the oxen would remain standing, still in their traces.

Under the loads of salt, the carretas would begin to creak in the night, as the rawhide wet from river crossings and the green wood heat-riven by the day began to twist and contract in the cooler temperature of evening, so that the wearied carts gathered around the salt traders sounded almost like living things themselves; and sometimes it was difficult to tell which sound was which: to differentiate the moans of the worn-out oxen from those of the wooden carts to which they were still harnessed, and with the carts' wheels lashed with the hide and ligaments of several of those same oxen's ancestors.

The traders traveled early, and again late, in the hottest months, and wore wide hats and white shawls, and sometimes carried self-made parasols of shirts and trousers that tattered quickly and gave the procession the appearance of a failing parade.

Back and forth the traders went, wearing their paths deeper into the hardpan desert, until to archaeologists in later years it would have seemed that the salt traders' trek must have been a religious pilgrimage rather than an economic one, and that they had celebrated, revered, and worshiped, and even loved, the salt.

• • •

The Mexicans camped and cut salt from the south shore in the nineteenth century, while the American colonists worked the north shore. In 1836, after the Alamo and the Battle of San Jacinto — after Texas proclaimed itself a sovereign nation to the world — the lake received its current name, Juan Cordona, after the man who held the original deed.

The American colonists stepped up their own salt-freighting operations, supplying not just the living and dying of the Civil War (those Pennsylvania farm boys succumbing with Texas salt dissolving in their bloodstreams; and those Alabama farm boys' wretched last meals the night before battle salted down with the same), but the cattle that were filling the country around San Antonio as the buffalo, and then the Indians, were killed off.

The face of the land changing quickly now, like that of an old man or old woman, even as the shape of the bone, the frame and structure of it beneath that changing surface of skin, remained essentially the same.

The salt cutters were as noted for their physical strength as for their prodigious greed. When the salt was dense enough, they loaded slabs and squares of it into their wagons as they would quarry stone; but often the salt was formless, so that they had to wade out into the lake waist-deep, as if into a warm ocean, and, working shirtless, or in rags and tatters not unlike those that festooned the spars of the farther skeletons, whose coattails still now and again stirred in the rarest breeze, the salt cutters would shovel the salt onto broad planks of wood they had brought for that purpose (which would later be reattached to their wagons to form a higher tier, enabling the freighters to transport even more salt).

Once the sleds were fully loaded, the mules would pull them to shore, where the salt would dry in the sun before being loaded into wagons.

The wagons themselves — prairie schooners — were the size of small clipper ships, thirty feet long, with front wheels five feet in diameter and rear wheels measuring slightly more. Each wheel was six inches wide, to help keep the wagon from bogging down. The wagon could sustain seven thousand pounds of salt.

The salt cutters filled their wagons to the limit, and then beyond. It generally took one man three days to fully load his own wagon; and in the blazing heat, standing waist-deep in the brine, with the grinning skulls and mummified carcasses of the ancient wayfarers stationed all around them, it must have occurred to more than one of them to question why they had opted to sacrifice any portion of their allotted earthly time in order to enter hell prematurely. It's tempting also to think that they, too, dreamed of cool rivers and ferns, and of love — though perhaps they dreamed of nothing at all; or, worse yet, perhaps their dreams were of shoveling dense loads of heavy salt onto broad planks half-floating out in the middle of the lake, to be sledded into shore by tortured mules, to dry blazing in the sun.

Despite the hardships, the salt cutters could not restrain themselves. Among them, August Santleben was most famous for loading his wagons over their limits. Often he would exceed those limits by a ton or more, and would have to stop and offload along the *camino,* leaving saline mounds that were many miles distant from their provenance, and to which wild animals were attracted, even decades later: pawing at the sand where the salt had disintegrated and drained back into the earth.

Santleben opened the San Antonio market first, and from his modest team of seven wagons routinely produced fifty thousand pounds a week, which he sold for $2,500 to the ranches on his route.

The ranchers fed the salt directly to their cattle and sheep. Their cattle and sheep were quickly overgrazing the thin topsoil, and the salt the ranchers were casting over the land to help their livestock retain more water weight was scalding and sterilizing the soil, so that it was as if they were sowing ruin purposely onto their own fields; and still Santleben could not sell them enough salt, for the ranchers' stock craved it, and it helped the cattle and sheep bring higher market prices.

Santleben, knowing he was the first to be supplying the ranches around San Antonio, understood also that he was living in halcyon days; that sooner or later other freighters would discover his market and undercut his prices, until the miraculous salt was selling for something far closer to its true worth, which was almost nothing.

"There is room for only one trader per market," he wrote in his journal. "The reason for this is that daily the sun replenishes the salt, and in so doing proves itself capable of furnishing an inexhaustible supply for eternity."

Freighters came from all over Texas to load a wagon or two, before taking it back home as easy money. As the price kept dropping, a caste system developed between the ranchers who used the salt and the laborers who provided it, while the grueling work remained the same, until eventually the gathering of it became the last resort of the economically bereft.

Cattle barons Charles Goodnight and Oliver Loving went right past Juan Cordona Lake with their famous Goodnight-Loving Trail, but never deigned to traffic in the lake's commerce, focusing instead on meat on the hoof. They drove their cattle northward, selling the steers at Fort Sumner, New Mexico, and the mother cows and heifers farther north, up in Colorado, before returning south with their bags of gold, hoping to tuck in with some of the salt drivers for security on the final leg home.

On one such return, still north of the relative safety of the salt cutters' caravans, Goodnight and Loving lost their mules in a stampede and were forced to ride by night to avoid Comanches and overheating their horses, which were carrying more than $12,000 in gold. There were but four men in the party.

They straggled in this manner across seventy-five miles of waterless desert, aiming for the distant relief of Castle Gap, and were nearly there when they spotted a Comanche war party.

Too tired to run, they accepted their fate.

Charles Goodnight recalled looking out at the long line of Indians and thinking to himself, *Here you are with more gold than you ever had in your life, and it won't buy you a drink of water, and it won't get you food. For this gold you may have led three men to their death—for a thing that is utterly useless to you!*

Goodnight moved to the front and told the others to flank him; he would lead a last charge straight through the Comanches, firing wildly and hoping to open a wedge wide enough for his men to pass through.

They were surprised to discover that the Indians did not scatter to deflect their approach, and finally they drew close enough to see that what they thought was a war party was instead the trader known as Uncle Rich, who — like Loving and Goodnight — seemed to make money at everything he tried, out on the barren plains.

On this occasion, Uncle Rich was freighting watermelons from East Texas to trade with the drivers of the Mexican carretas, loading his own wagons then with some of their salt to take up to North Texas. He traveled regularly through the hostile territory — making the four-hundred-mile round trip from Coleman County in North Texas twenty-one times without harm to himself, though no one could ever say why. All of his oxen wore cowbells around their necks, and it was surmised by some that the melodies of the bells had somehow cast a blessing upon him. When he grew too tired to travel on any journey, he would dig a hole in the ground and nap in such a dugout, like a badger or coyote. It was rumored that for this, too, the Indians revered him.

Everyone was after the salt; the routes of its export left the lake in all directions.

The Texas and Pacific Railroad was finally completed in 1881, a hundred miles to the north, and the salt cutters and prairie schooners became obsolete overnight, though there were still those who continued to eke out a marginal existence, peddling baskets and barrels of salt to small-time ranches around San Antonio.

Lacking any vision or talent beyond mindless endurance, grizzled salt cutters like Burro Jack, last name unknown, and Salty Bill Latham persisted deep into the twentieth century, freighting absurd loads of salt across the desert in wagons pulled by miniature donkeys, even as the railroad passed them by, as did later the motorcar and an expanding highway system. It was what their fathers had done, and their fathers' fathers, and as such, they believed it was holy work.

They traveled the old stone-lined trails that the carretas had once used, and each time they came through the area, the entire population of the present-day ghost town of Upland, just east of Castle Gap, would come running out of their homes and line the road to watch them, and call out greetings, and sometimes leave favors for them out on the side of the road.

Access to the lake's mineral resources ended in 1920 when the Cowden family bought the four-thousand-acre deed and attempted to convert the lake into a sheep farm, a scheme that resulted in spectacular failure. Although wolves were already nearly extinct from cattle country — only an occasional old loner would come limping clubfooted down from out of the mountains, wreaking havoc on a herd or two of sheep before being poisoned or trapped or shot — the smaller, more numerous coyotes were able to almost single-handedly destroy any sheep they encountered, and at Juan Cordona Lake, it was too easy; the coyotes had merely to stampede the sheep out into the suckhole bog of the lake, where they became stuck, and the ravens were free then to feast on the ones that did not sink.

The coyotes, lighter in weight yet with large feet, were able to struggle on out across the floating sludge of salt long after the sheep had been rendered immobile. The sheepherders had to keep vigil and even then were unable to protect the entire herd; the lake was too vast.

Trying to recoup their losses, the Cowdens ran larger and larger herds, and tried to keep the sheep bunched together for greater protection. The result was that often whenever the sheep overnighted, the next day they would leave concentrated deposits of their dung baking in the sun, supersaturated with nitrates, and rich in saltpeter.

The dunghills were flammable, and a stray spark from a bolt of lightning, or even a backfiring piece of machinery or a sheepherder's cigarette, could set off these mounds with a percussive explosion of orange-yellow light, followed by the odor of brimstone; and then the sparks from one dunghill would sometimes set off the explosion of another.

And on a stormy night, after lightning had passed by, it was possible to look out across the lakeshore and see several such mounds afire, as if in the storm's coming there had arrived also clans or encampments of a more secretive race of beings — the tribes of those who had once lived there, returning now to reclaim that which for so long had been theirs.

The fires always burned themselves out. They were dramatic, but there was no other fuel for them to consume beyond the dung itself; the sheep had already ravaged all else. There was only stone, salt, and wind; and again to a stranger it would have seemed curious as to why the ranchers had placed such a curse on their own land. As if smiting it in this manner only so that they could show that it was theirs to smite.

After the Cowdens had inflicted all the harm they could upon the land, they sold it to the young man of German stock, Max Omo, Marie's husband, who, having already amused the locals by having purchased such a suckhole of a tract, astounded them next by building a home on its shores, thereby becoming — in 1936 — the first known person to reside at the lake year round.

Not since the forests of the Ice Age had lined its shores had any-one considered camping there for more than a few nights; but Omo, who before he bought the land had worked briefly as a laborer for the Cowdens, and who had fallen in love with salt, built a little house out of stone and wood and sheet iron.

He brought Marie and his children — another son had been born two years after the first — with him into the dunes — seeking his for-tune, but seeking also salt: craving not the scent or taste or even the shimmering sight of it, but the mere accumulation of it; as if some switch had been flipped within him, some genetic tenuousness had been disturbed, finally and radically, by its interaction with the sere and withholding landscape into which he had been drawn.

Omo figured out almost immediately that it was not really neces-sary to wade waist-deep out into the sludge with a board and shovel, but that by constructing weirs, a man could trap and harvest the salt as it was driven each day by the prevailing winds that carried the waves in from the northwestern depths to the shallows, before receding each evening.

By adjusting slightly the depth and slant of the southeastern shore-line, near his base of operations, and setting up a system of rock flood-gates, Omo was able to lay out flat sheets of iron onto which the salt would be precipitated each day, so that every evening before he went to bed he would be able to empty his sheets of iron into barrels.

In this manner, he was able to harvest nearly two thousand pounds a day.

Omo was not a big man when he first came to the lake, but moving such prodigious quantities of iron and salt developed him into a caricature of labor, knotted and swollen with muscles whose contorted proportions seemed all the more odd in that they were little used for anything but the act of pulling in the iron sleds and leaning them against his barrels, and shoveling the salt into the barrels.

He had tiny little bird-calves, but ponderous thighs; no chest, but preposterous biceps and forearms. No triceps to speak of, but a neck like a bull's. His back was as wide as that of two men, so that he looked like some kind of experiment of nature, and a mistaken one at that.

He dug water wells too, finding the brackish water, in those days, at a depth of only twenty feet. He and Marie hardly drank any water at all, but kept buried in their hot sand cellar, which was lined with more sheets of iron, dozens of cases of white wine from Germany. (When they were first married, they had received as a wedding present from Max's uncle, a vintner in Germany, a hundred cases of cheap white wine, along with the promise that their lives would be blessed for as long as they had any of the wine remaining.) This was almost all they ever drank, except for a pot of salt-coffee each morning, and it was mostly the children who were subjected to the tepid taste of the brine water. The children were always thirsty, as a result, but one of the side effects of their diet, so high in minerals, was that they grew quickly, so that by the time they were seven and nine years old, they were already the size of adolescents, and able to do nearly the work of a full-grown man.

The richer the Omos became, gathering the salt, the poorer Marie's heart grew; and rapidly she passed from being a beautiful and vivacious young woman into a weather-beaten, dour hag. When the townspeople saw her coming into the town of Odessa for supplies, or to bring the boys to the Lutheran church, they would avoid her, where once they had sought her out.

The smell of sour wine was on her breath and somehow always on her clothes, even in the mornings, and, as well, the sulfurous odor of the lake itself, and the scent of dried mutton, which along with the eggs from a few parched chickens was all the Omos ever ate.

For the longest time, Marie had sympathized with the creatures that the coyotes herded out onto the salt, where they would become mired — the remaining sheep, usually, but also the deer, and even sometimes an individual from the fast-dwindling herds of antelope — *Had the buffalo ever been caught in such a trap?* she wondered. And as the years passed, and Omo's bounty increased (he could never sell nor even transport as much as he produced, so that there were mountains of salt, inland from the lee basin, up against the dunes), and as with the jettisoned or wagon-broke loads that lay scattered along the *caminos,* wild animals of every sort came all night long to paw and suck at the ever-increasing and miraculous salt mountain of Max Omo.

Deer and rabbits came, as did mice, coyotes, foxes, pack rats, antelope, wild boar, feral horses, bobcats, and once, down from the cool pine mountains and forests of New Mexico and the Big Bend country, a black bear, looking so uncannily like a human that at first neither Marie nor the children could be convinced that it was not merely a man dressed up in a fur coat, a man gone mad, clawing and gnawing at the salt, unable to control his desire.

After several years of living in the oven, however, and seeing her babies sprint past babyhood, launching almost immediately into grotesque musclebound imitations of their father, Marie found, at first to her horror but then to her slow-building pleasure, that she enjoyed seeing the parade of animals that the coyotes were able to haze out into the quicksand of the salt.

She began to view them as a kind of crop, something the land produced for her, even if she could not utilize it; and she would arise early each morning and move eagerly to the window, to see if the coyotes had sent anything new out onto the flats.

And then, still later into her unhappy career as mistress of the lake, it got to where she came to view the trapped and struggling, writhing animals with even greater pleasure, reserving a place in her heart for them as if they were guests who had arrived to keep her company out in the wasteland.

She would lie awake in the night listening for them, straining to hear if the sound of the wind carried with it the joyous cries of the coyotes, bringing her more visitors.

Her husband beside her, reeking of salt; the brute children above her, in the torturously hot loft.

Marie could hear the sand pitting against the iron walls and tin roof of her house. The old-timers who had told them that a house or other structure, if large enough, would anchor the dune, had for the most part been correct; though in the early autumn, when the heat abated slightly and the winds began to quarter, no longer driving relentless from the deserts to the west but easing down from out of the north, slipping through tall grass and then whistling and moaning through the canyons of Palo Duro and other time-cut slots in the earth, even the largest dunes would begin to shift.

And once or twice every few years, the dune above their house would envelop them completely: not with any final, thunderous collapse, but in a steady sifting, a stream-like pouring that was so sibilant, the sound of it barely entered their dreams.

Like badgers, Omo and his boys would burrow upward through the dune, pulling Marie on a rope behind them, sweating and sand-clad; and after about six feet of such digging, they would break back into the free and clear white sunlight, and their happiness at seeing it again might have raised a troubling question: why was a life of such hardship and misery so desired, even cherished?

Marie among them was happiest to see the salt earth again, and waded down off the dune and fell upon the crusty whitened hardpan ground, weeping and kissing it, while Max and the boys went out to the toolshed, which had been only partially covered, and began shoveling their house back out, working neatly and methodically in their labors as might a line of red ants whose path was temporarily blocked by some catastrophe.

They would have the house unearthed by dusk, and after exhuming it, they went out to their salt traps and gathered them in, and shook into their drums the salt, which sparkled in the light of the full moon.

For protection, they threw up a few more sheets of heavy iron, each time planting them vertically into the dune just above the roof of their cabin, to act as a kind of hood or shield; and each time, Marie refused to go back into the cabin that first night, so they would drag their mattresses up onto the hot roof to sleep.

That first such night, the boys fell asleep immediately, and Max Omo soon thereafter, leaving only Marie awake among them. She sat up and looked out at the shining lake, sparkling and glinting with every color of the rainbow, and appearing as a frozen pond in winter, upon which children might skate and play, or upon which young couples, new in love, might after winter's thaw canoe and picnic. She was awake for a long time, listening to the breeze, and hearing, or imagining, the rustlings of the sand flowing against the flimsy tin.

She drifted off to sleep just before daylight, though her dreams were terrible, and it was a relief when the stirrings of Omo and the boys awakened her a short time later. They dragged their mattresses down off the roof, and Marie went out to the iron cookhouse, built some distance away to avoid overheating the cabin, and lit a fire in the woodstove to heat a pot of the cloudy, salty water for coffee.

She cracked eggs into the skillet and laid strips of dried mutton alongside the eggs. She mopped the sweat from her brow. She poured half a glass of wine and felt the day's first trickle of sweat running down the groove of her back, bringing a strange chill and shudder.

She stopped and listened to a clanging sound out by the toolshed; Omo and the boys wanting to get a little work in before breakfast.

Later in the day, they all rode into town to buy a twenty-foot length of stovepipe, to install on their front porch as a crude sort of breathing apparatus, should the dune ever bury their house again. Omo joked, "If we wake up one morning and see sand pouring through it, we'll know to buy thirty feet next time."

As Marie shopped, she visited with some of the ladies with whom she had an acquaintance. When they asked how she had been, she informed them nonchalantly — no quiver in her voice at all — foolish pride! — that their house had been buried beneath a sand dune for a while, but that they had dug out and were all right now. And as she shopped, going from store to store, she pretended not to be able to hear the whispers behind her: as if the whisperers believed she lived in some other world, in which the normal physics of sound and conversation did not apply to her, or as if she were from a land so foreign that she could not understand the language.

"What do you suppose they do with all that money? They surely don't know how to spend it on clothes."

"Don't those boys look *feral?*"

"I feel sorry for the husband — married to such a cold fish."

For his part, Omo gave himself over to the landscape as might a lover made desperate. The movement of his days — the script of his routes and his activities — remained as constant as the meter of a metronome ticking for so long that its movements are no longer heard or noticed. But beneath the dull muscularity of his physical life, he was falling, falling without a rope; in love with the savage deprivation of the landscape.

And whenever he encountered excess in that land of deprivation — be it salt, or the heat, almost igneous in nature, that wrung all but the last of the water from his body and sent it in sheets down his chest and back — he fell even harder in love, without even realizing that was what it was; falling into the clefts between the abundance of one thing and the deprivation of another, falling through an incandescent pluming kaleidoscope of colors that belied completely the physical constraints of his salt-colored life and his methodical movements above.

As he fell, such was his lust for the act of falling itself, that in his gluttony he made no grasp for the heart or embrace of another with whom to share these wondrous flashing-past sights, as if the entire past as well as future of his life seemed to unscroll before him in each day's dreaming: as if no possibilities had ever been compromised or extinguished, but instead still existed, fully formed, below.

Marie stood next to him in the daytime, and lay next to him at night, and gradually came to know as if through some sixth sense his enthusiastic and selfish, silent leave-takings.

And in his dreaminess, he began to cobble together strange inventions, fantastic contraptions designed to summon even more salt from the landscape. And if there had been any spark of love or hope left in Marie's belly for him, some tiny spark that was somehow still alive, despite the inhospitality of the landscape, that spark was snuffed out as she came to realize fully the selfishness of those unshared imaginative travelings, recognizing that such imaginings were not merely escape from the barren landscape, but from herself as well.

There were a few tolerable years before her indifference grew to resentment; and in that graywater period, she would watch him go out to work each day with the boys, and held on to the thought or hope of him returning at the end of the day with a kind word, a pleasant touch, or (and as the years went past, she hated herself for even having imagined such a specific thing) some desert wildflower, or interesting small crystal, or the wing of a butterfly, of which thousands gathered at the lake in early spring and summer, sipping at the puddles along the shoreline and craving the salt — entire sections of shoreline alive, some mornings, with the feathered, arrhythmic stirrings and exhalations of their watering: as if the entire shoreline were breaking apart, and iridescent color was emerging from the salt plain, after millennia of sameness and whiteness.

In such large gatherings of others of their kind, the butterflies were not discomforted by the approach of potential predators, and on many occasions, drawn to the plenitude of color — the pumpkin and russet of fritillaries and monarchs, the corn hues of sulphurs, the periwinkles and azures of spring beauties — Marie had walked down to the lake and crouched hunkered next to the great massed gathering, to watch them feed and water at the lake as if they were the livestock of some finer, better shepherd.

But after the butterflies moved on in their migrations, and the damp shores were littered with the bright husks of those who had died or been left behind (even the most aged of them living for only a few weeks), it was Marie who had to wander the spongy salt-whitened quicksand of the beach, picking up the more interesting specimens that had been left behind, gathering them as she might pick up shells at the oceanside. She brought them back to place in a small bowl at their dining table, not as if some offering of a strange or ritual meal, but merely a tiny presentation of beauty.

Not once did Omo or the boys ever stop to pick up even a single butterfly to bring home to share with her; and she hated herself for wanting them to, and then again — later into her term — she hated them for not doing it.

The landscape lying as heavy upon all of them as a giant mound of stones or sand; and they made no effort to climb out by pushing up higher through all the rubble. Instead, their feeble attempts at escape came in the form of burrowing and diving deeper, as was the habit of most of the other desert creatures who were not free to migrate, but who had instead been selected to remain in one place for the rest of their lives, and beyond: until they and their kind went extinct.

Thousands of torn and ragged butterfly wings might be blowing around the shoreline, following such a migration — whirls of flashing color caught in the brief turmoil of the dust devils that swept across the prairie — so that it appeared the butterfly parts had come back to life.

Occasionally, sitting in the shade of her doorstep, waiting, just waiting, Marie would have a butterfly wing brought her way by the whim of the wind, deposited neatly at her feet by chance; and as she descended, broken, it often seemed to her that the weight of her breaking — one giant wave after another falling upon her — came not from the last-straw weight of a thing so insignificant as a single blue or red or yellow butterfly wing, but from the final crush of a thing even lighter than that: the absence of even a single shining blue or red or yellow butterfly wing.

For a while — before the pain had been lithified — she remembered a time even further back; the time of Omo's brief courtship. He had brought her flowers, and had been shy and gentle and delicate around her, and it had seemed to her then, as his attentions had gathered around her — this hardworking, quiet man, seeming unusually restrained in her presence — that she had somehow captured him: and she could scarcely believe the wonder at having done so.

And even after the boys were born, that feeling had persisted, for a while longer — that through some miracle, she had been blessed and gifted with such a man, and that she had been privileged to give birth to two fine and hungry, healthy baby boys.

It had seemed back then that good fortune had wandered into her life as might a strange animal she had been trying to coax or capture. It seemed as if the animal of luck had come wandering in from off the prairie, and had entered her corral in early evening, just before a summer thunderstorm, so that all she had to do was close the gate, sliding the poles in behind the animal, which appeared to be temporarily disoriented, lost, wandering.

Here is your home, she would think, rising from the porch and hurrying across the front yard to close the gate.

It would be some years more before her own unfillable hunger would be revealed to her. At that point however it became for her as if she had fallen through a thin crust: as if the animals she had captured, the herd of her family, had through their dull comings and goings worn that crust dangerously thin.

No amount of hazing or imprecations could drive these animals away, they had her cornered, and then the crust wore completely through and she was falling, arms upflung, falling with both hands splayed outward in a grasp for the life unlived, but it was no use, she had made the wrong choice, had bartered for attention rather than respect, for need instead of desire, for gluttony instead of generosity; and as she fell, it seemed that she was plummeting through a cavern filled with swirling brightly colored wings, but none were for her outstretched hands, all were instead ascending.

And in her lap, in her apron skirt, was a weight as dense and nonnegotiable as a farrier's anvil, carrying her farther and faster to the bottom of the well, with the butterflies all escaping, rising in flutters up the shaft of shining light to the surface above, toward the jagged crater of light she had created in her punching-through.

The brush of their rising wings against her face, and the chaotic swirls and glimpses of color, was as close as she was going to get to the thing she so craved.

For his part, Omo was falling even faster; and again he embraced the anvil as he would a greedy lover. He dreamed of salt, stared at the small inland ocean of it, looked forward to digging the shaftwells into it, and loved or was at least reassured by the warbled, rattling sound the iron made when he and the boys pulled in the loaded sheets of salt each evening — a sound that was sometimes answered by the thunder and jags of lightning out on the darkened prairie beyond.

In such moments, what it felt like to Max was that the answering thunder, and its simultaneous lightning, was knocking loose old crusts and plaque in his mind — releasing him from old constraints, allowing him to work more powerfully and confidently at the one thing that he did best: the one thing he did so well, it seemed that he had been neither crafted nor shaped for it, but born ready for it, and had, by grace and luck, found his way toward it.

In retrospect, he would have said that they were the happiest days of his life.

Spindletop had been discovered in 1901, and in the subsequent years people had begun drilling for oil all over the state, searching in every conceivable nook, and proposing outlandish hypotheses. When Omo was thirty-eight he came up with a vision for how drilling rigs might successfully penetrate the layers of subterranean salt through which they sometimes attempted to pass. Drilling through salt had always before been problematic, because as the drill bit entered and then drilled through it, the salt, flowing like a liquid or a plastic, would surge against the drill pipe, binding the drill stem and causing the bit to stick firmly in the hole, so that the drillers could go no deeper, nor could they pull out.

The hole had to be abandoned, in such instances — the drilling platform disassembled and set up at some other distance, in a location perhaps less conducive to finding oil, for often the green-black crude lay pooled warm and waiting only beneath those treacherous shields of salt.

Omo discovered that by mixing enough salt into the drilling fluid as the pipe was rotated down into the earth, the heavier weight of that newly mixed salt water acted as a stabilizer, neutralizing the tendency of the underground salt formations to cave in upon the drilling pipe.

The benefits from his vision were incalculable. Because the weight of the drilling fluid was now heavier due to the added salt, there were less blowouts whenever the drillers' bit encountered a buried pocket of gas. In the past, there had been little time to prepare for and evacuate a rig during such an encounter. A bubbling froth would come rushing back up the hole as the gas spewed into the drilling fluid, churning to the surface like the vomitus of some buried gargoyle. The mixture of gas and water would spray into the sky, and splash down upon the steel floor of the drilling rig in rude ejaculation. The driller and rig hands would have but a few short moments to run for cover, because any stray spark — the ash from a cigarette, or the sparking of magnetos from the engine of the rig itself — would be enough to ignite that gas, which would be converted immediately into an inferno, and the flames would melt the rig quickly into a puddle of steel. The vertical torches of such explosions burned sometimes for months, unable to be quenched or capped or plugged: burning until all the gas was used up.

How many lives had Max Omo saved with his invention, his idea? Such mercies could not be calculated, nor could the millions of barrels of oil and millions of cubic feet of gas that were able to be discovered and extracted now from beneath those previously inaccessible strata of salt; nor could all the good be measured that would come from the uses of that extra oil and gas: the hospitals constructed, the journeys taken by plane and car, the synthetic fabrics manufactured — the cities, and the nation, swelling, feasting on his idea.

He increased the demand for this product; but in so doing, a fine balance was tipped and lost, for salt now became valuable enough that enterprises sprang up to refine it straight from bubbling little outcrops in the Hill Country, and from the comings and goings of the ocean and tides. Max Omo's salt was still of the highest quality for feeding livestock, and the drillers would still buy his salt if he cared to transport it to them; but for the purposes of cramming it down into a hole in the ground, never to be seen again, one brand of salt was as good as another, and the cheaper the better.

And again, the landscape seemed to snap some fragile synapse within, for with the new earnings Max Omo realized from the increased demand for his product, he poured all that money back into the purchasing of more land, radiating out in all directions from his beloved salt lake — wretched, useless land, heaps and dunes and gullies of sand: leagues of sand, unmappable and unsurveyed, as capricious as the wind.

Because of all of Omo's purchases of useless land, the Omos were just barely hanging on, drinking warm salt water, and stale wine that was at the edge of vinegar, and eating moldy dried mutton.

Still Omo kept buying up one tract after another, voraciously extending his barren kingdom to a greater distance beyond his sight, even when he stood on the tin roof of his shanty, and then farther; his ownership extending beyond the horizon even when he shinnied up the hollow breathing pipe that towered above their sand hut like the crow's nest of a tiny ship.

It was a simple equation — the more the landscape withheld from him, the more he had to have — and it was with nightmarish clarity that Marie saw the salt prairie's effect upon him.

Why had she traded her childhood for this? She had been forced to give birth to the second child alone, save for the company of his squalling brother, two years older; even then, before they had moved out of town, Max Omo had been hieing off to the salt desert, and by the time he returned, the child had been born. (Out at the salt lake, she would later lose two subsequent attempts, each early in the term; she always imagined that they were daughters, and blamed everything — the landscape, Omo, the lake, herself, the odor of salt, and the odor of the boys.)

The house was invaded daily by scorpions, centipedes, tarantulas, rattlesnakes, and vinegarroons. The spiders and wasps she crushed with a blacksmith's shoeing hammer, sledging them into matted oblivion with gusto. Her forearms were overdeveloped from this practice, veinous and bulging, and the snakes she severed into multiple pieces with a hoe that she sharpened regularly.

She took to wearing her long dark hair in a bun. It was too hot to do anything else. Even before the boys reached adolescence and forgot her entirely, she had reached a state of despondency, perilously approaching insanity, in which her most pleasant moments were spent catatonic in the incredible heat of the privy, where she found herself, across the years, content to just sit in the darkness and let the world pass by.

For hours she would sit there, dress hiked up over her waist, purging herself, with the heat and her salty diet baking her feces into diarrhetic soup; but the darkness was soothing, and she would just sit there, praying quietly that the world would bring her no more disappointment.

Like a mason laying stones, she would build up around her an armament of numbness, as if fortifying herself for protection against ever-coming heat and brilliance.

Now it seemed but a short step until the end, and in both her dreaming and her waking, she could smell, taste, feel, and hear a different quality to the air rising from the abyss before her, though still she could not see it.

She stood so close before it now that almost anything could take her there. As she lay awake at night listening for the coyotes, the gentle sifting of a few grains of sand onto the metal roof above was enough to raise every hair on her body, and though she managed to lie still, she would find herself breaking into a sweat, more excessive than even the usual lake-dampness in which they all spent their nights perspiring.

Marie sometimes found in such instances that she would be growling quietly to herself, as she listened to the sand skate across the top of the roof, though other times she would be unaware that the sound was coming from her, and would lie there in terror, listening, even as the sound from her throat grew louder.

Omo and the boys slept on, three sets of snoring mixed with the sound of her growls.

She imagined that at any moment the growling would stop, and that Max Omo would stir in his sleep, possibly awakening, and would reach over and take her face in his hands, and begin murmuring kind things to her.

Little violet-and-green swallows had begun to nest in the stovepipe of their breathing apparatus, and these night sounds too would awaken her and unleash the panting terror that was sutured tight in her chest: the scrabbling sound of their little lizard claws as they shifted in their nests, jockeying for position and rearranging themselves ceaselessly in the night; and then once their eggs were hatched, the endless cheeping of the nestlings clamoring for food.

Sometimes one of the flightless young birds would tumble all the way down the pipe and out onto the floor by their bed and spin there, clawing and scuttling, and Marie would have to get up and open the door and fling it into the night, where the coyotes would come and find it.

She would try to get back to sleep, with the pillow over her head while the other birds in the pipe chirped and chattered with even greater agitation; and she could not be sure if she dreamed of the coyotes' laughter out in the yard, or if it was real.

A strange and powerful landscape summons strange and powerful happenings, just as beauty seems to summon beauty, or harshness beckons to harshness. One night Marie was awakened from her sleep (if her alternating bouts of terror and stupor could be called that) not to the sound of sand or bird or coyote, but to what seemed at first to be a complete absence of sound: as if the entire world around her had paused in order to listen to something so wonderful and unusual that it caught for a few moments even the world's uncaring attention.

Gradually, as her senses readjusted to the different pace of the silence, Marie realized that it was not a complete soundlessness she was hearing, but rather, the distilled purity of one sound: a gigantic and strangely rhythmic thrashing, out in the lake, huffings and suckhole gaspings, spews and sputters: enormous, lonely splashings unattended by any other sound.

Marie rose from her bed and went out onto the porch, damp in her nightgown. It was October, and there was enough of a breeze from the north to cool her. She wrapped her arms around herself; and in the night, and the just-awakened grogginess of things, she forgot for a moment who and what she had become, and believed herself to be a young girl again.

The moon was bright upon the lake. She listened harder as the sound separated itself from the nonsound, and as her sleep separated from waking.

There was an enormous hump-shaped animal, writhing and lunging out in the lake, powering its way through the moon-bright floating bog of salt. Marie gripped a front porch post for support — trying in that grip to pull herself up from the well of sleep and fully into the land of waking, so that the monstrous image might disappear — but the sight would not go away.

Disbelieving, she walked out barefoot into the salt-packed hardpan yard, the surface of it cool and smooth and worn beneath her feet, and dared to look closer, and saw that her initial dream had been correct: that there was an elephant in the lake, with immense flapping ears, and long shining tusks like scimitars, and a wild-waving trunk.

The exertions of the animal were sending shallow waves splashing up onto the shore.

Marie imagined instantly, in that first moment of knowing for certain what the creature was, that she could see, even across the distance, that one bright wet shining eye of the animal, filled with both terror and resolve, as well as a bottomless loneliness; and that the eye of the elephant was fixed upon her, even in the midst of the animal's terrific struggles: and in that moment, amidst such a surreal vision, Marie felt more grounded, sane, and hopeful than she had in years.

Like a sleepwalker, she walked down to the lakeshore to offer silent encouragement to the lunging animal, being careful not to break contact with what she perceived to be the desperate creature's drowning, thrashing gaze held fixedly upon her own.

At the lake, she crouched on her haunches and watched, unblinking and hypnotized, and silently urged the elephant on.

Behind the elephant lay a wake of furrowed salt, a wandering path as jagged as if sawed through chunks of ice. The elephant had already cut a great furrow across the lake, and Marie wondered what might have led it to enter the lake in the first place.

Strangely, she did not wonder where the elephant had come from. Already, it seemed to fit.

There was no telling how long it had been floundering, nor for how long the sound of its labors had entered into Marie's restless sleep.

From time to time the elephant would, despite its panicked frenzy, pause and rest, gathering its breath and energy, though during such cessations it would begin to sink slowly, drawn down into the summoning mire. When this happened, the elephant leaned over on one side to keep from sinking farther, and the great trunk would wag and loll plaintively, as if the animal was giving up; and it would be all that Marie could do to keep from rolling up her nightgown and wading out into the lake herself, to try to somehow help the creature.

"Hold on," she whispered into the great silence. "Hold on."

And soon enough, as if heeding her pleas, the elephant would roll back over — his eye fixed once more upon hers, she was certain of it — and would labor on, as if in harness, and pulling the whole of the world behind him.

Marie sat hunkered there for two hours, watching the struggle — the elephant's rests growing longer and longer, and — did she imagine it? — a shine seemed to be leaving the eye; but finally the creature dragged itself up onto the farther shore, crawling out on bent knees, and only then uttering, for the first time all evening, one weak and spent trumpeting: not a call of victory, but more a feeble, tentative inquiry as to the possibility of others of the elephant's kind, who might be hiding out in the dunes, or cached just a short distance farther into the darkness.

Marie had expected the elephant to take advantage of the firmer ground by rolling over on his side and resting once more; and if he had, she was prepared to go to him, to haul buckets of water and bathe the crust of glittering salt from his hide — at the far end of the lake, standing beneath the bright moon, he looked bejeweled — but she was surprised to see that he wasted no time upon his emergence.

He paused only briefly, having given his lone trumpet, and then strode off toward the dunes, lake water still trailing from his thick legs in sheets.

Every now and again he would punch through the crust of the shoreline and stumble and sink to a knee; but each time, he pulled free and continued on his way, traveling in such a straight line that Marie had no doubt he knew precisely where he was going, even if he never had been here before; and for this, too, she found that she loved him.

Still in her nightgown, she followed him for nearly a mile, walking along the lakeshore until she came to the intersection of where he had crawled out and gone off into the dunes.

She followed him into the dunes, tracking his cratered prints, which were spaced so far apart that it took three of her steps to travel the same distance. She hurried along his trail, the sand still wet from his passage and caking to her bare feet.

With each dune she climbed, it seemed to her he might be just on the other side, big as a barn and striding magnificently, head held high, tusks shining bright; or that he might even be holed up in a trough, resting, so that, descending that final dune, she would be free to walk up to him and put her hand on his leathery hide: to hold her hand out to his snuffling trunk for him to take her scent; to perhaps even climb the trunk, as she had seen children do in pictures — passing between the long ivory swords that would act like bars, protecting her from anything below — and to ride upon his hairy back then, on through the dunes and out of the desert.

Riding for a while, seeing all the sights from a newer, slightly higher perspective, as when she was up on the roof of her cabin, and then napping, in the heat of the day, taking her gown off and ripping it to fashion into a crude and flapping tent beneath which she could seek shelter from the sun, while the fanning of his enormous ears sent a slight cooling breeze her way, and as he kept traveling, leaving the lake, and the desert, and eventually all of Texas, so far behind.

Each dune scaled, however, brought her nothing. The sand in his tracks was still wet, and the scent of the lake upon him was still rank and strong, but when she got to the top of the dune and looked down, he was not in the trough below, nor was she able to see him anywhere in the distance; and she would stand there atop the dune, breathing hard, her thighs and calves burning, watching in the dimming moonlight (dawn not too distant now) the crests beyond her, and hoping that on one of those distant sand ridges she would see the dark shape of the elephant climbing his own dune and then disappearing over the back side, so that she would know the distance required to catch up with him.

It was an awful feeling, like being lost — hoping that he was merely in one of the troughs while she was on a crest, and vice versa — her chase of him becoming in that manner like the notes of a song; a teasing, carnival-like melody.

In the waiting there was rest, but there was also the taunting knowledge that the elephant might already be just over the horizon, and that rather than her gaining on him and closing the distance, he was moving even farther away; and after a while, and a few more staggering dunes, she realized her hopelessness. After a while longer, she gave up and turned around and walked back home, following her own tracks, and the elephant's.

Back at the cabin, she used a damp washcloth and leftover bucket of brine to wash her feet and ankles, and under her arms and between her legs. Then she got back into bed, trying to hold grief at bay. She slept for nearly an hour, dreaming the first dreams of hope she had dreamed in many years, and awakened slowly, unwilling to leave the dreams — waking as she always did to the ticking sound of the light heating already the tin roof, and Omo and the boys stirring, then pulling on their sour boots and splashing water on their sunburnt faces.

Omo, hawking phlegm and making animal-like morning sounds, and the three of them as anxious for work as stock animals for their morning feed.

She dressed and went over to the cookhouse to begin breakfast: kindled a fire in the rusting old stove. While the stove heated, she went outside into the rising brilliance to see if the elephant might have returned, even as she knew that it never would. She shaded her eyes with her hands against the glare and studied more clearly the churned-up path of the elephant's passage; noted how it had traveled past several of the skeleton sentinels, passing so near to some of them that had they still been living — had there not been a fifty-year gap between moments — they might have been able to reach out and touch its hide as it passed by; might even have been able to grab hold of the tail and be pulled free in that manner, and dragged to safety.

She saw Omo and the boys standing down at the shore and staring out at the jagged salt-rift and conversing among themselves — earthquake? buried caverns collapsing below? — and went down to tell them what she had seen, disappointed and discouraged that she would not be able to keep it a secret.

At first they did not believe her, but after she showed them the tracks, both hers and the elephant's, they did believe; and Omo shot her a puzzled look, as he saw the tracks leading off into the dunes — "How far did you say you followed this creature?" he asked, and when she answered, "A good ways," he frowned and said, "That could have been dangerous." He glanced at her again, largely uncomprehending but with some hint or wisp of dull understanding, an acknowledgment or the beginning of an acknowledgment of — what? the fact that she, like him, was falling, and that unlike him, she was not enjoying the plummet? — but then the mask came back over him, and he scowled and said again, "That could have been dangerous."

The boys were in favor of following the elephant, of tracking it down and somehow capturing it and bringing it back to the lake and keeping it in a corral made of welded oilfield pipes, and training it to use its brute strength to help them pull in the sleds each evening, and to load the buckets and barrels of salt into the back of the truck to take to market each week. But Omo stared into the distance, in the direction the tracks had disappeared, and said that it was a foolish idea, and that he did not want to have to rely upon the capriciousness of a living creature for his livelihood, preferring instead the reliability of machines.

They went back to the cabin and waited on Marie to finish making breakfast, and then went down to the lake and launched themselves into work as if no miracle had passed by or even been discussed.

Around ten o'clock in the morning they saw a shimmering mirage approaching them through the wavering heat: a wall, a phalanx, of a thousand soldiers, all girded in silver and gold and bearing lances and maces and leading before them immense lions and tigers and snuffling bears, leopards and wolves and what appeared to be a saber-toothed tiger on thick chains: the animals, like the warriors, clad in jeweled armament of silver and gold, and the animals lunging, pulling the soldiers along in their ferocious wake.

Behind them was the strangest and perhaps most horrifying sight of all, a battalion of tanks towering over the soldiers, glinting in the sun, soundless across the distance.

The approachers still seemed to be several miles away, though that could not have been possible, because the lions and tigers were so large. A hundred yards? A thousand? Through the magnifying glass of the bright and bulging swell of light that separated them from Max Omo and his family, the animals surged, and sometimes the thick chains restraining them disappeared for a while — another terrifying image — before reappearing, as if summoned back into existence by the Omos' fear alone.

Likewise, sometimes a section of the wall of advancers would stumble, as if being fired upon by unseen armies, and there would appear for a moment a ragged break in silver and gold; but then the light would readjust itself, so that the gap was quickly filled back in: as if there remained always behind the main wave of soldiers another wall of them; that no matter how many breaks appeared in the wall, there would always be replacements, and that they would step in quickly.

The Omos stood motionless, with some place inside each of them terrified and disbelieving, and yet another place in them not only believing in the inevitability of the vision, but accepting it, so that they remained there staring at the approach; and in their paralysis, the Omos would have seemed indistinguishable from the skeletons out in the salt bog, who appeared also to be giving the approach of the war party their slightly curious attention, as if they had somehow been waiting for such a sight, and whether it was a war party or rescue party did not seem to matter much.

The breeze stirred the tattered coattails and scraps of cloth, adding to the notion that the bones were eager to join the army, and that the army had come searching for them.

The pantheon was now close enough that the Omos could hear a rapturous singing, a pure ringing, like the choir of a thousand angels — a song of both desire and unrestrained praise — and before such a beautiful and all-encompassing sound, the Omos' hearts relaxed a little from their previous terror; and now they could hear a metallic, fearsome, syncopated drumming.

And yet even as the wall of soldiers drew closer, they were becoming smaller, shrinking and banding together, so that although their sounds were becoming louder and the warbled features plainer — the soldiers' faces, and the animals' teeth, and ears, and legs — it seemed that the great army was receding, pulling back away into the distance: that some journey, begun thousands of years ago, had nearly been completed, but just shy of its destination, the army was retreating, as if somehow frightened or unwilling yet to participate in the final engagement.

And now the Omos saw, emerging from the other side of that lens of heated, brilliant light, the metamorphosis of terror and unholy beauty and power into a ragtag procession of two large and dilapidated wide-tired trucks, with steam rising from beneath the hood of each, and the larger truck misfiring badly, its burned-out valves clattering a death knell.

Limping along in front of the two trucks was a posse of half a dozen bedraggled men, pant cuffs rolled up and straw hats askew, with four of the men being tugged wearily along by lunging, baying bloodhounds, whose peals grew clearer and louder.

The trucks rattled to a stop in the Omos' yard, and the men tied the leaping hounds to the bumpers of the hissing trucks and hobbled over to meet the Omos: walking toward them as if not clearly seeing them, limping along at the edge of heat stroke. When one of the men reached out his hand to shake with Max Omo, he missed Omo's hand entirely.

They were with the circus, the driver of the larger truck explained, and had come searching for their elephant. They had been tracking it since daylight — the circus had been in Odessa, two nights before — and they cast suspicious glances at the great mound of yellowing salt, and at the barn, as if believing that the Omos might be harboring the creature.

Marie went to get brine water to give to the gasping hounds, and Max Omo led the posse over to the small wedge of shade offered by his porch, where the men sat and then lay down in stages of collapse, rolling onto their backs and sides and even their stomachs, like children taking a nap. Only the elephant's trainer, an Indian gentleman who, despite the day's heat, was dressed in the traditional garb of his profession, refrained from collapse, and that only because he had been riding in one of the trucks the whole way.

In broken English he explained that they had already gotten their trucks stuck a dozen times that morning — the men digging out with their hands and shovels, and one truck pushing or pulling the other through the salt and the sand — and when Marie inquired about the nature of the elephant, the trainer, whose name was Mufti, informed her that he had had the old bull almost all his life, that the elephant was himself forty-seven years old, and in full musth, very dangerous and full of breeding hormones, and that they should consider themselves lucky he had not demolished their shack, with them in it, for the simple reason that it might have appeared an eyesore to him.

"A fleck," Mufti said, "a piece of dust." He had a whip and a holstered pistol on his hip and said that though he was very fond of the elephant, he feared he might have to protect himself against it, though he was hoping that the trek across the sand would be dulling somewhat the animal's excesses. He said this loudly, as if for the benefit of his associates, rather than the truth.

Max Omo wanted to know what such a creature was worth, and when Mufti answered that in India the animal could easily bring the equivalent of between $10,000 and $20,000, Max Omo stared with incomparable Germanic scorn at the assemblage of sleeping ass-whipped middle-aged men and then told Mufti, "I will go and get your elephant."

5

WHILE MAX OMO AND MUFTI gathered water for the trip, the other men continued to nap, snoring and drooling like the hounds themselves, which had crawled under the frames of the still-hissing, leaking trucks, where they had then dug holes in the salt.

The water was too briny to go into the trucks' radiators, so Max Omo had to pour expensive antifreeze gurgling into the maws of the trucks, as well as another of his inventions, a golden mixture of the glittering residue of aluminum hydroxide flakes, which would float in suspension in the radiator until the water became hot.

Under pressure, then, the flakes would be forced into the cracks through which the radiator fluid had been leaking, where the magical flakes would continue to hydrate in the warming waters, swelling to a thousandfold of their previous size, and aligning themselves into tiny warped sheets of a thin, metallic substance, as impermeable but brittle as a sugar glaze broiled quickly upon a cake.

More jarring would eventually knock those little false-welds loose over time, depositing in the bottom of the radiator a sludge of broken sheets of spent aluminum, which made the radiator run rougher and hotter than ever, and, when this happened, the engine was usually lost.

But Omo had not yet discovered that about his invention, knew only that it seemed to be a miraculous stopgap solution to the desert heat that plagued and finally consumed any piece of machinery that required water for its maintenance.

Mufti watched as Max Omo tapped, magisterially, the last of the sparkling flakes into the radiator, and Mufti murmured, "I have come to the right place."

The boys already saw their father as a wizard — their entire universe was but the shining wide skillet of the lake, through which elephants passed, they might have assumed, with some frequency, and whose tides and yields their father had not so much learned as commanded to perform at his beckoning. It was for them a universe beyond the horizons of which the world might as well have fallen off to nothingness.

It surprised Marie to see that her husband could be respected among the strangers of the world: competent, even helpful, and a leader — he who could not coax her heart, nor any of their hearts, out of the ivory cages of their rib-bones, with never a word of praise or other kind gesture for any job done well, or done at all.

And in some futile, helpless way of both possessor and possessed, it pleased her to see that it was this way. He might be wrong in his mistreatment of her, or he might be justified — perhaps she *was* unworthy — but either way, it appeared that he was strong in the world; not just within the confines of Juan Cordona Lake, but in the larger, wider world beyond.

Marie studied Mufti with a mixture of curiosity, attraction, and repulsion — the holstered pistol and whip, the scent of incense upon his body, as well as, faintly, the odor of the elephant that she had scented lingering in the dunes. She glanced at her husband as if seeing him anew, and was excited by the adventure upon which they were about to embark, though still, she hoped they would not find the elephant, or that if they did, that he would continue to make good his escape.

"We must hurry," Mufti told them. "He will burn in this sun. He drinks over forty gallons of water a day. It was madness, to bring him to this part of the world. Always, I have succumbed too easily to greed."

"Does he know how to find water?" Max Omo asked. "Will he be drawn to it, like a mule, a horse, or a cow?"

Mufti nodded. "He will not be able to stay away from it," he said. "Wherever it is, he will find it."

Max Omo hunkered down on his heels and with a stick sketched a rough map in the marbled salt floor upon which they squatted. As the twig scratched at the surface, Marie could smell the sharper, damper odors that were released, and the scents were familiar and comforting as well as nauseating.

"Once he gets out of the dunes, it's downhill to Horsehead Crossing," Max said. He sketched the path and direction that led to Castle Gap.

"Must we cross the great desert to get there?" Mufti asked, as if riding in the back of the circus truck, while the other searchers led their hounds, had been the hardest ordeal of all.

"We can take a dirt road down there," Max said, thinking out loud. He sketched that route, then looked out at the broken furrows the animal had plowed through his sleeping lake. "I don't care how good a swimmer you fancy him to be, he's likely to have trouble if he tries to drink there at the crossing. If he just sticks his trunk in, he might be okay, but if he gets a mind to wade in and try to cool off, like they do in Africa—"

"India," said Mufti.

Max Omo shook his head. "I don't care where he's from, he's likely to find that crossing more than he bargained for."

They rose and rousted the dogs and their sleeping handlers, and the circus attendants who had traveled with them. They loaded barrels and buckets of water into the back of the smaller circus truck. The larger one, an enclosed van, was as hot as the cookstove, a violent, stifling, dead airspace so superheated that it seemed even a single breath or stirring could ignite it into an inferno; it was into this enclosure that they would attempt to herd the elephant, if they found him.

Because it was too hot, the dogs and their owners rode high atop the covered van, where in addition to staying cooler, they hoped to be able to sight or take scent of the elephant in the distance; and they set out into the bright day in a swaying, rumbling caravan, the Omos all piled into their truck and the overcrowded circus trucks, temporarily revived, traveling behind them; and Marie felt more alive than she had in years, invigorated and rejuvenated by the hunt, and filled with the feeling that her life was going to change: that it had somehow just taken a brighter turn for the better, whether they found the elephant or not.

They reached the crossing an hour later, traveling down the last of the little sand roads that had led them there. The vehicles were all still running strong. They walked up and down the bluff—it was about a ten-foot drop into the rushing water—and looked for tracks to see if the elephant had passed through, but there were none.

A great blue heron was surprised by their approach and leapt into the sky with a troubled rasp. It climbed crookedly, seemingly suspended over the rushing waters, and then flew higher, finally finding its graceful rhythm.

Marie stared after the bird until it was gone completely, and still she stared. Mufti watched her watch the bird, and knew then more deeply that which he had already understood at first glance. He had seen and met perhaps a thousand women who, when the circus came to town, would gladly and desperately have abandoned their homes and husbands and families to travel with it, and to travel with him: not knowing the words of his new language, nor the rules or customs of the circus culture, but willing nonetheless to travel every other day to a new town, and to sleep each night bedded down amongst the caged animals; to learn new odors, new patterns, and new work: and to know, for the first time, a complete unraveling of the past to which they had each been chained for so long.

Some of the women came to him after the performance, asking or even pleading to join—believing, in some injured place far within them, that they would be happy in such a life; that no other place in the world could be so well-designed for them as the traveling cast of the freakish and the foreign, the wild beasts and aliens.

Mufti had learned, from those almost nightly encounters, how to differentiate, in even that first glance, the merely sad and hopeless from the truly disturbed; how to separate, and speak to, the troubled or forlorn as opposed to the crazed.

Only once had he relented and allowed one of the women to join the circus, and travel with them. The arrangement had immediately caused such jealousy and animosity among the other circus members that the entire act threatened to fall apart. The issue had resolved itself however when the new woman was mauled by the tiger one afternoon, as the tiger pushed open the door to its cage at feeding time. The woman survived, barely, losing both an arm and a leg. She was returned to the care of her family, where, largely immobilized, she received thereafter the attention she had been looking for, though not of the type that she had needed or desired.

What they all wanted, Mufti had noticed, was not so much freedom as a new set of borders and rules. They wanted to trade a familiar imprisonment for an unfamiliar one; and their unhappiness was, in Mufti's opinion, due to the fact that they were comfortable with neither boundaries nor freedom; that not since childhood had they had the experience of dwelling in both lands, passing back and forth freely from one to the other.

The modern world did not seem set up to accommodate such passages for either men or women, in his opinion.

When they stood before him outside the tent, arms outstretched, palms uplifted, they were weeping for their lost childhoods, and those days of dreaming.

"Jumpers," the circus members called them scornfully; and watching Marie watch the heron fly crookedly away, Mufti saw that if she was not yet a jumper, she was close enough: too close.

The men and boys and Marie sat in the shade of the circus trucks with the hounds and sipped the warm brine water they had brought, and Mufti and his two helpers told them stories of the circus for nearly an hour before Max Omo began to grow impatient. The noon sun overhead was baking his salt lake, squeezing riches out of it by the minute. He urged the other men to consider leaving one truck stationed at the crossing as a lookout, and taking the other two into the desert to search for the animal.

There was no circus scheduled for that evening, and Mufti was satisfied to sit in the shade a while longer and wait for the elephant to come to him. Max Omo, however, would hear nothing of it. He argued for the men with hounds to be deployed up through the center of the dunes while Omo's truck and the circus van flanked them on either side.

At first Mufti agreed — any plan was fine with him, he said, as long as he didn't have to go back out in the sun — but no sooner had he spoken than Marie, like a chess player hunting down the king, proclaimed that she too would stay by the river and watch, and wait.

That plan was more than fine with Max Omo — he knew that either of them, the woman or the Indian, would slow them down out in the dunes — but Mufti, wanting no part of a domestic calamity — he had been in too many already, and the sadness that always attended him in the days afterward had to it almost precisely the flavor of that sun-heated brine water — reversed his position immediately, volunteering to go out into the desert with Max Omo himself, or the dog handlers, or anyone; and cracked now if not broken, and too chastened to change her mind, Marie kept to her original pronouncement, and stayed with the second circus truck, in the shade, while the others went off into the desert.

She was numb to the sight of the posse striking off into the terrible whiteness, felt no pain or even discomfort or regret that she was neither traveling with them any longer nor whiling away the afternoon in pleasant conversation with the elephant trainer.

A younger and less time-hardened woman — even an earlier version of herself — might have felt pain, watching them set off — separated so completely from not just her goal but the general commerce of fellow humans — and a younger, less hardened person, or her earlier self, might even have still known hope, knowing that the day would end, and that they would return.

But watching the heat swallow them — it looked as if they were stepping through a white curtain — Marie felt only a jaded heartlessness. She was aware of something seeping out of her as one might feel faintly the blood trickling from one's nostrils. It seemed to her that whatever was draining out of her was leaving her in the fashion of water and seeping down into the earth, vanishing through the dried, platey crevices of sunbaked mud cracks.

But of true sensation, she felt nothing, only the last of an ancient vitality draining out of her, and traveling back down into the dust.

Max Omo and Mufti and the others found the elephant pretty quickly. Though there was no discernible breeze, the dogs had caught his scent. Max Omo, in the truck on the left, and Mufti, in the truck on the right, saw the hounds catch the scent at the same time, saw them lunge in a single wave, jerking the frazzled houndsmen along with them — the

houndsmen yanking back on the chains and leashes, sending up show-
ers of flashing sand around their ankles like the spray of sunlit water.

One of the handlers stumbled and went down on a folded ankle, but
did not let go of the leash, which was wrapped around his wrist. He
continued to hold the leash with both hands as his dog, a big bluetick,
dragged him on his belly across the hot sand and down a dune.

Both Max Omo and Mufti accelerated their trucks, Omo's engine
laboring, whining at the abuse, and Omo winced, imagining that he
could feel the friction of each straining stroke upon the delicate, lu-
bricated valves — and at the top of the next ridge, with their engines
beginning to smoke, they saw the elephant.

He was lying on his side at the top of a high dune, as if the effort of
reaching only that one single crest, rather than the cumulative effects
of the journey, was what had felled him; and even from that distance,
they could smell him burning, cooking in the sun.

It was an odor exactly like that of a roast baking in the oven, a huge
ham not of mutton or pork, but delicious beef, and even in the truck,
Max Omo could smell it, and it filled him with an immediate pleasure,
took him back to childhood, when his mother would fix a huge lunch
for their family on Sunday after church, the wheel of the century having only just clicked forward a few years, 1904, 1905, and the bones
and muscles and blood of the dreaded Comanches not even entirely
rotted away to worm-food in their countless unmarked graves and
nongraves, the repositories of the chewing beetles that remade history
daily.

The odor spurred him on. He did not plan to eat the elephant, but
he accelerated the truck toward the odor with anticipation or inexplicable and surprising happiness: as if some part of him far within
believed, however illogically, that he was going to meet up with his
mother again, and the rest of his family, and his childhood.

Mufti likewise was stimulated by the odor, though he had never
eaten beef, not even during his sojourns in Texas, and never would;
and he had certainly never eaten elephant, nor could he conceive of
such a thing. And Mufti did not associate the pleasant smell with the
hastening decomposition of his aged companion, but instead per-

ceived it to be merely some favorable background aroma — a barbecue at some nearby ranch: as if just beyond the last visible dune lay some mythic sylvan glade, where a happy, loving family worshiped their God not weekly but daily, and then came home midday to fix, in celebration of their life of prayer and hard labor, an incredible feast, dining midafternoon at a great oaken table with shimmering leaf-dappled light reflecting from the pond just outside the dining room window and a breeze stirring the curtains and tablecloth, bathing the diners with the odors of the kitchen, and the meal, and the green lawn and great farm beyond.

A pitcher of clear water would be standing in the center of the table, and a bowl of sunlit fruit, and the table would be filled with a family of all ages, the young through the very aged.

The man who was being dragged on his belly by his hound was finally able to regain his footing at the bottom of a dune, as the bluetick slowed slightly; but now another hound snapped free of his tether, and broke from the pack with such speed and enthusiasm that it appeared he had been chosen by them to take the lead; that they had marshaled the collective sum of their frenzied desire and assigned it to that one hound.

At the top of the final rise, the elephant received the hound as gracefully as if he had been lying in wait there all of his life: as if that one place was where the elephant, recumbent, best fit the curve of the earth in order to welcome, and return, the hound's charge.

As his millennial ancestors had done innumerable times with tigers, leopards, and lions, the elephant lifted his weakened trunk almost tentatively, even leisurely, raising it just in time to blunt the dog's headlong attack, and with seemingly no more effort than a man reaching into a refrigerator for a beer, the elephant caught the dog in midflight with his trunk, made a quick twisting motion — there was a sudden silence from that one hound, though the angelic shouting of the hounds below continued — and then with a whiplike gesture, and still recumbent, the elephant hurled the hound back down to the bottom of the dune, so that the advancing houndsmen had to stop and duck to avoid being struck by the flying object.

This was enough to give both men and beasts pause in their charge, and the hounds circled and milled around their lifeless comrade. Max Omo and Mufti parked their trucks on adjacent dunes — to an observer looking down upon them from far away, the arrangements and positionings would have seemed like those of chess pieces in some tiny game — and they got out of their hissing, ticking vehicles and walked down into the trough, where the houndsmen and hounds stood gathered over the campaign's first casualty.

On the ridge above, the baking elephant fixed them with a direct stare, with both reddened eyes seeming to drill straight through all those gathered below. His ears flapped, his enormous tusks were long against the sky, and now his eyes seemed to be searching the hearts of each of them; and to all the men, it appeared that the eyes rested longest and saddest upon Mufti, and that the expression in the elephant's eyes spoke of nothing but betrayal.

The elephant laid his head back down onto the broiling sand almost gently.

"I cannot tell if the musth has left him yet or not," said Mufti, quietly. There was no other sound around them save for the quicksilver panting of the dogs.

The men conferred, and decided that the elephant could not get up, or did not want to, and that he would be safe to approach, as long as none of them got within reach of his trunk.

The hounds still roared and strained against their leashes; but the houndsmen approached more cautiously now, wrapping the chains and leashes in bights around their waists, and moving slowly up the final dune like mountain climbers, belayed by the dogs: and as the staggered battalion of them neared the fallen elephant, his head did not even lift, nor did anything else move save for the slow, occasional flapping of one ear, seeming mysteriously communicative.

With the side of the elephant's huge-tusked and bouldered head pressed into the burning sand, it appeared to them all, as they approached, that the elephant was listening to some instructions coming from far below, and faintly heard: though the instructions might be more audible now to the elephant than they had ever been before, so that perhaps he was not even aware of the chorus of the hounds.

He paid them no mind, thus seemed at peace with them, even as the men and hounds drew nearer still, moving more fully toward the scent of the roasting.

They gained the ridge, sweating, and stood spaced about, still unsure of whether the animal might yet be transformed back into health and strength in some godlike metamorphosis of rage — the image of the flying dog indelible within them now — and they convened among themselves by calling out to one another in hushed voices, as if not wishing to disrupt the communion the elephant was having with the ground below.

"I do not know if he will be able to mind me or not," Mufti said. "I do not know if he will want to mind me. He looks and acts as if the musth is still upon him, but I do not think he can get up. Maybe if I crack the whip he will remember all the times before when he has obeyed, and will rise one more time."

The houndsmen shook their heads and muttered among themselves, disgruntled at the suggestion that the crack of a whip could accomplish the same effect as their dogs, and wanted to turn the hounds loose upon the elephant, with the hounds having worked so hard and led them so far. It was not good for the dogs' courage to draw so close to such a combatant, and then not finish the job.

The elephant still belonged to Mufti, however, and Mufti to the elephant, and so the houndsmen's dissent was tempered; and, as well, none of them was anxious to see another dog lost to the elephant's final throes: lost, and seeming somehow wasted in that manner, being vanquished by the elephant when the elephant itself would not be living long enough to even acknowledge its small victory.

Mufti advanced upon the elephant, whip trailing in the sand like some dead snake he was bringing to the elephant as a gift.

The elephant's eye glowed brighter for a moment as it caught sight of the whip, and a ripple of muscle tone quivered through the animal, a galvanic tension that none of the men would have thought possible from a creature so near to death; and the dogs sensed and smelled the life still within him, and set about their baying again.

And though the elephant had not yet lifted his head from the ground, it seemed that he was no longer listening to anything below but was attuned and attentive once more to the world around him, desert though it was.

Max Omo took a step backwards, glad in that moment that he had not yielded to his sons' pleadings that they go off into the desert by themselves after the elephant, in the hopes of subduing and domesticating it and training it to turn its labors and power to their good.

Mufti advanced.

When he was but ten feet away from the anguished animal — was it fear or anger or tenderness, or even joy, with which the elephant beheld the sight of the whip? Even Mufti could not be sure — Mufti stopped, and swirled the whip, readying it to crack upon the dry heated air that was rising in shimmers from the elephant's cooking body.

There was a part of Mufti that was lamenting the impending loss of his old friend — he had known and lived with the elephant now longer than any human — but there was a part of him too that was calculating the consequences of what might possibly be the end of his career, represented in the smoldering gross tonnage of the sand-bound creature that was fast becoming deadweight.

Mufti raised the whip as if to crack it — magically, the elephant raised his head, seeming now as alert as does a dog who has been waiting by the door for its master's return — and when he leaned forward, snapping the whip into the hot sky like a fly-fisherman casting into some still pool, the elephant rolled over with a great stirring of sand and leaned forward also, struggling to kneel upon its front legs, but still unable to rise.

Not blaming the elephant, but frustrated, Mufti cracked the whip harder and louder. The dogs were nearly uncontrollable, roaring, and this time the elephant managed to get its hind feet beneath it, and sought to stand, but lost its balance — it appeared to the men that the muscles and bones within the great sack of its hide no longer had any order, and merely shifted, spilled sideways, obeying no desire or willpower but merely flowing according to the laws of gravity — and the flagging animal tumbled over on its side, falling as if crumpled by a shot: and once again the dogs danced and howled and sang.

The elephant lay still, trunk outstretched and eyes catatonic, tusks no longer menacing but instead as harmless as twin beams of river-polished driftwood. But Mufti was encouraged by this show of valor, and knowing the animal as he did, and believing that for all its great bulk and strength, the animal's heart and will was stronger than even its body, he began popping the whip again and again.

And as he was cracking the whip, and as the elephant was lifting its huge head and struggling once more to rise, Mufti shouted to the handlers, telling them to turn their dogs loose, and they did so gladly.

The dogs darted in as both individuals and a team, their desires weaving and unweaving, seeking out and finding and snapping at the weak spots and seams of softness that the elephant could not protect; and in that deviling manner, chewing and howling, they helped to urge him, against the logic of his body, to his feet, where he did not spend or waste time standing his ground but instead broke into a swaying run, down the dune and in the direction of the river. He stumbled and fell often, piling headlong into the dunes with great fountains of sand but rising again, the hounds behind him now, euphoric. Max Omo and Mufti jumped back into their trucks and followed him up and over the dunes.

The houndsmen ran along behind, also stumbling and shouting and blowing on their huntsmen's horns; and to the sky above, and the curve of the earth, it would have seemed little different from the times when in this same country hunters with lances had pursued and harried the woolly mammoths and mastodons, over ten thousand years ago: as if all the time that had passed had been as if but a nap on a summer afternoon.

On a path to the river, blinded with fatigue, but somehow knowing where the river was, the elephant managed to pick up one more dog and hurl it, whiplike, a sufficient distance across the hard sand so that it would run no more, and he paused to stomp on two other dogs, leaving only four pursuing it; but it was not the hounds the elephant was fleeing now, nor even the men and their trucks behind him — Mufti firing his pistol into the air — but rather the desert itself, and this errant turn his life had taken.

For a moment, for several moments, there was nothing else in the world, just that one elephant galloping at full effort down that one steep slope of sand.

It was a sight so wondrous, one that perhaps no other human had ever seen, that Marie wondered in that breathless moment if the image of it did not unlock within her certain feelings and ideas, mysterious combinations that in some way freed her from earlier and older guidelines of being human.

It seemed that she could feel parts inside her, both physically and mentally, opening and closing like the locks and weirs of a dam, or the sluice gates to some innovative if not complex watering system that diverted creek water to parched fields. It seemed that she could feel and hear the sound of water running, as she watched the elephant continue his plunge down that steep slope, running with a steadfastness of purpose that seemed to indicate the destination toward which he hurtled was not one of a mere moment's opportune selection but rather the desire of a cumulative destiny; and that in his haste, the elephant was acutely aware that the last of certain puzzle-pieces were being assembled.

And it seemed almost to Marie, across that distance, that she could perceive joy in the elephant's tumult — though in this, she was completely mistaken.

She could not look away, could not blink; and as she watched, she continued to feel the gates and locks changing and shunting within her, felt the cool water rising.

She was conscious of the day's fierce heat, but the heat was no longer an enemy or an oppressor, and she kept watching the faraway elephant pluming down the dune like a ball rolling crookedly, not sure whether she was dreaming it or not, but not minding.

The waves of her pleasure and astonishment began to fade, however, as there appeared now behind the elephant the straggling, shouting wave of pursuers, the trucks and houndsmen strung out all across the landscape, struggling in that seam between earth and sky.

Then came the jagged, blaring sounds of the chase, the horns and bayings only now drifting across the expanse of sand and reaching her ears; and it was a disturbing sound, reminding her of the descriptions the missionaries of her former church had given of the ceremonies held by rank villagers in the Himalayas, who would surround a fellow villager, dressed as a devil or dragon, pelting him with rocks and banging on pots and pans and blowing on trumpets made from the hides of animals or the wetted bark of trees stretched tight around hoops of bone or iron, in the foolish hopes of driving demons and other evil spirits out of their village.

These villagers were worse than cursed, said the missionaries, for they believed in these pagan rites, and lived for months following each purging in a deluded sense of cleanliness and well-being, even as their souls were rotting.

Again and again the elephant fell, stumbling and sometimes rolling a short distance down the dune like a boulder seeking to both establish and yet resist its angle of repose. And always, if the elephant sought to pause and rest, the hounds would bite and worry his flanks, so that no rest could be had, and the elephant would rise and continue his headlong descent.

Near the bottom of the dune, his glittering eyes caught sight of the truck parked still before him, and he caught sight of and recognized Marie — she could tell this in an instant: some jolt, some awareness, across the distance. It seemed to Marie that his recognition of her spurred in him some effort even more pronounced, for he lowered his head with resolve and came on even stronger, reaching the bottom of the dunes and accelerating, lifting his feet and knees high, and running hard.

It looked like a charge — the ears flapping, and the tusks riding so smooth and level, aiming for the destination, which she assumed to be the river, Horsehead Crossing, but which she understood too might have been mistaken by an uninformed observer to be the truck, and Marie.

And as the elephant continued to close that last distance — so close now that the exhausted hounds still hectoring him no longer sounded like angels, but merely hounds — it began to occur to Marie, belatedly though still in time to consider an escape, that there was some error in the elephant's interpretation of events, and that it was not with comradeship or any feelings of commiseration or understanding that the elephant was hurtling toward her, but that it was powered instead by the ungovernable fuel of the betrayed.

Maybe Marie's perceptions were wrong, she told herself, even as she felt her own heart falling through some rotting planking. The beautiful image of the elephant crossing her lake, and then descending the dune to greet her, was destroyed like a mirror or glass vase broken into a thousand pieces — and now as the elephant drew closer, Marie was certain that it was a feeling of having been betrayed which drove the elephant toward her; though still she could not bring herself to run or hide or take cover, but could only do that which she had done all her life, to watch and wait: and when the elephant was close enough for her to smell it, and to see the pearly strings of slobber trailing from the hounds' jowls, she had another revelation, which was that the elephant was correct, that Marie *had* betrayed him — both in her passive participation in the hunt, as well as in her failure to stop the hunt, or even argue against it — and so overwhelming was this sudden, lucid awareness of her own unworthiness that she felt as if the elephant had already slammed into her.

She was standing in the wedge of shade cast by the truck. She stepped out into the light and sun so that he could see her better, and to better receive the full impact of him.

She thought she saw a wave of softening — the first release of emotion that precedes forgiveness — enter his eyes, a dimming of the enraged lights within, in the last moments before his body shut down, and his front legs tangled together, conspiring to send him down hard, coming to a stop so close in front of her that the impact of his collapse threw a spray of sand against her feet, and a wave of the heated air displaced by his passage washed over her, carrying with it not just the ripe scent of his cooking, but of his fear and anger and misery, too.

He lay there, ribs heaving, unblinking, staring at her without seeing her, while the dogs climbed atop him and began chewing and tearing at the thick hide. Blood began to run down the sides of him, glistening like the streams leaving a mountain's melting snowcap.

Marie waded into the fray, shouting at the dogs and laboring to pull them off — climbing up the elephant's tusk, running up over the top of his head and tugging and jerking on the hounds' collars and on the leashes and chains that still trailed from them — but even with her might and fury she could never keep more than one or two of the dogs from biting at the elephant at any one time, and she called out to the men to hurry down from the dune and help her.

"Ah, they can't hurt it," called out the houndsman nearest to her, "and it's what they've worked for." The others seemed to be in agreement, and it occurred to Marie that the men had lost hounds to the elephant and were seeking revenge.

One of the hounds snapped at her ankle as she pulled it down the slope of the elephant. It was a young hound, and it laid open the skin around her calf as if cutting into it with shears. She felt no pain, only the brief tugging, and when her boys saw that she had been hurt, they scrambled on top of the elephant to help her, and to wreak their own vengeance on the hounds, wrestling with the dogs as they would with another person, and winding the leashes around the dogs' necks and strangling them.

Mufti was scaling the bloody elephant too, crying out and slapping at the dogs with his palms, and then the houndsmen were up on the elephant, pulling their dogs off not so much to keep them from inflicting more harm to the elephant as to protect them from the attacks of Mufti and the children; and one of the houndsmen, in prying the oldest boy loose from his best hound, with the dog's eyes rolled back in his head — still the boy would not release his chokehold — was a bit rough with the boy, which spurred Max Omo in a way that witnessing the damage the hounds had inflicted upon his wife had not; and soon enough, Max Omo was into the combat as well, so that atop the mountain of the elephant there was not just hound battling elephant, but man against man, woman against dog, man versus child, foreigner versus native; and through it all, the elephant did not move, only lay there as if oblivious to the scrabblings above, and to the heated red rivers trickling down his back, and stared out at the crossing, not fifty yards away.

The houndsmen finally got the hounds pulled free of their quarry, and reattached to the trucks' bumpers. The dogs were still euphoric; if left unregulated, they would have continued to gnaw at their great treasure until they succumbed to the heat and their own enthusiasms; and even after they were leashed and chained to the bumpers of the trucks again, they continued to lunge and snap at the air itself, biting and howling now at nothing but the distance between them and their quarry: and for the rest of their days, their dreams would be filled with the memories, the odors and tastes and sights, of this one chase; and, greedsome, they might wonder if even more glorious quarry than this existed, when only days earlier they would never have been able to imagine even this immense and splendid wonder.

"What is wrong with you people?" the lead houndsman demanded of both Mufti and Max Omo. "We were only trying to help you find your damn elephant. We've just lost about three thousand dollars' worth of dogs, chasing your damn elephant across hell and back."

Mufti was silent, chastened, but Max Omo bristled, ready to jump into the fight again. "He's not my damn elephant. I see no good coming from him, and am just as happy to see him die as live" — but at this Mufti broke down in sobs, still jittery from the fighting, and implored them to try to save the animal.

"I'll pay for the dogs, if we can save him," Mufti said. "In the salvation of your enemy lies your restitution," he pleaded. "I stand before your mercy. Name your price."

"I'll help you," Max Omo said. "If you pay for the gas it took to come out here and back, and if you let my boys ride on that elephant in the circus, next time you come through."

"Me too," Marie said. "I'd like to ride on it. The three of us. The four of us, if you want to, Max."

Max Omo stared at her, then shook his head. "No, it'll just be the three of you."

"Fine," Mufti said. "A parade. A celebration for the elephant's saviors. We can all take turns riding on his back." He nodded to the houndsmen. "All of us. You, your dogs, the children, Mrs. Omo, myself — he can carry all of us."

They were all silent, then, studying the catatonic mass. There was no sound save for the hounds' plaintive whines and yelps.

"You are the engineer," Mufti said to Max Omo. "How can we get him into the river?"

But Max Omo was already hunkered on his heels, studying on it: watching the horseflies settling themselves into the crusting red calligraphy that decorated the still-heaving hide.

"Getting him into the river will be the easy part," Max Omo predicted. "Getting him out, not so easy."

"I think once he cools down his power will return to him," Mufti said. "He can leave the river on his own."

Max Omo turned to survey the limited machinery at hand. It did not seem fair to him that the elephant, in its infirmity, should weigh the same; by Omo's accounting, it seemed that in his reduced state the elephant should be becoming lighter and more tractable by the minute, as his life and will drained away, and it alarmed Max Omo to realize that the opposite was true. It probably took a creature that size a year to die, he supposed, or longer; perhaps several years. Perhaps the elephant did not even know yet that it was dying.

"He's going to have to help us some," he said. "If we just hook up to him with the chains and ropes and try to pull him to the river, the ropes will cut right through him." He walked over closer to the elephant and looked into his eye, trying to gauge what resolve might remain, but had no real idea of how to measure such things. "If we wrap the chains around his tusks, will they come out?"

Mufti winced. "They might." He considered the problem himself. "Maybe around the back and under the shoulders, if we have that much rope and chain."

The houndsmen looked at one another like card players who, having been beaten badly all night, have come to the point where they need to decide whether to play one more hand or turn around and go home.

They could not turn away. Even though down to four hounds, they could not quit. When would they ever have another chance at an elephant?

They brought buckets of water from the river and doused their fiery hounds before shutting them up inside the back of the circus wagon, leaving the roll-up-curtain door cracked only enough to allow a thin siphon of fresh air. The dogs clawed briefly at the door before finally being overcome by the heat. They lay on their bellies on the hot floor of the truck with only their muzzles pressed through that little seam, sucking in through flared nostrils the sweeter outside air.

The men laid their ropes and chains together and began fastening them into a pulley system, and with shovels began digging a small passageway beneath the elephant, in order that they might wrap the chain around him from below.

Two trucks would pull from the front while the third pushed from behind. They would drag and shove the elephant as close to the river's edge as possible, where he would then have to take but one or two final steps to tumble down the little bluff. They would have to work quickly to unfasten the ropes and chains when this happened, so that his plunge would not take the trucks and drivers with it.

The boys continued excavating beneath the elephant, while the adults positioned the trucks and readied the ropes and chains.

Marie kept going down to the river to haul up bucket after bucket of the silty water, which she poured on the elephant's head, and on his wounds; but it was to little avail, for the water seemed to evaporate off of him in shimmering waves, as when one splashes droplets of water onto a too-hot skillet; and in the process, Marie soon began to overheat, and had to stop and drench herself, not the elephant, with the bucket of warm water.

They each made dozens of trips, and through it all, the elephant gave no response, and finally Marie stopped, with her heart hammering and a crushing headache. She took refuge with the men in the hot shade of the trucks, from where they watched the boys dig.

"You probably don't want those little scoundrels to crawl all the way under," one of the houndsmen counseled, "in case their tunnel collapses," and so Max Omo got a piece of driftwood and fashioned it into a pole that could feed the chain and then gathered several more for the houndsmen to use as pry bars and levers.

Max Omo considered the weight of the beast again, and the capabilities of their overheated machines, and said, "He's going to have to help us. He's going to have to want to get there."

Mufti went over and peered into the elephant's motionless eye as if through a tiny peephole. "I don't think he's going to help," Mufti said.

With their first attempt, they merely got all three trucks stuck. The elephant did not budge, and seemed to hunker down into an even more unmanageable configuration, like some desert creature disappearing halfway into its burrow; and with their tires spinning in the sand, the trucks quickly buried themselves up to their frames, with tires and engines smoking, and the fumes of boiling, pressured sand burned back into glass beneath the roar and stink of their balding tires.

Once again the boys were deployed, though they moved more slowly this time, and the men and Marie helped, clawing with their hands and scraps of wood and leaning into the trucks with pry bars of river-polished cottonwood, gleaming barkless spars that must have appeared to the elephant in his delirium like the tusks of his ancestors, gleaned from some terrible quarry just on the other side of the bluff.

They got their trucks unstuck, paused to quaff more salty water, and set off into their labors once more, only to become stuck again immediately.

There was nothing to do but dig out. Shards of crude and hastily manufactured black- and purple-streaked glass lay scattered in the sand all around them from where the spinning tires had churned out more silicon, some of it into the fantastic and intricate shapes of lizards, serpents, camels, and even, in one piece the boys noticed and picked up, an elephant with tusks — and in the flattening light of the slowly lowering sun the cast detritus appeared as so many diamonds or other jewels hurled carelessly from some vast treasure-place, or extraterrestrial objects rained down from the night sky, bits of melted star.

As she walked through these shards, stopping to examine and sort through the glassine figures as might a walker on some seashore pause to look at seashells, Marie was reminded of the flakes of diamond-crust that had been furrowed upward in the wake of the elephant's passage through her salt lake. In her own fatigued and fevered state, she wondered if it was in the nature of the elephant's life to be attended thus, almost daily, with diamond-like detritus marking his path wherever he traveled; and she wondered what scent or residue or marker was her destined leaving; which story of hers would be told over and over again.

Her loneliness in that moment was as inescapable as if in a vise.

"It's no use," Max Omo said. "That creature isn't going anywhere. Besides, we've got to rest the machines." He idly kicked at a sheet of spun glass, fracturing it with a little tinkling sound that was strangely musical, and at odds with the barely restrained anger that rested just beneath him, sullen and dangerous as an eggplant-colored thundercloud.

"We have to let the engines rest," he said again, and then looked off at the sinking sun as if lamenting fiercely not merely the weight and cost of a lost day of work, but of some errant turn in life: as if all was now irretrievable, and that it was not one failed day that Max Omo was being forced to accept, but the template for some new pattern, some new way of being.

Mufti and the houndsmen let him smolder, as if knowing that even a single sound would detonate him.

They rested, and waited for his rage to bleed off as if in some synchrony with the setting of the boiling sun. They sat in the shade, drinking more salt water and smoking cigarettes, each of them becoming soothed gradually by the gurgling of the river below.

As if against their wishes, a peacefulness began to steal in over them; and after a while, Mufti dared to petition the men for another chance, and when they only looked away and shook their heads in silent rejection, Marie scandalized them all by placing both of her hands on her husband's bare sunburned arm in silent entreaty.

Max Omo looked down at her browned hands upon his arm as if he had never before witnessed such tenderness or vulnerability. He glanced at his wife with both a scowl and confusion, then back at her hands; and clumsily, she pulled them away, feeling as if she were like nothing but the spun and ground and cast-out glass that lay scattered in the desert before them. (In his grubbings, some years later, Herbert Mix would find some of these strange and, to him, beautiful glassine fragments, like the broken pieces of elegant figurines, and he would examine them between his thumb and fingers, and would wonder, unable to form a story.)

"I will pay you his full worth," Mufti said, "if only he can be saved, tonight."

"He can't be saved," said Max Omo.

Mufti paused, then renegotiated. "I will give you his full worth, whether he survives or not."

The houndsmen sat up a bit straighter at this offer, though they recognized also the ridiculous desperation in it, the womanly chords of heartstring.

"You'd never raise that kind of money," said one of the houndsmen.

"I would try," said Mufti. "I give you my word of honor as a gentleman."

"Shit, I bet you ain't no gentleman," said another of the houndsmen. "You're circus folk." Still, they readjusted their aching legs beneath them, as if willing now to try again: as biddable to the call of money as were their hounds to the music of the hunter's horn.

They turned their attention to Omo, waiting for his decision: knowing that neither their hounds nor their own imaginations would be nearly enough to salvage the great runaway; that the task could not be completed without him.

Omo considered the brief flash of the money, as quick and yet distant as the pulses of summer heat lightning that danced every evening to the north and west — storms that in the summer had no chance of ever making it out onto the salt flats. He turned his gaze from the lightning and back toward some inner, uncompromising, untempted, dispassionate place; and watching the expression on his face, the houndsmen knew that he would agree to continue rescuing, or attempting to rescue, the elephant, and that he would accept no payment for his labor.

There arose suddenly from the truck a mournful baying and howling from the hounds so strident and frenzied that even the least superstitious among the houndsmen, and even Max Omo himself, could not help but wonder for a moment if such unsolicited clamor was not protest against the unspoken decision to push ahead; as if the dogs had divined the shape of that desire, passing over their sleeping forms and waking them to full fury.

The houndsman who had accused Mufti of not being a gentleman went over to the truck and rolled open the curtain door to shout at the hounds. The stench of their enclosure, and their befoulment — rank urine, heat-greasy feces, and regurgitated, putrefying meat — came rolling out in waves.

The hounds were still leashed together, so that they could not leap free, though in the admission of new light and air to the zone of their imprisonment, the volume and intensity of their shrieking doubled yet again — and when Mufti, gagging, came over to see what had happened to the back of his truck, the houndsman clapped a hand on his back and advised, "Best to let it dry, cousin, then chip it away with a shovel in a couple or three days, otherwise it'll be an awful mess."

He and another of his partners fastened a chain to the four dogs and jerked the hounds down to the river, keeping them clear of the elephant; and at the bluff, and on the count of three, they lifted the chain between them and hurled the whole assembly of dogs like a stringer of vile fish into the rapids, as if intending to drown them.

Marie watched the darkened form of the elephant, which appeared to be sleeping — though she knew he was not; he was dying, not sleeping — and thought, *If this is the hidden cost of a single circus, cloaked or veiled from any knowledge, what similar costs exist just beneath the surface of all other things, both the mundane and the magnificent?*

Once the men had the hounds hauled back to the top, the houndsmen allowed the hounds to wriggle on their backs in the sand, cleansing themselves, before the men loaded them into the back of the open-air truck and fastened them down in a way that even Marie, in the confused state of her fatigue, found surreal: an indecisive mix of harsh disciplinary punishment and loving, treasured attention.

She made a low, moaning sound, but no one noticed.

"We could try one more time, right now," Mufti said, but Max Omo shook his head emphatically.

"You can stay here with him if you want," he said, "but we have to get these machines home, and oil and rest them. We will be back after midnight. We can bring you some food and water, if you want. It'll be about six hours before we're back."

Mufti studied the houndsmen, wondering whether to stay with his dying elephant or travel on with them, to help goad and turn them back toward the chore at hand, near midnight. He walked over to the elephant and placed his hand on its face, between the unseeing eyes. He thought of the weakness in all men, then — perhaps not in Max Omo, but in all others; certainly he was familiar with such weakness in himself — and with no trouble at all envisioned a scene in which, once back at the lake, well-fed and watered, a subtle alteration in plans might develop, if not an absolute mutiny.

The rescuers, exhausted, might nap a little too long, or simply slip or drift off out of sight, never to be seen again. Max Omo, once back in the familiar embrace of his work, might recover his good senses, and leave the elephant, which meant nothing to him, to die, and leave Mufti, like all the other weak and foreign strangers of the world, to fare for himself.

If they did not get the elephant to water that night, he would die. He would not survive even a few more hours of the next day's sunlight.

"I'll ride back with you," Mufti said, stepping away from the elephant, which was still radiating heat. Mufti wondered if there had been damage to the animal's enormous brain. He wondered if, were he even to survive, the elephant would still be able to do his little tricks.

Before leaving, he went back over to the elephant and spoke to it quietly. Tears glistened on Mufti's face as he spoke. The houndsmen looked away, disgusted, and Marie felt a sudden franticness in her heart — as intense as the feeling she got when the dunes swept in over her cabin and she was buried beneath the sand — and she wondered, barely able to breathe as she considered it, what it would be like to be loved by such a man.

They rode in caravan back toward the lake — Max Omo and Marie and the boys alone in their truck — the boys asleep, Max Omo watching intently the gauges on the instrument panel for signs of flutter or weakness, and Marie thinking about the way Mufti's tears had rolled down his face that was the color of butter heated almost to a scorch.

And each of the travelers, in their different vehicles, even the houndsmen, felt varying degrees of remorse and regret, and admiration for the heart of the beast they were abandoning; and in his vehicle, Mufti kept weeping, and in hers, Marie rode leaning forward, mouth slightly open, as if stunned, staring at the emergence of the desert's night stars, and marveling at both their distance and their proximity.

The stars fell regularly, as they did every night, and in the desert like that, there was very much the temptation to stop the truck and get out and go seeking the nearer ones, which appeared to have fallen only over the next dune.

6

AT THE OMOS' HOME, men and beasts drank quart after quart of newly hauled brine water. The men stood around the well like animals at a trough, taking turns hauling the oaken buckets upward and drinking it dry before handing it to the next man, each of whom was responsible for gathering only his own, and then, after they were all sated, each for his hound; and as the men stood around the shaft of the well, recounting the strange events of the day, Marie built a fire in the cookhouse and began slicing strips of mutton for both the men and the hounds, and frying eggs; and she opened a bottle of the white wine from their wedding.

Of the hundred cases that had been gifted to them, there were now less than five cases remaining, and she often had the uneasy feeling that once that supply of wine was exhausted, some troubling force or development would enter into their lives; though she could not imagine anything more vexing than the wasteland she already inhabited.

She thought of Mufti's golden-brown tears again and wondered if perhaps when the last of the wedding wine was gone, things might not actually turn better.

She carried the food out to them on rough platters improvised from sheets of plywood, with linen towels draped over them. Mufti helped her set up a long banquet table at the lake's edge with benches fashioned from the planks of lumber balanced atop the rusting hubs and rims of old tires and wheels, the table pieced together with the hoods and trunks of abandoned vehicles and sheets of tin, which still retained their warmth from the day's heat.

The men gathered at the table and sat hunched over their plates twin-elbowed, eating in a silence that was intruded upon only by grunts and smacking. They ate as if the meal was unquestionably their due, and they ignored the vision of the sparkling lake at whose edge they were seated.

Marie kept getting up to cook more food for them, and they did not begin to slow down until after all the mutton and all the eggs were gone, and three more bottles of wine; and they talked further amongst themselves.

Marie listened, thinking to herself that certainly she was going to go crazy, surrounded by so many men. She found herself wishing that one of them, Mufti perhaps, might miraculously, as if in the echo of all the strangeness that had already passed, transform himself into a woman. She found herself fearing, too, that in such surroundings she had become too manly, that she thought and spoke and acted as a man —and she stared out at her lake, at the bony sentinels that had attended almost all the days of her adult life, and found that she was acutely aware of the slight salt breeze stirring its way toward the table, and of its cooling effect as it passed beneath her arms and around her legs and brushed against her neck.

She stared out at the long furrow of the elephant's passage from the night before and wondered at the assemblage and sequence of the world's parts.

They would not be dining at the edge of the lake in darkness, in the starlight, if the elephant had not passed through on the previous evening — and yet, such scant hours separated the two events, the *then* and the *now,* that it seemed as likely, in retrospect, that the elephant *might* have just passed before them, like a great freighter churning the sea, while they sat at that table, dining. She found herself scanning the lake, hoping for such a thing, believing it possible, and then, worse yet, waiting for it: tuning out the inane conversations of the men, with their talk of engines, hounds, and weather.

She felt the firewall within her mind that had protected her thus far against the savage loneliness dissolving quickly now.

She rested for long hours with her eyes open but unblinking, just as, miles distant, the elephant rested before the river, on the bluff, his eyes also unblinking, and having also approached that final and now almost indistinguishable line between sleeping and dying.

She stirred to the sound of Mufti's voice, speaking gently to the houndsmen, who were sleeping at the table with their heads lowered into the crooks of folded arms, as if all that they had gorged upon had been poisoned, and they lay dead now before the banquet.

Mufti was speaking to them as if trying to calm their dreams; waking them as a father or mother might awaken children. "Come now," he was whispering, "we have rested, but time is short now, it is time to go and rescue the elephant."

And awakening or returning from her own vigil, Marie rose, determined to travel with him even if no one else could be awakened.

Max Omo and the boys stirred also, however, faithful as ever to the call of work — rising with an eagerness that seemed beyond their control. Though when the houndsmen roused to gather their hounds, they found that one was missing; and casting around the cabin for him, and calling out his name — Hondo — they were rewarded with a distant, plaintive whining that came from far out upon the lake, where the hound had followed the scent of the elephant out onto the salt and had become trapped.

At first they did not believe it was him, for they could see only the silhouette of his head and long ears above the salt-line, and believed it to be some smaller animal that he had chased out onto the salt; but when the dog realized they had him spotted, and were discussing him, he tilted his head upward toward the sickled moon and gave the unmistakable bay — sacrificing more position to do so, and sinking deeper, so that now the lower part of his jowls were barely above the surface, and his ears floated atop the salt sludge, the crust cooked dangerously thin by the day's heat.

"Gott *damn*," Max Omo muttered — it seemed certain that the precision of his entire life was unraveling, and for no reason other than that he had, in a moment of weakness, agreed to help a doomed stranger. He hurried over to strap on the flatboard wooden flippers he had made for himself and the boys, which allowed them to sometimes walk with caution across the firmer archipelagos of sludge.

The boys hurried along behind him, the three of them flapping huge-footed out across the shining lake, but by the time they got to the hound he had gone under, and the serpentine ripples of his struggles had already stilled, and the sludge had already congealed back over him.

The rings of where he had gone down were spaced like the growth rings visible in a new-cut stump; and by going out to the center of those ripples, and reaching down into the salt with their bare arms, reaching in up to their shoulders and groping, they were able to find him, and with great effort haul him back up to the surface. But he had already drowned, his lungs were filled with salt, as if it had been pumped into him for a preservative, and although they skidded and dragged him back out across the top as if muscling in to shore some great sodden fish they had caught on a drop line, and once to shore attempted to resuscitate him, he could not be encouraged back to the land of the living, and now they were down to three hounds.

They would have but scant hours to recover the elephant and return him to the circus, but they packed as if going off to war: a fourth truck, and a tractor, and a winch, two come-alongs, more chains and ropes, and — the thought of it made Mufti blanch — a branding iron, left over from the sheepherders' days.

Mufti watched Max Omo throw the branding iron into the back of his truck. He knew Omo was bringing it only as a prod, but there was some other undercurrent speaking to Mufti that suggested to him that there was another, angrier part of Omo that would, out on the desert plains, feel somehow obligated to use the brand, as if merely to test it out, whether the elephant was moving or stationary, or even alive or dead.

They gassed up, the gasoline fumes as rank and reeking as the slightly fluorescent salt crusts upon their scaly, wind-grimed bodies. *Money down the rat hole,* Max Omo thought, watching the gas disappear, canister after canister, into the gullets of their vehicles, East Texas crude refined, two cents a gallon, but at least it wasn't his money. *My God,* he thought, *what is the price of an elephant, how can the world afford an elephant?* — and the caravan drove back out onto the lonely desert road at half past midnight, with a slight breeze stirring, a breeze that sent ribbons of sand snaking across the highway like the trailings of ghosts just passed.

When they got back to the elephant's resting spot, they were surprised to find that he had moved slightly; that he had somehow been able to rise and drag himself another three feet closer to the bluff, but then no farther.

His eyes were shut. Mufti leaned in close against one ear and spoke to him, but there was no response; though still the elephant's ribs rose and fell, and some of the heat and odor of cooking had left him.

When Mufti and Marie began hauling buckets of river water back up the bluff and pouring it on him, he awakened and stirred, opening his eyes, and he tried to rise to his knees, so that they were all encouraged, and even the houndsmen thought for a moment not of the money to be gained by the elephant's survival but of the possibility of the rescue itself.

"Please," Mufti said to the elephant, speaking quietly, "please."

Max Omo watched for a moment, and then sent the boys down to the river to begin gathering more driftwood to build a fire for the branding iron.

"I think he is well rested," Mufti was saying, "I don't think that will be necessary" — but already Max Omo was igniting the little pile of tinder and kindling, which flared quickly, burning not with the accustomed flames of yellow, red, and orange, but with the iridescence of the burning salts infused within the driftwood: hues of copper, chartreuse, magenta, and turquoise.

The houndsmen watched this spectacle for a moment as if witnessing a sorcerer's work. Max Omo put more driftwood onto the fire, and placed the branding iron in the flames. The elephant trained its whale-like eye on those leaping colors, and none of the men, nor Marie, were comfortable with the emotion they saw reflected in the dampness of that single eye.

The houndsmen moved two of their trucks in behind the elephant, and with their bumpers shoved gently against the animal's heft, but again this seemed only to spread the elephant lower and wider against the sand, and the men did not seem to have the heart to push harder;

as if, in their rest, they had gained some inkling of maturity, and as if, in its almost-geological endurance, the elephant had begun to earn their respect.

Mufti looked on in a daze. He watched his elephant watch the fire fixedly — the animal paid no attention to the other goings-on — and was reminded of an elephant he had seen as a boy in India, an elephant that would paint with palette and brushes, on large canvases, renderings of exquisite landscapes, landscapes that that elephant could never have seen or known before, but which nevertheless existed in the world: mountains and golden prairies and seascapes and winding rivers lined with cool shady birch trees dappled with yellow light.

As if intoxicated, Mufti continued to watch but was not quite fully sensate as the men, under Max Omo's orders, maneuvered their trucks and winches into position. Working beneath the night stars as they were, Mufti was reminded of how it was in each new town when the circus first arrived and began setting up all the tents and tarps that comprised the Big Top: all the various rooms and chambers and compartments creating the architecture that must have seemed like a dream to the circus-goers, but which was the truest reality the circus members themselves knew.

Marie went over to where Mufti was staring at the fallen elephant and put her hand on his arm, uncaring of who might see her. So touched was she by his own heart's ache that she felt it deeply as her own, and felt her heart being drawn or summoned as if from some great depth; as if for all her life, her heart had been like a bird kept trapped beneath an overturned bucket, and that only this specific chain of events, *this* sequence, and a stranger's sorrow, an alien's sorrow greater than her own — had been able to lift or overturn that bucket.

The firelight washed across the two of them, her hand on his bare arm, and flickered across the rest of them, and the elephant; and if Max Omo noticed the consolation Marie was giving the outsider (Mufti's head now tipping into hers, and his shoulders shaking), he gave no indication of finding it unusual; or perhaps he simply did not recognize the heart in flight.

The ropes and chains were readied; the links of the chains jingled in their slackness, but then became silent as they were stretched taut, as the trucks were positioned for the pulling. Mufti's tears splashed onto the dry-spotted skin of Marie's hand, and she patted his arm once more and then released him, and the houndsmen, with the trucks now leaning full into their burden — the ropes and chains bowstring-tight, as if ready for music — rolled up the curtain door of the circus wagon.

Once more, the hounds clambered onto the back of the elephant, slashing and gnawing at the hide with as little discernible progress as were they to begin chewing at the thick bark of a tree. They opened a few more rivers of blood, but the elephant gave them no acknowledgment, kept his eye only upon the fire; and the men, under Max Omo's coordination, began pulling harder with the trucks, and the boys cranked on the come-alongs that were attached to each of the elephant's front legs.

It seemed now to all of them that the elephant was again trying to rise, and that, somewhat rested, he might even have had the power to do so, given just a little more time.

But Max Omo had not brought the iron to let it go unutilized, nor was there any way he would be content, once it was heated, to set it aside and let it cool slowly in the sand; and with heavy gloves he picked up the iron and moved toward the elephant. The glowing brand — two wavery lines forming the Cowders' initials "CC," with three curling lines beneath the letters, undulating waves — appeared to float unattached through the night, floating and yet possessing only one intent, never faltering in its path toward the elephant's flank.

The elephant's eye widened farther, and it struggled harder, but it seemed that the chains and harnesses that had been rigged in the attempt to help hoist it now conspired against it — that there was not enough yaw or pitch, not enough space for the rolling and leaning and lumbering involved in the elephant's standing — and when the brand found the elephant's flank (at the last minute, Mufti had run at Max Omo, trying to stop him, but had been unable to), the elephant trumpeted and shuddered violently as if seized by an electrical current, and the hounds on his back lost their footing.

The stench and steam of burning hide filled the night, and in the elephant's lunge, the brand was knocked from Max Omo's hand, with the poker-bar shank of it glancing and searing his forearm.

The elephant was standing now, had broken two of the chains that housed it, and had pulled the boys with their flimsy come-alongs off their feet as if their attachment to him was by nothing but the single strand of a spider's web.

The trucks dug in deeper, wheels spinning harder.

Steadily, the trucks were dragging the elephant in the direction of what the drivers believed to be the elephant's salvation. The children were behind the elephant, shoving the driftwood prybars under its belly and attempting, foot by foot, to hurry it along in that manner.

There were no other sounds except for the gunning roar of the engines and the tires spinning in and plowing the sand, bringing great rooster-tail cascades of sand down upon the backs of their necks, the sand still heated from the warmth of the day; and once the pullers had come as close to the edge of the bluff as they dared, they turned and traveled parallel to the river, traveling north, with the elephant following them unwillingly, sometimes stumbling though other times being dragged, with his tusks furrowing the sand like a harrow, and in so doing looking not so much as if preparing the sand for the sowing of any one crop or another, but instead like some implement designed to search for something lying just below.

Somewhere near the end, it occurred to Mufti to question the worth of the endeavor; somewhere near the end, he understood for only the first time the great and final distance that would always exist between the elephant's desire and his, even when the two appeared to be working in synchrony.

But what good was such brutal understanding now, with the other plans set so irretrievably and forcefully in motion?

Even as Mufti was processing the discovery, Max Omo, who had reheated the branding iron, was getting out of the truck and administering a second, duplicate brand to the elephant's hide, and then a third branding; though the animal had now come to a stop exactly where they had wanted it to, close enough to the bluff's edge that it could lean over and tumble down the bank, if it wanted to; or if it did not want to, where they could perhaps shove it over the edge with the aid of the levers of driftwood; or, if that was not successful, where they could dig out the ledge beneath the elephant, undermining it with shovels and pickaxes like miners hunting for some rumored cache of ore, until the meniscus of the surface on which the elephant rested thinned to the point that it could no longer hold his burden, and collapsed, the elephant spilling into the river it had once sought with such desire.

The men shut off their trucks and got out and began unhitching the chains and harnesses before reassembling them into one longer line, which they would keep attached to the elephant so that they could reel it back in, once it was sufficiently cooled and watered.

As if they each and all believed the elephant, if it recovered, would still be capable of making the next evening's show.

Upstream, they fastened their trucks together with remnants of chain, forming one solid deadweight that they felt confident not even the elephant's bulk, nor the current of Horsehead Crossing, could displace. For extra security they had the boys fill the backs of the trucks with sand. Then they set about building a sand bunker between the trucks and elephant, as a kind of firewall between man and nature, beast and machine.

Max Omo burned the elephant's flank a fourth time, and a fifth, though to no avail; the elephant sat perched on the ledge like some great roosting bird. Each brand smoldered anew, and though the pattern, the inscription, was always the same, the cant of each brand was always different, and the brandings soon began to overlay one another, so that they began to appear as crowded hieroglyphs, meaningless.

The elephant's eyes widened each time the firebrand drew nearer, and tears leaked from those glassine eyes with each clench of steam — the elephant's body miraculous in that it was still capable of producing any moisture at all — and with each branding, the same shudder rippled through all the thousands of pounds of life. And though thus attentive to the brandings, the elephant still disdained the river below, determined to settle in.

They tried shoving against the wall of the elephant, pushing so hard against the cottonwood lever-spars that the timbers snapped with the sound of cannon fire — and finally they gave up and set to work on the bankside, digging and clawing with boards and shovels and bare hands at the pale cliff wall beneath the star-backed silhouette of the creature.

As they worked, kingfishers that had been roosting in the nests and crevices and burrows of their making flew from their hollows in the earth as if from some magician's trick, or as if excavated and released by the frantic labor of the searchers.

For two hours, the crew worked beneath the towering, silent elephant, kneeling beneath it as if praying for absolution; or as if attempting, perhaps, to prevent the elephant from falling, rather than encouraging it to fall; for seen from any distance at all, their exertions would have been indistinguishable from any one goal to another.

Mufti was the only one among them who was thinking clearly; he was the only one who had not joined in the digging, and stood instead up on the bluff, tending to the elephant: speaking to it, scratching its ears.

Most of the others — Marie, and, amazingly, even Max Omo — were beginning to have the first flickers of self-doubt, despite their work: as if, in their furious burrowing, they were tunneling closer to some lucid, surprising truth, and that it was a truth they did not want to discover, and yet neither could they stop digging.

Because the ledge was not stone, there was no telltale buckling or fracturing to tell the miners below and the riders above when the shelf would suddenly give free, delivering them all into the river.

There would be only the briefest, hastened hourglass-trickling of sand pouring down upon the necks and backs of the workers below, and there would not be time to ponder or consider the meaning of this. There would be barely time to leap.

And when the workers below — the houndsmen, the children, and Marie and Max Omo — felt those whisperings of sand, in the moment before collapse, each threw aside his or her shovel and dived to the side just seconds before the world above fell upon them.

In his sorrow, Mufti was curled up on the elephant's back with his arms spread wide as if trying to embrace the animal, or as if riding the elephant in his sleep, at a great rate of speed, so that he had to lower and turn his head against the resistance.

When the ledge broke, crumbling into the excavated void below, it was fortunate for Mufti that he was already properly positioned for such a ride; and in their plummet it seemed to Mufti that he had caused it from his mere will alone: a metamorphosis as astonishing as the transformation from a graven image on a coin — a horse, or a hound — into the living object itself.

They flew past the others, man and rider, passing their comrades with a hushed roaring of sand, then sweeping past the place where the others had been standing only seconds before, sweeping past them as if the laborers had been but ghosts; and the crumbling assemblage collapsed into the rushing, muddy Pecos, which accepted them as readily as if such admixture was the very fuel on which the river ran. As if no other miracles could exist or be sustained without the regular stirring-in of additions, willing or unwilling, such as Mufti and the elephant.

The elephant's legs, summoned and working now from a place even deeper than where the pain of the firebrand had been able to reach, churned frantically, and like a gray boulder being transported by unimaginable force, the elephant spun and whirled, looking not so much imperiled but like some wild teacup ride in a children's amusement park, and Mufti clung to the animal's ear.

Had the river gotten wilder in all the years intervening since the cattle crossings? The old ranchers said that if anything it had gotten lower and tamer; and watching the elephant bob helplessly in its current, his starlit ivory tusks twirling and rising and falling like driftwood spars, and the trunk writhing upward, desperate for air, twisting like some great serpent that came up from the river's depths only once every century or so, Max Omo wondered how any of the cattle had ever made it across.

He tried to reconcile in his mind the vision of ten thousand cattle churning and lunging broadside to the current, a plait of flesh contesting the river's many electrical currents, each sheathed in its own pulse, while above that subaqueous song, little different from the baying of the hounds, the frantic legs of forty thousand hoofs gnashed at the water, surging for the other side: the mass of their cumulative desire so great that they often formed a temporary bridge, a living dam that the water still breached, but which raised the shuddering water upstream by a height of several feet.

The elephant continued downstream, spinning, tipping, and bobbing, with Mufti still hanging on (in his desperation he had seized the elephant's ear with his teeth, and with his eyes shut against the whirling, had committed fully to traveling wherever the elephant went — to be saved or lost, according to the fortunes and talents of the elephant), and Max Omo and Marie and the houndsmen ran alongside the river above them, stumbling across the sand; the houndsmen running for their claim, watching their tenuous chance for riches be pulled farther away from them, and unable, in the enormity of the moment, to let it go as only the cost of a lost day's wages, an education, and a spectacle.

The boys ran along the river like hounds, and Max Omo ran without knowing why. Marie ran alongside as well, with the hopes of somehow being able to rescue Mufti, or to provide consolation to him in his vanishing: and as she ran she entertained still, and despite her exhaustion, thoughts of somehow trying to rescue, or at least comfort, the elephant.

But their quarry spun farther away, as if unmindful of the desires that pursued him, and was whisked onward by some speed and power far greater than the hungers of the pursuers and the pursued.

Quickly, then, the elephant and Mufti disappeared into the darkness, and the followers ceased their pursuit; and in ceasing — strung out and straggled up and down the high banks of the river — each felt the release of a torment that none had realized they even possessed.

Even the boys felt the new peace, and stood there huffing, sweating, listening to the river.

Marie knelt in the sand and wept: and whether for Mufti, the elephant, or herself, she could not say, nor could she have identified the tears as being those of sorrow or release.

She cried a while longer — Max Omo and the boys stood rigid, mortified by this sprawl of rampant femininity — and the houndsmen looked away, slightly embarrassed but feeling sorrowful in their own manner over the loss of their money.

Without a word to the houndsmen, Max Omo turned and went back to his truck, heading home to work. His boys followed close behind him, and farther back, like a sleepwalker, Marie.

She noticed that Max Omo was walking gingerly, almost lightly across the sand — as if seeking to avoid being detected by someone, or something; and it was some moments before she realized, through the downward tilt of his jaw, and the whipped cant of his tense and stiffened shoulders, that that thing whose notice he sought to elude was failure.

For days afterward, and then weeks, Max Omo would feel stuck in place, mired in some awful morass of weakness and unoriginality, days in which the most mundane problems would appear before him, and where once before he would have evaluated them almost seamlessly, it seemed now that his rhythms had vanished, as well as his energy and interest.

A generator would not start, or would be firing on only one spark plug, or his diesel fuel would get some salt water mixed in with it, and he would stand flummoxed, motionless, on the verge of weeping. His strength seemed to be all unwound from within, and though he wanted to blame it on the elephant, he knew that the weakness, the rottenness, had to come only from within; that he had only himself to blame, for hauling off across the sands after that damn elephant; for having drawn too close to another's dream, rather than fashioning and pursuing his own, however dull and tame and uninspiring his own might have been.

The dream of rising daily and grappling with the salt in the muscular combat of steady immersion. The dream of unwakefulness. He had been gluttonous, had traveled too far beyond his world, and he knew it; and now his body and his mind were like aliens to him, and he could not seem to find his way back.

He began to stand at the edge of the lake for long periods of time, particularly in the evenings, just staring: a man who had never before wasted time or energy on dreams now plagued by them, with the notion or concept of failure a shadow or possibility now over everything he did or looked at or even considered.

In the river, options were more limited. There certainly could be no steering of the elephant, and as Mufti clung to the animal's back, it seemed to him that they were not so much being swept downstream laterally, but that their flight, their falling, was vertical, as when in a dream the dreamer shuts his eyes and lets go entirely.

It seemed to Mufti that he had become the elephant: or that he had always been the elephant, and only now, in the center of the stripping current, and pummeled by stones and logs, was that old mask or outer layer being pulled away, scouring clean the disguise of the man to reveal instead the essence, the elephant.

As Mufti rode — the elephant jarring against spars and jams, colliding and careening — there were nonetheless long rushing stretches in which they floated without striking anything; and in those unencumbered runs, with the elephant's thick legs churning silently under water, it felt to Mufti as if the elephant was dancing.

Sometimes Mufti could hear the clatter and rumble of rocks tumbling along the river bottom beneath them, their movements muted by the blanket of river. Was it worse to watch the stars, or the rushing dark river? Mufti imagined that he could see pulses of electricity beneath them, and it seemed too that on his journey he was passing through zones and pockets of sentience, if not full intelligence, and thinking, living processes: not his own sentience, but the river's.

From time to time, in certain sections of the river, he would find himself passing through waves of communication so strong that after he had swept through and past them, he would turn his head and stare back at the place he had just passed through, as if hoping to continue receiving the communication; but there was never a second refrain, only the once-calling: and then, farther down the river, he would pass through another place in which it seemed the river was more alive.

On they rode, with the night melting now back into the living red heat of the dawn that would have destroyed the elephant, had he remained collapsed in the sand; though even in the river, Mufti noticed, the elephant was riding lower: yet still, the legs kept churning.

Mufti leaned in close to the elephant and whispered encouragement to it, and marveled at the animal's power, and celebrated for so long having been associated with such an animal.

He knew it went against that which he had previously believed in, but he leaned in even closer (the waves had flattened out to mere swells, and the elephant was bobbing along almost effortlessly now, even if it did appear to be sinking lower with each passing mile) and whispered, for the first time in over twenty years, the elephant's name: "Tsavo."

He did not believe it was the end of the line for the elephant, nor did he believe that his own time was drawing near; instead, he wanted only to call the elephant's name out of respect and overwhelming gratitude, and out of mortification and apology, too, as he realized sharply that despite all the tricks and stunts he had trained the elephant to do across the years, it should have been the other way around, with the elephant the trainer, and Mufti the student.

"Tsavo," he whispered again, and as if Mufti had somehow driven a lance between the elephant's ribs, the elephant dropped perceptibly lower in the water, even though the current was no longer troublesome, but was instead mild and consistent, like a winding brook such as two young people might paddle upon in a canoe on a Sunday afternoon, out on a picnic, with a hamper of cheese and wine in the bow.

The sun was riding higher. Only a broad oval of the dry center of the elephant's back, and his head, sunk nearly to eye level, remained above the surface now; and though the current was easier now, the elephant was laboring harder.

Now the elephant's eyes were below the water. Could it still see? Mufti wondered. Was it observing wondrous wrecks of the past, the spars of old wagons, or even the ribs of its ancestors, the mastodons, embedded as fossils in the underwater cliffs?

Still the elephant kept swimming, its trunk swirling listlessly just above the surface, taking in air in that fashion, with the water up to the base of Mufti's calves, so that now it was as if Mufti was surfing; and he wondered again if it were his own weight, his own desire, his inability to part with and release the elephant, that was driving the elephant deeper.

He slipped off and swam alongside.

The sun was fierce above them now. Mufti was surprised by how strong he felt in the elephant's company. As if he could swim however far was required of him. He hoped that the elephant felt the same way; but even as this hope swelled in Mufti, the elephant began to sink again, forced down yet farther by the iron-weight burden of Mufti's need.

The elephant rising and falling in that manner like the musical notes from some calliope rendered somehow silent, though the piston-piping sound waves continued to pump away — inaudible to most, but possibly able to still be heard or sensed or felt by someone else, someplace else.

"It's okay," Mufti said, raising the elephant's ear like a fan and speaking into it, even as he swam, sidestroking. "You don't have to go back to the circus," he said. "You don't have to work for your keep anymore," he said. "We'll retire. We'll go home," he said. "Back to where you came from. Just don't give up."

It seemed to Mufti then that the elephant rose a little more.

They swam side by side a bit farther — another hour; a couple of miles? — and when next they passed through a deep eddy Mufti understood the elephant communicate to him that it was over, that he had covered all the territory he could, and that he would be going under now — that he did so with regret, but that it could no longer be helped, and that Mufti should swim to shore and save himself.

To the end, Mufti could not bring himself to let go; even as the elephant sank all the way under, submerging now like a sounding whale, Mufti dived with the elephant, seizing one of the giant ears, and held his breath for as long as he could, kicking and pulling with bursting lungs, endeavoring to raise the elephant back to the surface.

But the full weight of destiny had him now — the elephant seemed heavier than iron, was sinking at a determined rate, and Mufti too was out of air.

He released his grip and kicked hard for the surface, crying under water: and when he burst into the bright air, coughing and gasping, he treaded water, watching intently downstream, drifting with the current, hoping for the sight of the elephant resurfacing, or even the periscoping trunk — pleading with the elephant to keep on and to travel however many more miles were required.

But there was nothing, only the serpentine sheen of the river winding lonely and onward, silt-colored and silent, hungry only for the next bend, and the next — hungry only for the ocean — and Mufti turned and swam for shore, and pulled himself up onto the damp sand.

He lay there with his face down, covered with his arms, alternately crying and sleeping, with his feet still in the river, and tons of water sweeping past him each minute, and each hour: and the elephant a boulder now, rumbling and tumbling along the bottom, tusks clacking against the rocks, consigned now to the land of spirit and memory, and leaving Mufti behind like some strange alien or outsider not yet permitted to enter into that far more common territory, where all will meet again, and travel together again.

It was only another forty miles to Mexico, which was where the elephant made its landfall. His body washed up two days later in a small village just across the border, where it was discovered by a woman who had gone down to the river to do laundry. In the soft gray light of dawn, the elephant had been fog-colored, so that all she noticed at first were the tusks.

She had approached curiously, thinking them to be oddly tilted lengths of driftwood, and of how happy her husband would be that she had found them, so he could cut them up into firewood.

So slow had the horror been to spread, when she began to piece together the patches and outlines of what she was really seeing — her eyes, against her wishes, disassembling her dream of firewood, and reassembling reality — that when the final understanding came, there was still too much of a gap between that understanding, and the emotions of fright.

Instead of acknowledging her fright, she stood there mute before the monolith; and in her silence and disbelief, and in that morning fog, even standing but a few yards away from the astounding sun-swollen beast, she could not quite be sure of where the animal ended and the gray sky and fog began. Even as she was looking right at it, she could not quite be sure of what it was she was seeing.

She remained silent, with the terror that was filling her rising so slowly and so detached from the normal profile of fear that for the longest time she did not even recognize it as her own.

When she did, she fell backwards, as if pushed two-handed by some invisible force: *smitten,* as if in biblical times: as if she had witnessed some forbidden sight.

She rose in a scramble, looking around to see what might have pushed her, and ran back to the village, where at first she had trouble making anyone believe what she had seen. It seemed impossible, rather than simply improbable. They all thought they had already seen everything, and knew everything; that the world was a small and regular, finite place. That elephants could never drift down their slow and muddy river.

By noon they had the tusks sawed off. Even two days dead, the elephant did not look entirely mortal — or rather, stiffened as it was now, it looked dead, but somehow preserved, and capable, perhaps, of getting back up again and traveling on, and away from them. They fastened a chain around one of its bent and stiffened legs, lest the current undercut it once more and pull it away from them.

There was the consideration of meat, but even in their need, the villagers could not bring themselves to defile so strange and elegant a creature, and instead they merely gathered around it, sitting and visiting amongst themselves and preparing meals on driftwood cooking fires, speculating and storytelling. For some time it was debated whether to place the tusks over the entranceway to the church or the cemetery, and they finally decided upon the church, preferring to risk the sin of sacrilege among the living rather than disrupting the dead.

The elephant grew in the sun for another two days, the hide thinning and stretching tighter, until it was so taut that when the flies buzzing around the mouth and eyes bumped into it, there was a thumping sound, as if pebbles were being tossed at a drum.

There was at first only the faintest, sweetest odor of rot, though the villagers could hear the myriad intestinal gurglings.

The villagers kept moving their seats and their cooking fires farther from the elephant, in anticipation of when it blew; and each day, they marveled at the increase in size, and wondered if in olden times any creature so large had ever strode the earth, or if such size was and always had been limited to dreams and death.

Some of the villagers considered lancing the elephant to release the pressure, but each time the suggestion was made, it was overruled by those who wished to see further expansion for no reason other than the spectacle. The issue resolved itself, as all knew it must, on the third day, when one of the ravens that had been gathering was finally able to pierce the drum with its beak.

There was a blast as if from a cannon, followed by a piercing whistle (the raven was sent cartwheeling into the river, where it drifted, stunned, before swimming to shore like a small mammal), and a gouting plume of iridescent pink and green entrail soup that released from the rent in the elephant's side with the pressure at first of a fire hose.

The contents cascaded into the river, where the ejecta formed oily pools that rafted downstream, shining in the bright light, and the villagers backed away, stumbling before the toxic stench.

From a distance, they watched as the elephant shrank rapidly back to its normal size — the torrent of entrails lessening, after a few minutes — and the elephant continued shrinking, then, to less than its normal size: the gray sagging skin draping itself over and around the bones and clefts and angles that were no longer padded by fat or muscle, and with all the vital organs expelled vitreous now into the salty river.

By the time the expulsion had ended, the elephant seemed no larger than a logjam of bloated steers, a sight with which the villagers were more familiar; and with the elephant thus exposed and reduced, the ravens waded in, cawing and squabbling, pecking and feeding as if at a trough; and those that could not fit into the carcass perched upon the fallen sunken hulk, painting it with the chalk-streak graffiti of their excrement.

Their croakings and cawings summoned the coyotes and the village dogs, and even the golden eagles; and each day the feast grew, and each day, the elephant grew smaller — the world consuming it savagely, voraciously.

The villagers marveled at the speed with which so marvelous a creation disappeared, and soon enough the salt winds and heated sun, as well as the toothy gnawings and steady peckings of the birds, had scoured away the stench.

The villagers had at first believed the elephant would be too large to move, and had thought they might need to bury it beneath a salt mound, to keep its putrefaction from ruining their village and their water supply; but soon everything was gone except for whitened bone: and such was the size of the feast that the elephant had even summoned from down out of the mountains one night a grizzly bear, not the relatively rare *oso negro* but the mythic *oso grande,* which no one had seen in forty years. No one saw that bear, but the villagers heard the barks and howls of their dogs in a newer, more frantic tenor that could speak only to something rare and unusual and dangerous; and in the morning, along the river, they found the distinctive tracks of the grizzly, and for a moment, they turned away from the future and looked back into the near-past, back to a time when such creatures had still lived in the world, and when the sighting or existence of such a being had been neither improbable nor miraculous, but simply part of the fabric of the made and still-whole world.

Within a year, the elephant's ship of bones had collapsed into indistinguishable silt-wrack, and the massive fertilizer of his repository had nurtured the growth of an enormous clump of willows and tamarisks, in which perched yellow warblers and painted buntings, scraps of color flitting and singing at the edge of the women's vision as they crouched by the river and scrubbed their laundry.

For several years they kept a cautious eye out for the bear that had left the tracks, but were never gifted with any more sign; and though eventually the bear must have gotten old and gone off to die somewhere in the mountain, its own bones now a wrecked shipyard, in the villagers' minds he was still always out there; because it had shown up after all such bears were thought to be gone, they now assumed that it, or another, would always be hidden out there; that a mountain range could never be entirely shed of its grizzlies, for then they would no longer truly be mountains. And in the same manner — accustomed so quickly and easily to the miraculous — they watched regularly, frequently, upstream, as if believing that the river might one day again deliver another elephant to them.

East or west, north or south; Mufti had too much freedom, could have traveled in any direction, and he lay there on his own beach for nearly an hour before deciding to travel downstream, walking instead of swimming.

He stopped to sip from the river whenever he got thirsty, and for the first several hours he kept a keen eye out for the elephant, scanning downstream and watching both shores intently, searching for either the resting animal himself, or for tracks that might show where he had exited the river, and made yet another escape back into the desert.

By early afternoon, however — his stomach queasy from the salty river water, and his skull gripped by the heat — he had already become accustomed to his loss, and forgot to even be looking for the elephant. He forgot everything, even his own survival, and veered off into the brushland until the fatigue in his legs and the slope of the terrain guided him back to the river.

He came to a bridge at dusk, and climbed up the embankment — he kept sliding and falling back — and once he was finally up on the road, a hard-surfaced blacktop, he curled up and fell past sleep and into a deeper unconsciousness. In the last beaconlight of sunset, the pavement was still so warm that the blacktop was malleable, as comfortable as a firm mattress, and it accepted the shape of his body.

With the desert already cooling, furry-legged tarantulas came out onto the road, searching for that last warmth — crossing the road like pedestrians, or as if convening for some scheduled gathering; and likewise, desert tortoises, Gila monsters, horned toads, and rattlesnakes slithered out onto the warm road in that last red light, passing by the sleeping Mufti, who was blissful, dreamless in his exhaustion.

Later in the night, the road cooled, and the cold-blooded creatures went on off into their burrows, where they would wait to be summoned by the next day's heat.

Near midnight, a truck approached, a long-haul driver bringing walnuts from California — he would travel on to East Texas, offload the walnuts, and pick up a load of pecans to take back to California — and at first the driver intended to go on past Mufti, believing him to be a car-struck deer that someone had not bothered to drag off the road.

The driver, who himself had been in the land of near-sleep, his mind inhabiting a waking dream in which cocktail waitresses served him iced drinks by the blue waters of a Caribbean pool, shouted when he saw Mufti sit up, and then stand, just as the truck was bearing down on him.

As there had been with the laundress and the elephant down by the river, there was such a gap in the driver's mind between the space of his having believed the innocuous shape to be an old dead deer, and seeing it rise and attempt to flag him down, that he could formulate no thought other than sheer panic; and he drove on, trembling, for a couple of miles, before logic came back to him, and he understood what he had seen.

He turned the truck around and went back to pick Mufti up, and gave him a ride to East Texas, where Mufti helped him unload the walnuts and reload the pecans, and took him with him then to California, where Mufti worked with another circus, though not with another elephant, for ten more years: the next part of his life opening like the mere turning of a page in a book. As if it had all been but a story or a dream, and he had stepped simply from one life into the next.

Having lived all those years in the first, never dreaming that the next life lay full and waiting for him. As if all of the first, despite its splendor and detail, had been but an overburden that needed to be stripped slowly away, to reveal the undermost life next and further.

Strangely, it was Marie who reentered the rhythm of her old life most easily: or for a while, at least. While Max Omo began to spend more time standing at the lakeshore, staring out at the white haze that was once his never-ending quarry (the boys increasingly impatient with him, twitching and flexing their muscles like draft horses standing in harness on a hot day, unused and fly-plagued), Marie slipped back into her old routines as smoothly as any machine.

On her first morning back home following the adventure, she was up before dawn, starting the cookfire as she had innumerable others, preparing breakfast. If anything, for those first several days, she was almost thankful to be back in the comfort of her routine. It seemed once again to be the place she belonged in the world, and for better or worse, there was a reassurance in that.

As she worked, she admired the wooden handle of the ax she had wielded all of her married life, salt-stained with the sweat that had come ultimately from the old ocean that was now the remnant lake, being filtered through her.

She split the twisted ironwood as she had always split it, so unthinkingly as to approach some daily-murmured prayer; two pieces into four, four into eight, and the days falling away and then disappearing to near-nothingness, leaving behind nothing but the shaped and smoothed handle of a well-worn ax.

No prince was coming for her, but it did not matter, for it seemed to her that she was back where she belonged: even if the slot of that place had not been cut by her. She turned her back on the dream she had glimpsed — put Mufti almost completely out of her mind, and the elephant, too — and resumed splitting wood, and starting fires in the little iron stove.

Within only a few days the sun had melted the salt-cast trough of the elephant's passage back to its previous planar smoothness, and the wind scoured and buffed the salt back to its old iridescent sheen.

Sometimes when she glanced out at the lake and saw her husband standing there, staring into dreamland, she would mistake him at first for one of the ancient sentinels that had been claimed by the salt; the wind flapping his sleeves and coattails, too, as if the fact had already occurred.

7

A STRANGE AND POWERFUL landscape summons strange and powerful happenings. They return again and again to such a landscape, like animals drawn nightly to the same oasis. And perhaps it was in this pattern that Marie found herself unable to turn her back entirely on the dream; or as if, even in turning her back, she could not be separated fully from it, for now it followed her, even if unbidden.

A scratching, rasping sound within her, of new grooves being cut, and water trickling, flowing down those grooves; and in her dreams she began to follow those new slots and canyons, even while in the bright light of day clinging tightly to the old routines, and to the ax.

Men came to visit her in her dreams, in the new country. They moved close to her, and she to them, easily. In the dreams, she and he leaned their heads in against one another, rested upon each other shoulder to shoulder; and in the dreams, she was astonished to be the recipient of tenderness and affection: and not merely the crude pawings that masqueraded as caresses in the brief preliminary to sex, but tenderness and kindness of its own accord, existing for its own sake.

In the dreams, among these strange men (though sometimes there might be a boy she had known from grade school, grown up now — hardened, and of her age, and understanding too well her weariness), she felt surprised at first but then quickly confident that she was deserving of such gentleness and attention — that indeed, the cup of his hand seemed made for the fit against the side of her face, and that, as with a violin, perhaps, the point of that chin fit perfectly, was made for the calm and worn-out cleft just above her collarbone, halfway between her shoulder and neck.

The best ones were the men who came to her quietly and simply took her head against their shoulder, and leaned theirs against hers, and the two of them would just stand there, each leaning into the other like sentinels; and she enjoyed their company, listened intently to whatever it was they had to say, whether trivial or significant.

She grew more and more accustomed to the strange intimacy of these encounters, the freshness of possibility, so that she began going to bed earlier each night, and stayed in bed longer in the mornings. And even once she was up and about, she moved more sluggishly: and on the days in which there had been no dream at all, no visitor the previous night, she would be moody and irritable, so much so that even Max Omo noticed it, and though he assumed it was simply a part of the aging process, contentment or happiness disintegrating gradually, he was nonetheless concerned, as he would be were any of his machines to begin emitting a faltering sound, a skipped beat, a waning in output.

A strange land summons strange inhabitants, and shapes them all to its own desires. As if setting up a stone wall, Marie was able for the most part to keep dreams of Mufti and the elephant from pouring in, though the welcome strangers continued to drift in; and she had other dreams, too.

Though she knew nothing of the circumstances, had heard no tales or rumors of their existence, she dreamed frequently of camels. Caravans of them had been used in her country only several decades earlier, during Army Brevet Captain John T. Pope's staggering searches for water, in his years spent scouting possible routes for a transcontinental railroad. And although Pope had found very little fresh water, the camels had succeeded hugely, for a while. (Pope's failure was colossal, even by the standards of the landscape's harshness. Time and again he missed finding water by only a few miles. In his scratchings and diggings and drillings, informed by crude science and wild intuition, he often ended up drilling in the one and only place where he could *avoid* finding water. His own mental collapse, though slow in coming, culminated with his men wanting to mutiny, but still he pushed on, inflamed by the hunt. Near the end, with each new dry hole, he would become convinced that sweet water lay only a few feet deeper, and he would sometimes awaken in the night, and would attempt to steal the ash-tree ridge poles from the tents of his sleeping soldiers, hoping to attach them to the drillstring the next day, in an attempt to reach down another six feet. So spectacular was his strange failure that he missed — walked straight over the top of — the then-untapped Ogallala Reservoir, only thirty more feet below him, one of the largest freshwater aquifers in the world.)

What broke Marie, finally, however, was not the inattentions of any lover, nor the total absence of tenderness, nor even the terrifying whisper of the dunes slithering across her tin roof, but instead, the growling.

Despite his own new dreaminess, and the long sessions spent staring at the lake, Max Omo had not been able to sever his old ways entirely. In October, as the north winds returned to readjust slightly the cant and position of the dunes, he had completed construction on his latest invention, a salt-sorting machine that utilized a long steel cylinder, a barrel tube, which revolved endlessly, driven by the piercing, stinking labors of a steam engine that Omo had adapted to consume oil, coal, ironwood, sheep dung, or even the dried bones and hides of animal carcasses. Each day he and the boys fed the barrel tube as they would a penned but unruly animal.

A series of screens within the barrel tube led to various chambers that filtered the grains of salt according to all their different diameters, before pouring the salt, now sorted evenly, into gunnysacks waiting beneath the revolving tube. Omo was then able to sell the finest grade of salt, for fifteen dollars a ton, to sheep ranchers, who would place it in troughs or mix it with their feed, while the medium-grade salt went to the cattle ranchers for thirteen dollars a ton. The coarse grade was sold to individuals for twelve dollars a ton, where it was used for freezing ice cream: a delicacy that the Omo children had heard about, but never tasted.

It was not the gruntings of the steam engine, however, nor its dank and briny scent, that broke Marie, but the rattling of the dreaded salt within the barrel tube: the ceaseless grumbling as the machine ate the lake, day and night, before spitting it out into sacks, which were carried away on the backs of flatbed trucks (by now the boys, though barely twelve and ten, knew how to drive); and the tube refilling again and again, the lake replenishing its dreadful cargo always.

She began to develop tics and tremors, insuppressible tremblings within — she could barely light the fires in the cookstove each morning — and the pleasant dreams vanished entirely, as if there was something now unworthy about her, something in her that caused her to no longer be able to receive them.

This hunger and absence only aggravated the tremblings, and she dropped things often, and forgot what she was doing.

As all her other senses began to shut down, deadened by fatigue, it seemed that only her sense of hearing grew sharper, until it was unbearably acute: and against her wishes, she would find herself straining to hear the subtle intricacies of the barrel tube's sorting: the grinding of the gears constant and monotonous, though just beneath that, the faintest, occasional variations in the proportion of fine salt, whispering, and medium salt, murmuring, and coarse salt, groaning.

It became for her as if she was straining to pick out words and sentences from a conversation she could not quite understand, and made all the more maddening by her increasing belief that it was a conversation that was important and meaningful to her present circumstances, if no one else's.

Other mornings, the voices from the salt would sound as if they were being uttered in some foreign language, and she would grow madder still.

"She is a goner," Max Omo told the boys, and advised them to say their goodbyes to her while she still recognized them, and they, her.

And as if his pronouncement had made it so, a week later, as the big dune behind their house began to make its autumnal shift (she had been lying awake for three nights in a row, listening for it), she finally broke: unable to escape the growling that seemed to emanate from the barrel tube even when the motor was silent and the barrel was motionless.

Waiting, listening for the sand, she heard the first snaky slitherings, felt the first heaving deadweight of dune come leaning across their roof, up and over the barricade of iron: sand falling lighter than rain, and flowing around either side of their stalwart little cabin.

This time, so keenly prepared, she had them all up and awakened and out the door and onto the roof with shovels and brooms, fighting the rippling shift of the earth, the rearrangement of topography. But they might as well have been trying to sweep back the advance of the ocean's tide; and the sand came sweeping steadily in, up to their ankles, ten shovelfuls sliding back in for each one they tossed aside, and then the sand was up to their knees, and then to their waists, so that they were working only to save and extricate one another — handing the long end of the shovel to whomever was stuck and pulling, while the others burrowed quickly around the imprisoned human pillar; and once they were free, they abandoned their hopes of holding back the dune and instead leapt from its edge, went sliding down its slopes and ran toward the lake as if pursued.

By morning the dune had repositioned itself and lay sleeping atop their house as comfortably as an animal that might have gotten up from its bed and turned in the night; and Max Omo and the boys began digging out, working with great force in the rising heat merely to get back to where they had been the day before: and in their labors, they did not notice that Marie, still wearing only her nightgown and the tall rubber boots that they all wore when mucking around the lake, had disappeared.

It was midmorning before they thought of her at all — wondering where their breakfast was — and at noon, when they took a brief break, the three of them sharing one of the bottles of wine (which was tasting more vinegary every year), they were hungry enough to think to go look for her in the cookhouse.

They didn't find her there, and wandered briefly around the outbuildings, calling her name. Max Omo checked the privy, for he had noticed she had been secluding herself in there for increasingly longer periods — napping, he assumed, in the shade and darkness — and it was one of the boys who found where her tracks had gone down to the shore and out into the lake; and when they gathered there, they did not recognize her at first, out among all the other skeletons, sitting down in the salt with her back turned to them, the breeze flapping her nightgown.

She had lost weight all through the summer, shedding pound after pound until she was but a skeleton herself, her organs held within by only the envelope of her brown papery skin — even Max Omo had noticed it, but had told himself she would put the weight back on when cooler weather returned — and with a groaned curse, Omo had the boys put on their salt-bog paddle-shoes, and he put on his, and together they went out onto the lake toward her with their shovels and ropes and chains. She was kneeling in the salt, the lake up to her waist, her head tipped forward so that her chin rested on her sunken collarbone, and was whimpering, the tracks of tears dried to salt courses on her leathery face. Max Omo was nonetheless rude and impatient, half-believing that he too was stranded in some sort of beastly purgatory, in which all movements and patterns strove to repeat themselves; and that finally, what had once been a source of great comfort to him — the predictability of mechanical repetition, the flawless lift and rise of piston and cylinder, the safety and accountability of foreknown routine — was at long last becoming a curse and an anchor.

He fastened the chains and ropes around his kneeling wife and gave the boys the order to pull; and leaning in to the task, they dragged her back out of the salt's embrace, with Marie riding on her back looking up at the sky, offering no resistance to her rescuers, both hands clutching the chain wrapped around her chest as if it were simply a too-tight necklace, one that threatened to choke her.

Back on shore, the boys unwrapped the chains from her and sat hunkered by her, confused, and patted her salt-crusted hair and peered with dim wonder and curiosity at the new lightlessness in her eyes.

Max Omo went and got her old tattered parasol — festive, in early days — and leaned it crookedly against her shoulder to protect her from the sun — believing that her mental dishevelment had as its source but a single day's overexertion. He poured her a glass of wine, set it in the sand beside her, patted her back, and then he and the boys went back to their labors upon the house.

It was far into the deep end of the afternoon before they had all the sand moved, and their cabin (looking somehow slightly brighter and cleaner; scoured by the sand's tight embrace) revealed once more; and it was only after they had finished their task that they thought to check on Marie, and when they did, they discovered that she was gone again.

Once more, Max Omo groaned and cursed the purgatory of his existence — in his fury, a thought flashed like fire across his mind, which was to simply leave her out in the lake this time — and still cursing, he walked with the boys past the abandoned parasol and the untouched glass of wine (in which spun delirious sandflies) to the edge of the lake, where they again cupped their hands to their eyes and stared out across the distance, trying to pick out her motionless figure from among all the others.

And when they could not find her out there, the thought again leapt through Max Omo's mind that she had already gone under — that she had reentered the old loosened tracks of the morning's passage and gone straight to the bottom. Certainly, there had been enough time for it. He glanced back at the cookhouse, to see if any smoke might be rising from the chimney — there was none — and at the door of the privy, which was ajar.

He felt in that moment a dizzying combination of elation and remorse. "Boys," he began quietly, but was interrupted by the youngest, who like a bloodhound had found and begun following the fresh tracks of his mother, which coursed in seeming wandering stupefaction along the contours at the edge of the lake before veering off into the sand when they reached the point where the elephant, earlier in the summer, had also left the lake.

Now it was Max Omo's turn to fall to his knees in the sand — he too felt like weeping — but instead he only cursed more profanely, and pounded his fists in the sand while his boys stood by and wondered what he was so upset about, though such eccentricities had become familiar to them. The boys stood, waiting for him to tire himself out against the sand, as he pounded and cursed, and then he rose and bellowed her name out across the dunes.

It seemed that they could see the sound waves of his shouts travel a short distance in the heat and aridity before falling in pieces to the sand.

They set out after her, the boys mildly concerned but also partly entertained by the prospects of another chase, but with Max Omo so enraged at being drawn still farther from his work by what he perceived to be but a foolish and feminine indulgence that he was resolved to cuff her, when he caught up with her.

They trotted, not knowing how many hours' lead she had on them, but understanding that she would be headed for the river, and that she would enter into it at that same spot. And again Max Omo felt the confusion of two feelings, as he hurried behind: hoping to catch her, if only because she was running, and yet hoping to get there too late, even if only a little too late, and in that manner have his life returned to him.

After only a short distance, they found her nightgown, discarded as if she had disappeared — though still the tracks continued — and farther on, they found her rubber boots.

There was nothing else then but her trail, with her feet bare now, narrower, so that it resembled more the passage of some animal with cloven hoofs, a deer or a goat. The stride lengthened, which Max Omo knew meant she was running now, probably because of the sand's heat. He knelt and felt it with his work-hardened hands and found it barely tolerable. He took it to be a good sign that she was at least conscious enough to still feel discomfort — though the newly lengthened gait of her tracks made the trail seem even more like that of a wild animal, traveling across the shifting sands in leaps and bounds; and Max Omo and the boys hurried on, feeling that they might be losing ground.

They caught sight of her once, in the last wedge of day's light, the evening's cooling purple tide settling back down in over the desert and the last radials of red sun flowing across the sand, the setting sun perfectly level with their eyes. They could see her going up and over the distant ridge, appearing as a wild animal, moving with the grace of a deer, her nude body pale against the strange sunlit hues of the sand.

She disappeared over the back side of the dune. Max and the boys staggered down theirs, huffing and dead-legged, and when they came to the next rise and gazed west, the dunes contained no life, possessing only the varying shades of sunset's orange and gold hues, and beyond that, the first evening stars — and when they came to the next ridge after that, even the painted light was gone from the dunes, and they squinted into the dimness, hoping to see the pale object that was still moving steadily away from them.

They could see nothing; and on the next ridge, they found nothing but true darkness, and even their own hands held before them were barely visible.

They navigated by the stars, sometimes following her tracks and other times striking in the straightest tack toward the river; and after a couple of hours, Max Omo noticed that the gait of her tracks was shortening again, as the night chilled. He knelt and felt the sand, which was now as cool as that of a day-old dead animal — colder, somehow, in having had the warmth drain away from it, than if the warmth had never been there — and he noticed in her tracks where she had some- times stopped and turned around to look back in the direction of her pursuers.

They found her resting in a sand hollow she had carved with her hands, trying to scrape down far enough beneath the surface to find some remnant pulse of heat, within sight and sound of the river.

She had found some residual heat about two feet down, though still she was shivering when they came upon her, and they could see where she had already excavated several small pits in the area, milking the last of the fast-vanishing warmth from each one before moving on to the next; and when they approached, she hunkered down tighter into her sand-bowl, but made no further attempt to escape.

Max Omo took off his salt-crusted work shirt and laid it over her, fastened it around her with a couple of buttons at the top; and the boys, who had recently started smoking, gathered driftwood twigs and branches, and made a small fire beside her nest.

As the flames danced and leapt, the four of them squatted by the fire for warmth.

It seemed to Max Omo and the boys that in that shifting, waver- ing firelight, the dunes were moving again, flowing all around them, covering everything but them — while to Marie, with the last of her resistance having crumbled like ancient parchment beneath a heavy touch, it seemed that they were being buried.

She was still shuddering, trying through the simple side-to-side rocking of her body to burrow down deeper into the sand — desiring to be up to her knees in the sand's buried warmth, up to her thighs, her waist; up to her armpits, to her chin, and then submerging, like a swimmer — and it seemed to her that the dunes were aflame, in that reflected light, and that the sound of the river was fire, and that the stars above were glowing coals and embers, and yet still she could feel no warmth.

Max Omo sat close to her, his arm hooked clumsily around her to provide warmth, but it was too little too late, and she stared at the fire feeling nothing, and unable to travel any farther.

On the other side of the campfire, the boys kept smoking their cigarettes and getting up to add sticks and branches to the fire. They appeared disinterested, unconcerned with their mother's dilemma, their family's dilemma, or the strangeness of the evening, and from time to time looked around idly for the elephant, as if believing that because he had been in these environs once, he might be again.

Eventually Marie's fatigue carried her down into sleep. She leaned in against Max Omo and fell asleep with her head in his lap, both her arms stretched around his waist as if they were still newlyweds — and Max Omo instructed the boys to pile sand over the form of her sleeping body, to act as a blanket, which they did, covering everything but her head and arms, as if they were children playing sandcastle games on a beach.

They all slept until shortly before dawn, when Marie alone among them was awakened by the yaps of a pack of coyotes that had been running along the river and had stopped to investigate, and to bark at the smoke and ash of the dying fire.

When she awoke, Marie perceived again the coals before her to be the stars, and believed that for whatever judgment had been passed against her, she had been buried up to her neck in sand for all time — that she had not died, but worse yet had been assigned to the limbo of purgatory, neither living nor dead, forever; and that, worst of all, in the afterlife, she would forever be accompanied by the captors she had finally sought to escape.

She did not wail or offer any other protest — only a renewed shuddering — and further curious, the coyotes edged in closer, their little eyes shining red in the coal-light. Still shivering, Marie lay her head back down and went to sleep, and when she awakened again a short while later to the stirring of Max Omo and the boys, and the new-washed gray sky of dawn, the coyotes were gone, though in her fractured state she imagined that Max Omo and the boys, who were brushing the sand from her, were the coyotes metamorphosed: and whether they were trying to dig her back up or bury her even deeper, she had no idea, and no longer cared.

She wished for an ocean to come sweeping in again, quickly.

They rose and left the little fire burning and went down to the river to sip its salty waters. The boys were down to their last two cigarettes, which they shared among the four of them. They turned then and went back into the sand.

The night's breezes had for the most part obscured their passage from the evening before, so that they had to cut the grooves anew; though in other places their trail was still visible. They could see the bowl of sky that rested above their lake, the gathering of a few clouds like a small school of fish, far in the distance, and were able to navigate in that manner, trudging toward the spawning ground of those clouds.

They arrived parched and blistered shortly before noon. They fell upon the wine and splashed buckets of well water upon themselves to cool their cracking, scaling skin. Marie would not go back inside the cabin, even though it had been swept spotless of sand, and so Max Omo dragged an old iron bed frame from out of the barn, chipped off the flakes of sheep dung, made a crude pallet upon it, and built a little tin awning above it, and then with padlocks fastened one end of a chain to the iron bed and the other firm around Marie's bird ankle.

He left her with one of the last bottles of wine — he noted with a small sadness that there were only four left, and remembered the prophecy that had been made when his uncle had first gifted them with the hundred cases — and provided her also with a battered metal pail of the warm salt water, as he would for a goat or a cow.

Then he returned to his chores, and though Marie tried to escape again, she could not travel far, dragging the iron bed and chain with her, and leaving behind the unavoidable sand-furrows of trail.

She howled all night, arguing and singing with the unquiet growling she imagined she could still hear coming from the mechanical salt-sorter, and she was so strident that none of the others could sleep. Finally Omo and the boys went out into the night, and as if in self-fulfilling prophecy started up the barrel tube: and because they could not sleep, they set to work, dragging in trawl lines of salt by desert moonlight, and feeding the sparkling sludge into the barrels and funnels, carrying on their important work of feeding salt to the world.

They hurled themselves against that work as if believing that through some extra energy expended by them in the service of the implacable world, they might reverse the inequity between the mortal and the immortal; and while they worked, slaving at the trawl lines, Marie continued to howl, cautioning them to come back, that they were going too far out into the lake: warning them to turn around and head back in the other direction, wailing at them to come back and tend to her, and to be tender, not hard.

The next morning they bathed her as they would a soiled horse and took her to town — not to a doctor for any treatment, nor to her old Lutheran church, but to the Baptist church, for adoption, or incarceration, or whatever other mitigative procedure might be arranged — and though she was cleaned up and had stopped groaning and was able to answer politely the most general questions, the church's volunteers could see with clarity how her pale blue eyes had looked too far into the future, and how she had traveled too far into the past, and how something had been broken during that journey. And whether she would heal or not was anyone's guess, and would depend, they said, on God's will, God's mercy.

The church workers put her in a loft apartment they owned, which was used by unwed mothers from other towns and cities around the country — theirs was but one in a network of reciprocating agreements where young women vanished for a time to visit aunts and uncles, before returning a year or two later with the infant cousin or niece or nephew with whom they had suddenly been entrusted, and neither the specificity nor lameness of the excuses ever mattered, only the veneer of the code of manners at the surface that would allow other pretenses to proceed unperturbed.

It would be a trial run for Marie, the church workers explained. They would observe her for a week, then evaluate her for whatever tasks she might be fitted for with regard to the service of the church, and the earning of her keep.

The boys and Max Omo gave her clumsy, salt-odored, diesel-fuel embraces. They said something to her, perhaps something poignant or tender or meaningful, though it was heard by no one, for the only sounds she heard from them when they opened their mouths was the grating, rattling roar of the barrel tube; though after they had turned and left her, she noticed that a silence returned to her room, the first such silence she could remember hearing: and with the white walls of the unfurnished apartment before her — a cot, a sink, two windows, no curtains, no mirror — she felt freedom onrushing, carrying her away to safety.

She felt it as strongly as if she had been in a small canoe on a rushing river and had come to a fork in its path, and had chosen the river's smaller, quieter, backwater braid, and had been rewarded finally in that choosing.

A stellar calm and quietness. The rich odor of all the living things rising from the gentle slough. The sound of the water dripping from the blade of her paddle held motionless above the little backwater river as she drifted, surrounded by all-else silence: her silence, and nobody else's.

The sounds of the world returning slowly, then, along with their sights. The one guttural croak of a great blue heron, the color of fog, leaping up from the graveled shore and pulling himself up into the sky like a magician before flying away, each single wingbeat seeming to carry him farther than one would have thought possible — each slow wingbeat against the sky like the one-stroke of her own paddle, taking her farther down the little river, the forgotten and hidden river, her river.

In her mind, she reached down and collected the prettier stones, carried them on with her farther downriver in the canoe before setting them on the shore beside her when she made her camp for the night on a secluded gravel bar, tended by a small campfire as much for companionship as warmth; sleeping then to the sound of the murmuring river right beside her, a bower of scented branches beneath her for a cushion, and a blanket over her for warmth.

A morning swim in the river, a bath, and she was off, carrying those few best stones with her, and collecting more the next day — and when she returned to her apartment, she would bring the stones from that trip with her and place them on top of the dresser that was not yet there in her apartment, stones from a trip she had not yet taken and might never take: but no matter, she was in a clean, dry, comfortable place that was fully her own, the silence was her own and no one else's, history had already passed by, there was no need any longer to struggle with or battle against it.

She went over to one of the old windows and opened it to the height of its sash and leaned against the fresh-painted white of her bare walls and stared out at the sleepy comings and goings of the town, her new life, below; and in the coming days, the church workers could discern no problems, no failings, illnesses, or imbalances within her, and after first assigning her to the cleanup detail, she was soon promoted to full kitchen duties. By the end of the autumn, she had been fully embraced by and incorporated into the church, with its underlying gridwork and support system of endless potluck dinners and prayer lists, its sermons and lectures. The church members welcomed her with the zeal of the starving — as if with their opportunity to be kind to and supportive of her — even perhaps rescuing her, as was sometimes intimated had happened — they were consuming her, and were wild to do so.

She never engaged her heart in the full passion of the message of the church that had adopted her — she was too chary, too ravenous herself for the delicious new freedom, and the dreams of the little river, and the freedom of the bare clean white walls of her loft. Her heart remained only her own, like some wild animal even when among them, kept housed and out of their hungry reach as if in a small cage of bamboo bars.

And somehow, as if understanding this about her, and perhaps even slightly admiring of it, the church did not demand her heart, for they were only too grateful to have the opportunity to serve her, and to project upon her their needs and desires, and their own images of helping-selves — in this regard, they subtly, craftily sought to imprison her, even up in the freedom of that loft above the town — but they were easy to elude, compared to the years spent with her husband and sons; and whenever she felt panicked or enclosed, she was almost always able to slip away merely by placing her fingertips against one of those bare white walls, which she kept fresh-painted and clean-scrubbed, across the years.

And in the first year, when she thought occasionally of Max Omo and the boys, and of the scorpions and sandstorms and hot salt water, it was with a dizzying combination of elation and regret; but after those first four seasons, she thought of them almost hardly at all, and on the one or two times each year she might encounter them in town (the boys as large and passionless as heifers, now), she usually looked through them without even realizing who they were — and even when something in her clicked, and reminded her of who they were, or who they had once been, she still could not make the full connection.

And in looking at them — staring at them as they walked down the sidewalk on the other side of the street — it was for her as if she were viewing them through a riffling sheen of clear water, as she had stared intently in some of her visions at the blurry then clear passage of polished stones beneath her as the river, and her little canoe, carried her along.

She helped out in the church — filing books in the library, baby-sitting during services. A calmness came back into her life, if not a strength or enthusiasm. In the evenings she would return to her loft attic and, after preparing a simple meal on her two-burner stove, she would sit by the window like a cat and look out at the slow goings-on in the little town.

The football players rushing past, cleats pounding the pavement. The oilfield service trucks, as if on their way to some critical military engagement. The young people, occasionally walking down the sidewalks, heads down, new in love. Some of the young women were beautiful. *What would it be like,* she wondered once — not desiring it, only trying to imagine it — *to possess such beauty?*

The other Omos lasted but a few more years without her; and those years were even shoddier than before, in which Omo and his boys were plagued by bad luck and poor business decisions, increased physical clumsiness, slovenliness, malnutrition, and, gradually, a general inattentiveness to their subject, the salt, so that soon it became apparent to the boys that Max Omo was only going through the motions: not pining for Marie, certainly, but seeming somehow gutted nonetheless; and they missed the old days of groove and synchrony, when the salt had risen each day, and they had been there to meet it, and for a while had been its equal.

Now the lake swelled, dominating its weakened and imbalanced former oppressors, and as the salt miners' production dwindled, the lake's salt rose in small folds and ridges that accumulated in patterns similar to those in the sand dunes.

The lake had always before been planar, as level as cut or shaved ice, but now it began to look haggard, and when Max Omo went down to the shore in the evenings to stare out at it, he no longer stood as he once had, but sat in an old chair smoking a cigarette; and where once he had gazed intently at the lake, he now saw nothing, and thought nothing, only sat and rested, waiting.

And of the salt they did manage to continue producing, in ragged fits and starts, they had increasing difficulty selling it, and then even giving it away. Low transportation costs and large companies working on both the Gulf Coast and in the desert Southwest were taking over all the old markets, though still Max Omo and the boys continued to produce the salt, almost frantic now that the only thing they knew how to do well in the world was no longer sufficient to keep them afloat.

And whether the neurosis ran in their blood or came trickling up from out of the ground, to then be shaped and directed by the wind, they could not know, but both boys began to notice that the lake was expanding, creeping inward with a subtle but noticeable steadiness, so that by the next spring the legs of the chair in which Max Omo sat smoking his cigarettes in the evening were eventually several inches into the lake: and still he did not move the chair back, but sloshed out toward it each evening in his rubber boots, and sat there slouched and exhausted in the blue dusk, the end of his cigarette glowing as he pulled on it, as if that lone spark now was all that sustained him, and perhaps even all of the world in motion around him: as if it were all but one spark away from freezing solid, as lifeless as stone.

And in the same manner that their mother had once lain awake nightly, listening for the approach of the winding, slinking sand, the boys — fifteen and seventeen, now — lay there and wondered and imagined how much ground the lake might be gaining on them each evening. They began to develop tics and stutters, jerks and twitches; and only in their work were their fears and troubles able to be absorbed.

The barrel tube broke down, as did one trawl line after another, and there was no money to fix the machinery, and then no money for gas. For a while they sorted the salt by hand, drying it and shaking it through large sieves, but once they realized they would not be selling any more salt, there was no longer any need to sort it, and they grew even more haphazard in their harvest and their storage, working now only with big shovels, simply piling the sludge in great heaps all around the edge of the lake.

Their well began to go dry, recharging more slowly, and with greater salinity each time — when they sweated now, they could feel the salt pushing its way through their pores, as if seeking to return to the lake. It seemed that the salt in their sweat was comprised now of coarser and coarser crystals, so that the once-pleasurable act of perspiring was now painful — and as the heated winds dried their skin almost immediately, the evaporating perspiration left salt crusts everywhere upon them, gritty as sand, so that to anyone who would have observed them, they would have appeared to be creatures made of salt.

Their well went completely dry, and Max Omo went sixty feet down into it, and was shoveling the salt out bucket by bucket, searching for one more seam of fresh water, and attempting to deepen the well, when the salt — as if, patient all his life, had only now become eager for him — shifted slightly, the shaft filling in on itself and swallowing him as if the bore hole had become a gullet; and though he had a rope fastened to him, and the boys above pulled and pulled, they couldn't raise him, and then the rope broke.

They went and got their shovels and began working, trying to find and clean out the well shaft, but it was four days before they reached the old water level, and they were not quite in the bore of the old hole, and had no idea whether their entombed father lay preserved to the north or south of them, nor even if he lay deeper still, or if they had passed him by, and he was floating somewhere in the salt above them.

They had been taking turns, hauling out bucket after bucket, as if carving out the marrow of a living earth; but now, down around the sixty-foot level, and without the reinforcement of timbers and spars, the salt began trying to flow back in over them too, so that they had to exit.

They constructed a cairn of old truck wheels and axles, old rusting cogs and gears, to mark the spot (within ten years, the salt had completely eaten that iron, leaving not even the whispers of clues), and they fled.

One went to work in the oilfields of East Texas, laboring to help drill shallow wells on the flanks of some of the old anticlines. He died of liver cirrhosis at the age of forty in a three-dollar-a-night hotel room outside Beaumont, and his last conscious thoughts were of the evening the elephant had come through, and of the excitement of pursuing it — the hounds baying, the men leaning into the great animal with driftwood pry bars, the multicolored campfire, and the small, quiet, strange foreigner — and of being below the elephant, digging with his brother, when the sand began to trickle past, the ledge collapsing, and someone shouting for them to get out of the way . . .

The other went north to Chicago, to work in the meatpacking industry, utilizing his great strength, which would stand him in good stead yet another twenty years before he, too, vanished from history, less than an asterisk, disappearing as Richard would: like seed-drift.

Neither of the boys ever saw their mother again, and in their wake, years later, young boys on the town's football team, almost men, continued to thunder down the streets of town, galloping like wild horses, perspiring, glorying in the quick breath of the brief strength, a strength not unlike that which the Omos had once possessed—a strength whose fullness had not even been reached yet: running each morning, pulling a wagon loaded with an orchestra, charging out of the dawn as if released from behind some gates or portals hidden deep within the earth; as if these children, only these and no others, had been waiting forever to be let out, and to storm the world with their power and quickness—almost giddy with the fierce belief that anything they did mattered. As if all the generations before them, the strata of dry bones, was but a rampart building for this generation, the true and important one—the living one.

Book Two

8

Mexico, or Underworld

1967–1975

A FTER LOSING CLARISSA, Richard fell in with bad characters down in Mexico: liars, thieves, charlatans, conmen of the
blackest hearts imaginable.

He had always moved among and amidst these men, working in the
oilfields of West Texas, but had been able before to keep them at arm's
length, focusing instead upon his labors.

In Mexico, however, isolate amidst a foreign culture and foreign
tongue, the oilmen were forced to band together in a small clan on the
outskirts of the village in which they were making their latest big play
(relentless self-dramatizers, they referred to it as their Last Great Play,
at the base of the Sierra Occidentals — though what Richard believed,
even as a young man, was that the world was huge, and that there
would always be one more great play, and then another, and then another).

Besieged as they were by loneliness, the independent oilmen — a
disparate and mongrel mix of Texan financial backers and renegade
politicians with part-time connections to the Mexican and United
States governments, Cajun roughnecks and north Mississippi and
south Alabama roustabouts and South Texas water-well drillers, self-
taught engineers who could drill a well with a broomstick and a rubber
band — men who could not, would not, be diverted from their goal,
regardless of what that goal was — gathered in the evening to drink
and talk.

United not just by their goal — cheap shallow oil and gas in a nation
not yet bound and hamstrung by environmental restrictions — the den

of rapscallions became not unlike a small community, gossiping and begrudging and yet remaining intensely loyal to one another.

They played cards in the evening and went into Rio Hondo, drinking and whoring and commandeering entire restaurants. They flew their little planes through the night sky and across and around the mountains while drunk, flying wherever and whenever they wanted, as if the little buzzing aircraft were nothing more than toy rides at an amusement park.

They flew with powerful spotlights and shone them down onto the desert floor, and into the oak and piñon forests of the mountains, where the beams, bright as comets, sought the reflecting red eyes of foxes and coyotes, deer and little wolves, jackrabbits and javelinas, which the oilmen pursued for sport. Sometimes they poked rifles and shotguns out through the popped-open vented windows, angling to get a shot.

Owls flew beneath them, ghostly in the glare of the spotlights, and the worst of the reprobates fired at the gliding birds below, as if the owls were not hunters like themselves but acted as some kind of shield, providing a net or layer of intervening grace separating the denizens of the desert floor.

They staged mock dogfights too, games of chicken in which their little planes would buzz one another, flying straight-on toward each other before flaring away at the last second — always, the rule was for each fighter to peel to the right. Sometimes, after they had fired into a herd of mule deer, securing what they called camp meat, they would land their planes on the desert, landing whenever and wherever they wanted — a gravel road, or even the floor of the desert itself — and with the rich scent of freshly chopped prickly pear sweet in the air from where the propeller had whacked out a swath upon landing, and the gin scent of crushed juniper beneath the plane's wheels, the oilmen spilled out onto the chalky, dusty desert and ran whooping after their wounded prey, baying like bloodhounds, following the injured animal sometimes by sight though other times by the crimson trail of blood.

They tripped and stumbled in gopher holes and ran over the backs of buzzing rattlesnakes; and often, the wounded bucks got away, leaving the oilmen to come straggling, lost and breath-heaving, back toward the plane. Often they could not find the plane again in the darkness and were forced to spend the night in the desert, bivouacked beneath a scraggly mesquite tree, no longer omnipotent, but as meek and lost as coyote pups, until the harsh flat light of desert morning revealed to them the next day the distant glint of their carriage, and they could stagger back to it, holding their heads with both hands to minimize the jar of each hung-over step.

Other times they found their quarry, sometimes stone dead though occasionally still living, in which case the rougher of the oilmen could be counted on to leap upon the dying animal with pocketknives or stones, putting the animal out of its misery, as they referred to it, before gutting the animal and then dragging it in a wandering backtrack that roughly approximated the blood-painted markings of the flight; and being the youngest, it was usually Richard who was called upon to sledge the carcass back toward the plane.

The brow tines of the deer's antlers would dig into his palm and wrist and forearm as he pulled it across the sand, and although he found the ritual unpleasant, he chose not to perceive that his own life had any other route; or rather, that this path to his other desires was the most feasible as well as the most mythic: and in his desire for the oil and gas just below, there was not much that he would not have done.

The men would shove and bend the taut carcass of the deer into the back of the plane as best as they could, smearing the fuselage with blood as they lifted the deer through the small door, so that the plane appeared to be anointed with some biblical waiver of immunity, some endowment of Passover: and crowding themselves back into their little chariots, and ascending back into the sky, the oilmen behaved as if they believed this was the case.

They knew no restraint, possessed no sense of governance, and they seemed to Richard — particularly in those brief moments when they were airborne — to possess a singular power, not just the strength of confidence, but of destiny. It seemed to him that their unending hunger was a source of liberation rather than a captivity; and although he knew better, he followed them, and sometimes even pretended to be one of them. Still falling.

On the return flights to their village, the excesses of the night before would conspire with the bounciness of the little planes and the heat of updrafts to release from some of their membership great expectorations of vomit. The pilots, flying in crude staggered-wing formations like miniature bombers, would call out the various updates of such distress to the passengers on the other planes, gleeful at the turmoil of their lily-livered compatriots, though chagrined, too, at having to experience it themselves; and while providing such reports, they would often key the microphone next to the face of the afflicted as he leaned bent over gagging into whatever makeshift container he had been able to snatch up.

The airwaves amidst all the planes would be amplified with the sound of that retching, the sky would rage with tortured gags, and the pilots ferrying those passengers who'd fallen ill would push the throttle all the way in and make downwind landings with flaps full up, fairly flying the planes into the ground in an effort to be free of the stench as soon as possible; and bailing out of the open doors even as the plane was not yet finished rolling to a stop, they would lie there in the blazing heat, gasping at fresh air, looking as if they had fallen straight from the sky.

Always, after such sojourns, they summoned one of the many slave-wage paisanos they kept at beck and call ready for such tasks, and while the oilmen crawled off to their air-conditioned bunkhouses to sleep the rest of the day away, if their drilling schedule would allow it, the paisanos would scrub away the damage, hosing the planes down, polishing and waxing them in the sun, and cleaning and butchering whatever bounty the great hunters had procured.

Later in the afternoon, the servants — "employees," the oilmen called them — would build a great fire in the open-pit barbecue ring they had dug in the center of the compound, and by nightfall the glowing mesquite coals would be radiating enough heat to bake to a porcelain glaze the sidewalls of the pit, with the deer being rotated slowly on a spit, basted with chipotle barbecue sauce, one small child applying the sauce with a broom as another child turned the crank of the spit like an organ grinder, both children's faces blistering from the heat, and with the succulent odor of fresh meat-juice spattering onto the coals.

The oilmen ate only meat — no fruit or fiber, no vegetables other than fried onions and fried potatoes, and drank salty margaritas, and smoked cigars and cigarettes, all except for Red Watkins, the driller, who would be dead before any of them.

Unlike the others, who tended to career through life with wild amplitudes of oversteering followed by violent correction, Red Watkins was neat in almost everything he did. On the rig floor, he made sure that his crew kept every tool in its precise place, so that in the event of a blowout or any other calamity, a roughneck could find the proper tools, even blindfolded. He insisted that his rigs be tended more carefully than would be animals or even men, resting them every seventh day (though he was not religious), and seeing that the filters and oil and other lubricating fluids were changed on every operating engine far in advance of schedule.

"Making hole," they called the act of drilling, just as "pulling pipe" meant they were coming out of the hole, for any of a number of different reasons, while "setting pipe" or "running casing" meant only one thing, that the oil or gas had been discovered, and the production pipe would be sent down into the hole and cemented, so that it could stay there forever, and would be perforated then, so that the oil and gas could flow out of the earth and into the wellbore and up the hole into the waiting world above, ready to be ignited — the oil industry composed of but perhaps half a hundred such two-word commands, as if even language was an impediment to the yearning to drill farther, drill deeper, make more hole, find more gas.

And even when the roughnecks were not making hole, even when the rig was resting, being hosed and cleaned and cooled for its Sabbath rest, Red Watkins made sure his workers were neither idle nor relaxed. He busied them with painting the pipe stands and the legs of the derrick in bright silver paint that was the same color as their hardhats, and the driller's doghouse cherry-red, and the stucco and adobe temporary office buildings near their encampment snow-white, even if they had just painted these things the week before. It was expensive and wasteful, they went through hundreds of buckets of paint each week, but Red Watkins was determined not to let the men go slack or soft with even a single idle or lazy Sunday afternoon, and so he worked them as if training them for some upcoming physical challenge for which they were not yet adequately prepared.

And once the new-old paint was scraped clean from that one item with its one blemish or imperfection, the roughnecks would begin painting again, working carefully in the heat to apply smooth and cautious strokes, so that there would be no roughness, no striation, only a bright and perfect gloss; and Red Watkins would follow along behind the workers, cruising past in his jeep (itself an open-topped, unpainted, sandblasted wreck of a thing), sipping a cold beer and squinting through his cat-eye glasses, his silver flattop haircut still burnished with the flecks of the same red he had been born with and once possessed in such abundance.

When the job was being done according to his satisfaction, he would smile a sweet smile of pure contentment — and this was a thing the roughnecks strove for, without quite understanding why, just as they sought to avoid the blue curses and tantrums, the scorn and invective Red Watkins would pitch if he discovered the job being done improperly.

But he never made a mistake, and for this he was viewed with awe and fear, if not quite respect. As well, he did the hiring and firing, and so for the roughnecks and roustabouts who populated the little camp (sleeping in their own separate bunkhouse, kept apart from the geologists and engineers), Red Watkins was more powerful than God. He did not deign to serve as the judge or arbiter of disputes, but instead merely sent both or all disaffected parties packing back to the States, so that beneath his command there was no dissent at the surface, only humming, straight-lipped efficiency, even if grievances and complaints writhed below in the men's souls like grubs in wormwood: and together, without exception, they chased the oil.

Red Watkins loved to cook. From his travels in the South, he had learned a great many recipes, knew the uses and tastes and sources of spices most of the other men had never even heard of, not just cumin and paprika and chili, but saffron and cardamom, Chinese five-spice and mirin; and he knew the effects of their various combinations.

At first glance his concoctions seemed flavorful, but simple — high fluffy creamy cathead biscuits, fried doves and quail, frog legs, venison tenderloin, roasted peppers stuffed with goat cheese, basil, and, strangely, peanuts, or olives, or the poached cheeks of fish; huge slabs of steak, embedded with nothing more than cloves of garlic and dressed with but a crust of olive oil and rosemary, nothing more.

But there was a perfection, a ferocity of control, both in their preparation and in their cooking, which brought out their best; and he knew how to arrange a menu, pairing those items — meat, potatoes, and a dessert — in a way that seemed to allow the food to transcend itself. He did not cook all the time, but the men looked forward to it when he did, and all that day, their work would be inspired.

He would puree Bing cherries and ancho chilies in his molasses and brown sugar barbecue sauce, would slice coins of ginger in with the mysterious black beans he kept simmering over a campfire in the desert heat for days on end, the beans taking on a vitreous, iridescent sheen of sweetness. He mixed shredded coconut into his cold buttered flaky pie crusts — almost always, just one or two slight and different elements were thrown into the mix, so that the food continued to masquerade as normal or average, only to explode with richness upon the palate — and, as with everything else in their lives, the men could not get enough.

Despite Red Watkins's neatness, there was waste, excess, in their temporary village, and at the well sites scattered beyond, across the desert and along the base of the mountains, and — as the searchers discovered more oil and gas — up into the mountains themselves, scabs of bright new roads ascending the canyons like stitches, with plumes of dust rising from the bone-white roads like the drift of smoke from ascending fires.

Because there was no surface water in the area, save for an occasional thin creek, each drilling well needed its own pit dug beside it, broad and shallow, in which the drilling fluid was kept, which was then circulated down into the hole to help lubricate the drill bit, to assist in better cutting and grinding, and to condition the hole to keep its shape.

The drilling mud — with tiny flecks of the gnawed-out stone floating in suspension — was then circulated back out of the hole. The drill cuttings were strained out of the fluid and examined minutely for any clues of oil or gas, scrutinized for lithology, color, taste, fossil content, all variables that might help the geologists ascertain where exactly they were in the lost landscape of their imaginations, two miles below, and poured back into the waiting open pit of brown froth, where a mud man, diligent as a baker, kept close watch on the density and pH and clay content of the vile brown soup, which steamed slightly from its brief contact with the heated innards of the earth's distant interior.

There were no regulations, requirements, or restrictions regarding the construction and maintenance of the mud pits (which also housed waste oil and diesel fuel from the various workhorse engines required in lifting the great gleaming tonnages of drilling pipe in and out of the holes); and because the mud pits that were springing up around the drilling operations represented the only surface water for miles, all manner of wildlife began flocking to the pits, seeking nourishment and respite from the desert's anvil of heat.

Rendered bold by their need, the animals usually waited until night to get into the pits, though when they came (the drilling rigs ran twenty-four hours a day, six days a week), the animals did so wantonly, walking right past the roughnecks' parked cars and trucks and on out into the shallow mud pits, wading straight in like penitents seeking baptism.

The animals — coyotes and deer, foxes, skunks, bighorn sheep, wild turkeys and bobcats, and an occasional black bear — would drink greedily from the thick, toxic slurry — which usually had a skim of an inch or two of water floating atop the heavier drilling mud, like cream separating from the milk below — and then they would roll luxuriantly in the chocolate-milkshake-colored mud, splashing, while the roughnecks on the drilling platform above looked down in wonder, the mud pit illuminated at night by the brilliant halogen blaze of the rig's Christmas-tree lights, wattage so powerful and incandescent that the lights of each rig were visible at any distance upon that planar landscape (a flatness that belied the exciting jumble of topography below, the architecture of the past), and even visible, or so the geologists had been told, from space.

Once the animals had drunk from the toxic pond, it usually took fifteen or twenty minutes for the sickness to settle in. It afflicted the smaller animals first, so that sometimes they died outright and sank to the bottom of the pit, where they were later fished out by the roughnecks, bloated carcasses slimed elephant-gray with the silt at the bottom of the pits—though usually the animals were able, despite their discomfort, to lunge back to the banks of the pit, where, with a caking of mud draped over them now as heavy as concrete, they would collapse a short distance away, lungs heaving and internal organs poisoned.

On their brief smoke or lunch breaks, the roughnecks would hurry down from the catwalk and hose the gray and brown drying layer of mud from the coats of those animals still living, and would drag them over into the shade of the drilling rig, so that by the time the stalking heat of the day returned, the sick and dying animals might know some peace and comfort; and just as the mounds of chipped drill cuttings grew like anthills at the site of each well's location, so too did the pyre of bloated carcasses of the bestiary that had been summoned by the allure of the mud, and the promise of water in the desert.

Birds, too, settled into the mud pits, not just migratory waterfowl but colorful little songbirds passing back and forth to the tropics, struggling in the mud with oil-soaked wings, as bedraggled now as moths: and in the early years, the oilmen had attempted to pull these victims out, dabbing them each in a bucket of valuable fresh water, and spending hours, sometimes, on each wing—the same men who days earlier had been machine-gunning the night sky, and shredding even the beauty of the stars with their violence: though the searchers had other tasks and chores, and the sky was filled with birds, they could in no way begin to keep pace with the steady supply of birds that kept funneling into their pits, so that eventually they gave up and allowed their hearts to harden, and became accustomed to that waste.

Richard would lie there some nights, occasionally in the bunkhouse but more often crooked and cramped in the back seat of his car, catnapping between bit trips, with the diesel clatter of the rig as familiar and even lulling to him now across the years as the sound of distant surf breaking, and it would seem that Clarissa's leaving, her fear, had carved in him a gash or rend, the exact shape of which he could still feel, and that even with years passing, the flow from that wound could not be stanched; that he could still hear it trickling away.

Lying there, just before sleep, in those fragments of moments where he was not occupied by his work, he would be forced to wonder, *What do I want — what do I want next?* He felt off-balance, not knowing what he desired — desiring nothing, really, hunting the oil below almost dispassionately, in cold blood — as anomalous, with that absence of desire, among the other oilmen, as might be a foreigner who did not speak their language.

He envied the oilmen, with their crude and simple and seemingly bottomless desires, chasing a past that lay miles below. They seemed to him to be hostages of another kind, but intensely and deeply alive. They did not seem to be visitors in the world.

The desert, with the blue-and-buff chaparral of the Sierra Occidentals just to the west, the soft foothills reminding him of the contours of a woman's body that might never age. What was it about a desert landscape, he wondered, that produced such needs and appetites, such oversized dreamers and flash-in-the-pan pretenders?

Was it this way always for any landscape of outer limits, he wondered — landscapes defined by absence, rather than presence? Perhaps some excessive, even childish, yearnings arose as if from the soil itself in some inhospitable environments, any strife-filled borderland near or even just beyond the edge of comfort.

And yet: these pirates with whom he was associating were not all charlatans; and their dreams and desires, even if outlandish and fevered, were not unattainable. They had dreamed a thing, scenting it at first as an animal might imagine cool and distant water, and they had moved toward it like men possessed by a purer truth, abandoning their past lives and stepping recklessly into the future: and what they had found in the desert and the foothills was not a dream, but tangible and real as the men themselves.

Always, they found just enough of their treasure to be termed successful, to sustain and reward them, and to lure them and encourage them to proceed onward: *Más allá,* farther on.

The entire consortium possessed the most hardy and enduring of constitutions. Many of the men had significant physical strength, but also a toughness. They would crawl away from their semicontrolled crash landings, and their twenty-four-hour nonstop revelry, and go straight back to work when the occasion called for it, which was often.

Back into the fields the oilmen threw themselves, laboring for forty or fifty hours at a time, unabetted by any drugs: doing whatever was required of them — logging the wells, drilling out bridge plugs, analyzing cuttings, and skidding rigs to new locations; and they gloried in their labor and their desire, reveling in it every bit as much as they did their play times. They were like sailors, Richard thought. He had often envisioned the unseen stony landscape far below as being implacable as the heart of a frozen sea; and in the oilmen's after-hours revelry, they seemed like crewmembers on wild shore leave.

It was estimated that it would take them eight to ten years to properly define and tap into the reservoir, whose shapes were still unknown to them.

Only the rigs above the reservoir moved, probing and searching, penetrating; and if the stone below was the deepest and most unknowable of oceans, and the men above (he never wondered why there were no women; who would want to be among such men?) were indeed sailors, then, in the moving waves up at the surface, they were all chasing the slipstreams of wealth that snaked and wound their way in wild and mysterious arcs, ancient loops and patterns of logic that existed just beneath the feet of the unsuspecting.

In addition to the curiously aggressive Red Watkins, with his wildly alternating spells of placidity, even tenderness, and ill-temper, there were two others within the consortium who took an interest in Richard, and who were grooming him for the arc of a longer future, a corporate life spent pursuing the riches of South America and China, Russia, Africa, and — always the prize plum — the Middle East.

Simon Craven was a financier from Dallas, and previously London, whose dreams and appetites were so large that he was frustrated by the smaller successes, deeming as failures any wells that tested initial flows of less than five hundred barrels per day. Impatient and edgy, he had a hawk's face and dark brown eyes, was tall and dressed always in white, and wore a Panama hat.

Only occasionally had Richard seen him look happy. Whenever a wildcat blew out or tested in excess of a thousand barrels a day, Craven — the consortium called him Sy — would burst into song, with tunes and lyrics that seemed to bear no connection whatsoever to the event at hand. Present on the scene of such success, he was as likely to begin braying "The Yellow Rose of Texas" as he was "Oh, Danny Boy," or even a gospel hymn; and in some instances he had launched into song even as the bodies of workers who had been killed in the blows were still being hauled away.

The laborers he utilized were neither skilled nor rare, they were as common and relentless and desperate as ants, and he was not shy about admitting his values — the discovery of one more rank wildcat was worth, or superior to, any number of Mexican laborers — and not shy either about his hopes for and interest in Richard, who, having sharpened his skills on the distant Paleozoic oceans beneath Odessa, was proving, despite his youth, to be one of Sy's better geologists.

Richard had never seen Sy look relieved or at peace — only taut and pensive, or exuberant — and, even more so than with the aging Red Watkins (whose blotchy face belied countless cold beers drunk, and countless sunburns), Richard received the impression from Sy Craven that such a lifelong leaping between ferocity and exuberance was not sustainable, and that Craven's days might be even more numbered than the frail and fading old driller's.

As Red Watkins's ill health seemed to be etching itself more and more plainly upon Watkins's surface, across the years, so too did Sy Craven's seem to be building within him far below, and all the more potent and deadly for its not being seen.

The other investor in Richard's well-being and development was a semiretired prospector, a man named George Waller, who possessed just enough geological and financial and drafting skills to be able to ex-plain and sell the prospects generated by the staff. Whereas Sy Craven seemed to take extra caution in mollycoddling Richard, and making sure he was treated with respect — grooming him for future continents — George Waller was uneasy with Richard's skill, and the reliance he found himself having to place upon the young man.

George Waller dreaded ceding control to anyone or anything, and it unnerved him greatly that Richard had so much more knowledge of the world beneath the world, the world that Waller was responsible for selling, sometimes to dupes and stooges, though other times to qualified and knowledgeable partners and investors who sought, at great premium, to join in on the play.

If Sy Craven's relationship to Richard was cautious and delicate yet candid and open in its predatory nature — not unlike that of a man choosing twigs in an attempt to start a fire, upon whose flame the fire starter's continued survival depends — then George Waller's relationship to the young geologist was almost the exact opposite, an exhausting and debilitating mix of passive-aggressive bullying and wheedling that was completely fear-based.

Craven's fear was not that Richard might leave — he understood the young man was too wounded, and needy, and too desperately hot, like all the rest of them, upon the elusive slipstream trail of the oil and gas — but feared rather that Richard might simply not develop to the fullest of his talent.

And so Sy Craven sought to nurture him, almost as if in love with him. As if in love with the future.

Waller's fear was more immense: that Richard would fail, or that he would abandon the consortium at their most critical time of need. Some of the structural and stratigraphic traps that Richard was mapping were so complicated and unlikely-seeming that they were often hard for Waller to fully comprehend, much less sell to other partners.

Waller was usually able to mask his unfamiliarity or discomfort with the strange prospects and their fractured logic (the unconformities in time and lithology, the radial faulting, and the overreliance, in Waller's opinion, upon delicate and invisible permeability barriers) by referring to the prospects as "sophisticated" — even as he himself knew better than anyone that at this level, there was no investor worth his salt who would buy into any of these larger prospects without understanding them inside and out.

And yet, the prospects kept striking oil and gas, and the consortium kept pumping and siphoning it up out of the ground, so that soon enough, a not-so-subtle transformation began to take place, in which George Waller found that investors were wanting to know which geologist had authored the map they were looking at; that George Waller was now selling the geologist as much as the geology. And again, this reliance upon the surface, and upon the present, made him uncomfortable, resentful of the power Richard held — even if unasked for — over the success or failure of George Waller's selling of the packages.

In a perverse way, Richard's successes were even making it harder for George Waller to sell other perfectly good prospects — and for this, too, Waller found himself nurturing a swelling resentment.

As a way of reasserting some degree of control over the younger man (George Waller was in his early sixties, had spent all his life in the oilfield; had been present at the end of the Spindletop play, had made and lost half a hundred fortunes, and twice as many enemies), Waller had taken to calling Richard by nicknames, which he did with anyone by whom he felt threatened, or toward whom he felt aggressive, which was almost everyone. An investor who had fallen on hard times and who had had to leave the consortium, Buckminster Williams, became Bucky Boy, and then, falling farther into the abyss of gone-by time, Buckfuck, while Waller sought to imprison other associates with simple names like Mr. D and Happy Man and Señor Maximum.

His various attempts at redefining and owning Richard, even if briefly — for the few moments in which the shadow of the name lingered — included Cave Man (due to the fact that, unlike the others, Richard eschewed the opulence of the oil culture) and Wonderboy. (Other times, when the aggression was barely manageable, it was Boy Wonder.)

Richard had been confused by George Waller at first, taken in initially by the man's manners and smile and general effusiveness. It made no sense to Richard, but it seemed to him more than ever — particularly since he had dared to see all the way into, and still love, Clarissa

—that the more experienced he became at peering beneath the flat surface of a landscape, reaching down into the unseen vision of the folded layers hidden below, the more accurately he was able to likewise cipher the hearts of the men and women he encountered.

A human being was nothing like a mountain range, nor was even the coldest heart like any stone. But it seemed to Richard that in learning to look for, and see, the one thing, he had developed skills that allowed him to perceive the other. He understood immediately that the height of George Waller's grimaced-smile fawning — teeth bared like those of a skeleton's — was matched only by a corresponding depth of resentment and loathing; and he was cautious around Waller, even as he spent an increasing amount of time in the older man's company, explaining the prospects to him. And when Waller still failed to understand them, Richard would explain to him how to at least talk about them as if he did; how to sell them, how to promote them. And this was deeply frustrating to Richard, for it took away from the time in which he could be exploring and generating new prospects.

And though if Richard had been asked about it, he would have opined that he considered himself to be outside the club, isolate and separate not just in his talent, but also by disposition, a truth he had not yet realized was that he had been absorbed by the oilmen nonetheless. They had not yet consumed him, but he had been swallowed. He had no goals other than the finding of more oil. In this, he was not quite a taker — was more of a giver — though his appetites were no different from their appetites, and there was nothing in the world before him but oil, and nothing in his life now but the past.

They were all dying, all of them — Red Watkins, Richard knew, and Sy Craven, quavering between his torments for more, always more, like a leaf of paper that has just settled into a flame but has not yet ignited, and George Waller, whose soul was not so much rotting as simply funneling down some vast drain, with Waller not even making the slightest attempt to grasp or claim it.

They were all in varying stages of spiritual decay — even Red Watkins, with his old man's childish rages, a hostage, as in infancy, to his temper — and yet still Richard considered himself apart from them; as if, by virtue of his observing these things in them, he had rendered himself immune.

Their emotional deaths were masked, too, by the wrack of their aging bodies. A lifetime of exposure to Halliburton fracturing fluids, benzenes and acetones, ammonia nitrate and sulfuric acid, and all the other brimstone aromas of their profession, coupled with long hours, the hot sun, and wanton alcoholism, had conspired to dash against the rocks the strength they had once possessed in their youth, little different from Richard's own strength — and yet here, too, Richard thought that because he could see these things clearly, he was immune.

As his years in Mexico advanced and he rose higher in the company, being assigned greater interests and royalties in his various prospects, assembling more wealth and gaining ever-more knowledge of the secret and tangled traps of the old lands below, he watched as one by one the older geologists and drillers began to totter, nearing collapse: though still they soldiered on, as if the oil was their god, and their work their prayer.

Goiters began to mount on some of the oilmen while their muscle mass withered year by year, so that it was as if they were being turned inside out, becoming as knobby as a blighted riverbed, bright cobble baking chalk-white in the sun.

Syphilitic chancres began erupting like tiny geysers on many of them, legacy of countless trips to whorehouses around the world, the sores drying and cracking in the desert sun as their immune systems faltered.

Only Richard moved among them untouched.

Tough as nails, however — tougher, he suspected, than he could ever dream of being — they kept on, in many instances hiring their surgeons and physicians to come work on them out in the field to save time, and to prescribe fairly radical treatments. They had all had their prostates sawed out at one time or another, and even those who fell prey to the most dire of prognoses chose work over everything else, so that more than ever work became a prayer for them; and Richard moved with them, adjusted his rhythms and patterns to match theirs, and continued falling, tumbling with them through space and time, even as he continued to believe himself apart from them.

There was a tally, a running total of interest points, charted by Sy Craven, in which each geologist (as well as the engineers and production personnel) was assigned little ownerships in the world below, which, at the end of their service, they would be able to convert to ownership in the company, claiming their proportionate shares not just of all the oil and gas the company had produced and sold, but all that which had been discovered and claimed, residing beneath the desert floor and stretching up into the mountains in hidden lobes and fingers.

None of the geologists or other specialists had ever claimed their percentages — the caveat in doing so was that they had to retire — and though any one of them could have done so and walked away rich, heirs to the spoils as well as the fruit of a foreign country, so deeply had they fallen into the spirit of the chase — so fully had it become the sinew of their lives — that they would have been bereft without it, and would sooner have renounced their names or even their lives before they abandoned their profession, or the joy of and glory in working in the Sierra Occidentals, and one of the greatest inland plays in recent history. It had been decades since such a reservoir had been found, and almost anyone who knew about such things said that there would never be another one like it.

There were ten-year packages, and twenty-year severances, and thirty-year plans designed. The most durable among them, Red Watkins, had been with Sy Craven for forty-two years. No one left.

Each day that they went out into the flat pan of the desert and then up into the foothills of the charred landscape that was often still burning or smoldering from their recent revelry with the planes, they were each keenly aware of their power and luck. "Luckier than pigs in shit," was how Red Watkins described it some evenings, standing up on the throbbing derrick floor, watching the dusk of the desert come creeping in, painting the mountains in alpenglow.

Richard would study the old driller and wonder what Clarissa might

202 • RICK BASS

have made of him. It was possible there had never been an uglier or more grizzled human being. His beauty lay in the fact that he knew how to get the oil, any oil, all oil, out of the ground. His beauty lay in the volume of oil and gas he had sucked out already over the course of his life, like some mythic dragon, enough to belch plumes of flame that would scorch the world; enough oil to erase the beauty that had yielded it.

His beauty lay in the fact that he alone among them had transcended his hunger — finally — and yet still, he continued on, farther on.

Sy Craven was not a slouch of a geologist himself. He recognized what Richard was doing with his prospects, understood the aggressiveness with which Richard approached his maps, pushing or following his pencil into unknown territory. Like Richard, Craven had learned to see clearly beneath the surface of men as well as mountains, and like a conjurer, what he saw below Richard's surface troubled him; and although Craven felt fairly certain that he would have no trouble getting Richard to the ten-year mark — another two years' worth of oil — he sometimes had trouble convincing himself that he could be guaranteed another ten years of labor on top of that, much less another twenty or thirty years.

There were so many other places in the world where Craven wished to turn Richard loose, like a hound on the scent of a wounded stag; but with that sorcerer's clarity, Craven saw the possibility that once Richard's pain and disillusionment settled, and the scar tissue formed thick enough, Richard might not see the need any longer to construct maps as daring — and successful — as he was now drafting.

Sometimes Sy Craven would probe like a physician, trying to find and open back up the scars of memory. "A young man needs a partner," he said. "Someone to go through life with. Or some young men do." He studied Richard, pretending to only now be speculating about such matters. "But you had your shot, didn't you?" he asked.

"Yes," said Richard. "I had my shot."

Still, Craven would be worried, would feel vulnerable and exposed, but could find no way to gain control over his youngest geologist. He knew that Richard was not by nature a quitter, and yet it seemed to him increasingly that Richard was like some of the wild animals that sometimes came through camp, down from out of the mountains.

Wilder than the deer and antelope that bent their heads to drink from the toxic sludge-ponds, or even to wade out some short distance into and then wallow in those ponds, were the occasional visitors from farther back: not just the black bears and coyotes, but the little Mexican wolves, and, in a drought year, an occasional grizzly bear, and once or twice, a jaguar. The crew rarely saw such animals — the animals managed to stay just beyond the throw of rig light, just on the other side of the pond — though the next day, checking the mud pits, the crew would find their fresh tracks in the powdery dust, and would sometimes even find the carcass of a deer or antelope which the predatory visitor had pulled out of the mud pit, as if to save it, only then to consume it.

The carcass would be torn open, and the pooling blood still warm and uncoagulated, with the destruction so recent that the desert flies had not yet even discovered it: and though the roughnecks and drillers would hurry back up to the rig floor and stare out toward the mountains in that morning's first light, they would never see the departing visitor; though each time, they were convinced they would be able to glimpse the shambling hulk of bear, or the gliding shadow of dappled jaguar, its coat the color of sunlight, tail floating behind it like a kite string: or even the lobos, half a dozen of them spread out and loping.

Always, however, there was nothing, only those tracks, which might as well have been left by ghosts, were they not as fresh and recent as the pencil erasings from the readjusted contour lines on one of Richard's maps from the night before: as if the landscape below was returning to life and beginning to flow once more, no longer secretive, but known, and emerging, or reemerging.

The past less of a ghost now than the present.

Sy Craven grew more convinced that he was losing Richard. He refused to believe that Richard would leave before his ten-year investiture — but beyond that ten-year mark, he could no longer envision a future with Richard attached to either Craven's leash, nor the earth's.

There was no one thing, no particular clue, which led him to believe this, only his own fears and instincts, his own subconscious ways of knowing. Some nights he dreamed that Richard had gone out into the desert at night with the wolves and bears and jaguars — that he moved among even larger creatures: elephants, and the shadowy visages of mammoth-like hulks. He dreamed that Richard was crawling through the desert on his hands and knees with a little pickax, digging small objects from out of the sand and stone and pocketing them — that he was keeping them secret from the rest of the consortium, that he was not reporting them — and in his dream, Sy Craven leaned closer, desperate in the darkness to know what treasures Richard was pursuing, but was unable to identify them, sensing only that they were objects of incalculable worth, somehow possessing more value than all of the oil and gas that lay buried at various depths beneath the disintegrating sediment of the Sierra Occidentals.

And Sy Craven would wonder later that same day, or the next, about the nature of the woman who was no longer with Richard; wondered if he would survive her or not.

There were times when Richard went into the mountains not in dreamtime, but in real life, in the full daylight; times when, increasingly, he chose not to accompany the rest of the consortium into any of the border towns or parlors in which they sought their entertainment, but instead traveled farther up into the hills, and then up into the black volcanic rocks, the reefs and castles and turrets of the mountains themselves, where giant golden eagles nested, and bighorn sheep climbed like magicians up and over improbable spires.

He found springs in the mountains, in which clear water trickled two and three feet deep, little pools with black sand beaches stippled with the fresh tracks of the comings and goings of every denizen of the mountains, and with — and this seemed to him to be the wildest miracle — little fish, top-water Gambusia minnows, flitting back and forth through vertical beams of underwater sunlight, their eyes as bright as coins, each no larger than the head of a pin.

Had they been swept up in waterspouts or the violent dust devils that sometimes caterwauled across the lowlands, spinning and whirling before being deposited here and only here, guided and directed to this pool by nothing less than the hand of God? Had passing birds likewise brought them to this one spot, in desiccated eggs or packed tight in the birds' gullets, regurgitating them accidentally and yet by fate into these saving waters?

Richard had no idea. He could reconstruct a deadened earth below, and every one of its mysteries both vast and minute; but of the processes of life above, such as how a minnow made it up into a mountaintop vernal pool, he was uncertain. He would lie there for hours, on his belly in the cool sand, watching the minnows: sometimes trying to figure it out, and other times just watching them.

The birds' songs would surround him. They darted out over the hidden watering hole to snap and peck midair at translucent shimmering-wing insects rising from the water's surface, and then returned to their perches in the willows to consume the insects, nipping them into pieces in three neat bites, head, thorax, and abdomen, while avoiding the delicate wings, which, when disembodied, fell fluttering to the sand like the scales of dragons, and gathered in small glittering wind-drift piles.

No one knew of the vernal ponds. There were pictographs on some of the blackened basalt faces from travelers hundreds or perhaps thousands of years ago; rock etchings on the brooding boulders, stick figures of men with spears, men hunting, dragging the carcasses of deer and antelope and bighorn sheep behind them, as he and his compatriots had done: though in none of the pictographs was there the image of a man lying on his belly in the black sand, staring into the clear waters.

And for some reason this made Richard feel better, made him feel that he was on some grand adventure, and was to some degree different from all the thousands of generations of the race of men who had lived before him.

No one had traveled this path ever before: not the path he had taken, nor — and this was what began to remind him to feel joy, and to know courage again — the path that remained before him.

There were no other sounds but the tanagers and warblers, and the desert-dry summer clack of grasshoppers, the occasional buzzing wing-clatter of dragonflies — outlandish primitive dinosaurs whose fossils, like the horsetails, he had found in his diggings.

No other sounds. No drone of planes from the geologists engaged in their mock dogfights, no lisp and hiss and suction-gasp rattle of faraway pumpjacks: only mountain silence.

What if, he wondered during one such outing, his entire life, and all that he had already known and lost, had been, instead of the peak of excess, nowhere near enough?

What if all that — Clarissa's beauty, and the freedom and exploration in the country beyond Odessa — had been as but a paucity, compared to all that was yet to come?

He listened more intently to the silence beneath the birdsong and blaze of sun, and beneath the whorl of dragonflies. It seemed there was another sound, one that had been present all along, but which he had not noticed, and which only now in his mind was he able to separate and unravel from the thread of farther silence.

It was a murmuring, trickling sound, fainter than a whisper. The water at the far end of the pond was stirring slightly, as if the breath of a breeze had found it, or as if some small creature labored just beneath the surface, preparing to rise.

Some of the water was dabbed up by the birds, and some of it, without question, had been drunk by humans, century after century; and that which was not utilized by ferns or flowers or wolves sank then unclaimed back down into the sand and the basalt fissures below, draining away surely into nothingness, and never-knowingness — a quick glimpse of the sunlit world above, and then back down into eternal darkness — and yet the pictographs bore witness that no matter how low the pond got, the spring always filled it back up, patient and ceaseless; and that over the years, the world had adjusted to accommodate the taking with the giving.

It was this balance, the equipoise, that he felt so deeply, lying there at water's edge, staring at the minnows. He could feel, finally, his own well recharging; and being at heart and by practice as much of a taker as a giver, he began only now, finally, to believe that it was his time to take again: that all of the millions of barrels of oil, and billions of cubic feet of gas he had found and taken in the last few recent years, had been as but a sport and a pastime, compared to what he had had, briefly, before, and had lost.

With even those blessings — Clarissa, and the strength of his innocence — having been, he saw now, not enough.

There was a creek, a small river, the Rio Madeira, that wandered along
the country between the foothills and the desert, some twenty miles
south of the consortium's main play. They had sunk a few test wells
down in that region, trying to define the farthest reaches of the field in
that direction, and had pretty much satisfied themselves that that was
the outer reaches of their play — that the Rio Madeira was the remnant
of an old fault that climbed from deep beneath the mountains, the
same fault that had birthed the mountains and estranged them from
the desert — and that on the other side of that river, no oil or gas could
be found.

Nonetheless, because it was the nearest known surface water of any
significance (Richard had told no one of his discovery in the mountains), this was where the geologists went to recreate, now and again
— to ride in the ripply current in inner tubes, leather-skinned paunchy
old men gripping cold bottles of beer and smoking cigars, wearing
sunglasses but hatless, broiling to the color of lobsters beneath the sun,
drifting and bumping along beneath sycamores and cottonwoods, riding the Madeira past bleached-white beaches as if content to follow the
lost river all the way into some nether world.

And it was a lost river. In times of drought it would disappear beneath the surface for hundreds of yards at a time, so that, cursing and
grieving, the oilmen would have to stagger to their feet and tuck their
inner tubes under one hand and grip their ice chests in another, and
stumble on bruised and tender feet across the bare stones, limping and
gimping bowlegged that farther distance like penitents, if they desired
the pleasure of riding again with the river, which reemerged always
some distance ahead.

Campesinos from as far away as sixty miles would show up at the
river likewise, to swim and picnic, with the ambiguities of the river,
the challenging path across the hot bare stones, the cold beer, and,
above all, always, the broiling desert sun providing a great democracy
of equality — and on those occasional off-days when the oilmen traveled down to the Madeira to cool off in the water and to leer at the

wives and sisters and daughters of paisanos, it was possible for almost all of them, both castes, to forget that just to the north the oilmen were presiding over the creation of a wealth that would eventually prove to be so vast as to subsume perhaps even the biblical descriptions of heaven, with streets of gold and gates of marble and pearl.

Some of the campesinos worked as drill hands at the compound, while others labored in the kitchen, or as janitorial staff, at subminimum wages that were still greater by a factor of ten than anything else they could be earning. (The drug trades had not begun flourishing, but instead lay nascent, like a river gone back underground for a stretch of time.)

Millionaires and paupers alike sat in the shade beneath the sycamores, the white and tan bark flaking in great puzzle-piece peels, and the pale-skinned oilmen brilliant ivory, and few in number, compared to the dozens of native river-goers, their own skin dark and coppery.

In the early autumn of Richard's eighth year in the Sierra Occidentals, during the period of lowest water, on a Sunday, while driving down to the Rio Madeira one day — the geologists in a long caravan of open-topped jeeps, drinking beer already at ten o'clock on a Sunday morning, and bouncing along dusty cowtrails and crossing back and forth across the cobbly river, splashing over the shallow fords and crossings in which the water barely even came up to the axles — George Waller, who was driving one of the jeeps, looked downstream into one of the deeper holes and happened to see an immense black shape suspended in the clear waters, finning slowly.

He stopped the jeep midriver, disbelieving — it was easily the biggest catfish any of them had ever seen — and what was more amazing to them was that it was trapped in the deep pothole; that due to its great size — as large as a hog — it had run out of water sufficient to sustain its mass.

It must have slithered and bumped its way down from some series of upper, deeper pools, they speculated, until finally it had run out of water just below the crossing, and had taken refuge in the pool into which they were now staring, the deep hole that was not much larger than a tub, but with no way out until the river rose again, which would not happen until the rains of winter.

"That motherfucker is ours," George Waller said, getting out of the jeep and splashing out to the pool where the fish lay trapped. The other oilmen followed.

They gathered around the stony basin, the warm shallow water flowing past them in a sheet. Little minnows darted past, collided against their ankles, and the catfish's only response was to sink deeper, lowering himself another three feet, to the bottom of his tomb, though there was no movement of fins or muscle that the oilmen could discern: he appeared simply to decide to sink.

"He's sulking," George Waller said. "My God, what a fish." They stood there admiring him, and before a full second had passed, George Waller announced, "Let's eat him."

The other oilmen knew what he was talking about. It was their custom every several months to hold a cookout, partly as a way of treating the local workers and their families to a feast to engender continued goodwill toward their employers, though also out of some deeper need for hunter-gatherer or even agricultural ritual, for they usually planned the barbecues to coincide with the logging of an important well.

A cow would be slaughtered and butchered and cooked in its entirety, or three or four hogs, or a dozen goats, while the oilmen tried to visit among the locals, who stood in the heat next to the blazing coals with plates heaped high and who smiled nervously at the cluster of oilmen who approached them, attempting their pidgin Spanish.

The oilmen were jumpy, too, on such occasions — nervous about the well's chances for success — and this act, this offering, was as close to prayer as any of them got.

This fish, despite its immensity, wasn't large enough to serve all the part-time workers and their friends and family, but George Waller wanted to take it downstream to show the families congregated on the beach nonetheless; wanted to capture it and display it as a symbol and marker of his prowess in the world — though there was still some salvageable part of him, some dim place of instinct, that rebelled against the notion of killing such a magnificent animal, and that desired to keep it alive for as long as possible.

The men continued to stare down at the fish as if into a well. The engineers began to consider the logistics. George Waller was of the opinion that someone "young and strong" should lower himself into the pool, gaff the giant fish through the mouth — there was barely room in the pool for the fish to turn around — and then fasten a rope to the gaff and walk the fish downstream, leading it through the shallows, as if walking a dog.

Richard laughed; he was willing — he envisioned himself riding the fish briefly as he wrestled it, its back nearly as broad as a pony's — but in the end, the capture was far simpler than any of them could have imagined, for the fish was famished, having been trapped for weeks, and when they lowered a crude hook made of twisted wire into the well, baited with nothing more than one of the rolled-up tortillas the cooks had made that morning, the catfish swallowed it immediately, then whirled as the point of the hook bit through its lip and sunk deep into the cartilage of its mouth.

For fishing line, the geologists were using the cotton string with which they marked and surveyed new well locations, and as the fish cleared its pool and began trying to slither and muscle its way downriver, wriggling through three or four inches of water like some changeling unleashed upon the world, some of the men turned and ran, and slipped and fell down hard in the shallows.

George Waller commanded Richard to "Get him!" — shouting in an urgent falsetto that the men would later mimic, and for which George Waller would not forgive Richard. And without quite knowing why he did so, Richard splashed along behind the fish, which, despite its mass, was making slow progress, its strength robbed by the absence of water; and Richard was able to subdue it easily by wrapping his arms around its broad back, as if he were bulldogging a steer in a rodeo.

The other men gathered themselves, bruised and dripping and embarrassed now, and came sloshing over to examine the stilled and panting fish. Red Watkins, who had not entered the fray, but who had been standing on shore watching and laughing, called out to them to be sure to keep its skin wet — the fish didn't have to be kept in water, only his gills needed to stay wet, and as long as they kept water splashed on him, he would stay alive — and so now, like children, the oilmen crouched beside their strange prize again and began to splash him, tentatively at first, but then with purpose, splashing Richard and the fish together, and they began to laugh, not mockingly nor as victors or conquerors, but only because they were happy.

They led the catfish back upstream, three and four of them hauling on it at a time. The engineers piled up towels to plug the seam along the tailgate and filled the back of the jeep with water, scooping it from the river with an empty ice chest. They lifted the catfish into the back of the jeep — despite the fish's weeklong fast, its white belly sagged and hung heavy, as if it had been swallowing basketballs — and they finished fording the crossing and drove on south along the river road, passing beneath the dappled shade of the riverside trees, the broad green leaves of summer casting rippling shadows upon the men and their jeeps, so that seen from above, it might have seemed that they, too, were just beneath the surface, and swimming.

The villagers who were down at the river that day gathered in great numbers around the fish, disbelieving as it banged around in the back of the jeep, unruly as a calf. The villagers reached in and touched its wetted back, thrilled by the power of the shudder that ran through the fish and into them as they did so, and they regarded the oilmen anew, as if having misjudged them, for most of what they did was below ground, as little seen or understood as work performed by smoke and mirrors; but this fish, real and tangible, seemed to offer some evidence of worth or talent on their part, and appeared to give refutation to a previously held opinion of the oilmen that had been less than favorable.

The landscape would be altered and then broken here, as it was everywhere they passed, made eventually unfamiliar even to the old men and women who had been born there — each new well, and each new road crisscrossing the desert and the mountains, burying their homelands with incremental abuse, and with their rarest and most vital of fluids, the groundwater, being slowly poisoned by the contamination and intrusion of all the drilling fluids — and yet, fifty years later, when the villagers were asked about the oilmen, and of what those times had been like, it would not be the pristine, immemorial desert landscape that had existed before the geologists had arrived that they spoke of, but instead, almost exclusively, the big fish.

They had seen the fish only briefly, that one day, strange as an alien, and stranger still for having been neither summoned nor suspected. It would become the watchword for how they thought of, and discussed, the oilmen ever after — not as the ones who had built a glittering civilization of pipelines and wellheads in the desert. Instead, they would remember them as the men who had produced from the desert a far more miraculous thing, the giant fish, glimpsed briefly but more real than any vaporous gas or rumor of wealth below: a creature twice as large as any of them would have guessed could exist, black as the desert sky at night, with long whiskers and sharp little teeth. A devourer of ducks and rabbits and perhaps even fawns; a behemoth and leviathan, and a creature wholly and totally dependent upon water, great amounts of water.

Rather than inviting the villagers, laborers, and their families, George Waller decided to throw a party for the fish, and he hired a boy to keep the fish alive for the three days before the event. Prostitutes would be flown in from Mexico City, a band from Vera Cruz, and caviar from Russia, via Houston. (None of the oilmen cared for the taste of caviar, but they ate it at such soirees nonetheless, suffering it as one of the necessary prices for asserting the privilege of flaunting their wealth. There was not a man among them who came from old money; they had each scrapped and fought their way into affluence, and in this, too, they were united.)

There was no clean water pit or tank in which to place the fish. The geologists did not want him living in the back of any of the jeeps, which were needed for field duty, and so for three days the boy, Tomás —fourteen years old, but small for his size and appearing younger— squatted beside the gasping fish, which was laid out on a wetted burlap bag in a small sandy pit, in the shade between the bunkhouse and a toolshed where he kept the fish hosed down with a steady trickle of cool ancient water that had been mined from a well that reached a thousand feet into the past.

The boy aimed the steady silver trickle first at one side of the huge flapping gills and then the other, watering the inflamed and feathery, irritated crimson gill linings as he would a garden, while the catfish, his eyes bulging, lay otherwise motionless, save for those gasping gills: a perfect hostage, connected tenuously and utterly nonnegotiably to that slender thread of cold silver water, and to the boy who was providing it.

The boy rested, squatting on his heels in the dust, and studied the fish as he hosed him and thought of the money he would earn for caring for the fish — a few dollars, or maybe, if the oilmen had been drinking, ten or even twenty — and as he moved the steady stream of water up and down the fish's broad back, the fish in turn studied the boy with its obsidian-round eyes, which had a gold lining to the perimeter, like pyrite. The fish panted and watched the boy, all that first day, and on through the dream of the night, and into the next day, while the heat built around them, rising steadily through the day. The heat gave birth in the summer-blue sky to beautiful white cumulus clouds, each one a distant world.

The boy grew dizzy in the heat on the second day — he was having to sit cross-legged now, had taken only the briefest of breaks to use the outhouse — and one of the cooks brought him a sandwich. A hypnosis began to overtake the boy, until it seemed to him that it was the trickling from his hose that was inflating the clouds; that he was watering the clouds as one would water a garden. And as the water trickled off the catfish's slick gray back and passed over its gasping gills (which were pink now, no longer bright red), his slimy whiskers grew bedraggled and droopy, making him appear sad and defeated.

The water pooled and spread across the gravel parking lot before wandering into the desert beyond, where bright butterflies swarmed and fluttered, dabbing at the mud the water was making, and it seemed to the boy that he and the catfish were frozen in time, and that the great gasping hulk of the fish would forever be hanging on to life, and that he would forever be a small boy watering it and keeping it alive, and that the huge fish would forever be somehow creating, birthing, those beautiful clouds against the summer sky.

Throughout the afternoon, one or two of the geologists would wander over to examine and admire the monstrosity — Richard was out on a location, up in the foothills — and after a few words they would all sit there hunkered, watching and listening to that silver stream of water, and the fish's gasping; and each time they gathered like that, the boy would guard himself, would become even more diligent, more perfect in the watering.

He would scowl at his task, trying to present himself as a man to them, so that he might be hired for more work at some near point, though he knew that the odds of the geologists noticing anything other than the fish were long. Nonetheless, the boy continued to glower, fierce and intent in the regularity of his task. He would be the best catfish-waterer they had ever seen; better than any they might ever have imagined. He would be the equal of the catfish. He would match his heart to it, and he would become its partner in its final days, and would destroy it.

Late on the second day — the boy bleary-eyed in his hypnosis, and falling asleep sometimes, the hose loose in his hand for long moments at a time — the first of the planes began to arrive, buzzing like dragonflies. Cars began arriving, too, dust plumes rising like a single long row of unfurling feathers, hurrying toward the oilmen's camp, drawn from all directions. The planes began to stack up down at one end of the runway, and the long cars began to accumulate in the parking lot; and one by one and two by two, the visitors wandered out back to examine Tomás's fish, and to ask questions about it; to be awed, terrified, revulsed.

For many of them — bankers, politicians, upper-class drifters — the sight of the fish would have been worth the journey alone; and it seemed to Tomás that some of them were even envious, and properly respectful of, his one task. It seemed to him that they lamented the lack of such a purpose in their own lives.

In the desert dusk, furry tarantulas crawled out from beneath their burrows and marched across the warmth of the gravel airstrip as the day finally cooled slightly. Some of the spiders were as large as a man's fist, mammalian in their size and appearance; and likewise, seeking to extend the heat of the day, the rattlesnakes came sidewinding out onto the runway, milking the last of the airstrip's warmth.

In the red dusk, for Tomás, the appearance of the tarantulas was as lulling as the constancy of a clock ticking in one's own home each evening, as was the occasional, fretful buzzing of the snakes' rattle-tipped tails as they slithered into and then negotiated their way around each other.

Each evening, all of his life, had been marked thus, so that it seemed to him the tarantulas' appearance, and the snakes', was more regular than the hands of time on any clock; that the tarantulas, each with their eight furry legs, *were* time, time itself becoming alive and creeping up from out of the ground, as were the snakes, and that the world of clocks and watches was but an abstract approximation, a crude representation of an infinitely more complex process.

He kept watering the fish, into and then through the second night, his head bobbing with fatigue. Sometimes he fell asleep so deeply and suddenly that he pitched forward, sprawling in the mud next to the fish; and for a while, on that second night, it began to seem to him that the fish was his friend, and that he had neither captured it nor found himself as its caretaker, but had in fact somehow created it, through his ceaseless watering, bringing it to life, up from out of the desert sand, like some miraculous gardener; and he began to consider how he might help the fish escape.

There was nowhere nearby for it to go but to the mud pit — even Tomás, with no understanding of the oil and gas industry, knew that the fish would not survive for long there — but it occurred to him that he might be able to somehow muscle it into the back of one of the jeeps, and steal the jeep, race the thirty miles to the river, splashing cup after cup of water onto the fish's gills before releasing it into one of the deeper stretches of the Madeira.

The fish continued to scrutinize him, as it had all the days before — he could not be sure if it was requesting anything of him or not — and farther toward dawn, he considered again the needs of his family, and the expectations brought about by the job, and he made the decision not to free the fish, but kept watering it, still half-hypnotized by the sound of the cool water draining onto its back. And by the time the red light of day began to return to the desert and the mountains, and the tarantulas began crawling back off into the sagebrush to take refuge against the coming heat, it seemed to him that the fish had reached some state of transcendence itself, and understood now there would be no release, and was accepting of that fact; that it did not blame Tomás for having failed to deliver a miracle that was the equal of the fish.

On through the morning he watered — a fire seemed to be going out in the fish's eyes, and an uncaringness seemed to be entering them; as if this was now just any old fish, instead of a great one. The cook who had taken to caring for the boy brought Tomás a burrito and sat with him for a short while, even held the hose for him while Tomás got up and went for a short walk to stretch his legs, and to visit the outhouse — and when Tomás returned, five minutes later, he was chagrined to see that the cook was haphazard with his watering, was sloshing the water over on one side of the fish and then the other — and the fish, discomforted by this erratic flow, was thrashing and shuddering, as if trying to swim some short distance farther forward to find once more that steady silver stream which the boy had been able to provide.

Tomás thanked the cook and took the hose from him and settled back in to his task; and eventually, the fish stilled itself again, relaxed back into its previous trance; and Tomás told himself that in this regard, he was being kind to the fish, in bringing it a few more moments of ease. It was not as great a gift to the fish as might have been a complete and daring escape, but it was a gift — another few hours.

On that third day, both Red Watkins and George Waller checked in on the fish. And although Tomás was surprised, having previously thought that all of the oilmen were identical, godlike in their powers, he saw now that despite the power of their excessive appetites, they were no different, really, than perhaps any other grouping of mankind; that the insipid could stand shoulder to shoulder with the noble, and the virtuous next to the wicked. That although there was a sameness in all men, there was also always some wedge of difference, some rift or fracture into which the character of a man seeped, and took root, and then grew or died.

It was simple and evident in even a single spoken sentence — Red Watkins placing his old liver-spotted hand on the boy's shoulder and asking him how he was doing, speaking to him in his own language, *Cómo está?* — while George Waller, having been absent during the entire process, was perturbed and critical of how bedraggled the fish looked, chagrined that it was not nearly as vibrant and formidable as it had been when he had first captured it, and disappointed that his guests might find it lacking, or less than he had described it.

"What have you done to him?" George Waller asked, then muttered "*Fuck,*" and might have kicked the boy had Red Watkins not been there; and Tomás knew a sadness and an anger then, that he had not ferried the fish back to the river, or at least tried to: though still his decision-making returned to the question of what was best for his family.

And sensing George Waller's useless and to some degree unearned opulence, he hated him, and shifted on his heels as if adjusting himself to accommodate the new weight of his hatred. He did not discard it, and it burned bright in his dark eyes even as all light continued to drain from the catfish's gold-rimmed eyes.

The two men left, with Red Watkins murmuring a few more words of encouragement, and abandoned Tomás to the heat of the day. The cook came back a short time later for the third time, bringing a bell pepper and Swiss cheese frittata with garlic and green onions, still steaming — which was so delicious that Tomás's eyes filled with tears at his fortune, as well as the fish's misfortune — and the cook also brought a little stump for Tomás to sit on, as he continued to water.

All through that last day, the guests continued to arrive, appearing like mirages from out of the desert heat, their droning planes wavering above the horizon, growing larger, then floating down onto the runway with a spray and clattering of gravel, the planes' maneuverability mushy in the thin hot dry air; and the cars appearing tiny and vaporous in the far distance, but finally coalescing into their true size when they arrived, with the engines groaning and ticking in the heat, and the windshields and grilles splattered with grasshoppers, which Tomás would be asked to scrub clean later in the night, after the fish was flayed and fried, and while the party was going on — Tomás scrubbing with hot soapy water and a washcloth, cleaning every inch of chrome, removing the remains of tens of thousands of grasshoppers and butterflies like confetti, so that by daylight, after the party, all the cars and planes would be gleaming again, and the princes and princesses, the kings and queens who still slumbered in drunken haze, would be able to rise noonward and, blinking at the desert scald of brightness, be handed a bloody mary as they emerged from the air-conditioned bunkhouse and went out to their chariots, into which they would fold themselves before roaring off into the void.

On through the third day the arriving partygoers kept wandering around behind the bunkhouse to inspect the grotesquerie, the monstrosity, of their dinner, as Tomás kept watering the fish.

At dusk, with the fish's gasps coming more slowly than ever, and with the silver stream of water no longer seeming to bring him any relief — with every gulp of air a rasp of sandpaper against the fish's gills, and no oxygen transfer to be gotten at all from that transaction — the tarantulas came out again, regular as clockwork.

The guests were sitting out in lawn chairs by the airstrip, drinking and watching the sunset, and Tomás heard the women shriek and the men hoot drunkenly as the arachnids revealed themselves, walking with delicate high-step deliberation — as if the remnant warmth of the airstrip was something to be savored, and as if each step, and each moment, was a calculation of utmost deliberation.

The cooks lit propane lanterns and set them up and down the airstrip, to guide any night-arriving flights, and lit candles and placed them on all of the picnic tables. Moths rose from out of the desert, swirling like a sandstorm, or like the ghosts and spirits of the grille-splattered grasshoppers reanimated. The moths swarmed those lanterns, burning their wings and falling crippled and smoking to the ground, half-cooked already, where the tarantulas found them, hunted them down, and began consuming them.

The cooks came and placed lanterns around Tomás and the fish, as well, and told him that his work was done, that he could stop watering the fish, though he only shook his head and told them that he would continue until the very last moment; and Sy Craven, who had come outside to view the fish, looked down at the boy and smiled at his grit and fury and focus, and thought how he would like to pluck this boy, too, wondered how he would like China, and pulled a hundred-dollar bill from his money clip and handed it to him; and Tomás took it, thanked him gratefully and enthusiastically, and folded it carefully with one hand into his shirt pocket: though still, he kept watering.

There were lanterns gathered around Tomás and the fish now like candelabras at a dinner setting. Tomás wished for the fish to die before the men began skinning him, but realized also that that was a child's wish, not a man's, and he would soon step away from and outgrow such trivialities as kindness or compassion for such irrelevances as a gritty, dying fish.

Moths cartwheeled off the lantern and landed charred and fuzz-singed upon the fish's glistening back, where they stuck to his sticky skin like feathers, their wings still flapping.

Someone accused Tomás of wasting water, and finally he rose and turned the hose off; and immediately, or so it seemed to Tomás, a fine wrinkling appeared on the previously taut gunmetal skin of the fish: a desiccation, like watching a time-lapse motion picture of a man's or woman's skin wrinkling as he or she ages.

The thin summer breeze, and the heat from the lanterns, seemed to be sucking the moisture from the skin already. It seemed to Tomás that the fish's eyes searched for, then found, his. What was it like for the fish, Tomás wondered, straddling the land now between the living and the nonliving?

George Waller stepped up and pulled out a hunting knife. It was his fish to kill. He would not be the one to cook it, but it was important to him, Tomás and the others saw, to lay claim to it, and to remind everyone that he was the one who had caught it.

He made the first cut lightly around the neck with the long blade as if opening an envelope. He slid the knife in lengthwise beneath the skin and then ran an incision down the spine all the way to the tail, five feet distant. The fish stopped gasping for a moment, opened its giant mouth in shock and outrage, then began to gasp louder.

In watering the fish all day, and into the evening, Tomás had not noticed how many men and women had been gathering. Now that he was standing he saw that there were dozens of them, and he wondered if the fish could feed them all. He saw Richard, who had just returned from the field, and, though he did not know him, scowled at him, disapproving that a man so young and still possessing the capability for fuller freedom should place himself in such company.

"Someone put that fish out of its misery," a woman said, and a man stepped from out of the crowd with a pistol, aimed at the fish's broad head, and fired — the noise was tremendous — and people yelled and screamed.

"Cut that shit out!" Red Watkins yelled, stepping toward the man with the gun, who retreated back into the crowd, grumbling an apology, then raised a bottle to his lips.

The bullet had made a dark hole in the fish's head. The wound didn't bleed and, like some mythic monster, the fish did not seem affected by it. It kept on breathing, and Tomás wanted very much to begin watering it again.

George Waller, with the knife, kept cutting. When he had all the cuts made, two other men helped him lift the fish. They ran a rope through its cavernous mouth and out its gills and hoisted it up into a mesquite tree, where roosting birds rustled, then flew out of the branches and into the night.

The fish writhed, sucking for air, finding none, but was somehow from far within able to summon and deliver enough power to flap its tail once, slapping one of the men in the ribs with a *thwack* that sounded like a woman beating a wet rug with a baseball bat, and the man, who was drunk, was knocked down. His glass spilled and then broke when it landed.

"Give me that gun," he shouted when he got up, and he took the gun from the man who'd fired it earlier and stepped up and put another bullet in the fish's broad head, so that now a second, balanced, nostril appeared; and still the fish seemed unfazed.

Red Watkins intervened once more, grabbed the gun from the drunk man, knocked the man down yet again, then threw the gun out into the desert. Tomás's eyes followed the arc of the gun beyond the candlelight into darkness, and he resolved, after the party had ended and the partygoers were lying comatose and tangled amongst one another, to go and search for, and claim, that pistol.

Another man passed through the crowd, pouring tequila from a bottle. Red Watkins's knuckles were bleeding from where he had hit the man, who was still lying on the ground, not moving. The fish was making guttural sounds, and George Waller said, "Well, I guess it's time to cook him." He found a pair of pliers in the toolshed and came back out and gripped the skin with the pliers up behind the fish's neck and then peeled the skin back, skinning the fish alive in that manner as if pulling the husk or wrapper from a thing to reveal that which had been hidden within.

The fish flapped and struggled and twisted, swinging wildly on the rope and croaking, but there was no relief to be found. The croaking was loud and bothersome and so the men lowered the fish, carried it over to the picnic table beside the fire, and began sawing the head off. When they had that done, the two pieces — head and torso — were still moving, though with less vigor — the fish's body writhing very slowly on the table, and the mouth of the fish's head opening and closing just as slowly, and still the fish kept croaking, though more quietly now, as if perhaps it had gotten something it had been asking for and was now somewhat appeased.

The teeth of the saw were flecked with bone and fish-muscle, gummed with cartilage and gray brain. "Here," said Waller, handing Tomás the saw, "go down to the mud pit and wash that off." He looked at the gasping head (the rope was still passed through the mouth and gills) and said, "Take this down there, too, and feed it to the turtles — make it stop making that noise" — and some of the men and women laughed.

He handed Tomás the rope with the heavy croaking head attached to it, and Tomás took it and turned and went down into the darkness toward the shining round mud pit — the full moon was reflected in it like an eye — and as he walked, there was silence down by the mud pit, except for the dull croaking coming from the package he carried at the end of the rope: carrying it almost like a basket or a purse. He could hear the sounds of the party up on the hill, but down by the mud pit, with the moon's gold eye cold upon it, there was silence, save for the deep-purring fish head.

Tomás lowered the fish head into the warm water and watched as it sank down below the moon. It was still croaking, and the gasping made a stream of bubbles that trailed up to the surface as it sank, and for a little while, even after it was gone, it seemed he could still hear the raspy croaking — duller, now, and much fainter — coming from beneath the water; and like a child, he held the brief thought or hope that maybe the fish was relieved now; that maybe the water felt good on its gills and on what was left of its body.

He set about washing the saw. Bits of flesh floated off the blade and across the top of the water. After he had the blade cleaned, he sat and listened for the croaking, but could hear nothing, and was relieved. (In later years, Tomás would have the occasional dreams that the great fish had survived; that it had regenerated a new body to match the giant head, and that it still lurked in that pond, savage, betrayed, wounded.)

He sat there quietly and soon enough the crickets became accustomed to his presence and began chirping again, and a peace filled back in over the scuzzy pond, and over the night, like a scar healing, or like grass growing bright and green across a charred landscape. Out in the desert, chuck-will's-widows began calling once more, and Tomás sat there and listened to the sounds of the party up on the hill. Someone had brought fiddles and they were beginning to play, and it was a sweet sound, in no way in accordance with the earlier events of the evening.

Tomás could smell the odor of meat cooking and knew the giant fish had been laid to rest atop the coals.

The light from the lanterns on the hill was making a gold dome of light in the darkness — to Tomás it looked like an umbrella — and after a while he turned and went back up to the light and to the noise of the party.

In gutting and cleaning the fish before skewering it on an iron rod to roast, the cooks had cut open its stomach to see what it had been eating. They found a small gold pocket watch, fairly well preserved, though with the engraving worn away so that all they could see on the inside face was the year, *1898*. It was decided that in honor of his having the barbecue, George Waller should receive the treasure from the fish's stomach. (There was also a can opener, a couple of handfuls of pesos and centavos, a slimy tennis shoe, some bailing wire, and a large soft-shelled turtle, still alive, which clambered out of its leathery entrapment and with webbed feet, long claws, and frantically outstretched neck scuttled its way blindly down toward the mud pit — knowing instinctively where water and safety lay, and where, Tomás supposed, it later found the catfish's bulky head and began feasting on it.)

In subsequent days Red Watkins would take the watch apart — George Waller wanted nothing to do with it — and clean it piece by piece and then spend the better part of a month, in the hot middle part of the day, as he babysat all the various rigs and their crews, reassembling the watch, after drying the individual pieces in that bright September light.

That night at the party, one woman stood out from the rest. She was dressed like a flapper, and she went up to where the fish skin was hanging from a nail on a mesquite tree, still wet and shiny. She turned her back to the bonfire that was burning, lowered her dress to her waist, and slipped into the fish skin, wrapping it tightly around her like a vest, then turned to face the crowd, and started to dance in front of the fire, and in front of the partygoers.

The fiddles slowly stopped playing, one by one, so that the only sound was the crackling of the fire, and Tomás could see the woman doing her fish dance, with her arms clasped together over her head, and dust plumes rising from her shuffling feet, and then people were edging in front of him, a wall of people, so that he could not see.

More plumes of dust came hurrying down the road, cars traveling toward the party as if knowing that the fish lady was dancing, and hurrying to see her; while beyond, in the desert landscape stretching to the blue mountains and then up into the mountains, they could see the flares of the gas wells venting fifty- and sixty-foot plumes of flame into the night sky. The natural gas was rarely worth selling, was cheaper to waste than to utilize, its removal necessary to get to the sweet dark oil below.

A hundred, then two hundred, then three hundred such flares were

visible, delineating the developing ghost-shape of the giant oilfield below, the columns of flame appearing perhaps like the burning bars of
a cage to the partygoers, or, to those passing over in a plane, the shape
or outline of a great dragon or sea monster below, or even an immense
fish.

Tomás left the encampment after a solitary breakfast the next morning, the cooks and he the only ones awake at the bright hour of nine
o'clock. Richard, who had not participated in the evening's revelry, had
already gone back out into the field, and Tomás, with the prize of the
fish-killing pistol hidden in his ancient canvas rucksack, was paid an
extra twenty dollars for washing the cars and planes.

He had worked through the night, catnapping amidst the sounds
of the party — he had awakened at dawn to the sight of the tarantulas
creeping past and around the scattered bodies of several of the partygoers, who lay felled like soldiers defending a homeland or a cherished
cause, rather than simple victims of folly and ill-considered choice —
and as he was leaving, Sy Craven came out and thanked him, asked for
his full name so that he might contact him at some point in the future
about other work, and then Tomás left, declining Sy Craven's offer to
have one of the pilots fly him back to his hometown, twenty miles distant.

Instead he set off on foot. By noon, he was back to the upper reaches
of the Madeira, where he lay down in the tall autumn-dry grass beside
the river in the cool shade of a sycamore and napped for two hours,
listening to the sound of the river running like blood, and the yellow
grass rustling.

He slept peacefully right until the end of his nap, when he dreamed
that he had lost all the money he had earned — that he had gone swimming in the river and it had floated out, gotten wet and deteriorated,
simply vanished — and he sat up in terror, felt frantically for the money
and, even after discovering it was still with him, had trouble calming
his heart.

He rose and followed the river downstream, eventually passing by
the ford where George Waller had spied and caught the great fish. He
observed the tire tracks where the brigade of jeeps had crossed the

shallow water, bruising the white limestone and its thin sheet of algae, and paused to watch a swarming school of tiny catfish, black as ink, the underwater cloud of them drifting in writhing nucleus downstream, the entire school of them ravenous, just hatched. Some would be eaten by crows and belted kingfishers, others by shrikes and frogs and turtles and raccoons. Others of them would be charmed, and might go on to live for several years. One in ten thousand of them, or one in a hundred thousand, might go on to become giants; or perhaps none at all, perhaps never again.

He patted the money in his pocket, shifted the heft of his rucksack to reassure himself that that prize was there, too, and marveled at all that could happen in the world in only a few days. Still, he had decided that he did not care to work for Sy Craven, or any of the others — not anywhere, not ever again — though the wealth he had gotten from the last three days' work would last him and his family for weeks.

The lullaby of the river and the sound of the leaves rattling in the breeze above conspired to help him forget, for a while, his betrayal of the fish, and by the time he arrived back at his village that evening, where his family was astounded by the sudden wealth, he felt properly hardened, sufficiently encased and rigid against the possibility of that memory ever returning with its full emotional debts and obligations. A man, already.

It wasn't so much that Richard kept dreaming of Clarissa — only occasionally, once a year or so, would she return to him in his sleeping dreams — but, more problematic, thoughts of her invaded his waking moments, quiet moments that should have been filled with peace and forward-looking.

He wanted in no way to become one of those wrecks of human beings who is haunted by the past, imprisoned by regrets and the plague of *What if?*

Yet as the years went past, he felt himself getting no better. The pain was gone, but not the ache.

Is she more beautiful still? he could not help but wonder, and, *Perhaps she is calmer, perhaps she is less frightened.* The thoughts and memories and desires returned to him on their own, as if they had achieved some enspiriting and now moved in the world with their own clockwork logic, arising and sleeping and then arising again, searching him out and intersecting with him for a while, then departing, yet returning: not just at dawn and dusk, but at any odd time of the day. And he began, finally, to understand that he was going to have to try to set the weight of her aside or be crushed, that he could go no further without attempting that: but that he would not let go of the old weight of her without attempting to find some new weight to carry.

I want one more chance, Richard told himself. The Sierra Occidentals meant nothing to him, were insufficient as a substitute for passion — they had never meant anything to him — and so it seemed to him therefore that there was no choice but to backtrack to the last place on the path where anything had mattered to him, and to begin anew.

Here, too, in Mexico, the earth began to cave beneath the oilmen's weight, and their consumption. By Richard's eighth year, enough oil and gas had been pulled out from below, and enough water had been mined to use for the manufacture of all the various drilling fluids, that, as in Odessa, the desert floor began to sag and buckle in places.

Pipelines ruptured and sprayed fountains of flame a hundred feet into the air, and pooled blackish-green oil across the desert, creating little lakes and ponds of oil. Red Watkins was kept busier than he'd ever been, racing from one location to another, shutting off pipelines and ordering backhoes to dig up and refit the broken lines. Bulldozers shoved the oil-sodden earth into huge piles, blackened cone-shaped mountains appearing incongruously out in the center of the desert, with the tangled pipes still protruding from those piles, and then the workers ignited them, where the burning oil-sand would go on to smolder for years, clouding the desert sky with ribbons and tendrils of black smoke, and the odor of burning tires.

It was abysmal, none of the geologists were happy about it, but it was the cost of doing business, they said; the price of the world's growing appetite for their product. "The blood of the past," Sy Craven called it.

It seemed to Richard that he began to lose his nerve. He dreamed some nights that the ground he was walking upon was collapsing, insufficient to hold even his own insignificant weight. In the dreams, he usually fell in only up to his waist or his armpits, and was able to crawl out, though there were also dreams in which he fell endlessly, fell all the way into wakefulness, landing with a shout and finding himself sitting up in bed in the bunkhouse with his heart sore and raw from having pounded so hard.

It would take him several minutes to calm and convince himself, in the darkness, that he had indeed not fallen off the face of the earth — had not been swallowed and consumed by the thing he had spent the last many years pursuing — and he would sit there for a while longer, sweating and remembering the dream in its clarity, while surrounded by the snores of the other men.

Is this what it felt like to the great fish? he wondered. Was there a moment of sudden illumination when it first found itself trapped in the last deep hole?

Was there immediate chagrin, or did the regret and despair seep into the fish day by day and hour by hour, as it waited for the executioner, George Waller, to appear?

There was a fracas, later that autumn, when Richard went to Sy Craven and informed him that he had decided to retire from the company; that he understood he would waive full benefits, that he was only fifteen months shy of being fully vested, and that rather than walking away with millions, he would be leaving with far less than that amount. His annual salary had been generous and adequate, and his expenses almost nil. He would have to work again someday, particularly back on the other side of the border, but not for a while; in his last eight years, he felt as if he had already worked a lifetime. He could devote himself to other pursuits. He could reconsider other, past desires. He felt that he was finally rested enough to do so — to reenter the past — and believed fully that he would do so, if only because that was what he had always done, all his life.

Is it always this way? he wondered, staring out at the blackened and ruined landscape. *Does even a single scratch upon the surface reveal, almost always, the identical results, over and over again?* Despite the lessons of his profession, he did not want to believe this was true, and yet, too often, the evidence before him seemed incontrovertible.

Sy Craven cursed him, then pleaded with him, telling him he had built entire drilling programs around him. He offered him outlandish incentives, then cursed him again when he refused. The eight years, nearly nine, had been necessary, but had been too long already, there could be no comparison between them and the four months he had had with Clarissa. He dared not try to explain these things to the other geologists and engineers, but simply shook his head and said that his heart was no longer in it: and they, with their alcohol-shrunken livers and emphysemic lung-hackings, their goiters and syphilis and gout, only stared at him uncomprehendingly. George Waller was not-so-secretly thrilled, and winced when Sy Craven suggested that Richard consider it merely a leave of absence, that he take some time off to do whatever he felt he needed to do, and then come back tan and rested and ready.

Only Red Watkins among them seemed to understand. With his rheumy eyes and rickety teeth, his shallow, labored breathing and otherwise-fading body, he regarded Richard with a mixture of surprise and respect that encouraged Richard to keep to his decision and to tell Sy Craven that no, it would not be a leave of absence, that it would be the real thing.

Richard thought that Craven was going to strike him then, but instead he simply cursed again and then turned his back on him and left, walking out of the room before Richard could — and disbelieving at the folly he had witnessed, George Waller followed quickly, shaking his head in delighted confirmation at this final revelation of the younger man's instability: and Richard smiled and waved goodbye to him, knowing that George Waller could easily spend the next ten years berating him to Sy Craven, and redefining his success into failure, even as the desert around them continued to collapse beneath the weight of all indications to the contrary.

It was the worst and most shocking thing any of them could imagine — many of them wondered afterward if Richard had been ill, or if there had been a death or illness in his family, or if — as George Waller continued to suggest—he was suffering some sort of breakdown, some collapse of nerve. Among them all, only Red Watkins remained nonjudgmental, and his firm, gnarly handshake seemed to Richard to be more than approving.

Richard didn't think the car he'd arrived in almost a decade earlier would survive the journey back, and Sy Craven wouldn't let him buy one of the company jeeps, so Red Watkins had to drive him north to the border crossing where Richard could then catch a bus to Texas.

The two men drove through the darkness—Craven had refused to let Red Watkins take off any time from work, so that he'd had to leave at night, like a truant schoolboy rather than an aging man, in order to be back by daylight.

As they drove, Red Watkins told Richard about the brief period of time before he'd begun work in the oilfields, his first twenty years. He had learned a lot and seen a lot and had no regrets, he said—in many ways, he believed that he had been made for the oilfield, that no profession could have suited him better—but that he did wonder sometimes, especially now that he was dying, about the path he had not chosen, the other path, and where it might have led.

It made him feel lonely, he said, as if there was some other part of himself out there that he had never known, or had known ever so briefly, but then abandoned, and which judged him, somehow, for that abandonment.

"You could come on across with me," Richard said, and Red Watkins shook his head and said that Richard didn't understand, that that path and that life had died long ago, and that there was no way to reclaim it now even if he'd wanted to. The gravel road turned briefly to pavement, and glittered in the headlights with flecks of dark silica. A hundred yards of pavement, as if from this point forward, the way for all travelers would be easier, faster.

The two men stepped out of the jeep and Red Watkins handed Richard the watch taken from the great fish's belly and then did a rare thing for the old man, and embraced him. He wished him good luck. "You're going back because of a woman, aren't you?" Red asked, and Richard nodded and said that he was, and that if it worked out, and Red ever wanted to look him up, he would be in a place called Odessa.

He watched the younger man for a moment and tried to remember what it had been like to still be between the past and the future, and with the luxurious buffer between the two: able to go back and look for the lost pieces of a life, if one desired, or able to forge on ahead into the future, hungry and eager and unafraid, and unweary.

"Good luck," he said again, and watched as the younger man turned and walked across the bridge, back into the country of his youth, and with so much treasure abandoned behind.

Behind him, Richard heard Red Watkins laugh out loud. It was not a mean or sarcastic laugh, but a laugh of plain happiness. Richard heard it clearly, but did not turn back around and look. It was dark on the bridge and the stars above were bright. The river glinted silver, far below, and he felt a brief wave of vertigo, but there would be no more dreams of falling. He gripped the watch in his pocket and in that darkness felt the thud of each second, each coil-spring tremor, ticking within its case.

9

1976

THE YOUNG GIRL who was Richard's daughter, Annie, and whom he had no idea even existed, was living with the aging, faltering Marie, who, in the last several years, had been visited increasingly by Mr. Herbert Mix. (Whenever Mix addressed these visits to anyone, he acknowledged that he was "calling on" Marie. The farther Marie fell toward physical ruin — her long years at the salt mines overtaking her — the more she seemed to be an object of interest to Herbert Mix, who, to his credit, was drawn not just to the physical spectacle of her mortal flesh — her skin growing thinner and thinner, her frail old-woman's bones becoming nearly as pronounced as some of those in the skeletons he had spent his life collecting — but attracted also to her calm and endearing nature, her steadfastness.)

He admired the way she had taken on the task of raising the orphan girl in a swelter of Bible-belting fundamentalism, despite her not being an enthusiast of that sect, and of her commitment to be as good a mother as she could to the young girl, despite her advancing age and limitations.

In his later years, Herbert Mix, no Holy Roller himself, had taken to perusing the Bible, as fascinated by some of the sagas of wealth and apocalypse in Revelations as might be a young boy with a stack of action comics; and he had come to think of both the old woman and the young girl as being Ruthian, capable of, and even prone to, eloquent declarations of devotion. As if the two had been shaped for each other from the beginning. It was not that way at all; but in their isolation, they found themselves crafted into the closest of partners.

Together, the three of them were not so much like a family as a band or clan that gathered occasionally, reassembling in need or opportunity — but the two of them, Marie and Annie, had become like a family over the years, knit more closely than anything Annie would ever have known with her mother, the flight-driven Clarissa, and closer than anything Marie had ever known out at Juan Cordona Lake, or even among the peach orchards of her own childhood.

Marie and Annie had moved into a house on the outskirts of town, and had stopped going to the church the previous year, when Annie was eight, for a reason that seemed incomprehensible to Odessa's leaders at the time, stating that she, Marie, as well as Annie, who was a precocious child, had already read the Bible all the way through, twice — that they already knew it all, knew how it all turned out, and preferred to spend their Sunday mornings quietly, at home, cooking and reading and working in the garden, which they were able to always somehow keep protected against the heated winds that rippled through the days.

It was an avocation for which Annie had a surprising aptitude, and she loved to awaken at first light and go out into the garden — melons, corn, berries, peas, lettuce, okra, cucumbers, zucchini, half a dozen varieties of tomatoes — and Marie would join her there, watering and weeding in the early hours of the day.

The work reminded Marie dimly of her own childhood among the orchards, though she sensed that here her life seemed freer than it must have been for her father, who had been so bound to one crop, peaches and only peaches. Here, too, there were challenges — cutworms, webworms, weevils, borers, blight, gophers, stinkbugs, rabbits, coons, skunks, drought, heat, and wind — but when one crop failed or faltered, there were others that were less affected; and the size of Marie and Annie's garden was manageable, and far less ambitious than the acres of her father's orchard, which had ended up subsuming his life in a brutal and, to Marie's way of thinking, unsatisfactory, trade: his life, for x-numbered bushels of peaches.

A thousand, a few thousand — a hundred thousand? What of it? A man should be more than a peach, she mused, and a man should be more than a pile or pillar of salt, or a hole in the ground.

After watering and weeding each morning, they would raise gauze sheets around the garden's perimeter, the gauze flapping in the wind and hooked with curtain rings to a series of bamboo and willow poles that Herbert Mix helped them erect. They would raise the billowing sheets a couple of feet midmorning, just enough for the softest part of the morning sun to make it over the top and down into the garden, and then would go back out and raise the sheets another few feet at noon, and then higher still, all the way up, midafternoon, before lowering the sheets back to the halfway point shortly before dusk, and all the way down at night.

To Annie it seemed precisely like raising the sails on the oceangoing ships she had read about in her adventure books. The crops might have been her dreams, with the soil her imagination, or the crops might have been some lost civilization over which she was the queen. She felt keenly the pleasure of wanting to take care of something, and it likewise pleased Marie, who, in raising and lowering the sails each day, was reminded of how she had cared for Annie from the very first day she had arrived; of how she had draped sheets around Annie's baby bed as she slept, to keep the afternoon sun off her.

As a baby, Annie had been extraordinarily pale, but was tan now from her garden work; even with her black hair, no one would ever recognize her as her mother's child. Her eyes were not that light wolfish green, but darker green, like river stones, with a mosaic of black-flecking, shiny as opal, appearing at times as if they had clear water running in fast sheets across them.

As Marie grew older and less robust, Annie stepped up and performed more and more of their little household's tasks. She was not yet caring for Marie as she might for a child, but that transition was already in progress, the ship was leaving its harbor. And it did not displease either for this to be the case.

They lived on the east end of town, out past where even the football players ran, in an area that had previously had no name, but which was now known as Mormon Springs, named for the schoolteacher who lived out there, a young woman, Ruth, who had always wanted to teach in a one-room schoolhouse, and who had gotten her wish, though not quite in the manner she had envisioned.

A Mormon in a sea of all-else Protestants, Ruth had begun her career teaching at the middle school in Odessa straight out of college.

She loved the children, was an excellent listener and motivator, volunteered for and coordinated numerous clubs and projects, and by her third year had been voted Texas's Teacher of the Year, the youngest ever to receive that honor, and won it again her fourth year, when never before had an educator been awarded the prize twice.

Her faith and heritage, however, had proved to be her undoing, as the town, increasingly uncomfortable with her influence over the children, became concerned that she might corrupt them with her outlandish ideas about religion. The townspeople were approving of her values (twice a month, she got up early on a Sunday and made the long drive to San Angelo, to attend the church in the small town where she had grown up), but they were alarmed by the claims of her church that the Latter-day Saints' religion was one born of this country, rather than olden Israel.

They were troubled most of all not by the fact that Ruth kept a Book of Mormon in her house, on her bookshelf, where any visiting child might see it, as well as possessing what seemed to those who had investigated the situation an extravagant number of other Mormon tracts, with mysterious, occult-like titles such as *The Pearl of Great Price,* but that she was writing and publishing occasional essays about what her faith meant to her, and what life had been like for her growing up Mormon.

It wasn't as if the essays were red-flagged in the Odessa paper; instead, they appeared in places like her church's newsletter, and a couple of church magazines published in Utah, including the alumni magazine of Brigham Young University, where she had attended college. But as the Texas press began to pay more attention to her teaching methods and her own persona, curious about her success — numerous accounts reported on her calming and radiant "aura" — her essays were eventually rounded up, republished, excerpted, and analyzed, and she was, in the words of some of the patrons at the daily diner, "outed."

They clucked and tsked when the next school board election — essentially a referendum on whether she should leave or stay — went to a candidate who ran on an anti-Mormon platform. The vote was close, a handful either way would have changed it, but in the end, fear had won out over courage, and at the next board meeting, she was asked to leave.

It would have been easy for her to return to the town where she had grown up, or to go to work in the well-financed school district of some larger city, or even to take a high-paying job at an endowed private school, where surely she would have been just as revered and loved by the students as she had been by her desert children.

But there was a feistiness running through her, a strength that was sometimes overlooked, like the sheen of red that burnished her otherwise brown hair in angles of sunlight. She withdrew from the middle school, but spent hundreds of hours studying the complicated legal strictures of tax codes and apportionment systems, filed the necessary forms, and opened a new school on the outskirts of town, building it with her own hands, using her own tools and funds, along with the help of some of her ex-students and their parents.

She had befriended many of the other school's teachers, who were not envious of the success of her awards — Ruth had always been gracious in deferring her attention to the entire faculty, and to the nature of the children themselves — and, wishing her well, the football coaches from the high school had donated the services of the team's labors, to help her pour the foundation she had dug, and to then frame and truss and roof the one-room structure, which was the schoolhouse of her dreams all along.

It was quintessential small-town craziness, the sweetly supportive abiding side by side with the maliciously venomous. There could be no reckoning that might present dualities itself on any given day, nor was Ruth interested any longer in guessing. It was much better to simply stay away from it.

When Ruth opened her doors the fifth year of her teaching career, there were only four elementary students whose parents were brave enough to send them to the alternative school, though slowly over the next several years, that number had doubled, and then increased again, so that by the time Annie entered the third grade, there were thirteen students in the school.

It was an ideal system, Ruth thought, in which the younger students could learn at their own speed — Annie, for instance, was sitting in with the eighth-graders as they made their way through *The Odyssey,* creating costumes and dressing up for dramatic readings each day — and the older students could help instruct the younger students.

In the beginning, Annie had not attended the Mormon Springs school, but had been going to the main school in town. It was before Marie had completely written off as malicious and heartless the church folk and townspeople who had offered her a hand up, and who had also given her, even if indirectly, the great gift of her life, the child herself, as loving and attentive as her own two sons had been numb-spirited.

Annie was advanced, and initially it was Marie's belief that the larger school would be able to offer a greater array of teachers and services. But it was Annie's very precociousness that challenged the lesser teachers at the school, leading them to dislike the child, who, unaware of diplomacy, sometimes corrected her instructors. By the time she was in the second grade, it grieved Annie to hear her teacher say "acrost" instead of "across," and there were children in the larger school who, in addition to resenting the ease with which Annie skimmed through her lessons unchallenged, looked down on her for the fact that she was orphaned, and possessed so ancient a caretaker as Marie, an old washed-up, gone-by granny woman.

There were mothers of the children, too, who were discomforted by Annie's odd brilliance. One, in particular, encouraged her child to spread lies about Annie, not just amongst the other schoolchildren, but to Annie's teacher as well. The mother conspired to get her son to tell another girl in the class that Annie had said she thought the teacher, Mrs. Blaronski, was dumber than a box of rocks and that she was "a fucking idiot."

Weeks later, after the accusations had in their small-town way finally wound their way from accuser to accused, Marie heard about the rumor, and scheduled a meeting with Mrs. Blaronski to set things straight: to let her know that never in her life had she heard Annie utter those two words, although she had to admit, she had heard the boy's mother use such language. "If she had called you an 'imbecilic termagant,'" Marie said, trying for lightness, and shaking her head, "I might be able to believe there was some substance to the allegations. But 'fucking idiot' . . ." She shook her head again.

Marie thought the matter was over then, and went on to a discussion of Annie's special needs — she did not use the phrase "stultifying boredom" — and she believed the issue had been resolved, until, two weeks later, she heard that the teacher had been down at the local diner lamenting to all and any in earshot the blow-by-blow specifics of her and Annie's cross-wayedness, complaining about the child's character and absent-mindedness.

As the evening went on, Mrs. Blaronski's lamentations degenerated into weeping, so that clearly she was the wronged party, and the child, the wrongdoer; and the diner patrons tsked again at the malice of a child who could reduce a grown woman to tears.

It was a month later, at the town Halloween party, before Marie heard indirectly of the teacher's betrayal; one of the men who'd been in the diner during the performance came up to Marie and asked what the heck was going on, and filled Marie in on what he had seen and heard; and by the end of that week, Annie had calmly been instructed by Marie to gather her pens and pencils and notepads, her scissors and crayons and glue, for she would now be attending the school at Mormon Springs, which was but a short bike ride from their house: and although Annie regretted leaving her classmates, she was intrigued by the adventure of starting anew.

Ruth was thrilled to have another student, and particularly one as bright as Annie. Annie fit right into the system, adjusting day by day to all the richnesses, the crannies and alcoves and crevices of wonder, afforded by the school at Mormon Springs, and afforded by Ruth as a teacher.

The old charlatan Herbert Mix came into Ruth's class once a year to display his wares, and to take the students on a field trip into the dunes to search for treasure. (Having grown more tender in his old age, each year he salted away a few prizes in the desert, to be sure that the children each discovered something.) A Mormon congressman from Utah came and visited the class each year, while another of the faith, the chief executive of a telecommunications company, paid to have the class travel annually to Washington, D.C., to visit the House and Senate chambers, and to learn about the Constitution and the Bill of Rights and see all the judicial and legislative warrens.

A sports star, also a devout Mormon, came to class once a year and played basketball with the children out on the gravel half-court, with Ruth leading the opposing team; and because she had captained her high school team her senior year, she always managed to sink a few perimeter shots over her famous visitor, a feat that awed the students more than anything else she had done or said.

Ruth had secured a grant for a five-week artist-in-residency, during which time Ruth and the children, with the young visiting artist, constructed giant puppets and wrote their own play, culminating in a parade down Main Street, the children and their teacher costumed in the giant-headed cloaks of brightly painted creations: a multipartite thirty-foot-long Red Dragon, breathing real fire from a portable gas grill converted to a flamethrower, and a twenty-foot-tall Comanche warrior, a herd of buffalo, and a giant oil derrick.

The town was totally unprepared for the shenanigans of the parade. Conceived in secrecy and constructed in privacy and anonymity by the outcasts of Mormon Springs, the giant puppets merely appeared in town one day, beating on tin-can drums and sawing wildly on screeching violins and shaking handmade, brightly painted gourd pea-rattles, looming and canting and teetering sideways past the front windows and doorways of shopkeepers, pivoting their enormously oversized and grinning heads from side to side to take in and, it seemed, evaluate the town through which they were passing.

In addition to the sacrilege of the parade not having been previously advertised or even authorized by the town fathers and mothers, there was further scandal in that the play had the audacity in one scene to project a future that was no longer based on oil and gas, but alternative energy, including an array of little bright blue solar panels attached to the dragon, drinking in the desert sun and glittering like scales.

Still, what could the town do? They had already fired Ruth.

The children had constructed a giant papier-mâché prickly pear cactus, and an equally oversized scrubby-looking range cow, which they pulled along behind them on a flatcar not unlike the wagon the football players used. Near the end of the parade, the dragon (operated by Ruth, in the head) turned and looked back at the lime-green cactus, and at the ribby cow (its skeleton beneath the cardboard not fisted-up wads of newspaper, but the real thing, bones gleaned from the desert and reassembled in anatomical correctness, including even the great horned skull); and tilting its sloe-eyed visage sideways, stretched its long neck closer, articulated like an accordion, then let loose a blast of flame that ignited and quickly incinerated first the cactus and then, more horrifically, the scrubby range cow: again, a blasphemy and a mockery to the old ranchers who witnessed the spectacle.

The artist-in-residence, a young woman from Philadelphia named Beth, was athletic and tireless; she had worked with the students ceaselessly during their five weeks, had things hidden in store for the town that might not have appeared before them in their wildest dreams, puppets that not even the children had seen before the great parade.

Working in her off-hours, and living in a windowless shack out east of even the windblown outskirts of Mormon Springs, she had labored each afternoon after school, and into the night and early hours of the morning, with her battery-powered tape-player booming out Steppenwolf, Billie Holiday, and, seemingly paradoxically, Marty Robbins, Johnny Cash (she liked to sing along at the top of her lungs to "Ring of Fire"), and Mozart — weeping, sometimes, at the nighttime beauty of the *Requiem,* as well as at the beauty, she had to admit it, of her own creations, which she understood were summoned only in part by the greatness of spirit that resided in any artist's heart, with the rest of the creation appearing unaccounted for.

Beth had constructed dozens of puppets without the children's help, puppets that would not be a part of the children's self-scripted pageant, but would instead exist only for the children's enjoyment, and as an exercise in her own ceaselessness: her hands' inability to stop creating, once the flow had begun, once the vent shaft that was the source of her inspiration had opened; she found herself standing over it and peering down into a maelstrom of color and emotion and old unreplicated wisdoms, a roiling carnival of all the world yet to come, hidden and waiting only for her to release it.

In the creative haze of those hot afternoons and the slightly cooler nights, the puppeteer had constructed a giant Santa Claus, coyotes, space aliens, UFO rocketships, an elephant with sweeping tusks (knowing nothing of the history of Marie and Tsavo, but instead, merely staring down into the swirl of the muse), giant sailfish, dogs and cats, a King Kong character, and a thirty-foot-long rattlesnake with clattering coffee cans for a buzz-tail.

There was no electricity out at the broken-hinged Art Shack, as Beth called it, and so she worked by lantern light, and did not have to worry about spilling paint on the wide-cracked floorboards.

Moths circled her creations as she labored to bring them to a glossy sheen, and the insects often became entangled in the new paint, giving some of the puppets a furry, fuzzy look, which, rather than despairing over, she decided she liked, so that she even took strands of rope and binder's twine and unraveled the braids to create a similar fuzz, which she glued onto the lion, the lamb, and, in an impulse that she knew was sinful and would be a direct affront to her host community, the cherubs and angels, and even to the woolly Baby Jesus in a cradle.

Lightning bugs likewise sometimes found themselves adhered to the paint, continuing to blink as the paint dried in the evening breezes, with a result that pleased Beth so much that she incorporated that design into the rhino, swaddling him with a string of Christmas-tree lights, and attaching to his tail a hundred-foot-long cheap extension cord. She papier-mâché-mounted votive candles in the eyes and along the backs of other creatures — roadrunners, gamecocks, vultures, jackrabbits — and left her creations behind the shack to dry in each day's sun before covering them back up with blue plastic tarps.

On the night before the parade and with Ruth's help, she loaded Ruth's old truck with the secret puppets, making trips back and forth from Mormon Springs to town. She and Ruth used a long extension ladder to climb onto the rooftops of nearly all the two- and three-story buildings on Main Street, in addition to the seven-story oil and gas building, where they had positioned the puppets in hiding — "Ready for ambush," Beth said—and then laid out the ziplines that were part of her stock-in-trade.

Made of urethane-coated airplane cable, the ziplines could be anchored to the ground at a distant point, with their puppets looped to the cable far above, from which point the puppets could then be launched into Peter Pan–like flight manually, or even released electronically via the command of a series of transmitters that Beth carried in the pocket of a fly-fishing vest she had designed for such events.

The two women worked through the night, that last night, obscuring the puppets behind blank sheets of newsprint through which the weighted forms could then crash, like football players running through paper stretched between goalposts at the start of a game: and to camouflage the paper from the notice of the regular workaday routines of the townspeople, Ruth and Beth painted the obscuring paper in the same tones and designs as the respective buildings that housed and held the puppets-in-waiting.

They engaged two of the students' mothers to crouch hidden on the rooftops on either side of the street, stationing themselves to light the votive candles and plug in the extension cords at the appropriate time, the mothers running from rooftop to rooftop like train robbers, and thrilled to be participating in such daring.

Beth would leave soon after the performance, but the awe and force of what the mothers up on the rooftops had done, as well as the empowerment that resided in the children afterward—not just through the creation of their art, but through their presentation of it to the community, unbidden, and with the community—bankers, lawyers, bakers, geologists—coming out onto the street one by one and store by store to stare, in puzzled thrall of the children and their power—would burn in their hearts to some degree always, burning like the candles that were set into the pie-plates-for-eyes of the wing-stretched giant birds that the children's mothers were lighting now and then sending swooping down onto the tower near the parade's finale—a spectacle which even the proud children had not anticipated.

The wings of raven and red-tailed hawk, and of a golden eagle carrying a lamb in its talons, tipped and wobbled as they gained speed, nearing the bottom of the ziplines, and when they bumped or crashed to the ground, an occasional wing was torn loose, and the candles and candlewax spilled, igniting the paper, so that some of the creations, still tethered to the cable, burned brightly, sending up the burning black and green smoke of their paint.

The children in the parade moved carefully past the hulks of this flaming wreckage, as if through a battlefield in which the campaign had just ended, and marveled as, just ahead of them, the blinking rhinoceros wobbled and creaked as it hurtled overhead, passing from one side of the street to the other before bashing its head against the side of the bank building.

The rhino cracked open from the impact, and, hollow-shelled like a piñata, gold-wrapped candy coins spilled out, which the children fell upon with chocolaty zeal — and when the electrified elephant, seemingly as large as a blimp, came gliding down the final zipline, settling unharmed in the center of the street, even the scandalized townsfolk, who had not yet decided if they were being mocked or not, were overcome by the spectacle, and wandered out into the street among the strange creatures, amid the can-pounding and bean-shaking and marble-rattling, the xylophonic washboard-scraping, and examined the elephant admiringly.

Annie, who had been raised on the lore of Marie's elephant, lifted the giant buffalo mask off her costume and was among the first to reach the elephant — she looked back at Marie triumphantly, and yet not overly surprised, as if believing that into each and every life there might always appear at least one elephant, completely unexpected, and completely beautiful.

And as if in a dream, Marie, who had been wearing a Kiowa headdress and shaking a gourd rattle, went over to join her adopted daughter, and all the other children and townsfolk, around the elephant — she was seventy-two, that autumn, and it stunned her to realize that some forty years had gone by since her own elephant had passed through — and she laughed at the incongruity of it, the elephant on Main Street, reappearing when she had least expected it. She thought she had known what Beth was up to — she thought, in fact, that she surely knew the world, could predict with near-numbing regularity its comings and goings — and the surprise of it was delicious, so much so that she, like the others, felt compelled to simply stand in the elephant's company, and to examine its lacquered sides, the glossy tusks, the stiff wide ears, and the thick legs: almost as pleased with its presence as if it had been the real thing.

The children, believing that this puppet, too, contained chocolate and other candy, quickly laid into the elephant, stripping it of its glow-lighting and leaping upon its back to smash it apart, and wrenching its tusks from their sockets and reaching their hands up inside it, searching.

Finding nothing, they began unpeeling the cardboard, working in a frenzy now — certain that great glories were housed within — and in a matter of only seconds, the elephant had all but vanished, leaving in its place only a flattened jumble of painted cardboard, some wadded-up newspaper, electrical wiring, and twin eyebolts hanging from the zipline: and the children were mortified by what they had done, though Beth was amused, laughing at the speed with which her handiwork had been disassembled, and she gestured to the children to step back, then motioned to Ruth to step forward and with her barbecue-grill flamethrower vaporize the remains, as if the animal had carried some awful disease and had had to be incinerated.

And when the children saw that the elephant's creator was untroubled by the creature's demise, and that their teacher was leading the cremation, they felt less guilty, and gathered back together in post-performance glow, their choreography completed, while the elephant puppet smoldered and crackled in flame.

Ancient Herbert Mix was in the parade, too, dressed in no costume of his or the puppeteer's making, but instead a snow-white suit of spangled sequins and fringe, his one leg's white cowboy boot, a white Stetson, with toy six-shooter cap pistols in a toy holster, perched side-saddle on a tiny white Shetland pony. Mix quivered with joy as he rode alongside the dragon, and the buffalo, and the towering Comanche with his spear — and it was this day, and into this inexplicable but wonderful pageant, that Richard returned to his old town, the site of his old battle for the impenetrable heart of Clarissa.

He had gotten off at the bus station a mile west of town and, no longer knowing anyone, had walked into town, duffel bag slung over his shoulder: and when he came down Main Street from the other direction and beheld the townspeople on the sidewalks, and saw the one-legged, wizened Herbert Mix all dolled up, snapping off shots with his little pistols, and the dragon breathing fire, and then the flying elephant soaring down into the street, he was not sure what to think, other than that once again he felt he was somehow in the right place at the right time.

He had not known it the first time, but this time he was starting to understand and be aware of his fortunes, as well as the responsibilities of those fortunes, the eternal second chances that the earth itself seemed determined to keep delivering up to him. The replications of history.

It took a while to get things sorted out; it was an hour or two before the streets were cleaned and the excitement died down, and the businesses were able to return to their sleepy paces. The loft in which Marie and Annie had lived before moving out to Mormon Springs was available, and Richard was able to rent it from the church. From the upstairs balcony, he watched the Mormon Springs students loading the last of their costumes into the trucks, saw the diminutive puppeteer coiling up the ziplines — saw the two women climbing down from the roof of the bank, breaking down their extension ladders like workaday painters or plumbers and toting them back to the trucks, where all the carcasses of puppets, some charred and broken and others still intact, were piled high — and Richard marveled at how much the town had changed in the ten or so years since his departure.

He had no way of knowing he was witnessing an anomaly — that the puppeteer, Beth, was but a random seed cast by the wind, as were even the tiny handful of others whom he had not yet met. Nor would he have been able to guess as to their viability, their chances for enduring, and affecting change.

To him, from that window in the spartan white room, it looked as if all the change had already occurred, and as if the roots of those seeds had already, in his ten years' absence, reached deep, and had found both water and nutrients: and as if the once-cautious, once-conservative town of Odessa had not cut down those plants, or those roots, but had embraced them.

He showered and shaved, hung his clothes neatly in the tiny closet space, sat down on the bed and opened the phone book, three years out of date. Her parents were gone, and she was gone. For a moment, he held on to the idea that she had gotten married and changed her name; but then he laughed at himself, at having held on to even a shred of hope that it might be that easy, that she might have changed her character, embracing that which she had once reviled—and he admonished himself for having even dared to wish that this might be so, for he would not have been drawn to her without that fear and that hatred, just as his associates the oilmen had been drawn to the ancient deaths, the sulfurous black-green pools and vats.

The white room felt alien and yet familiar to him. Either way, it felt as if he fit it, at this point and time in his life, fit it as comfortably as if it had been made for him, or he for it.

He had not felt fearlessness in a long time, and sitting in the white room, staring down at the town that he thought had finally awakened, he realized that at some near level, he was not, or once had not been, all that different from her: that he might once have been as frightened of the future, and a world without her, as she had been of the past and the present.

I knew how to be fearless, he thought, remembering those days spent in pursuit of her heart. *Do I know how to be fearful?*

Like Max Omo, or any other of the millions of men and women who had ever walked the face of the earth—like Clarissa herself—he had run for cover, had allowed himself to go underground, before his time was due.

After visiting a few offices, Richard was able to find some of the men and women with whom he had once done business—a drilling contractor, a land manager, an engineer, a production geologist—though even among these familiar haunts, there were not many whom he remembered, or who remembered him, or him and Clarissa.

The turnover was high, out in the desert. He finally found someone who was able to tell him that her parents had died; but as to Clarissa, no one had heard, no one knew. *No,* to the best of their knowledge, *she had never come back. No, they couldn't think of anyone he might be able to ask.*

The people he questioned regarded him with pity. *You were lucky to have her,* their looks told him plainly. *You will never have her again.*

Richard called on Herbert Mix, wandered by the old skull gatherer's warehouse later that afternoon. It was the first time in nearly a decade in which he had not worked two days in a row, and he liked it.

Mix was out in the backyard, having just laundered his sequined suit, and was hanging it to dry on the clothesline. He had not sold a dousing rod in years, his willow garden was overgrown, an impenetrable rainforest that he kept watering anyway. Inca doves, bright tanagers, buntings, and vireos nested in its farthest reaches, and odd-gaited neighborhood cats, dingy and pink-eyed, their brains cooked to delirium by the desert heat, skulked the perimeters.

Mix carried a BB gun, a toy rifle on a sling, and whenever he spotted one of the marauders he would set his cane aside, lower himself to the ground like an ancient commando, and lob a stinging round at the cat before levering in another round and firing again. His aim was good, and the first time Richard witnessed this — standing at the back gate, unannounced — he understood why the cats were limping, and wondered idly why Mix did not just kill them, if he was so intent on protecting the precious songbirds, but then understood: the old man was lonelier than ever. Not crazy, just lonely; and watching him, Richard felt for the first time ever a touch of fear, a questioning about his own distant Clarissa-less future, and wondered if perhaps he should have stayed down in the Sierra Occidentals with Sy Craven and the others, where at least he'd had a home, a routine, and a future, even if it was no future at all. China, and Africa, and relentless root-hog grubbing: more oil, then death.

Herbert Mix pushed himself back into a standing position, then limped over to where he had stung the cat and scratched through the sand with the tip of his cane, his gimlet eyes squinting. Spying the pellet, he bent down and picked it up, polished the tiny gold piece on his shirtfront, then put it back in his ammo bag, more frugal than ever; as if by a fierce enough accounting, the old man might be able to stave off his immense fears, which might not even have been those of the simple void of death, Richard saw now, and a loss of all the senses, but amounted instead to some darker reckoning, both of the void below and the realm above, where time was wasted, less significant even than the sand sifting through his fingers.

And disturbed suddenly by such a sobering interpretation of the world — *Is this what Clarissa had seen,* Richard wondered, *and if so, how had she remained sane?* — Richard was about to turn away and depart, unannounced, leaving the old man free to grub for his spent BBs in peace.

But from the corner of his eye — hungering, as ever, for a passing-through treasure seeker, a pigeon, a mark — Herbert Mix caught the glimpse of movement, and waved to Richard, and hurried over to greet him, recognizing him instantly, as a father might his son; as if ten years was nothing.

Believing, perhaps, that there had been only a dull cessation in the relationship, and that Richard had returned with some grand object of commerce to trade or sell to Herbert Mix: a treasure all the more rare and wonderful for the waiting.

And for a moment it seemed that Mix was caught in the ten-years-past, for he looked around as if expecting to see Richard's partner with him. He even inquired after her, unable to quite remember her name, though certainly remembering her image. "Where is — she?" Mix asked, faltering over the name — "your friend?" — and Richard's face fell as he answered, "I was hoping you might know."

They sat on the back patio listening to the cheeps of the birds hidden back in the willows, drinking the iced sun tea that Herbert Mix had made that morning (stirring so much sugar into the pitcher that the last five or six spoonfuls did not dissolve, but remained on the bottom, gritty as sand), while Mix filled Richard in on all that had gone on in town in the last ten years, which was next to nothing; indeed, the day's parade, and the new school out at Mormon Springs, were about the only highlights.

There had been more drilling going on, there would always be more drilling—there were more caverns opening up out in the desert, abysses and sinkholes, and people's water wells were getting lower and sandier, and were starting to taste sulfurous in this, the eighth year of the drought—but the land had been through drought before, Herbert Mix said, and would be all right again after a couple of years of good rain.

"Not this year," he said, looking up at the great blue above, the heat almost nauseating, "but next."

He changed the subject away from the meteorological, then, and rather than veering toward the entrepreneurial, as he would have in the old days, he began to speak of something else.

"I've got a friend," he said, delighted to have the opportunity to talk about her.

And what else might he have told Richard? That his hungers were abating? That he was happy? What world revolution or climactic upheaval could be more interesting, immediate, or necessary than that?

"I go over there two, three times a week," he said. His heart leaping, wishing it were six or seven—so little time remaining!—and yet, the two or three times a week was enough that it seemed he was somehow with her even in her, Marie's, absence; even in their absence, Marie and the young girl Annie, of whom he was also proud, informing Richard that she was smart, quiet but smart.

"There's an artist in town," Herbert Mix said. "That was her parade you saw this morning. She's leaving tonight on the train. We're having a party for her, a celebration before she goes. You're welcome to come, it'll be fun. We're going to burn the puppets. It's something she says she does after every performance." A pause, then, after this lengthy run of words, to stand before the nutmeat, the true essence of the day.

"Marie will be there, you can meet Marie," he said. The pleasure of saying her name twice. And were he to say it a third time, the pleasure, the dizziness he felt, would be no less. Richard could see it in Herbert Mix's eyes, could see it in his general posture, could hear it in his voice, could feel it radiating from his mere presence, like a shout.

Goddamn you lucky savage, Richard thought, and was both saddened and stricken to think that his own road ahead might be as lengthy, improbable, and lonely.

Richard turned and looked back up toward the bluffs east of town, the Castle Gap country, as if waiting. As if she were due back on some certain schedule, and as if at last he understood that the form of the land would, must, deliver her back to him.

"I'd love to meet her," he told the old treasure seeker. "Where, and what time?"

The burning took place out near one of the old well sites. The puppets were arranged around the edge of one of the sinkholes, and a bonfire was already burning when Richard and Herbert Mix arrived, so that at first, from a distance, they thought they were late, and that the puppets were already aflame. They rode out in Herbert Mix's old truck, suffering stiffly but without complaint every jounce and jolt, and in their ride, and in the old man's calming mix of eagerness and peacefulness, his relaxation at moving closer toward the company of his beloved, Richard again felt a twinge of envy: and in the ride out to the party, he understood more about the old bone collector's bliss than he could ever have gleaned from awkward conversation.

The stars burned above them like sparks from the campfire itself; and feeling the cooler air of night rushing in through the open windows, and looking up at the familiar clockwork of constellations, Richard relaxed too, and felt himself for the first time to be in a place more like home: felt the curve of the earth accepting him, as might the flow of some powerful river.

They wound down sandy roads toward the distant fire, the color of it a brighter yellow than the orange flares of the gas wells scattered across the desert. Richard found himself remembering the specifics of each wellhead they passed, the abandoned dry holes as well as the productive, snake-hiss pumping oil wells and the silent hydrant-like wellheads of the gas producers. He remembered being out on the well-logging trucks at each location they passed, midwifing each well into existence, the life or death of the well to be decided by each logging job, and by his interpretation of the data.

He found himself remembering with remarkable intensity the squiggly lines of electrocardiograph-like responses of the logging tool on the computer's screen as the radioactive tool was lowered and then raised slowly back up through the geological column of the just-drilled hole: little blebs and nips of electrical response revealing hidden ledges and beaches and old creeks and canyons thousands of feet below; hidden oil and gas, the treasure, and lenses of water, sometimes salty (Devonian) and other times fresh (Pennsylvanian), always the enemy, always indicating failure.

And in the remembering of so many tiny geological details — the intimacy of specific sand grains from various core samples, the sand from long ago held in his bare hands and rubbed between his fingers to gauge grain size and hence perhaps porosity, and sniffed for traces of hydrocarbons, and even tasted with his tongue to determine the presence of silt or clay — he remembered also the often-nameless well operators and drillers and roughnecks who had been out on the rigs helping him deliver each of those wells.

He remembered the taste of 4:00 A.M. scorched coffee — always, it seemed the wells were delivered at night, gave up their secrets at night — and the odor of the workers' harsh cigarettes mixing with the even more astringent eye-stinging odor of the ammonia that was used to make the blue-line prints of the electrical logs, so that Richard could spread them out on the little table inside the logging van as if they were the thing itself, rather than a representation.

And with his calculator and various formulas, he had begun his computations that would help decide where into the subsurface world he had fallen, and what was to be done about it: whether to push on, drilling deeper, or to turn back, and walk away.

It was like the dreamworld, the otherworld, that Herbert Mix was in right now, as they headed farther out into the desert, as leisurely in their night drive as a pleasure boat chugging out of a harbor, with all of a grand day's trip lying ahead. It was similar, that deliciously imagined underworld, but it was not quite as good. It was but a substitute for the world above, and Richard, riding out to the bonfire and the burning of the puppets, felt as if he was perched on some ledge midway between the two worlds, the higher and the lower, and yet that he had no route, no path, to take him from the one to the other; that after thirty-three years, he was finally stranded.

And realizing this, he tried not to panic, but leaned back in the seat of old Herbert Mix's ancient truck, and tried to let the shape of the land and the force of time deliver him to where he needed to be.

He knew Clarissa would not be at this party, he acknowledged his fear that he might never see her again, and yet he found the courage to continue to hope that he might somehow again; and from behind the steering wheel, old Herbert Mix hummed quietly, both hands on the wheel, with the bonfire growing finally closer.

The little handful of puppet-children and their parents were already gathered, roasting hot dogs and marshmallows over the fire — half a dozen cars and trucks were parked around the throw of light — and perhaps Richard might have recognized the girl as his own immediately, had he spied her out on her own, separate from the small crowd.

As it was, when he first viewed her, she was surrounded by others, in the midst of three generations of girls and women, standing with one of her classmates, her closest friend, a quiet, younger girl named Maeve, and Beth, the puppeteer, barely twenty, and Ruth, almost thirty, and then Marie, whose silver hair shone in the firelight, and whom Richard intuited immediately was Herbert Mix's paramour.

They went straight away toward the assembled group and were handed paper cups of warm apple cider, which Beth acknowledged was an old pagan-Yankee tradition of hers, one that was necessary to accompany any and all of her puppet-burnings. She made it sound as if she had been doing it all her life, and when Richard asked when she had gotten started, she told him that she had been making them and playing with them for as long as she could remember, but that her first professional job had not come until she was thirteen.

"I had a happy childhood," she said, laughing — as candid with the stranger, Richard, as if, by virtue of his having made it out into the desert, he was one of them, rather than an outsider — as if she had worked with him, too, for all the long hours of each of those five weeks, as she had with the children and their parents. "I had a great family, no neuroses or anything, but I don't know, I just was really into making up all these weird worlds, and surrounding myself with all of these really weird creatures."

Her eyes were gleaming in the push-and-pull light of the fire, she was still riding the ecstasy of the post-performance high, as were the children and the parents and townsfolk who had witnessed the spectacle; and her thralldom in a place of otherworldness so reminded Richard of his own comfort and joy found in exploring other worlds that he was both attracted to her and yet somehow unsettled, for how could one dare or even desire to draw too near to one so like one's self?

Still, he found himself thinking, *How you would love to know of the ammonites, the giant horned cephalopods lying up in the hills, just beyond this fire* — and he marveled for the thousandth time at the confluence of fate that had led him to the place and time of loving Clarissa, rather than any other, rather than all others. She, who had cared almost nothing for such things, or even, it seemed, for the world itself. But almost: he could not shake the feeling that he had *almost* convinced her to love the world; to dare to love the world.

He should have noticed Annie then, should have caught a glimpse of her and had his head turned by a shock of recognition, or invisible current — she even looked like he had looked, at that age — but he had not thought about what he looked like as a child in a long time, nor was he even now a devotee of mirrors, so that even if she had been his twin, it might have meant nothing to him — though still somehow, standing so close to her, he should have known; should have come up from the lower world enough to take the fuller measure of things.

Instead, he turned to meet Marie — Herbert Mix was introducing him — and then the teacher, Ruth. He was put off by Ruth's guardedness, her defensiveness, and its implicit assumption that because he was a stranger, he might end up being like one of the townspeople who had judged and then turned against her — that he might be one of those who would get in the way of her life's passion, of teaching, and of making a difference in young lives.

Then he was being introduced to the other parents and their children, with old Herbert Mix continuing the introductions; and the others accepted him immediately, for that reason. Richard saw how Herbert Mix had outlasted his eccentricity, had ridden it like a mount to some far enough point where it had become a form of respectability — that the old treasure hunter had become like a geological fixture, and had altered the community around him, forcing them to respect him simply by virtue of his endurance, having prevailed over those who had once ridiculed him.

Only one of the parents asked Richard what he was doing there, and when Herbert Mix interjected that he was a geologist, that was all the answer that was needed, though it seemed to him that there might have been a thing like pity in the polite smile that followed. *Oh, yes, a geologist. We know about the indefatigable and insatiable hearts of geologists.*

He stared at Herbert Mix and Marie for a moment, the old gentle-man's arm resting lightly around her waist in a way that was both bold and shy, then looked over at the schoolteacher again, caught just a glimpse of her looking quickly away.

Of course she was wary of him, she was right to assume he might have come to interrupt her life somehow, or to take something away: she was listening to her instincts, and her instincts told her to beware; that he had about him the residue, the aura, of taking.

It bothered him that she perceived him so, and he wondered how he might convince her otherwise.

Perhaps I can work with the children, he thought, *perhaps I can come up to the school and teach them about geology, and the place where they live.*

Beth had detached herself from the parents and had called the chil-dren to her, crouched amidst them as if they were all football players in a huddle. A couple of the smaller ones appeared near tears, and the older ones were somber, as Beth explained how the puppet-burning was to proceed.

"It's supposed to be a celebration," she said. She was herself but a few years older than the oldest among them, and diminutive, lean as a boy; with her short curly hair, from a distance, she might have been mistaken for an elfin boy.

"I'll light each puppet," she explained, and then turned to address Zachary, the kindergartner, and raised a finger — "Never play with matches. And then once they're all burning, I'll give a signal, and we'll each use a stick to push our puppets into the Great Pit of Everlasting Purge and Rejuvenation, where they will be purified and preserved forever as memories in our hearts.

"You will always remember this," she said, speaking to all of them now. "It's human nature to want to hold on to something you've worked so hard on, and created" — she glanced over at Herbert Mix and then at Richard, and smiled — "but the spirits of our puppets have fulfilled their human obligations, they've brought us joy and happiness, and now it's time to seal them in our hearts so that those feelings will remain in us forever."

She looked around at each of the children, and at the pit that had been dug for the ritual. "If we try to hold on to them, they'll just end up in attics and basements, in lofts and garages, all dusty and cobwebbed, dull and cracked and heat-stricken," she said. "Their power and beauty will leave them. We have to resurrect their power to thrill us one more time," she said. "We have to have a finale."

The children nodded, not understanding, and perhaps not even believing such things: but they trusted her. Richard saw that Ruth was smiling, and that he might have misjudged her: she was not all hard, she possessed some softness. He saw the quiet, serious girl, Annie, tucked in tight against her, the teacher's arm folded over her chest pulling her in closer, and he thought, *Oh, her daughter.*

"All right," Beth said, "remember this," and she led them over to the trucks parked next to the abyss and pulled out their puppets, each to his and her own. The children brought the creations over to the pit and arranged them around its edges, buffalo and demon and alien and Kiowa, Comanche and heron and raven and hawk, each puppet towering like a stone megalith, realistic in silhouette.

A stillness fell over the little audience as the play of light from the bonfire wavered back and forth across the artworks in a way that brought them to life, seemed to be propelling them forward now into the world under their own desires and momentums. As if now they must be destroyed, in order for the memory of them to be owned: in order to prevent the puppets from becoming their own things — mortal, and, as Beth had explained, prone, then, to disintegration.

The children did not understand, but trusted her.

The puppets needed no gasoline in order to burn. Each child made a little setting of twigs and crumpled newspaper at the base of their puppet. Beth gave a brief invocation — "Thank you for the pleasure you have brought us," she told the puppets, and then, turning to the makers, "Thank you for what you have created, and brought to our hearts" — and then she knelt and lit one of her own puppets, the divine and gigantic King Kong, and the other puppetmakers did the same.

On the other side of King Kong, Herbert Mix and Marie were igniting the buffalo, and all else around the pit, the mammoth puppets were becoming quickly shrouded in flame.

It seemed to them that the puppets were stepping, of their own volition, into chambers of flame, and it was a surprise to all who witnessed it, for if such yearning existed in the puppets, then did it not also exist in the hearts of their makers?

All around the pit, puppets plumed in wreaths of bright flame burned in hues of magenta, cerulean, and chartreuse as the paint cracked and flaked and then vaporized. It was a rainbow of fire, a kaleidoscope of fire — Richard looked over at Beth and saw that she was watching as if hypnotized, her face fire-rimmed with an expression of Technicolored rapture — and then, just as Beth had hoped, the puppets began to ascend.

It was a phenomenon that occurred only infrequently, in the puppet-burnings. The conditions had to be near-perfect: a calm, cooling night, stable barometric pressure, and low humidity, so that the puppets burned hot and quickly — and when it worked, the flaming puppets were lifted a short distance above the ground, like hot-air balloons, as their hollow husks filled with the combustible gases, and as the heat of their self-made flames rose all around them, in the same manner in which smoke and heat swirl into the updrafts of a chimney.

One by one, all around the pit, the puppets began to hop and tilt and lift in a syncopated dance. Some of them floated several feet into the air and appeared to hover, stricken or perhaps exalted, seized, even if only briefly, by the current of life, before settling back down upon the ground, where, their gases spent, they began to crumple and shrink to blackening char.

Other puppets ascended only to fall over on their backs as they settled back down. Still others — the majority — were drawn toward the pit, canting and tipping toward it as if pulled there by some unavoidable summons; and encountering the cooler, denser air above the pit, they hovered longest of all, before toppling in.

They fell upon one another, a cascade of burning puppets, sailfish upon rhinoceros upon hawk upon Comanche, with the burning outlines of these apparitions alarming, surely, to any rigworkers who might be staring off into the desert in their direction.

The heat from the burning paper and cardboard was terrific, as was the roar of the flames. The heat singed the hair of the onlookers, curled the hair on the backs of the men's hands, and melted the tips of the eyebrows of any who did not step away quickly enough.

With rakes and shovels, the onlookers shoved those fallen puppets which had not yet made it into the pit down into the bed of fire, with rafts of spark and ember showering upward in brilliant fountains each time a new body part was added to the brew: the wing of a raven, the head of an antelope. Herbert Mix himself shoveled in the leg of a miner, wobbly on his own good leg.

The cremation was so intense that it fused the sand into a giant, iridescent, swirl-streaked glassine bowl, which would, in coming years, hold water, with bushes and then small trees growing up around it to provide shade and prevent evaporation; and the children would come and swim there on hot days, and would remember their earlier childhood.

That was all to come later. That night, as the puppets burned, and the old and glorious past fell away, the onlookers watched, fascinated by Beth's wizardry, as the glowing pit below, a caldera of heat and color and noise, flashed and flamed and roared. The fire burned hot for a long time, a single giant glowing ingot, burning far longer than any of them would have guessed.

It continued to send up a single heated breath, like some collective final exhalation; but as it finally wavered, the onlookers were able to edge closer and peer back down into the glowing bowl of their making, and in the wormy traces and ruins they were sometimes able to make out the shadows and outlines, framed by the ashen lines of the cardboard's corrugations, of certain of their creations: and they stared into this strange amalgam as if into a wishing-well mirror.

And in that viewing, they felt banded and bonded closer together — less the outcasts of Mormon Springs, and more than ever like community, family, clan — and although they all felt special, it was the children who felt this most keenly of all; and they felt assured and confident when they considered the future, now that they understood it could hold such marvels for them as Beth and her puppets.

It was a little lonely, after the last of the flames died down to glowing coals. The onlookers stood closer together, not for warmth but in affection — husbands and wives, parents and children, and the two lovers, Herbert Mix and Marie — and Beth herself felt the bittersweetness of it deepest of all. It was a feeling as if some good part of all of them was draining away back down into the sand. It was not the best part of them, however, and the emptiness they felt would be refilled and recharged — they each knew it — as if the going-away helped make space for the new and better part to come in.

Their bonfire had burned down. They gathered their shovels and rakes, their aluminum lawn chairs and ice chests, and loaded them into their trucks. Beth was leaving soon — the eastbound to Houston came through just before midnight; the next morning, at sunrise, she would transfer to New Orleans, then north, back to Philadelphia — and she told the children that she hated goodbyes, that she would come back and see them, and that she wanted to tell them goodbye here in the desert, that she did not want a big farewell at the train station.

She felt her own heart detaching, even as they clung to her and pleaded with her to stay just one more day. She felt herself ascending, burning, toppling, as she stepped into the chamber of belief that it was better to leave immediately, and to remember their time sweetly, even as she knew she would likely never return to Odessa.

She gave each of them fierce hugs, then stepped away, though still they followed her as if in a parade, and hugged her again and again. The smaller ones, Zachary and a girl named Sarah, made a game of wrapping their arms around her thin ankles, each of them a Lilliputian attaching to Gulliver, and she felt herself having to detach even further than she had intended: and though not in a panic, not too close to sadness or sorrow yet, she nonetheless felt herself tensing, and twisted in the children's grasp to find Herbert Mix, who had volunteered his truck.

It had been decided, agreed, Richard would drive her out to the station — there would be no grief, no attachment, there; a perfect stranger, a chauffeur — and now she found Richard's eyes and pleaded for help and understanding, and he went and got her two small duffel bags (one of personal articles, clothing and an extra pair of high-topped tennis shoes, the other a larger, heavier bag of puppet gear: coiled ziplines, PA-28 staplers, X-Acto blades, paintbrushes) and transferred them to Herbert Mix's truck. Mix would ride home with Marie and Annie, would stay out at their house that evening.

It was hard even for Richard to watch — he who had no investment in the leave-taking. They simply would not let her go. Their parents intervened, but no sooner had they succeeded in separating Zachary's and Sarah's grasp than other children rushed in, playing tug of war with Beth, even the older children, and Annie and her friend Maeve; and in the end it was Ruth who had to negotiate the departure, explaining to the children that she would ride out to the train station with Beth to tell her goodbye, but that they had to leave immediately, or else Beth would miss her train.

"She's anxious to get back to her home, and her family," Ruth said, "and her family is anxious to see her."

Still the children protested, though they finally released her — satisfied or at least reassured that she would receive a proper farewell with Ruth accompanying her — and the three of them climbed into the old truck and pulled away; and only then, with the safety of the desert's darkness swallowing them, and the night air swirling in through the open windows, as warm as if at the ocean, did Beth feel herself successfully detach, able to step away without heartbreak.

She laughed — she was sitting by the passenger-side window, Ruth was in the middle — looked over at Ruth's swirling hair, slapped her hand a couple of times on the truck's window jamb, and said, "Good job, Teacher."

The old feel of freedom, the old release, returning to her as it always did, a feeling like running for the open sea; though some certain times, it was harder to pull away. And yet, she had done it again.

They passed one after another of the flaring gas wells, the flames wavering like far-spaced candles on an immense birthday cake. "You drilled all these?" Beth asked, leaning forward to look at Richard — clearly more pleased with the nighttime appearance of them than by any intimations of material wealth they might foretell below — and Richard laughed and looked out to the horizon — trying to remember the outlines of the buried fields below — and corrected her, and told her that he had probably only drilled or worked on about a quarter of them.

"Cool," Beth said, and they rode a while in silence, Ruth holding her hair back from her face with one hand, before Ruth said, "Good, you're not responsible for *all* the cave-ins," and Richard, unsure of whether she was joking or serious, chose to perceive the former, and laughed and said, "No, only about a quarter of them," and they rode on some more in silence.

They were the only ones at the station. The conductor had a habit of not stopping, if he saw no cars or trucks in the parking lot; and by the way the train came roaring in, it was clear that he had not expected to encounter anyone this evening. He piled on the brakes, the squeal of steel caliper on drum shrieking from a thousand wheels, sparks tumbling from them, with the scent of burning railside cinder and the scorch of coal smoke acrid in the desert air.

In departing, Beth showed little emotion; she hugged both Ruth and Richard, though without the passion with which she'd enlivened her King Kong and flying elephant. She promised again to come back sometime, and then greeted the conductor (who appeared ready to be angry about something, until he saw how small and alone she was), handing him one of her bags as she climbed the iron steps, through the iron darkness, the coal-black sky silhouetted by the jewelry of stars.

And reaching the top step, without looking back — to Ruth and Richard, it seemed that the set of her mouth was cast in a straight line — Beth stepped into the horizontal husk of train.

She took her seat. The train hissed and yowled, began to bull forward. She leaned her face against the glass, eager to see the desert at night. During her entire five-week sojourn, she had gone nowhere other than into Odessa for supplies, then back to Mormon Springs; and as the train accelerated into its soothing, clicking glide, she handled in her memory those five weeks as a fossil collector working at night might examine with his or her hands the ridges and indentations of specimens just discovered.

She watched, dreamed, remembered. She considered, and reconsidered, each child, each adult. As if all of them, for that short space of time, had been her creation, a product of her shaping. As if she had been, for that time, responsible for them all.

Ruth and Richard, gathered to bid her farewell, saw her light-limned face against the window and waved. In the darkness, Beth did not see them, and they both experienced a gutted, empty feeling as the train pulled away — Ruth, in particular, bore it heavily, saddened not just by the loss of Beth from their lives, but by the hard reality of the return of the hammer-and-tong work that would be required of her again, without the benefit of the artist-in-residence.

Once alone with Richard, she presumed that, because he was her own age, and because he was a man, he would try to court her while he was in Odessa. She was not in the mood for such a thing. She had her fourteen children, her furious desire to remake the world, and to help coax a blossoming love in each of them that would last for all their lives — fourteen children multiplied by another eighty years each, calculated to eleven hundred and twenty years of pure love — and though she was not a man-hater in the least, she had no intention of pursuing, or being pursued by, a man outside her faith, nor any man, right now.

Show me a man who can compete with, who can create or provide, eleven hundred and twenty years of love, she might have said, when asked about the subject.

And perhaps that was the sadness she felt, on the drive back to Mormon Springs. Beth had given that kind of love, that joy and spontaneity and creativity — call it a year and a half of love — but now it had been taken away, pulled away, and there was an emptiness within.

On the other side of the truck, she imagined that she could feel

Richard, who was driving, preparing to speak; considering his approach.

For a moment, in her emptiness, she thought, *Oh, let him try, what would it hurt? I'm empty.* But she thought then of the work and challenge before her, and chose instead to begin fashioning a defense, even before his sexual gambit had officially been launched.

"I came out here to teach," she said, anticipating his first question, the lame one with which everyone led, male or female, young or old. Then she adjusted the message quickly. "I've never married, and may never. I've never found anyone brave enough, or active enough. Everyone's too complacent," she said, "too easygoing. There's no rage, nor exultation — *nothing*," she said. "I guess that's what attracts me to the children — they're still so *whole*." She pretended to change the subject, then.

"What about you?" she asked, almost challenging him, and paused, letting her words hang, so that it might seem she was asking why *he* was so damned complacent. Why he was willing to let the world, and the river-flow of time, happen to him, rather than him happening to the world. "What brings you out here?" she asked finally, a little more gently, cutting him a bit of slack, which surprised her; it was not her way, with adults. "Oil, right?"

Unsure of what bee had gotten in her bonnet, and feeling somehow scolded — a sentiment all the more troubling for the sense he had that she was correct in scolding him, as he himself was not quite sure what his offense had been — he said nothing, but instead just drove, and pondered her litany.

Richard thought about Clarissa: how, ten years earlier, it would be he and she who would be in this old truck, traveling over this same old country; and he wondered again, for the hundredth time, what she would be like, what she *was* like, now, at thirty. How she compared, for instance, to this interesting woman beside him, who clearly was more engaged and more caring, and perhaps more passionate, and yet who — for no reason that he could discern — seemed almost to be attacking him.

He continued to ride in silence. When he finally spoke, all he said was, "Maybe you should consider not being so harsh. I don't think you can always tell who's complacent, and who's not, just by looking." He turned to watch her for a moment, as he drove — examining her now: and her face burned as she remembered the times that she herself had been judged in such a manner.

She could think of no argument. She rode in silence, feeling completely stripped of her defense; though unlike the gutted, empty loneliness that had accompanied Beth's leaving, this was not a bad feeling. If anything, she felt lighter, and they rode comfortably, breeze-stirred with the gas flares on either side of them acting as familiar guides — as if it were a lane they were traveling that they had not been on in a long time.

They found themselves upon it, and there was an absence of fear. It was comfortable.

Maybe she is just beyond those flames, Richard thought, considering Clarissa. *Maybe she is out there in the darkness, biding her time. I will wait here for her a while,* he thought. *I'll wait here, just hang out here for a while, and wait for her to step back in from that darkness.*

As they drew closer to the little town, they began to see the silhouettes of what they thought at first were animals running down the road — stray range cattle, spooked by their approach, they assumed — but saw then that they were runners, football players scattered here and there, training not in any official regimen of their coaches' making, but simply running on their own, running miles and miles in the hours long before their 4:30 A.M. scheduled training: and although Ruth and Richard both thought they had already seen the full breadth of the players' devotion to their god, they were surprised and troubled by the revelation of these previously unknown depths, and they passed by them uneasily, feeling now more like travelers in a foreign country than residents in their own land.

If the players were running so maniacally as a symptom of love, Richard reasoned, they would not hide in the cool of night, they would haul themselves down the road in day as well as night, hurling themselves out into the desert as old Herbert Mix had done, in younger days. It was the fear of failure that drove them, masquerading as love;

it was not, they both saw, the incendiary thing itself. It was just old-fashioned fear, dug down extra-deep, as if into some farther reservoir; it was not the other thing, the mythic thing, the thing people clamored for and believed they deserved.

Richard and Ruth came into the sleeping town of Odessa, passing down Main Street, the town scoured and sterile again, as if no parade had ever occurred — and then they were out the other side, as if having traveled through a husk or tube, and were back out into the desert, driving on the short distance to the outcast village of Mormon Springs. As they drove, they could see now, farther out into the desert, at the end of long pale driveways, the occasional small clapboard ranch houses, yellow window squares still burning, one or two homes every mile or so, and they knew that these were the residences of families who had participated in the spectacle, still too stimulated to sleep: as if a comet or some other natural phenomenon had passed through, compelling them to remain awake far into the night, visiting about it and reliving it in the telling and retelling.

They passed half a dozen such houses, and then a dozen more, scattered in all directions to the east of Odessa, on the road to Mormon Springs and beyond, and it seemed to both of them to signify a kind of secret society, a clear demarcation between those who were asleep and those who were not.

Like angels of Passover, Ruth and Richard traveled farther, east of Odessa, noting who had participated and who had not; and when they drove by Marie's house, they saw that not only was her light still on, but that Herbert Mix and Marie were sitting on the front porch swing in which Annie usually curled up and read, in the afternoon, waiting out the heat of the day.

Richard slowed down and almost stopped, but then thought better of it, not wanting to intrude on their privacy, and continued on. It seemed unimaginable to him that an old man and an old woman would have anything left to visit about, at two o'clock in the morning; and when he remarked to Ruth how he found this to be rather wonderful, she shot him a look that he could not comprehend, but which seemed surprisingly to contain a mixture of disbelief and scorn.

"They're just people, is all," she said, "like you or me, or like two kids, for that matter. And the world is still filled with interesting things. Why shouldn't they be talking at two in the morning?"

Richard couldn't be sure whether she was a closet romantic or if the source of her anger was that he considered such a thing to be unusual. They were pulling up to her darkened little house. The schoolhouse lay a hundred yards farther on. He tried to explain himself, tried to agree with her.

"That's my point," he said. "The fact is, most people *don't,* and so it seemed wonderful to me that —"

"Don't try and brownnose," she advised him, and got out of the truck. Not sure exactly where she stood, but knowing that above all costs, she had to protect herself.

She smiled politely, thanked him, and shut the truck's door, walked up the flagstone walkway to the dark house, and once inside, did not turn the lights on, but went straight to bed, after slipping off her sandals, jeans, and shirt, turning the fan on, and washing the dust from her face, arms, and chest with a washcloth.

She was mildly displeased with how she had treated the visitor, and it took her a long time to get to sleep. She lay listening to the fan, and felt the waste of her body, unloved and unknown, like some map of little-known territory, across and through which no traveler, no explorer, had been in a long time. Her body — for now, for these brief few years — as real and finite as were her dreams of purity and passion and nurturing for the children abstract and amorphous. *Why,* she wondered, *is there not time or space in the world for both?*

Richard drove home. The lights at Marie's house were now off, the sleepers dreaming puppet dreams. He headed west back into Odessa, left the truck at Herbert Mix's museum, and walked the half block down to his apartment, climbed the wooden outside steps to the loft, even though there were no tenants below. Not wanting to pass through the empty shell of the interior, but desiring, like all of the various frightened dreamers, to remain somewhat outside.

He stood on the landing at the top of the stairs for some time, hesitating to go inside: invigorated by the passage of Beth, and by the newness of the turn his life had taken. He looked down on the sleeping town, with neither risk nor ambition rising from it, and he thought he felt again a stirring of what Clarissa must have felt, long ago.

Mormon Springs, on the other hand, seemed to him to be a community worth knowing, sufficiently outside the placidity of Odessa. Maybe not east of Eden, but newer, finer, rawer, edgier.

Ruth was just covering herself, trying to put up a wall without first ascertaining whether he was a threat. He laughed, looking down at the empty street across which earlier that day the elephant and all his fantastic kin had flown. Standing again in Clarissa's old town, and looking down upon the space where she no longer was, made him remember her all the more, and want her again even more intensely than ever: but in the meantime, here was this interesting woman who had not run from this place, but who had instead sought it out. He still wanted Clarissa, but at the same time, he was intrigued by the schoolteacher; and in her resistance, there was a part of him, the geologist, the taker, that found her irresistible.

10

THE CHILD WAS NOT so much standoffish and aloof as she was absorbed in a deeper world, dwelling for hours in a world others were not privy to, and sometimes for days and even weeks. She was a special project — burdened with an intelligence that had threatened her teacher in Odessa, and which even Ruth found challenging and sometimes problematic — but she had a stubborn sweetness within her, too, Richard saw, the first time he came into the classroom to talk to the students about geology.

He had been told a little of Annie's history by Herbert Mix. She had always been quiet and introspective, it seemed — but he could see the sweetness in the nine-year-old immediately, in a way that surprised him. It felt like a kind of clairvoyance, this instinctual knowing, and was of the sort that he usually experienced only with the earth, when drafting and assembling subterranean prospects, pursuing the old oil and gas.

He felt immediately, in this odd, underground perception, a close affinity with her. He could tell by the intensity of interest she directed toward objects and subjects, in her first moment's examination of them, that yearning was the source of that intensity and intelligence, and that when she did not perceive like-in-kind being returned, she turned away, and descended.

Of course the teacher in Odessa had not known what to do with her. Of course the parents of other children had been distressed by her. Of course they had believed the made-up stories cast by a bitter and puzzled few, the malicious surface-dwellers with too much time on their hands, and the inability to descend into and explore the lands that Annie was so comfortable frequenting.

And yet — she was only nine. Even as the deeper, older world was familiar to her, as were the lands of calculus and trigonometry, and the terrain and territory of Shakespeare and Latin, the sinuosity and contour of language, and the logic of chemistry, physics, and biology, the rest of the world was entirely new to her: subtleties and nuances, small curious things such as, again, the surface choreography of manners.

When something bored her, she turned away.

She spoke occasionally, and when stressed or troubled or confined, communicated in emotional truths, rather than planing along on the surface of facts. Of course the teacher in Odessa had not known what to do with her. Of course the town had not.

The fossils were a big hit. All the students regarded them as treasure, the day he passed them out in class, lecturing on each one, and detailing, on the blackboard, the chronology and duration of various geologic epochs — Silurian, Ordovician, Devonian — in ways that the school in Odessa would never have allowed. *Demonology*, they would have cried, *heresy, hypothesis, blasphemy.*

The children handled with reverence the bones of their faraway ancestors. It was too much to contemplate, the distance and journey between then and now. It made so much sense to them to break it down into seven workdays. Neither side was right, neither side was wrong: it was all here in the geological record, as plain to see as the typeset characters in a book. The establishment of the firmament, the separation of stars and moon from earth, the Great Flood; the Age of Reptiles, the Age of Fishes, the Age of Fruits and Flowers, and lastly, and so late, the Dawn of Man, birthed from a land of fire and ice, volcanoes and glaciers, beneath a mysterious sun that summoned each year, as if in the delicate greenhouse bubble of a dream, the shouting vegetative tropics, the poison-cleansing oxygen-producing botanical uproar of the world.

It was all the same, he said, for the benefit of any Christians among them, as well as for Ruth, unsure of what sect or cult of Mormonism to which she might belong: all the same, whether hardrock geological fact, *evidence,* or emotional truth buried sometimes far below.

It was one of the things he liked best about looking for oil and gas, this rare overlay of truth and fact — the emotional truth, able to be held physically, tangibly, in the palm of one's hand, as proof — and as he talked in this manner, the students listened attentively, having never consciously considered such distinctions, but willing to consider them now — willing to expand their boundaries of perception further. And among them, Annie listened most carefully of all, though she was guarded with, even enigmatic in, her response to the lecture.

And when Richard told the children to choose which fossils they wanted to keep and take home, they were thrilled, clutching the stony bones and carcasses of ammonites five hundred million years old, and Richard promised to take them up into the mesa soon, to teach them how to conduct their own excavations.

He was not offering this in exchange for any tenderness on Ruth's part, but neither did it pass unobserved by him that she did seem to be softening her stance toward him somewhat, viewing him as a possible asset rather than a danger. Beginning, perhaps, to see him for who he was; beginning to dare to consider looking — even if only in a glance, at first — beneath the surface.

The other children were parceling out their fossils, debating and ne-gotiating, selecting and trading them like baseball cards. Annie had al-ready chosen hers — a single snail-sized trilobite, one of the rarest and most ornamented. In all their months of searching, he and Clarissa had not found more than a dozen of that particular species, and it pleased him that Annie's hand had gone straight to it.

He noticed Annie beholding him, fixing him with her eyes, and sensed that she was about to ask him something about the subject at hand, the fossils — some point of theological contention, he might have guessed, based upon the directness of her gaze — but it turned out she was contemplating his previous statements, and had circled back to them after traveling some distance ahead, for she commented now, regarding his old affinity for searching for oil and gas: "The ge-ologists have messed up our water. Could you find us new water?" As if it was her personal water that had been taken: hers and Marie's, or hers and Marie's and Ruth's. Hers and the other children's. *Ah,* Richard thought, and not unkindly, *a public defender. But what is the source of her rage?*

Even Ruth was nonplussed by the child's near-accusation. "The children are concerned with groundwater contamination," she said, her face flushing in a way that let Richard know that Ruth herself had not been sparing the whip with regard to her assessment of the takers, the corporate exploiters who had filed across these hallowed homelands. "We've been studying about desalinization in Israel," she explained, and then, in her embarrassment, did a rare thing, something she abhorred in other adults.

"She probably means, 'Do you know anything about desalinization, or is it a viable alternative for this region?'" And she was confused immediately as to why she was cutting Richard slack and why she was speaking for Annie. As were the children, when not two weeks before, she had been grilling Richard's profession with fearsome incandescence. Lamenting the sulfurous taste of the drinking water in Odessa and, they claimed, even in certain wells in Mormon Springs, and the ever-expanding, pimply eruptions and collapses of sinkholes and caverns.

Annie glanced quickly at Ruth, surprised by this betrayal, but saw in a glimpse that Ruth was not responsible, that she knew not what she was doing, and she turned her attention back to Richard. "No," she said, "I mean, if you know how to find oil and gas, can't you also find water? Can you draw up some maps to show us where the water is — the good water — and then help us go after it and get it, before the oil companies poison that, too?"

A pall fell over the classroom. Richard felt his own face turning red, though with what emotion, he could not say. The feeling in the room was like the one that follows when an egg is dropped from a table and cracks on the floor; and that initial tension hung in the room, and then hung further, with no one, not even Ruth, knowing what to say. But as the tension began both to spread and dissipate, and the color began to leave Richard's face, he found himself nodding slowly, adjusting himself to whatever scale of rage and reason and innocence she was operating on, and he heard himself saying, "Yes, I suppose I could. Would you like to help me, would you like to be my assistant, would you like to learn how?"

He had come across the border with nothing, had not envisioned disappearing beneath the surface again so soon, if ever. He had imagined himself taking a job in town, in some nongeological volunteer position, where he might be free to listen for and hear any whispers of her coming: a position up in a second-story building, where he might be able to watch the horizon for the first stirring of dust from any approaching traveler: continuing on about his work, but glancing up from time to time at that distant rise of dust and, once the plume was nearer, lifting a spyglass, a seafarer's golden monocular, from his desk and peering through it, watching and waiting to see if the individual emerging from that far-off cloud of dust might eventually metamorphose into the one he awaited, like smoke becoming animate matter, spirit becoming flesh: and he would go to meet her.

Instead, he dove. As if unable to help himself, and knowing nothing else, he went into the oil and gas professional building, chatted with some of the newer geologists, who were only too eager to ask him for some tips about working in the area, and he came away with the loan of a handful of slide rules, some HB drafting pencils and erasers, long scrolls of blank linen, silken to the touch, on which they would sketch their contours as they probed and explored and remade the old world below; and best of all, when he explained that he would be working with schoolchildren, he was given, enthusiastically, full privilege to the electrical log library, so that he could go in after hours and work at the drafting tables on the seventh floor, accessing all the records from all the thousands of wells drilled in the area in past years. The control points of hard data, facts — anchorpoints for the dreams and desires to be imagined, and pursued — perhaps accurately, perhaps not — between those points.

He had to start slowly. It was not what he had intended doing, it was not how he had intended to spend his sojourn, his new life: returning yet again to the buried lands, and revisiting, remaking his own past.

But he had told the girl *yes,* had told her teacher and the other children *yes,* and so once again he found himself pulled downward, with his back turned almost obstinately to the future.

To one who did not know him better, it might even have appeared that he was avoiding the future. To one who had not witnessed his bravery in the pursuit of Clarissa, it might have seemed that he was frightened of it.

The work went quickly. He often labored on through the night before napping in his loft, rising at intervals to scan the horizon, as if convinced through the faith and force of prophecy that that was where he would see her, that she would be returning on foot from some point beyond the desert.

He dreamed that it would be so, and yearned for it, until the image of it was so strong in his mind that it seemed sometimes it had already happened that way, and that he was only waiting for it to happen a second time.

He built a base map, reassembling from memory and from the data in the log library a geological foundation from which the children could work, and across which they could witness and begin to understand the flow of time, and the secret sequestering of various valuable things, the old treasures of oil and gas and water.

Sometimes as he was mapping he was so reminded of the old days that it seemed she had returned to him, was still with him: if not in the same room with him, at his elbow and peering over his shoulder at the terrain unscrolling, then just down the road a ways, still living in the little house with the screened-in porch upon which they took their leisurely weekend breakfasts.

When he finished the baseline maps, he scrolled them up and took them out to Mormon Springs for the children to work on. Sometimes he had second thoughts about what he was doing — *What am I teaching them,* he wondered, *to take rather than to give?* But they were engaged and enthused, and the raw knowledge, new knowledge, ran like a grassfire from one discipline to the next as they incorporated the math, and the biology of ancient life forms, and wove principles of oil production and engineering into the earth history lessons: and although Ruth's opinions, and the foul taste of their drinking water, and the treacherous sump holes, had predisposed them to look less than kindly upon the petroleum industry, it was nonetheless a part of their own history; and they were able to use those lessons as a departure point for going back further, to the time of the salt traders, and the struggle for independence from Mexico, and further — to the Comanche wars — and then deeper still, to the prehistory of the Paleolithics, and then to the time of ice and mastodons, which seemed to them the most incredible thing of all.

And as the map progressed still further, he expanded his mapping sessions with the children into field trips, twice a week. It was one more trip per week than Ruth really should have budgeted for, but she loved the field trips, and the collecting and chronicling of their findings; and her pet, Annie, loved the excursions most of all, was more engaged than Ruth had ever seen her. Annie stayed with Richard, shadowing his every move, up on the mesa, and often spied the tiny traces of ancient life even before he did.

She was precise and diligent, practiced and cautious, in extracting them from their rock matrix and cleansing them, first by putting them in her mouth, and then in the bowl of dilute hydrochloric acid, brushing the sediment away with a wetted whisk; and sometimes, watching her reach for a certain fossil, up on the mesa — the shape of her hand, and the gesture of reach — the sudden current of longing, of grasping — Richard would feel disoriented, as if he had tumbled back in time not merely to the part where he and Clarissa had once been up on the bluff, but to some further time: one he had never inhabited, but which he somehow knew, and which had always been waiting for him.

Always, even in her focus, Annie kept the larger goal in mind; was always mindful of cant and slope of strata, and the thinning and thickening of beds, and what implications they held for trapping water.

She was a natural at it, so much so that Richard got the feeling she might soon be better at it than he.

The search for water often took place in the opposite conditions from those favoring the accumulation of oil and gas — searching for synclines rather than anticlines — so that for Richard the search was often one of confusing reversal, like trying to back a trailer down the road while looking in the mirror, whereas for Annie, it was all new and natural, she had no habits to overcome, no routines to step out of.

They picnicked on the mesa in the early afternoons before returning to the school. They sat on the edge of the bluff in the high dry wind, staring out at the vastness of the desert below, and at the far-flung scattered grid of pumpjacks rising and falling as if feasting eagerly on some nectar below. They used field glasses to point out familiar landmarks — the town of Odessa looking like a postage stamp — and then, farther on, the mote of Mormon Springs.

They saw the dust rising chalk-white from the slow progression of the football team, trained the binoculars on them and saw through the wavering haze of heat the tiny ant-figures pulling the wagon out past the main street and into the desert, and watched in silence, and with a feeling almost like pity or puzzlement, as they ate the sandwiches Ruth had prepared for them, and the cobbler, and poured cups of lemonade from the thermos, and felt the sun warm on their arms and on the backs of their necks.

As if the football players far below were lost, or had tumbled into the most gigantic of pits, and were circling, searching for a way out: earnest, dedicated, but clueless, and owned, ultimately, by the affections of the town's expectations and ironclad traditions.

The outcasts of Mormon Springs sat there and watched the prairie below, ate their pie and watched the red-tailed hawks and golden eagles sweep past below them on gusts and sheets of wind.

"How will we drill the wells for the water?" Ruth asked, "and how will we afford the leases?" Sitting next to Richard, still a professional, but barefoot, swinging her browned legs in the sun as if sitting on a dock. Annie next to her, chewing thoughtfully, watching the horizon, but dreaming, Ruth suspected, her vertical dreams.

Richard shrugged. "The leases shouldn't be a problem," he said. "We'll go places where they've already drilled dry holes and have abandoned them. I can get those leases for a penny on the dollar." Swinging his own bare legs in the sun. So much air below.

"What about the drilling?" Ruth asked. "Even a shallow well costs more than we'll ever have. I can maybe find some science grants, but it's a long shot, and I really don't have the time for it."

"We'll figure something out," Richard said. "I might be able to get one drilled."

There was no need to tell her that he could drill a hundred of them, or a thousand, if he wanted. They continued watching the desert, swinging their legs. He wondered how Red Watkins was, and the others. Wondered if they had already gone on ahead to China.

Annie got up and came around and sat down on the other side of him, took a fossil out from the pouch she wore around her neck and asked him what it was, how old it was, and what it meant. Leaning into him as if he were trusted. It was not normally her way, and Ruth was surprised by the twinge of jealousy she felt, and wondered at its source: if she wanted Annie to give her her allegiance, rather than sharing it with a near-stranger — or if she, Ruth, wanted to lean in closer and ask Richard questions about such ancient things.

This won't do, Ruth thought, shifting uncomfortably. *What's going on here, what's the problem? Do I want him to stay, or do I want him to leave?*

They descended a timeworn trail, a slot in the cliff, pressed smooth from the passing of countless deer and bighorn sheep, as well as the boot heels of bandits and pilgrims and wanderers. The children spilled out into the desert and began lowering themselves into the lesser of the various caverns and sump holes. Like explorers upon the face of glaciers, they dug footholds and handholds in the slumped strata, rivulets of dirt and sand pouring down the walls like seeps of water to the collapsed floor of rubble below.

They lowered themselves over the edges of the larger caverns with ropes they had brought and explored the despoliation below, finding the bones and claws and antlers of creatures that had stumbled into the caverns at night and perished. Occasionally one of these would have expired only recently, so that its carcass was still being attended to in the day by ravens, vultures, and eagles: and as the children approached any of these caverns, there might rise a feathered, flapping stagger of black-and-bronze birds like a cyclone, climbing straight into the blue sky like blackened sheets of cardboard and newspaper being lifted by the heated exhalation of the earth; and the children would hurry toward these sources, eager to see what calamity the birds might have been inspecting.

Sometimes there was no calamity, only mystery: as if the assemblage of birds had been gathered there only to cool their sun-heated black feathered bodies. Other times it was water the birds sought — puddles and seeps an inch or two deep.

Small trees and bushes grew in such sump holes, as if in little vases, so that climbing down into them was for the children like lowering themselves into a terrarium; and they would lie down in the cool grass that had leapt up there, or sit beneath the shade of those young but fast-growing trees, while the adults stood above them, peering down.

It was important to Ruth, she said, that they learn to own the world; that they come to view their outsiderness as a strength and an asset rather than a liability. They might or might not change the world, and the world might or might not change them: but it was important to her for them to know that they could make their way in it, anywhere they went.

She and Richard sat at the edge of the caverns on these field trips, as they had sat earlier on the bluff above, and watched and visited, talking about things that mattered to them. Up until this point, Richard had been more interested in the landscape than in people or their ways. He was astounded, listening to Ruth talk about children, having never met anyone who gave them — or perhaps anything — such attention.

"Does it fill you, or does it hollow you out?" he asked one day.

"It hollows me out," she answered, without hesitation. Often her discussions with him continued to be tinged with defensiveness. But she turned to him now to be sure he understood; and even if he had not heard her words, the radiance on her face would have made her answer clear. "It hollows me out," she said again, smiling.

The shouts and cries of the children rose from the various caverns around them like the pipings of organ chamber music, or the sound of flutes and bagpipes, swirled by gusts of wind. They climbed up and out of one series of sumps and hurried down into another, playing hide-and-seek and tag. The boys in particular, it seemed, eager to demarcate and claim territory, scratching and etching with sticks and rocks various graffiti and hieroglyphics on the walls of their pits.

They were like the Paleoliths who had come in at the end of the last ice age. The ticking of their hearts little different, surely, from only ten thousand years ago, and he felt a surge of discomfort, watching them scramble across the desert floor, disappearing into the holes and then emerging again.

He felt a wave almost like panic; he understood even more clearly that Clarissa would not be coming back — he believed, intuitively, that she *should;* he believed that all things, all natural processes, replicate in circular rather than linear fashion — and yet, if ten thousand years could hurtle by so fast, like the space between two heartbeats, then what was his obligation to that river of time, and to himself?

What were the chances, were someone to ask him, *Doesn't it hollow you out?,* for him to turn to the questioner and answer, *Yes, absolutely,* with such radiance, such fullness?

All of the children were pleasant, comfortable in the world, curious and loving, but it was Annie whom he found himself thinking about at different hours of the day, as if smitten or owned by her. At some point not quite known to any of them, the project, though still available and present to all the children, had become largely his and hers. He had noticed, as they worked on their map, that there was a tingling that began in his lower jaw and then spread into his teeth when she leaned in against him, working on the map, not just totally accepting of him, but more, incorporating him into her world. It was a sweetness that passed through his teeth, causing him to nearly shiver; and other times, there was a fullness like a burning in his chest, which spread to his shoulders and down the length of his arms, whenever he considered her work: and not just her potential, but who she was already.

It was hard for Ruth, watching them. Marie was pleased with this apprenticeship, made happy by the good fortune of it, and by the fact that Annie was learning a trade — that she would at least know how to make her way in the world, and Marie's work, Marie's obligation, would be done — but about this sharing, this growth and cleaving, Ruth was less sanguine, and again could not quite figure the source, nor the direction, of the currents of envy.

Annie thought the same way Richard did, seemed to understand intuitively, immediately, the logic of his work and explanations, and yet in other ways Annie was his opposite. Often, in the drafting and redrafting of their contours, sketching their maps level by level and horizon by horizon, descending through time, they would pass by little overlooked and undiscovered pockets of oil and gas, the very treasures that had once made Richard's heart leap.

Annie had no interest in such treasures, and was drawn instead to the water, only water: and when they discovered it, they celebrated, and they posted their maps on the walls and blackboards of the little schoolhouse, like field generals posting campaign maps in some far-flung war room. And though each of the children understood what the focus was, to find clean water, they understood also to keep the mission, the goal, secret; and they did.

It was their water, Richard told them, it belonged to them and was just waiting for them to find it and then to go out and get it. But if someone else found out about it first, he said, it might be taken from them. They had to keep it secret, had to work beneath the surface.

He bought a truck from Herbert Mix, a sandblasted wind-whipped pewter-colored old Ford with rounded fenders and goggle headlights. The back bumper was held on with baling wire. The truck gave off a distinctive squeak and rattle, one that the children could hear from a distance, their ears more attuned, like those of dogs, to the higher pitches of the world, and they would be aware of his approach several minutes before Ruth was. They were each beginning to regard him as critical and important, if not powerful and magical, and understood, far better than the adults of Odessa, the nonnegotiable nature of their need, and of the difference that existed between the taste of fouled water, and the taste of sweet.

And noting the ever-increasing attendance by him to their classes, they perceived that he had a crush on Ruth, and teased her about it, at first in his absence, but then teasing them both about it.

And as if to prove otherwise, or to at least discourage the continuance of such rumor, Ruth allowed herself to entertain the brief attentions of a young Mormon businessman from Waco, Joe, a seller of mobile homes who had served two years as a missionary in Asia, and who had clear goals about where his life was headed, and how his success would be measured. He came over to Ruth's house on a Saturday, and they cooked hamburgers on her grill in the October light, with the desert's temperature still not too distinct from that of the grill.

They sat out in her sandy backyard, Ruth barefoot and the businessman awkward in his black lace-ups, but unwilling to disrobe. He cut straight and dispassionately through the surface of the matter, the fact that both of them had a shared heritage and beliefs, their Latter-day Sainthood, and moved earnestly, doggedly, to the heart of things, which was his desire to build an empire based on the sale of preexisting modular homes.

Joe leaned forward in his lawn chair, setting his paper plate of food aside, and became more animated as he spoke, generating what almost anyone might have accepted as true passion — Ruth imagined that, indeed, it was possible that he had sold quite a few homes already — but whenever she found herself listening to the substance of his words, rather than the delivery, she could barely keep from laughing, and finally it was too much; at the tail end of a phrase expressing his longing to go back and capitalize on the overseas contacts he made during his missionary work in the hopes of "developing a joint-venture-based strategic alliance," and of "becoming dominant in that relationship," a snort escaped from her, and she bent forward on her seat, trying to imagine what in the world she might be able to do or say that might ever break his fixed gaze upon his ludicrous empire: and knowing that she could care less whether there was, or wasn't. An evening, nearly half a day, ruined, except for the relief of laughter.

He probably knows how to love, she thought, considering Richard, and the way he was willing to follow the world, rather than trying to lead it or control it or worst of all own it. That he would as lief give something up as take it away. *Damn it, he probably knows how to be in love,* she thought. *Now if only I was in love with him, or even desired to be.* The space in her heart for that was neither dead nor vacant, not lacking as much as simply not activated. It just didn't feel like the right time. She didn't feel like she had the available resources to do both. There was no summons, and even if some such summons arrived, she believed she would do well to resist it. She could not bear to think of failing the children, or her own goal of launching each of them, as many as possible, strong into the world, durable against the forces that would try to marginalize and ultimately ignore them.

Joe was looking at her with puzzlement. "What?" he said, his color rising, and she laughed again, sensing his outrage, and imagining what a feisty competitor he would be in pursuing those strategic alliances. "You don't think I can do it?" he demanded. "You think I can't?"

"No, no," she said, placing a hand on his arm, as if to stay him from rising to leave, such was his affront. "No, absolutely, I believe you can, and *will.*" He relaxed a bit then, and settled back into his chair.

"I may make it sound easy," he said, "but it's not. These folks I'm dealing with, it's not like they're — " He cast about, searching for a metaphor. "It's not like they're *children,*" he said. "These are boardroom kind of people, they're sharp customers, you've got to be on your toes."

"I'm sure it's very taxing," Ruth said.

She had made a pie, a triple-berry crisp, using berries Annie had grown in her and Marie's garden — both Annie and Ruth were wild about blackberries — and she had planned on bringing it out after dinner, served warm with vanilla ice cream melting over it, but she withheld it now, could not bring herself to reveal it, even though she was certain he had smelled it baking in the oven.

Instead, she rose and went into the kitchen and washed and sliced a single peach, which she brought out on two dishes, and served it without explanation.

They sat there in silence after they had finished the peach, the sand quickly cooling against Ruth's feet as the orange sun settled below the horizon, and then abruptly she stood and thanked him for coming all this way, that it was good for the members of their church to check in on one another, but that he would have to forgive her, she needed to get back to her lesson plans.

"I wish you well in your ventures," she said, shaking his hand firmly; and sensing her rejection, he felt compelled to lean forward, to pursue, and asked if he could come visit her, could come call upon her, again.

She laughed, started to say the first thing that came to her mind, an emphatic *no*, but instead shook her head and apologized for perhaps having misinterpreted the reason for his visit as being church-based — that she had no interest in suitors.

Even as she was seized, while she was speaking, with the odd notion, almost like a prophesy foretold that within a month she would be Richard's lover, entangled and frightened and in the midst of all sorts of unwelcome chaos, the responsibility of new affections; and she was both alarmed and intrigued by this sudden idea, impressed upon her almost with the force of revelation.

"Goodbye," she called to Joe as he went down her walkway, back to his green-and-white sedan, to face the lonely drive back to Waco. "I'm sorry my heart's not available, forgive me," she called out after him, making him look over his shoulder in face-scrunched disbelief; and he had not been gone three minutes before she took the pie out of the oven, and the quart of ice cream, and got in her own car and hurried over to Marie and Annie's, where they sat on the front porch and ate it warm, watching the night descend over the desert, with Marie and Ruth shelling late-season peas from Marie's garden then, and Annie curled up in the porch swing, reading *The Pickwick Papers*.

And as if attuned to the same premonition, for no words had been spoken of Richard, nor of school, nor the water maps, Annie announced nonetheless, without looking up from her book, and with no other prefatory declarations, "I like him." And Ruth and Marie gave no comment, but merely went on with their own discussions and work as if she had not spoken, and Annie returned to her book.

Unbeknownst to his friend Herbert Mix, or anyone, some evenings Richard did not return to his loft apartment, but would stay out at Clarissa's abandoned house, his old gray truck parked in the garage, the barnlike doors to that shed closed.

The lilac bushes, unpruned, had grown larger, subsisting in the drip line all around the house, and had risen to nearly roof level, almost completely obscuring the house. Except for the small chainlink fence around the barren yard, and the weedy flagstone walkway leading up to the little copse, it might no longer have even appeared as a place of human habitation, but instead only a strange grove in the desert.

The once-vibrant garden was a tangle of thistle and tumbleweed. Feral cats stalked mice through the concertina maze of it, and at night the wind flapped the tin patchings on all four corners, until it seemed that the entire house might be lifted into flight.

There was no power, water, or phone, only husk, and some nights he went to bed early and dreamed that he was back in those old times, though other nights he lit a miner's carbide lamp and moved from room to room, tilting his head this way and that to illuminate in the weak dull light individual objects of attention, their position unchanged in the last decade — a coffee cup and saucer, clean but still resting on the dusty kitchen table; the grocery list next to the telephone — such mundane concerns, bananas, butter, flour, and in the meantime, a life had slipped by.

Some of the lesser fossils that they had found but been unable to sell were still on the windowsill, dust-shrouded, and the fact that none of it had changed in ten years filled Richard with alternating currents of hope and despair.

And what of me? he wondered. He barely dared to handle any of the objects, so dense with power as to possibly possess the ability to summon her one last time, though also possibly able to sever once and for all that possibility.

How have I changed in ten years, he thought, *if at all?*

Some nights he lit a lantern and walked out into the garden, where once he and she had nurtured cilantro, rosemary, hot peppers, and basil. Tomatoes, corn, cucumbers, berries, and lettuce, in the months before the summer heat grew too intense. Now the bobcats and other unknown things scuttled from his approach, fleeing the ring of light cast by the lantern.

He stood waist-deep in the tangle. Part of him considered setting fire to the whole structure, while another part gloried in the rot and senescence, and in his ability to hold out and hang on, hoping and believing and then hoping again: and for this part of him, the old house was more worthy to him of enshrinement than incineration, and his visits to it sacrament.

He stood motionless, his shadow giant upon the mesa beyond. Moths swarmed his lantern, fell wing-singed into the clutter of weeds. The coyotes in the sand hills beyond saw his light and began laughing, shrieking, coming closer, and he turned the light out and listened.

Later in the night, on toward morning, sleeping in her bed, he would be awakened by the sound of the football team, the collective hope and fury of them cantering down the road, their wagon-cart rattling behind them; and in those first few moments, lying on his back looking up at the ceiling, and with all the furniture as it had always been, and the curtains half-open, and the window raised, and the morning birds beginning to stir and call, it would seem to him — for half a second, a full second, and sometimes even three or four delicious seconds — that she was still with him, that he had been successful in capturing her, and in capturing his own happiness: that he had not failed.

Most evenings, however, he hung out with Herbert Mix, going over to his house and visiting with him in his backyard amidst the cool shade and sweet odor of the willows. They drank iced tea, and only occasionally visited about lore and sagas of the past-stagecoach treasures. Instead, Herbert Mix talked about future plans, about upcoming projects, and about his new clan: and in particular, about Marie, and Annie, and Ruth. He had volunteered to be the school handyman, which afforded him still more opportunity to be over in Mormon Springs, and he soon had the school and its grounds looking first-rate, pastoral and idyllic, even as the elementary and middle and high schools in Odessa languished.

"She likes me," he said, "but she says she's lived alone too long to ever get used to having a man around full-time. She says a little goes a long way," he said. "She says she'd rather not see me enough than too much. She says it's not my fault, but that sometimes all the attention makes her feel like she's being buried. She says that some nights she has dreams of being dug up, and that's a good thing, but other nights she has dreams of being buried alive."

Herbert Mix looked down at his hands, and Richard knew that in those dreams, it must have been Herbert Mix doing the burying, on at least some occasions: and he did not know what to say, did not know what counsel to give the old man.

"You're happy, right?" he asked. "I mean, look at you, you've changed. You're a new man. You're not . . ." He paused, looking for a word other than "greedy."

"Greedy?" Herbert Mix said. "No, I'm not. Yeah, I'm happy. It just seems like I could be happier. Like I'm so close. And like time's running out. Which it is." He looked at his old shovel-digging hands again. "It's like being hungry," he said. "You always know, or are almost certain, that you're going to eat again. You just don't know when."

Richard nodded. He knew that he should try to dissuade the old man from looking at it that way, but he couldn't, and still call himself a friend. "You're right," he said. "That's what it's like."

And slowly, and generously, Herbert Mix brought him further into the fold, inviting him along whenever he traveled out to Mormon Springs, riding out there in his truck and then staying over at Marie's, while Richard drove his truck back to town, returning for him later the next day. And on such occasions, Herbert Mix knew pure bliss, nestling into the old wrinkle-sacked gray-haired skin-and-bones nest of her at night, his own ancient body thrilled by the feel of the crisp cotton sheets, and by the evening wind that stirred through the house; and it felt to all of them in the household that it was as if Herbert Mix was a grandfather, and Marie, a grandmother: and the three of them, Annie and Marie and Herbert Mix, accepted this new braiding, this new identity.

It seemed sustainable and natural and durable, and the whole of them accepted, day by day and increment by increment, the arrival of Richard, in a way that not even the Republican oilmen down in Mexico had accepted him, nor even, so long ago now — suddenly, it seemed long ago — the way that Clarissa had taken him into her life.

He began to feel embedded, cemented, like the fossils they discovered in their diggings; and many nights he found himself dreaming Marie's dream, in which he too was being buried: and it was the entire population of Mormon Springs that was wielding the shovels, incorporating him into their combination, their community, and yet there was no darkness, even as the dirt rained down over him, there was still light, he could still see all that he had been able to see before.

As Herbert Mix knew bliss on the nights when he spent the night in Mormon Springs, Marie, at least, knew comfort, sleeping or sometimes merely resting in the bony cage of his arms and his one leg, his knees and elbows. She knew pleasure if not rapture, contentment if not ecstasy. And she did not quite know what to make of it, sometimes straddling that middle country between receiving the attention of another, after having previously been ignored all of her life, and yet finally possessing also true freedom, after having been for so long a captive or hostage, to one thing or another.

She would lie looking up at the ceiling, aware of her sleeping household — the old man asleep, and pleasantly proximate, but making no claim on her, and the young girl, well on her way to becoming a strong young woman — and Marie would know contentment. Never would she have imagined that her life of deprivation might ever have been moving her all along toward a place where such deprivation no longer existed, yet here it was, real, the child was in her house, and the man too.

And yet, in those same moments of night-wakefulness, she was aware that a hunger still persisted. Almost as if, now that these first pleasures were being met, they were as but the seeds or scratchings for some other awakening, some long-ago hunger she had forgotten or never known.

In Mexico, the water had been poisoned by the residue of toxic chemicals used by miners in the mountains, cyanide and arsenic, which stripped away the overburden of ore and sediment, revealing faint traces, here and there, of gold, copper, and silver — and as such, the geologists drank mostly beer, and had had their drinking water flown in from distant sources — Idaho, Montana, Oregon — though Sy Craven had said that there were mines up there that would curl their hair, entire mountainsides stripped away, leaving oozing pustules of suppurating earth, and with so much lead leaching into the creeks that all the fish died or grew mutations, and the men, women, and children downstream grew enormous tumors, became feeble, brain-stunted, and anemic. Whenever a shipment of water arrived, Sy Craven would wipe the dust from the top of the heavy glass milk bottles in which it had been shipped, would open the seal and sniff the water as if it were the most expensive wine, and then he would sip from it, and after a moment would pronounce it either fit or unfit.

He claimed to be able to tell by that method alone the purity or impurity of waters, though his concerns were not health-based — all of the geologists, intimate as they were with the brutalities of time, the roughness of the scale against which their flashes of life were measured, understood too well their lives were but chaff blown by the wind. Rather, he simply loved the taste of good water, and abhorred the taste of bad.

But the water in Odessa tasted even worse than the water in Mexico, which had been merely rank with metal. The Odessa water was sulfurous, with the taste growing worse in the summer months as the level of water wells dropped. Some in town had likened it to what water would taste like were it to be filtered through the carcass of a rotting cow, claiming that a single glass of it left out overnight would by the next day have filled the entire room with the odor of its putrescence — and in Odessa, too, people had resorted to trucking in water from relatives elsewhere, or treating it with chlorine or halazone or iodine tablets, or boiling it.

The water at Mormon Springs had always been better — fresher, and cooler — though it possessed a higher iron content, which the townspeople of Odessa had scorned for the way it discolored their laundry, their dishes, and, they claimed, even their teeth. But to the residents of Mormon Springs, it was what they knew, it tasted sweet and delicious, and it did not bother them that the town, the big city, reviled their water as it reviled nearly everything else about them.

In the year that Richard arrived, however, some of the children had begun to comment that the water did not taste as good as before. It was hard to describe — but it tasted *warmer,* they said, so much so that they began chilling bottles of water in the refrigerator each night, to use in the coming day, chasing and trying to return to the taste of that sweeter water, the specifics of which were already becoming harder for them to remember.

And although Richard had nothing to compare it to — the water he had drunk out at Clarissa's had been from a different reservoir, more alkaloid than the water at Mormon Springs — he believed them when they said there was more sediment in the water than before, and tiny motes of particles, and air bubbles that had never been there before. They said the water even sounded different as it came out of the faucet.

On through the autumn, the problem became worse — late in the afternoon and evenings, the pipes shuddered and heaved and clanked, as if laboring to produce the water.

Occasionally the faucets would spit out gasping chunks of air, as if the water had become animated or enspirited and was struggling for breath, and it was unsettling to the residents of Mormon Springs, who had always prided their water as being better and more dependable, than the town's; and it was troubling to Richard, too, as he and Annie continued to work on their map, searching for more sources. He had the feeling that what had begun in leisure was now accelerating to need, and he felt, far in advance of the residents of Mormon Springs, the accruing weight of an unasked-for and undesired responsibility.

All he wanted was his old life back. He was not asking for riches, nor promise of better days from the future; no bounty, no golden horn of plenty. He had been happy, and he just wanted to go back. He did not want to reengineer the entire subterranean plumbing of a remote desert community. He did not want to be responsible, in his failure or success — and in the luck of the draw, in the outcome of the story that was already set in stone below — for men, women, and children having to abandon their homes and move, meekly, beaten back into the very town that had already cast them out.

And yet: they had begun it; and just as the residents of Mormon Springs claimed to be able to notice almost daily now a deterioration in the quality of their water and well pressures, it seemed to Richard that he could discern also daily the growing pride and intelligence of Annie as she became more confident, and took greater possession of the map.

It occurred to him that she was mothering the map, almost parenting it: treating it the way she might have wished to have been treated by her true parents.

He tried to shake the thought from his mind — it was no business of his, and certainly not his place to judge people he had never met or known — who knew what the circumstances were that had led to her being orphaned? It could have been any of a thousand reasons, or ten thousand, all beyond her parents' control — and yet it returned, larger each time, as if having grown from his efforts to shove it aside.

Surely she had to think about such things.

They worked on the map at school, and after school. They continued to make field trips, often Richard and Annie alone, borrowing Herbert Mix's jeep and traveling as far into the desert as Richard dared, carrying extra water: out past Castle Gap and Horsehead Crossing, out into the country around Juan Cordona Lake, crossing back over old territory. They climbed up into the mesas, not just to continue the search for fossils, but to observe from that greater vantage the network of landforms below, not just the muddy artery of the Pecos itself, but all the dried-out and gone-away traces of past tributaries, draws, and arroyos, and the secret confederacy of streams that had once flowed there; and the rise and fall of mesa and butte, the vertical escarpments of stone whispering the secret location of faults, and all other manner of secrets of the earth.

Ruth was beginning to let go of her jealousy — reminding herself to choose always what was best for the children, to choose always what was best for Annie — and she had commented to Richard how unusual it was for Annie to take to a stranger.

"I think it's a real growth step for her," she said. "I worry that I'm just filling her with knowledge, but that she's not learning how to be with other people — nonfamily members. I think you're bringing her a balance she's been hungry for."

"I do too," Richard said.

Time and again, particularly in the quiet moments between them, up on the mesa, Annie would seem to perceive or divine what he was thinking. Once, when he was thinking about the untapped, unmined water they were pursuing, Annie asked him straight out, "You're rich, aren't you? Rich enough to go out and take those leases, and to drill some of those wells?" And he had to answer her truthfully, telling her that although he didn't think of it as being rich — it was just money, was all, the leftover residue of his work, and his old life — that yes, he would be able to take the leases for them, and drill the wells, once they had all the water hunted down and trapped; and she seemed satisfied with that answer, uninterested in any further particulars as to how rich.

Another time, when he was thinking of Clarissa, she asked him, out of the blue, "Have you ever been married, have you ever been in love?" — and still another time, when he was pondering Ruth and her aloofness, and yet her quiet allure — not passion or even hunger, but an allure — when he went into the schoolroom, or any room, his eyes went first to her — Annie asked, "Do you like Ruth?"

And when he acknowledged that yes, he respected and admired as well as liked her, Annie nodded and said, "She's hard to like. It took me a long time to see beneath her."

There weren't a lot of peers — Ruth would have liked to have three or four more older students, for what she would have considered the perfect mix — but from the standpoint of family, the school could be considered large, not just with many siblings, but numerous aunts, uncles, cousins.

The closest thing Annie had to a best friend was Maeve, who was three years younger than she, and whom she'd befriended as much out of a mix of obligation and need as true friendship. The upside for Annie was that she got to know better a girl she might have known only barely, otherwise; the downside was that many days, she felt her differences attenuated even further — her intellectual life stretching out toward that of Ruth's and Richard's even as her emotional life regressed, at times, to that of a girl who still played with dolls.

The best she could make of it some days was that Maeve was a kind of living doll: though on the days when she did not want to play with dolls, there were frustrations for both girls. The situation was better for Maeve, who could not help but drift along at a little quicker pace, academically; though there were days when Maeve too was aggravated by the stretch.

In all, it was a ragtag and sometimes disjointed procession over which Ruth kept constant vigil, and worried about, encouraging each child academically, but keeping careful watch also over their social development, and general happiness. Annie foremost, of course — parentless, and the pet — but all the children. Ruth watched them almost all day, and then in her dreams at night.

She would have denied fiercely the assertion that she watched them too much; that she was obsessed, partly as a means of holding at bay the rest of the world, and her fright at the emotional demands of adults. She would have countered that the children were both purer and more deserving, and that their demands and needs were at least as complex as those of any adult.

As one of the ways to help plug some of the fractures and disconnections that occurred in the children's classroom lives, Ruth had enlisted them in an educator's pen-pal foreign-exchange network for the broader good of instilling in them the sense that they mattered to the world, beyond the confines of home. And it was touching to her to see the joy with which they received the simplest of letters, opening them like talismans and then reading and rereading them at various points throughout the day.

In each reading, the children would gaze at their letters as if attempting to see not just between the lines, but behind them, focusing on a different sentence in each reading. It did not matter that the sentences were almost overwhelmingly simple; the world behind the sentences was rich and immense. They saw the gerbils, saw the interior of another child's house, imagined the consternation of one parent and the amusement of another. They saw the lawn out front, saw the clothes, heard the birds in the hedges outside a child's window fluttering in the night. There was treasure hidden between every word.

And some days, when it was all going well — when the children's lesson plans were falling by the wayside, when they were blowing past the old plans — growing deeper as well as broader — some days, Ruth felt the glide going, in her classroom and even in her life. Some days, it all felt right.

By Halloween, Annie and Richard had the water shaped and identi-fied, though still not yet fully trapped. The rough shapes of the aquifers were beginning to take form, lenses of water in the Rorschach outlines of jaguars, parrots, serpents, and dragons. Some of the aquifers were like vaulted cathedrals, while others were like low basements, tunnels, and caverns. Annie and Richard had color-coded those aquifers they knew had been contaminated by oil and gas drilling, and those which they were pretty certain had not. They also identified the major sand bodies that provided the drinking water to the families in Mormon Springs.

The only thing they had not yet completed were the final con-tours between aquifers. They had sketched dashed lines where they thought the reservoirs were bounded; but they could not yet be ab-solutely sure if their aquifers were isolated, or thinly connected. If the latter, then there might exist sinuous little tendrils of escape routes, through which their water could be drained by the efforts of another, or through which toxins could intrude.

For those final contours, Richard was going to have to purchase and process seismic data and perform geophysical interpretations, as well as chemical analysis of whatever water samples he could obtain. The relatively easy work had been done, and some of what remained might now lie beyond Annie's range: but he kept coming over almost daily, keeping up that near-daily progression, until it began more than ever to seem to both of them like some alternative world; and in some in-stances, there would be no way of knowing those final contours until they actually drilled a well.

In some instances, the imagination, as well as all their powers of sci-entific reasoning, would fail, and they would have to physically grasp the subject itself, drilling into it and exhuming it and examining it with their own two hands: and they were anxious for this process to begin, though Richard had to caution her, telling her of the countless operators he'd seen go out of business by rushing their drilling, working more on emotion than on science.

"Do more field work, and more map work," he advised. "You can never do too much. Do it until you're sick of it, until you can't stand to look at the map another day — until you think you know it so well that you could draw it all over again, blindfolded — and then *keep* studying it, and suddenly things will shift, you'll see something a different way.

"That's when you're about ready to drill," he said. "That's when the map comes alive. It starts to move.

"It changes you," he said. "It's worn you down, at that point. The map's not changing — you're just rotating to look at it a different way. And you see different angles, different perspectives, and you can incorporate them into the map. And then you're ready to drill."

"It's pretty exciting," Annie said. "I think I could do this all my life. And I know our map's right. I believe what you're saying, and I'll look forward to seeing it. But I know the map's right. Sometimes it already does that for me — comes alive. I was scared the first time I saw it do that. I thought it was going to *leave* — that all of a sudden, it couldn't make sense any longer. But it just moved a little ways, and then it stopped. I've already seen it move," she said.

He didn't know what to say. And didn't know what to think about the upwelling of pride in him.

Beginning in his lower jaw again, and spreading through his teeth. Glowing in his chest again, as if afire, and then spreading warmly out through his shoulders and arms again.

"Well," was all he could think of to say, "I think you'd be good at it."

Like old bachelors, some evenings he and Herbert Mix did not go to visit the ladies, but instead grilled steaks out in Herbert Mix's backyard and drank vodka and tonics with ice cubes rattling in tall glasses, one lime wedge and then two and then three decorating the bottoms of their glasses, and their plates empty save for the watery residue of the juices that seeped out from the knife's cutting.

Sometimes they talked about the old days — Herbert Mix about the

Butterfield Stage and the Sublette gang, while occasionally Richard regaled him with tales of Mexico — but mostly they talked about the present or the future: not just about Marie and Ruth, but also Annie, whom Herbert Mix was beginning to regard as a granddaughter.

Richard wondered aloud if most young girls were like her — if she was a miracle of her age — and decided that most were probably not like her, that she was one in a million, one in a billion.

They visited about the water, too. It was running out fast now, but so what? They would find more. There would always be a second chance.

Herbert Mix was glad that Richard had come back. He might never have thought of Richard again, had the younger man not reappeared. He would certainly never have thought of Richard as someone who could heal damage — much less the damage that Richard himself had helped wreak. He might not have even imagined that the problem was solvable. He and the others might have accepted the diminishment of water quality as a fact of life. They might have limped along for a few more years, remembering the good old days, but tolerating now the taste of sulfur and clanking pipes that were as likely to spit out wads of sand as cool clean water; and then, when the pipes exhaled nothing but a dry warm hiss, they might have gathered their belongings and moved on, seed-drift, disconnected.

Richard was the last person Herbert Mix would have thought could help hold things together. Ruth, maybe, or even a child like Annie, once she had grown to adulthood. But he would not have guessed Richard to be such a person. In the old days when Richard had been running around with Clarissa, Herbert Mix had thought of him as nothing more than a well-off young person, indulging himself in the pleasures of a beautiful woman.

He had not blamed him for it — remembering it, Clarissa's beauty filtered back to Herbert Mix like smoke, so startling all these years later. When he had thought about it at all, he had classified Richard as a taker, like himself. He had not seen him as a giver.

He wanted to ask Richard what had changed him, but didn't know how to address it. It would be like acknowledging that he'd once thought Richard to be something of an asshole. Certainly, people were free to change without the impetus of some single dramatic event. Sharp edges got worn down by the harsh glances of time deflecting off a life, day after day, and the current in which a traveler moved rarely stopped carrying the traveler along.

Herbert Mix knew that he himself had changed, had finally had his own awful emptiness filled — as if some wound in him had finally been healed. He rarely knew hunger of any kind, now, other than to be in Marie's company.

But listening to Richard talk about his pursuit of the water, and watching Richard and Annie work on the map, and seeing them journey back into the desert, was causing old stirrings to resuscitate. Herbert Mix thought this might be how it was for an alcoholic or other addict, who, after long abstinence, feels glowing within the return of the first single filament of ignition, the strand of destiny or chemical attachment reawakening.

As if, upon entering such a place — such a cave or abyss — the only source of light to be seen was that single glowing filament that went far beyond desire, and even beyond need. It was something even purer than that, it was an object of worship, it was the essence of all existence. Suddenly, to such a person, and in such a situation, there was no more darkness.

Richard chose to be crafty. Their goal was too great to entrust to strangers. As the map grew ever closer to life, security became paramount. They chose not to trust another land manager to go out and take the leases for them, but decided instead upon a strategy in which Richard would target first the lands that were most undeniably dead to oil and gas, attempting to give the appearance to his old associates that he had some long-shot belief that he could find oil where they had not.

The name of the searcher's desire, "water," would not be mentioned. Richard would allow his old associates to believe that he was still pursuing the same grail he had pursued before. He would allow them to think that he had lost his talent; that he was crashing and burning, foundering, as so many did. That he was pouring money down a rat hole, that he was on the road to ruin.

He would allow them to think that they would help show him the way to that ruination, by selling him their old subsurface deeds and mineral interests.

He approached them with just the right mix of confidence and uncertainty. He was down on his luck, looking for something cheap, he was a little arrogant, hoping for one big play.

They sold him their old leases, the dead and dry and abandoned, their cluttered failures from the past, for a nickel on the dollar, and did so gladly, as if he were but an amateur, a hobbyist; and now the children at Mormon Springs school had a new map to color and hang on their wall, the map of their leases, with even the youngest ones pitching in.

It seemed to be coming to life — they seemed to be bringing it to life — even as they understood that the map was already alive, and had existed as if waiting for them long before any of them had been born.

The gateway of the flesh, as ancient and timeless as mountains of stone, as fleeting as a day, or a single season: the shock of hunger he felt when he saw Ruth in shorts for the first time, on a weekend, the three of them working on the map down at the school. It made no sense, he was waiting on Clarissa, but suddenly there were Ruth's legs, brown and strong, and something else he could not name at first.

She had noted his attention with pleasure, and with some pride and surprise. She thought about teasing him, about asking him how long it had been, or if he had a girlfriend, but refrained, not wanting to make light of or discourage his notice. And knowing that he might ask the same questions of her.

Instead, they mapped. It was like a covenant, a trust increasing slowly each day. It was not a leap into the abyss, not a plummeting nor a freefall. It was a steady, cautious edging forward, it was prudent and cautious, sustainable, it was informed by observation and sometimes even restraint.

I'm not in love, not at all, Richard thought. *I can back out at any time.* And Ruth felt much the same way.

She invited him over for dinner one night, along with Herbert Mix and Marie and Annie, not to work on or even talk about the map, or even school for that matter, but simply to make dinner. They rolled their own pasta and sliced it thin with razor-sharp knives, oiled it and dried it on a rack while they diced the last of the season's tomatoes from Marie and Annie's garden and put them in a bowl with chopped mincings of garlic, their fingers sticky and fragrant from the dicing. They chopped basil, Parmesan, black olives, and poured in olive oil, and a sprinkling of red pepper flakes and oregano. Annie sneezed as the five of them worked.

A loaf of bread was baking in the oven, an old Mormon recipe, Ruth said, and the fragrance was overwhelming. Coarse salt and pepper were added to the spaghetti when it was all done and being served, and they ate out on the porch and watched the dusk come in, with the warlike trooping of the football team visible, briefly, on the horizon.

The bread steaming, the butter sliding into and then through the bread. More salt: they all craved salt, Annie and Marie particularly. Herbert Mix's old treasure-digging hand resting in Marie's, and Marie, that evening, welcoming it.

She is not coming back, Richard thought, when he thought about Clarissa at all. Other times it seemed that she was already present: and still other times, it seemed that his life was better than he could have imagined, and fuller than he remembered it being when she had been present.

The next week, scarcely believing her own daring—the magnitude of her trust, and the recklessness, like letting an infidel or barbarian in through the gates of the kingdom—Ruth invited him over for dinner by himself.

They ate inside, not by candlelight, but by the light of a single low lamp. The evening was cooler, it was mid-November. She told him about her childhood and her young adulthood, and about her sojourn in the Church, as she still called it, borderline apostate though she was becoming. A flank steak, baked potatoes, a salad, and a cheesecake made with four different types of cheeses, and her own bottle of wine, and then the bottle he had brought.

They went out onto the porch where they could hear, faintly, the occasional echo of the fans banging the pipes against their helmets, and sporadic cannon-roar. The glow of distant stadium lights so far away that when, later into the night, it finally faded, there was not even a sadness.

It was his turn to talk more about himself, and he did, telling her about Mexico, and about geology — about how comfortable he felt down in the muck of the past, and even some about his old days, his former dealings with Herbert Mix. He told her almost everything, and when she asked about Clarissa, saying that she remembered having heard from someone, maybe Herbert Mix, that he'd had quite an attractive girlfriend for a while, Richard nodded and said, "Oh, her. Yes, she was really beautiful, she was something else."

They were both quiet for a while, and then the conversation moved on, as if they had both buried her — as if it had been that simple, and that unsustainable, too; as if she was able, finally, to be put down and away in a single sentence — and in the desert coolness, and beneath the same bright stars of autumn that he had known as a younger man, it felt to Richard as if a thorn had been pulled from him, and that a thing that had long been in him was free at last to begin flowing out.

It was after midnight. He started to tell her about how he used to swim the rapids at Horsehead Crossing. He tried to remember the man who had done such things, but dismissed this thought, having no real interest in that; and instead, they talked on further, moving ahead, talking until nearly 2:00 A.M., before the rigors of the week caught up with Ruth, and she could stay awake no longer.

It seemed to her that it would be easier for him to stay, easier for them both to undress, and for her to take shelter in the refuge of his body, to crawl into the cage of his arms and legs, and to love, and then sleep, on through the last of the night's darkness and into the bright light of Saturday morning.

She nearly suggested it. And if he had suggested it, she believed she would have.

Instead, they pulled back. The wine bottles were empty, as were their dessert plates on the ground next to them. They did not preclude love in the future. They did not avoid or evade it, stepping laterally away from it, nor did they turn away from it and move in the other direction.

They simply paused, that evening, and looked out at the night sky and considered where they were and what they were looking at, beholding it as they might a single distant strand of light.

Slowly, the cheapest leases assembled themselves on the map. It was tempting to make a run on all that he could reach, but Richard did not want to panic any of the other geologists; he worried that one of them, in looking at the whole of his assemblage, might piece the rather simple picture together.

Occasionally, he even pursued and bid upon leases that — to him — almost surely held oil and gas, just to keep the foolish preconceptions of the unobservant continuing their sleepy-lidded gazes in the same direction.

Even at nickels and dimes on the dollar, the costs were adding up. He and the school had hoped to be able to find a hundred years' worth of water, though that had been in a perfect world; as the leases were assembled, with certain tracts unavailable or unaffordable, it was looking like they might eventually end up with only about sixty or seventy years' worth.

Still, it was better than the day-to-day uncertainty of wondering if each time a sink faucet or showerhead was turned on, it would be the last, and that one day no water at all would issue forth, not even the sulfurous bile-water that was turning up, but instead only a thin stream of grit and sand, sand pouring from the faucet as if it were some form of wealth and they had suddenly become rich in it, the endless glittering silica of mountains worn down to nothing, hundreds of thousands of years in the wearing-down.

Beautiful sand, hot and dry, sand the color of pearls and ecru filling their sinks, and spilling onto their floors, and rising to the windows; flowing out through the windows then, and rising to the roofs: filling their homes, running them out of their homes — destroying and yet preserving them, embedding them in sand, encasing them in the disassembled detritus of those long-ago mountains, mountains on which blue ice had been capped, with cool green forests of fir and spruce, and through which giant tigers and long-legged camels and sloths and mastodons had once passed.

The sand flowing into the streets, rivers of sand eventually erasing all signs and evidence of commerce and habituation, and scaling over all the old ruinous pockmarked slumps that were the remnants of the geologists' activity, and of the civilization's hungers for the black oil and the flames and flares of the sweet and bitter gas.

Should I have stayed in Mexico for the extra year and a half? Richard wondered. Like some thin and final distance, would it have not, in the end, been a simple matter to travel those last five hundred days, with wealth — so much wealth — awaiting him at the end?

Had he remained to travel that last and lesser distance, he would have been in a position to take ten times as many leases, and could have procured all of the water. He could have built, or at least saved, a kingdom.

But I would have missed her, he thought. *The water might not have lasted a year.*

They might have been able to truck some in from somewhere, for a while. But they might also have folded, dispersed, disassembled. Things would have been different.

I had to go, he told himself. *I had to leave that very day. Not another hour, not another minute.*

Why do I feel full? he wondered one day, sitting up in his loft, reading and looking out over the town of Odessa: watching, as if from habit alone, the horizon. *Why do I feel content when my need, my goal, is not being met?*

Still, the other came to him, again and occasionally in dreams. Still, he imagined seeing that rise of smoke, plume of distant dust.

Thanksgiving was held at Marie and Annie's. They watched the professional football game on television, the Green Bay Packers playing the Dallas Cowboys, the latter the beloved icon of much of the rest of the state, and whom Ruth could not resist referring to as "the Cowpies," pretending to not be able to remember the correct name. They cooked a small turkey in a fire pit dug in the backyard, a tiny cavern covered with grasses and limbs and leaves — they had been reading about such native methods in social studies — and rubbed the bird with paprika and black pepper and cumin seeds and brown sugar. They baked sweet potatoes in the pit and roasted sweet corn, and made pumpkin pies and pumpkin-chocolate cheesecakes. They baked sweet-potato biscuits, rumored to have been Thomas Jefferson's favorite, and talked about Jefferson, read some of his writings out loud, while the game, attended to now only by Herbert Mix, played in the other room.

They drank apple cider and spiced tea, the taste of cloves as dense and rich as wood, and they cooked some more, then spent hours cleaning dishes, hoping that the water would hold out for one more day, which it did.

Later in the evening they began preparing the multitude of leftovers into various side-recipes, freezing some and parceling the others into Pyrex dishes to keep for the coming week, and then they sat around in the living room and visited further about all the things for which they were thankful.

Ruth, and the school, of course; and this year, Richard. They were thankful for the children, for a country at peace — there was another war going on — and for their health, the latter acknowledged for their own sake, but also for that of their elder statesman.

Food, water, shelter; freedom of speech, freedom of assembly — all of the time-tested rights, seemingly as durable as to be almost geologic in nature; though still, they were acknowledged.

Annie was even quieter than usual, and Ruth hoped that it was because she was missing her playmates, the sole child that day in a house full of adults — though later when Annie commented how she was grateful for Marie, Ruth knew the real reason for her quietness, and felt the bottom of her heart go out in a way she was usually able to guard against.

They went for a walk that evening after dark. They walked down the gravel road to the east, on past the window-lit squares of occasional other homes, and past the dark schoolhouse silhouetted by starlight. Farther on, the road went from gravel to sand, and still they followed it, Herbert Mix wanting to stop and rest or turn back, but unwilling to abandon or be abandoned by them, and certainly unwilling to see Marie draw away from him: and finally when they reached the top of a small rise, from which they could see the purple velvet of the desert below, with a lopsided three-quarters moon rising above the horizon, they sat in the cool sand and watched the swollen moon struggle to ascend as if from beneath them.

There was a cooling breeze sliding across the sand from the north, and they listened to the cries and yaps of the coyotes, and looked out at the little lights of Odessa, and the nearer, scattered lights of the houses around Mormon Springs, and at all the gas flares, some far-flung and others closer, the flares appearing festive, reassuring — and Herbert Mix, though weakened by the walk, sat tucked in close against Marie, and she against him; and Ruth likewise edged in close against Richard and, after a while, reached for and found his hand, and took it with both of hers, and held it for a long time, until Marie finally announced that she was getting cold.

Like travelers or even penitents nearing some long-sought destination, they walked together back down the rise in silence, back toward their tiny community, which was darker now: and the walk was peaceful, and yet they each glimpsed for a moment, here and there, like shutterings of images, the size of the country beyond them, dark and complete. And Annie and Richard were aware also as they walked of all the pods and lenses of water beneath them, stacked sometimes like schools of fish amidst the darkness of all-else stone: some of the water already gone away, and some of it poisoned.

But threads and ribbons of it, still sweet and usable, still miraculous, in other places; and just beneath their feet, as they walked.

The going-away of the water was most stressful upon Marie. In the twenty years since she had been gone from the salt lake, she had gotten used to not hauling her water, to not being held hostage by its paucity, and she did not intend to ever go back to that sort of life. Worse for her, however, than even the threat of the water going away for good, or being poisoned, was the occasional sandy rasp and hiss of the faucets, which each time reminded her of her days and dreams out at the lake: of the terror she had felt as those sheets of sand had come sliding in over the tin roof of their shack.

And in that memory, she was humbled by the recollection of her weakness, her breaking-down. She knew that she could break again

— that no one was unbreakable — and so she beheld Richard and the strangeness of his arrival with gratitude, and wondered occasionally at the source of the impulse that had drawn him back, and from so great a distance.

In the first week of December, a gift came for Marie, though at the time, no one had understood that it would be for her, for in its conception, it had been planned for the children.

In his brief visit, and his short run at the queen, the Mormon businessman Joe had mentioned to Ruth that during his missionary time in Asia he had met a group of women who were refugees from Vietnam. They had been injured by land mines set along the Cambodian border — some maimed by mines in the most recent war, others by mines set by the British during the imperialist campaigns of previous decades — and though each of the women were missing at least one limb, with some of them missing two or three, they nonetheless were able to weave, on looms specially designed for them by a Quaker relief organization, the most incredible silk scarves and kimonos, which were quickly in demand.

For a while, Joe — in addition to pursuing mobile home sales — had had an interest in being one of their product importers to the United States, but had eventually declined the opportunity, as it had seemed to him problematic that no two scarves, no two blouses or kimonos, would ever be the same. He had not been able to envision a way to catalog and market items which had not yet been created, and for which no pictures existed.

He still had the contact information, however, and when Ruth expressed an interest in learning more about the organization, he sent it to her, and she had written them.

The women were scheduled to travel the southern United States, with exhibitions of their work and methods, beginning in the textile communities of North Carolina, down into Alabama and then west to Texas and on to California, before returning home; and Ruth was able to secure a grant that allowed them to incorporate a program in Mormon Springs.

The weavers would be able to stay two weeks — there had been a gap in their schedule between their venues in Austin and Santa Barbara, and their plans had not been fully formed, other than to drift from town to town as they could, staying an indeterminate number of days with an informal collective of Quaker hosts around the country; and so they were delighted when they arrived at the bus station in Odessa and were greeted by Ruth and the students.

A support van was being driven from community to community, and it arrived not long after the bus. Richard and several of the parents spent the rest of the day helping them unload and set up out at an old abandoned stone granary near Ruth's schoolhouse, where the women would live for those two weeks.

Their looms were designed so that they could be operated either by foot pedals or by cams and pulleys turned by hand, or, in the absence of hands or feet, by the flipper-like revolutions of their arms, churning like a swimmer's, or by revolutions geared by the scissoring of their legs, working like those of a cyclist, with a slow road of raw silk scrolling beneath and before them.

The canvas walls of their weaving tent were constructed so that they could be lowered during stormy weather or raised during heat waves. Mosquito netting draped all four walls, but when the canvas sides were rolled up, the workers felt as if they were working in the desert itself.

In their tour of the South, as in Vietnam, they had need of the netting constantly, where the mosquitoes had swarmed, desiring the blood of those who had already given so much: but in the desert, there were no mosquitoes, and it was a joy to the women to work amidst such freedom.

There was a separate area in the tent where the women painted and dyed the strips of silk in unique patterns, and still others — a few of those accompanying the exhibit who still had the full use of their hands — sewed the painted silk into scarves and dresses and blouses.

There were false starts, errors, flaws and tears in the silk occasionally, or a poor mix of dye in which one section might be paler than the next; or something might go wrong in the drying process, causing a finished piece of silk to be unusable; and from these discards, with their barely noticeable flaws, the women fashioned their own clothes, and curtains for the doorways of the tent, and windows of their homes back in Vietnam, and sheets for their beds — wild, bright, bold, and brilliant colors of cobalt and lightning gold, cinnamon, melon — and still they had scarves and lengths of scarves left over.

With the most beautiful ones, they made prayer flags, which they sewed to the outer walls of the drab canvas tent, until it was covered with thousands of the wild-hued ribbons, like the plumage of birds, the scarves stirring in the breeze and making the occasional whispering sounds of silk against silk. The sight of the tent attached to the back of the little stone building, with the sere desert heat-dazzled beyond, and beneath the December-blue sky, thrilled the children each morning when they came to school, as it did all who saw it.

There was another, smaller tent, in which the women raised the silkworms that spun the silk. This was their gold, the secret engine of their existence, which helped power the fluttering soul of the scarves' wild colors — the plain white moths and their progeny, the plain pale-gray silkworms — and the children of Mormon Springs, and of all the communities that the women visited, were put in charge of feeding them, and gathering the spun silk each day, and keeping the silkworms from overheating in the most stifling weather by providing them with a spray of water, just a mist, twice daily, like the faintest of rains.

Whether the winter migrations of neotropical birds were drawn first to the blazes of the fluttering ribbons attached to the women's tent, or to the shadowy silhouettes of whirring moths in the separate, isolated tent, no one could be certain: but by the second day of the women's arrival, the birds were swarming and flitting around the tent and the schoolhouse — blurs of neon red and blue and yellow and green like the fluttering scarves themselves. And for all of the days that the silk weavers of Vietnam were in Mormon Springs, the birds remained, roosting in the eaves of people's homes and in the little wind-and-heat-stunted scraggly trees in their front yards, the birds stirring before dawn to swarm once more around the silkworm tent, to feed upon the trickles and streams of moths that escaped from the tent each time a flap was opened. The birds fed on the steady supply of aging moths, too, which were turned out from the tent whenever their silk production began to decline, replaced with the next wave of younger, stronger moths.

The birds roosted in the yard of Clarissa's old house, taking refuge in the tangle of tumbleweed that pressed against the walls; and they flocked also to the towering lilacs that shrouded the house, so many of them in the evenings that it might have appeared that the tree had begun to blossom once more, and in all different hues, despite the lateness of the season.

Richard had stopped going out to the old house, though there were still nights when, in his loft, he dreamed that he was there, and so the birds slept undisturbed by anything other than the feral cats that rustled in the tangled maze beneath them; there were no lanterns, lamps, or candles to trouble their sleep, only the shell of darkness, with the birds' great beauty unseen in the night.

The weaver women were made to feel at ease right from the start, in part by the immediate help and welcoming by the community — each night, a different family hosted them for dinner — and also by the visitations of Herbert Mix, and by the respected if not revered position he occupied in his community. But they were made most welcome of all by Marie, with whom they seemed to identify immediately; and she spent almost all of her time out in the tent with them, or helping the children take care of the moths.

And although Herbert Mix was happy for her, he felt also uncomfortably as if she was being taken away from him, as if lifted into flight by some greater force, while he, with his one leg like an anchor, remained below, flightless and abandoned. It was a feeling that was accentuated for him each time he approached the tent and saw from a distance the silhouettes of the workers, and their ceaseless, shifting industry within the tent: the sheets of silk rising and falling on the looms like the wings of great birds or dinosaurs trapped within, and the silhouettes of the weavers attending to the looms — some seated, others standing, but all startling in their asymmetry.

To Herbert Mix it seemed as if the strange figures were either trying to attack the winged creature, or to subdue and calm it; and yet then the desert wind would stir, the gauzed sheets of mosquito netting would billow, and it would seem that the laborers might be trying to encourage the dragon, or whatever the fallen creature was, back into flight: and as if somehow their own survival depended upon the success of that resurrection.

And in the smaller tent, also illuminated by the rising sun to create yet another stage of silhouettes, Herbert Mix could see the shadows of the thousands of swirling moths, their wings flashing and folding frantic semaphoric messages.

The sun pierced the moths, igniting every wing, turning each vein into a filament that magnified the sun's light and filled them with an electrical charge. That light shuttered as the moths continued to swarm, and the entire canvas tent filled with flashing incandescence, so that it seemed to Herbert Mix that the tent was burning; and as he watched, the sun climbed and clicked south and west another notch, and the moth-fire subsided from the tent, the image cooling before his eyes.

Despite his missing leg, he felt self-conscious in the women's presence; and although they knew a fair amount of English, he had trouble understanding them, due to their accents. Marie was better able to comprehend or intuit the women's directions and moods: and though he would have liked to have learned how to operate the looms, seating himself at one or another of the stations, he sensed that there was an immediate lowering in the level of joy on the few times that he had entered the silk weavers' tent.

He could not help but ascribe it to the notion that on some level they associated him, because he was a man, with warfare, and the weapons by which they had lost their limbs. He would have thought that because he shared that loss with them, there would be more intimacy, not less, between them, but it did not seem to be working that way, and so he retreated, left them to their private weavings and their inscrutable communications.

Marie told them about her life, about the elephant that had once passed through, and they understood, for they had each had elephants in their villages, and in their lives, at one point or another.

Other times they spoke no words, but gave themselves over to the looms, became lost in the clatter of the operation, feeding the silk into the guides, choosing not through any previous day's foredesign the color and texture of the new creation, but deciding such things only in the moment, often only at the last instant, even as one rocker-arm was rising and another falling: and in this, they were free, freer than they had ever been; and later in the day, when they began to paint their own designs and no other's onto the silk that was utterly of their making, great beauty arising and then blossoming out of the random barbarities of war, they felt each time — whether they had been weaving for only a month, or for years — that they had transcended even freedom, or the need for freedom: and in this state, they felt a strength they had never known.

Marie felt it, too. Though hers were not physical, she too had absences, caverns and abysses and long-hollow crevices, and she felt the rush of color, the blaze of the scarves, flooding into those vacancies.

Nor was it all about taking. She felt the color rushing out of her, too: flowing, as if from her fingers, her eyes, her mouth, color rushing back out onto the sand-colored landscape, and into the little town. She felt herself giving, as she had always given, but this time there was a pulse and a rhythm, a balance between the two, taking, giving, as synchronous and graceful as the gearings of the strangers' clattering looms. She had never felt fuller or stronger; and from the first day, she began to dread the silk weavers' leaving.

They stored the best of the apparel in tin chests decorated with scroll-work and rhinestones, and lined with strips of cedar to keep the clothes sweet smelling, and to protect them against insect damage. The slightly flawed garments they reserved for themselves and distributed also to the communities through which they passed.

They fastened the remnant scraps of silk to the rim of the basketball hoop at the school, and to the school's cedar rafters, and to the few light posts in Mormon Springs, and to the fences and gates outside people's homes, and to the lone stop sign.

Still they had scraps left over, and as the weavers' work progressed, they began sending them into Odessa: lining the streets there, too, and the buildings. Richard decorated the outer sills and ledges of his loft windows with long trellises of remnant silk, and when he took the schoolchildren out into the desert, they tied the colorful strips to the pumpjacks of oil wells and the casings of gas wellheads.

There had never been so much color in the desert, not in December or any other month, and at night, the children as well as the adults dreamed in color; and even those who had not led lives as rough as Marie or the weavers felt nonetheless fresher and stronger. That old wounds they had not even known they had or remembered were beginning to heal, and they too began to wish that the weavers would stay.

And each day, Herbert Mix stood on the outside of their tent and watched the silhouettes within, the flashing and leaping ascent and slide of the crofter and the laird. *She is happy,* he thought, *she is so happy.* And he felt his old hunger, his hollowness, returning.

Marie continued to work with the weavers in the tent, learning to operate the various looms. She was of great value with certain tasks, such as the threading of the silk into the looms before each shift — and she had also been spending time with the silk painters, and already had created some beautiful patterns and colors, and had sewn several suits and dresses.

She hung these blouses and skirts and scarves on the racks in the display section of the tent, next to those of the other workers, and was overjoyed by the communion she felt in doing so: not just the acceptance and approval, but the admiration.

The joy she saw on their faces when they viewed a scarf she had painted that day, bringing it up to them from the depths of her concentration and presenting its beauty; their brown hands, or stumped limbs, touching the silk for the feel of it: as if the color cobalt felt slightly different from chartreuse, and chartreuse from magenta or fuchsia. The pleasure of the dream-journey of the painting and sewing sweetened for Marie by this second joy, the joy of her ascension to these other things.

What more, she wondered, could anyone ask for in this life? The mask of her identity seemed to be dissolving into a kaleidoscope of color. New air was entering her lungs and her blood, and she felt to be no more than sixteen years old.

She tried to explain it to Annie, late at night: and although Annie could see how happy she was, she could not understand entirely how happy, nor why, but was glad for Marie, and sensed that things were far different from how they had been even a short time ago, before the silk weavers had arrived.

Each day, in the heated, sleepy middle part of the day, Herbert Mix continued to watch the silhouettes of the women working, and was mesmerized by the speed of the silk being spun, and by the rise and fall, the flapping wings of the looms, and by the fluttering of the brush strokes as the dye was applied to the finished silk.

Often he lounged by the tent, in the shade of one of his old umbrellas, and was both soothed and stimulated by the gracefulness of the movements, and by the flashing colors; yet he continued to feel the old rift opening in him, and despaired at what he perceived to be a failure, on his part, against the test of desire; for should not the beauty strengthen and fill him, too, as it did the others?

Marie was all but unattainable, in her daily and nightly schedulings with the weavers, and for once he did not want to draw closer to her — afraid that his backsliding, his sin of hollowness, might somehow be contagious.

And eventually Herbert Mix withdrew, and brooded, and plotted, and wrestled with his weakness, and despaired in his failing, before finally succumbing.

His old tractor had not run in years, mice and dirt daubers had built their nests in its pipes and pulleys, and the oil and grease had hardened as if to stone. He was up most of the night disassembling and reassembling the iron beast, trying to coax it to run — a couple of times, the engine nearly turned over — but in the end it would not crank, as if trying to convince him to choose a path other than the one he had fallen back onto, and at dawn the next day, he gave up on the tractor and instead loaded his old jeep — a risk, he knew, but again, he perceived no choice, had given himself over to the immensity of his hunger.

He packed a lunch, a shovel, a couple of gallons of water, a sunhat, and a tent, and set out for Castle Gap just as the disk of the sun was clearing the desert floor. The morning was cool, and as he passed the procession of the football team, driving through the just-stirring town of Odessa, he waved and they waved back.

He lifted his hand in greeting to the men and women walking out into their yards to secure the morning paper, and walking their dogs on leashes, and as he drove past the scarf-fluttering homes of Mormon Springs, a wave of sadness came over him, knowing that some of those colorful remnants were Marie's; and knowing, too, that when it was time for the silk weavers to leave, and to travel on to California, that she would be leaving with them: that no force on earth would be able to stop her, nor should it. He knew that it would be this way, knew it by the deadness of his broken heart.

And yet, farther out of town, drawn down the familiar path of all his many journeys from the years before, he felt almost good for a while, traveling freely, the promise of the day's treasures not yet revealed. He took his straw hat off and let the wind stir his silvery hair, looked back over his shoulder to be sure that he had brought his shovel, and continued on, searching for his treasure, whether bones or gold, no matter; he was on the hunt once more.

He decided to choose skulls over gold, this fine first day. He drove along the Pecos for a while, remembering his vitality, and got out and went down to Horsehead Crossing, where, on that bright, cool, blue-sky day, he was treated to such a sight that he laughed out loud — clear simple laughter flowing from him as if from a child, laughter that seemed like it might not end, and that seemed, for a while, to be synchronous with the river as the water rolled past, lapping and gurgling.

It was a dry year, and the river was lower. It would still have been a dangerous feat for anyone to attempt its crossing, the current still strong, but in that period of lower water he was able to get closer to it, crabbing his way down the plunging washboard-cobble of accretia and conglomerate, toward the chocolate-colored gurgling water.

What his hands found there, as he clutched and inched his way down as close as he dared, and what he saw on the other side of the river, similarly exposed, sent an explosion of pleasure through his body.

On either side of the river, there was a new strata of bones, scoured to brilliance by the ages of passing water and the scrubbing of silt and gravel — the bones as polished as pearls, as white as ivory — and disbelieving, despite the authority of touch, he ran his hands over the cobbly smooth matrix of them, the steep bed of bones upon which he rested.

And in the ancient lacunae, there blossomed beneath his hands the map of the future, and he felt the map beneath him moving, shifting as if in a quarter turn and sliding, slipping down into the water.

He tensed and held on, tried to dig in with his heel and to clutch the sidewall of skulls. His fingers found the gaping eye socket of horse or steer, he was not sure which, and tried to find purchase there, but the fragile brow crumbled at his touch, and slowly, bumpily, he rode the map down a little farther, a little closer to the rushing river, which he saw now was only masquerading as a river, but was really something else entirely, something far more immense than he had given it credit for, voracious and perhaps immortal.

He could taste the breath of it now, saw that the river was a living thing that had to be fed steadily — that it was hungering for him with an intensity far beyond that with which he himself had ever hungered for anything — and even in his old man's fright, he found this to be a thing of awe, even as he prepared to be consumed by it.

Still, he fought against it. Now and again his foot found brief and tiny purchase on the skull plate of a buffalo, or his hands were able to clutch and grasp at a momentary cleft between the ribs of some unknown creature as he slid ever so slowly down that washboard ossuary, with all the skulls grinning as they faced the bright mild morning sunlight that was illuminating them.

He thought of Marie, he thought of Mormon Springs, of Ruth and the children, of Annie, and of Richard, and the town of Odessa. He thought of his jeep up above him, and of himself as a younger man (though he had long ago already slid past that corollary strata), back when he had had both legs, the second of which would have now served him in good stead.

It was rough, sliding over all those knobs and protrusions, the time-crafted and time-carved minutiae of suture and indentation, each dimpled bone perfect for the attachment of long-ago muscles that were now so completely vanished as to no longer even exist in a single memory — every bit as gone, beneath that bright sun, as if they had never existed. His hands read it all as he slid, his old hands groping and fluttering, still cataloging all the way down, and when his booted leg splashed into the water, he was surprised at how warm it was, and not unpleasant.

He was not the first to have tumbled down this slope, drawn to this one final resting spot by the path of gravity and the contours of the surface, funneling him to the same place where it had funneled so many others; and falling no farther, he found that he was resting on top of something: a crude delta of boulder and bones.

He stood braced against the wall, the scrim of bone, and then, wobbly and trembly-legged, he sat down in the warm splashing water, the living water, and like a raccoon washing mussels in a riffling current, he felt and groped in the subaqueous nether for some clue to the identity of his benefactor.

Warm grit and sediment stirred beneath his probing, and once, it seemed to him that the mass upon which he rested stirred, as if coming back to life, or as if it had never left the living, but had been only resting and waiting — waiting, perhaps, the release that could be granted or vested only by the arrival of one such as himself.

He turned and looked up at the wall of bones and skulls that towered above him: and whether he had been outcast, or had stumbled in through the palace gates, he could not be sure; though again, he was surprised to not feel sadness, and to feel instead a kind of happiness spreading through him — or if not happiness, then peace, and — again — a dulling, a waning, to his hunger.

The river's hunger was enough. In its presence, his own hunger was puny, so insignificant as to be nonexistent; and in that vanishing, he knew an even larger and more secure peace — one which he did not think could be taken from him now, not even by Marie's departure.

It pleased him to think of her bright flags and ribbons, and of the traveling troupe of weavers, the crews of color she would be joining. So much vibrancy that even years after it had passed on, it would leave the echo of that color like a wash upon the sand, and in the minds of those who had seen it, and who had seen it made.

He looked now at the tapestry of bones all around him, and at those on the other side of the river. He read those closest to him with more leisure now, with his fingers and with his eyes. Some he recognized, while others were not known to him — the bones of creatures come and gone long before the likes of Herbert Mix had ever crawled up out of the sea. He could only examine them and marvel at his place now among them.

In the tidy stratification of time and gravity, the cataloging of bones appeared to be resting in abacus-like arrangement of column and row. There appeared to be order and assemblage, even in the falling-apart and storing-away — it seemed surely that there was even reassembly going on — and down at eye level with the beast of the river, it seemed wider to him than it had from above.

And still, God help him, he wanted to live; and still, God help him, the bones on the farther shore looked more interesting and desirable than those over which he had just passed, and among which he was now stranded.

Is it this way, he wondered, *can this be true?* He wanted, in his enlightenment, to believe otherwise, and to accept the bounty before him. But he could not be sure.

Once more, he groped the substrate, the submerged promontory on which he knelt, but could divine no history. Each clue that was revealed to him seemed to lead in a different direction; and again, it seemed to him that the object upon which he rested was beginning to move.

He felt a wave of vertigo, and imagined that he was about to sink farther; that his sanctuary was brief, and that it, too, now, was about to fail him. That perhaps it had even lured him to this point, in order to be able then to deliver him to the river.

And to that farther shore!

He had not swum in many years, and never since losing his leg; but he pushed off from his resting spot and entered the current, not riding on his back with his foot pointed downstream as he should have, but instead breaststroking, trying to traverse the current.

He swam like a fish or a snake, breaststroking, but with his leg undulating rather than kicking; and as he found his rhythm, he became more comfortable in the current, more attuned to its runs and eddies, and he began to glide through it as would a fish or a snake: though still he could not breach the current's turbulent center line, to gain the other shore.

He traveled for a long time, ascending and descending, swimming and writhing sometimes completely beneath the surface, before rising again, blowing a spume of air and spray of mist; and he rolled over on his back and floated, back-paddling, and watched the cliffside bluffs scroll past with their litany of exposed skulls, and he wished again that he was a young man, so that he could explore all that he was seeing — a man so young and strong that whatever his eye beheld was his dominion — but those days were so far gone as to barely even be worth remembering, and he drifted on, growing tired, the waterlogged weight of his clothes wanting to pull him down now. And riding lower in the water, and feeling the fatigue settling into his limbs, he began to look for a place, a nice sandy beach, where he could make his landfall.

He had no idea where he was, on the river; he had swum and then drifted into territory where he had never been before.

Little fish began to bump against him, skittering into him from various directions, as if in confused flight from the shadow of his passage. Something large dashed against him, like a bullet, and then a larger something, hard-shelled, like a turtle, drifted up against him from below, then pushed away: and he was certain that in its pushing away, he had felt claws.

He began to imagine, and then sense, that his one remaining leg was vulnerable — that to certain things, he looked helpless, and *was* helpless.

He imagined snakes, fish, frogs, desiring his flesh, and as he continued to be buffeted by the whirlwind of smaller fish, he began to feel certain that some single larger creature — a great fish — was chasing them, and following him.

He knew it was panic. He knew such fish no longer existed. He had found pieces of their platey skulls in his excavations, their reptilian armor and their dagger teeth, but they no longer existed, they were all gone.

And yet in his weakness and his fear, they returned — or one of them did — and he could feel it following him, nosing him from behind, bumping and prodding him as if into position for just the right bite. He could feel the swirls of water behind him as it opened its fierce mouth for a bite or perhaps to swallow him whole, and he rolled over onto his side, flapped his arms behind him and attempted to veer wildly, trying to throw the fish off course; trying to buy himself one more moment of life, and one more, and one more.

It was exhausting work, causing him to ride lower in the river, and summoned more energy than he had left. He knew he should abandon the centerline, where the current was quickest, and give up on his efforts to reach the other shore.

He was still witnessing the flashing-by cobble of the past, and if anything, his side of the river appeared as alluring now as had that farther shore — and as the current quickened still further, he began to smell a different odor upon the river, the frothy muddiness of increasingly agitated water, complemented by the underground clacking of large rocks: and rather than considering the possibility of what might lie ahead of him in the form of even more turbulent water, and rapids, Herbert Mix continued to concern himself with the danger behind him.

Logs and branches, seized by the unruly current, rose from the bottom and scratched against him as the spiny monster prepared him for its feast, positioning him just so with the shapings and urgings of its caudal and dorsal fins.

He could feel the fish's entire presence now, dense as gravity — and once or twice, out of the corner of his eye, he caught a glimpse of one of the fins breaking the water.

He could smell the vile creature itself, even from beneath the water, and he began to tremble, and did something he had never done before, and gave up; he stopped paddling, and began to call out for help. He knew that he was an old man, too old, and that as the river prepared him for its feast, it had every right to do so — that it was finally his turn to join the wall of skulls — but still he fiercely wanted it to be otherwise.

He was struck by a rare and sudden vision of the future, his mind casting forward in a way that it had rarely done before, and he imagined himself a day beyond the moment: a single day into the void.

No one will even know what became of me, he lamented, *I will be encased within the jewels and armor of the fish, my bones will be encircled by his bones, and taken into his bones, and someday someone will catch that fish and open it up, but there will be no trace of me, they will never even know I existed.*

Or the fish will go uncaught, will die instead a distant death, and take its place in the wall of bones. Perhaps some further traveler will dig it up, will rap on its calcified bones with hammer and pickax, and will think it is merely a fish, and not the echo of a man, not the echo of myself. Perhaps . . .

He shot through the river-slot of center current, between the two boulders guarding the entrance to the rapids like a gate, and was bounced into the air, upended, like a salmon ascending a waterfall, or a beach ball flipped skyward by the nose of a trained seal.

He did not wave his arms and legs wildly, seeking balance as if running in place, but instead remained perfectly still, scarcely daring to believe his luck, and unsure as to whether he had been saved, summoned by some benevolent force, or had indeed been shoved violently into the air by the snout of the leviathan that pursued him.

It seemed to him in the half second in which he was above the waves that he could see farther than he had ever seen: that he could see the entire length of the river, beyond the rapids and beyond even the deltaic sand beaches that lay hundreds of miles downstream. It seemed to him he could see the calm flat gray water of the sea; but when he fell back into the waves, the fish was upon him in a roar, attacking him as if with a dozen baseball bats, bruising and clubbing and stoning him, and as he reeled along through the turmoil, he thought strangely of the rise-and-fall action of the looms, and of the clack and clatter of those wooden bars, the movements so like those of a great bird preparing to take flight.

His old heart was in tatters, shot through with adrenaline and riddled by strain. He could go no farther, yet fish and river continued to carry him along, and he imagined, at the end, that he was a sheet of silk, still being lifted and stretched by the pulleys and crossbars of the looms — that his billowing colors, brilliant in the desert sun, filled the entire tent, casting ripples of color over all who fell beneath the shadows of his furl.

He perceived crimson, he perceived flashes of gold, and he paused and stiffened and stared upward with wonder and fascination at the brilliance above, and hoped that Marie would somehow be able to see these colors, to know that about him; and he continued to gaze upward, waiting for them to descend and fill him, as he had always waited and wanted to be filled.

It took them a long time to find him, that next day; he had traveled a long way, beyond the reach of roads: past high cliffs and bluffs and pinnacles, as if passing beneath the walls of civilizations in which the searchers were not welcome — civilizations from which they themselves might have been exiled, as had perhaps Herbert Mix himself, but to which he had returned.

They found his jeep and, fearing and then expecting the worst, found the telltale scrabble marks of where he had clawed his way down the steep bank and into the river. Both Richard and Ruth had driven out searching, as had two other men from town, and Marie had insisted on joining them also.

They spent much of the morning searching up and down the river in that general area, trying to find a sign of where he might have worked his way back to shore and managed to climb out, or perhaps might still be holding on, gripping valiantly to a rock ledge or root-wad, exhausted and current-shuddered, but still with them.

They cast out into the desert too, searching the pristine dunes, which were smoothed over from the day-before's winds, for the stippled or slithering evidence of his escape. They were dressed in brightly colored shirts, so that they could each see where the other was, even across the distance.

Marie wanted to cry, and felt a pulling apart in her old chest — an ache at both the loneliness and familiarity of it — but she felt a fear, also, at what she perceived as the inescapability of it; and in that fear, and that closing-in feeling of constriction, she knew anger, too, and re-solved not to let her heart, fragile and ancient though it was, be pulled any further apart. She tensed, tried to protect and harden her old heart, and continued the search.

It was Richard who found him, so many miles down the river, the body as brilliant as the white belly of a beached whale, visible from a distance on the ivory-colored sand beach onto which he had managed to crawl, half-washed there by the rapids and half-arrived there under his own final labors.

And across the expanse of sand behind him, Richard signaled to the others to come join him, that he had found him; and from all di-rections and distances, they converged, and climbed carefully down a rubbly slot canyon to the white sand beach below, where the old man, so clearly identifiable even from a distance as Herbert Mix, lay stretched out on his back, staring skyward.

Had his eyes still been sighted, he would have seen them appear over the bluff, would surely have welcomed the appearance of their bright shirts moving toward him, their wavering figures conjoining then separating again.

Through the heat and the miracle of mirage, they might have ap-peared, in that shimmering curtain of sunlight, like some apparition from the past: a runaway stagecoach, or a band of Kiowa pursuing a caravan of Mexican salt traders.

Instead, he saw nothing, his hungry eyes finally as sightless as a skull's, and his breath finally stilled. The wind stirred his silvery hair. The images converged into the present, including among them a woman and a man who had loved him; and in the present, they hur-ried toward him, carrying their grief now as if burdened by heavy bags of gold.

The funeral was held on a Sunday, a raw and windy day in Mormon Springs in which the new scarves flapped and swirled in all direc-tions. There was a community potluck that evening, held at the school — Marie was in the midst of packing, preparing to depart with the weavers, or it would have been held at her house — and the next day, the townspeople helped the silk weavers fold their tents and carefully disassembled the looms, storing each in its proper place in their trunks and crates and steamer chests.

The aging silk moths were turned loose that evening — as if from out of nowhere, birds began to appear, swarming them — while the younger, more vital moths and worms were stored in mesh containers and loaded into the back of a van in which blocks of ice were set in brackets atop mounted tables, to help keep the interior cooled.

It was harder for Marie to leave Annie than anything she had ever done; far harder than enduring the terrors of the salt lake, and harder than the discovery of her gentle lover washed up along the beach. And yet even in her tears, she felt herself filling with a happiness that she supposed was almost as strong as the love of a partner, and which she suspected could in some ways be its superior, in certain ways that had been lacking from her life. It helped her to know that it was the right decision for Annie — that the child needed someone far younger, that Ruth would be a perfect mother for her from here on out — but still, it grieved her, and she wondered too if her grief at losing Herbert Mix was affecting her.

There would be no more children — no Annie — but she would be able to come and see her again someday, perhaps on another tour. Or perhaps Annie would come and see her, traveling to Asia.

How would my life have been different if I had gone with Mufti, she wondered, *so long ago, and where would I be? What would I have seen, and what would I have missed?* She felt a current of understanding for Herbert Mix, felt for a moment his clamant ravenousness for the joys and treasures the world had to offer. Of course he had wanted them all. She considered those that might only now lie just before her, and again, despite her sadness, she knew excitement and wonder, and a thing that surely had to be happiness, she had seen it in the faces and lives of other people, it seemed characterized by a lack of emptiness. Surely this was it.

It would soon be Christmas break. The plan was made for Annie to move in with Ruth: Annie the loser yet again, seemingly, in these shifts of affections in the hearts of adults, these nearly tectonic yearnings and adjustments not dissimilar to the ones that stirred and broke apart and reformed in her own heart, but about which she could not yet do as much, other than to submerge.

There was no will, no probate. Richard moved into Herbert Mix's old museum and converted it into an office for the school's water-finding venture. He let dust gather on the relics Herbert Mix had spent his life accumulating and cataloging and cleaning. The willows in the backyard, unpruned, grew still wilder, casting shade over the entire warehouse, and here, too, the bright migrant songbirds gathered.

It was lonely out at the warehouse, and lonely in town, so Richard moved out to Mormon Springs: not into Clarissa's old falling-down house, but into what had been Marie and Annie's home — almost as if following them, always a few years behind; to the loft, first, and now to their little house in Mormon Springs: and with more of the path still open and available to him.

They drilled their first water well two days before Christmas, completing it on an evening when the wind was strong from the north and the stars burned so fiercely it seemed they might melt their way down through the night's blackness.

They were all gathered, children and parents alike, and Ruth and Richard, with a bonfire going, much like on the night of Richard's return to Odessa.

There was no spectacle this evening, only quiet murmurings of excitement, and when the drillstring was pulled and laid on its rack, the heavy pipe flashing and glittering in the starlight, the drill bit as jagged as the jaws of a dragon, they could all smell the scent of the fresh water, the isolated subsurface aquifer that had never been entered: fossil water that had not seen the surface of the world, neither the heat of day nor the stars of night, in over a hundred thousand years.

The drillers ran a swab down the hole, a piston, to pull some of the fluid up from the depths. They had brought a little gas-powered pump, and they attached it to the wellhead, and began pumping up some sample water for all those who had gathered to taste.

It was like no well birthing, no drilling, Richard had ever been to. There was no scent of sulfur, no belch of flame, no burp of gas; no sour-sweet smell of oil. Instead, it smelled like a deep cold lake at night, or like a trickling creek running over clear stones beneath the arbor, the canopy, of oaks.

They had brought all manner of cups — paper and plastic, crystal wineglasses, coffee mugs, tumblers — and one by one they filled them, sampling the delicious, ancient water that was theirs; and it seemed to them all to be the best water they had ever tasted, and nearly intoxicating.

It was not Richard's water, nor was it exclusively Annie's. They had all helped find it, had carefully tracked it, and now they claimed it.

They had brought empty bottles and thermoses, empty cans and bottles, and like migrants who have come upon a distant oasis, rather than the residents they would continue being, for a little while longer at least, they filled their containers to take home with them that night, filling them with the same intensity of pleasure with which another might fill a treasure chest with gold doubloons. Then they drove home, a procession of community, taillights blinking through the desert; while beyond them, as always, the towering, scattered candles of the gas flares wavered and leapt in the distance.

The children and Richard's wells continued to find water — new water, clean water, water not contaminated by the oil or gas or any other residue from above. It was the last of the last, and Richard knew it, at some level they all knew it — but there was suddenly so much of it again, and it was so delicious: and they had earned it, there was the pride of discovery, pride of ownership, pride of independence, again.

The water was secure in their lives once more; they were no longer hostage to the vagaries of its imminent going-away. They showered in it nightly in their own homes, they built a community fountain for the children to play in, they filled their birdbaths with it in their backyards, they watered their roses with it.

The village shone, glinted in the winter sunlight. Their gardens prospered and the trees grew shadier around the town's perimeter; and for a long time, the villagers knew neither deep want nor hunger, and felt they had no need of second chances. There were unresolved needs and desires among all of them from time to time — Annie, in particular, wanted her parents, her real parents, and Ruth — with Richard, now — occasionally wanted more space and time. She wanted the world, and something more, for which she didn't know the name — and even in his happiness, his peace and contentment, Richard still sometimes felt as if he should want Clarissa back, even if he didn't.

One year, a circus came to town. Annie was nearly grown, a beautiful young woman who looked more and more, the townspeople thought, and as is often the case in such instances, like her adopted father.

The tent, the Big Top, was erected, not in Odessa or Mormon Springs, but out in the desert. People came from both towns to see it, parked out in the desert amidst the caverns and walked carefully along paths lit by lamps to reach the tent, which was similarly lit from within, glowing in a huge dome of gold.

One by one, the performers and their acts entered the ring: clowns juggling, lions roaring, circus masters cracking the whip. Beautiful women walking dangerous tightropes high above the audience, with no sign of a safety net, and no harness: the crowd rapt, conjoined as if one. Annie's hand clenched tightly in her father's, Ruth shoulder to shoulder with her husband. And then the elephant, looking as old as time: looking as if he was bound for the boneyard, and yet appearing durable and dignified, too.

The circus master scanned the audience, peered up into the many bleachers, asked for a volunteer.

"I need someone brave, I need someone beautiful," he called through his megaphone. "I need someone to ride on the back of this magnificent beast while lions and tigers leap about beneath his ancient feet. I need someone unafraid to die," the circus master bellowed, "I need someone unafraid to *live*."

Ruth and Annie were elbowing each other, teasing each other to volunteer, each on the verge of raising their hands.

Richard leaned in front of them so that they couldn't raise their hands. No other volunteers were forthcoming. He raised his own hand, laughed at the startlement of his wife and daughter, and at the circus master's gaze.

The elephant, who had seen it all before, pivoted a quarter turn to see who had answered the challenge. Across that distance, the elephant beheld him, and Richard rose from his seat in the bleachers and went down to meet him.

Acknowledgments

Novels don't come easily. I've been fortunate to do three, now four — one with my beloved editor Camille Hykes, and one with the late Harry Foster, and a previous one with Nicole Angeloro, all of Houghton Mifflin, via the publishing imprint of the late Seymour Lawrence. One per decade, or thereabouts. It's an intense relationship — editor and writer sitting on an ever-changing, ever-stirring hatchling, while the rest of the world as well as the animal of the novel changes across the days and across the years — and I'm amazed by the fortitude, talent, passion, and endurance of these editors. If those qualities aren't somehow the underpinnings of a kind of reckless courage, I don't know what is.

I'm in deepest gratitude to Melissa Dobson for inspired copyediting and line editing, and to Patrick Barry for the haunting, striking cover artwork and (again!) the jacket design. Likewise I'm grateful to Melissa Lotfy for the book's elegant interior design, and to Michael Hill for the book's title. Thanks also to Dan Janeck for his proofreading and to Beth Burleigh Fuller, the production editor.

I'm in debt also to the editors of quarterlies who edited and published excerpts of this novel — Tom Jenks, Carol Edgarian, and Mimi Kusch at *Narrative;* Ben George at *Tin House;* Michael Ray at *Zoetrope;* Cassie Nelson at *Camas;* and Ron Carlson and Aaron Peters at *Faultline.* I'm grateful to my father, Charles Bass, for teaching me how to find oil and gas, among other things, and to my agent, Bob Dattila, retired now, after having been ridden hard and put up wet, financially speaking, while in the service of literary authors for his entire career, who is in this novel in so many ways.

Present throughout, too, is my editor for this novel, Nicole Ange-loro. I do some teaching these days, and while it is easy enough to be a curmudgeon and even a hard-ass with students' prose that isn't quite working, I will try always to remember that there can be no four more powerful words to a writer than "I believe in you."